Praise for _____
Book 1 of Queen of the Orcs

"An unusual tale . . . Howell's depiction of orc culture is fascinating—these orcs are as big, strong, and dangerous as any in fantasy, but they also have moral and ethical issues of importance. This is not a book to read for fun on a rainy night—it's a book to think about."

—ELIZABETH MOON,
Nebula Award–winning author of
The Deed of Paksenarrion

"Dar never loses our admiration and compassion—qualities at the heart of any struggling hero. _King's Property_ tests your presumptions of 'the other' and brings to mind the cultural prejudices and wars born from betrayal that are so sadly evident throughout our own history."

—KARIN LOWACHEE,
author of _Warchild_

"In a crowded field, Howell has succeeded in creating an original and vivid fantasy. [The] characters display unexpected depths of humanity—even when they're not human. I was captivated by Dar. Highly recommended."

—NANCY KRESS,
Nebula Award–winning author of
Beggars in Spain

THE QUEEN OF THE ORCS TRILOGY
By Morgan Howell

King's Property
Clan Daughter
Royal Destiny

QUEEN OF THE
BOOK III
ORCS

Royal
Destiny

MORGAN HOWELL

BALLANTINE BOOKS • NEW YORK

A Del Rey Books Mass Market Original

Copyright © 2007 by William H. Hubbell

Published in the United States by Del Rey Books, an imprint of The Random House Publishing Group, a division of Random House, Inc., New York.

DEL REY is a registered trademark and the Del Rey colophon is a trademark of Random House, Inc.

ISBN 978-0-345-49652-2

Printed in the United States of America

www.delreybooks.com

9 8 7 6 5 4 3 2 1

This book is dedicated to
Jeanne d'Arc, Yanan,
and Carol Hubbell

When she gazed upon her land, it seemed that clouds moved over it. But those shadows were hordes of soldiers. Steel lightning flashed amidst their darkness as they brought death, not rain.

—From the Deetpahi of Tarma-goth

One

♛

Othar's sense of smell returned first. He breathed in the stench of corpses. Then sight came to his open eyes, and he saw a black, starless sky. His flesh felt on fire. With pain came awareness. With awareness came rage. *She did this to me!* Othar recalled her name. *Dar!*

When his fury hardened to stony hate, the sorcerer considered what had happened. *How could a branded woman become queen of the orcs?* Othar pondered that question. *She had a clan tattoo. She said she'd been reborn.* He was unaware such things were possible. Othar wondered what had happened to the old orc queen. He knew she had died, for Dar had used her body in a ruse to get the orcs inside the city. *Did Dar kill her?* He suspected not.

But I killed Dar! Othar smiled despite his pain. *I stabbed her with a poisoned blade. And she . . .* Othar recalled Dar throwing his precious, magic bones into the fire, destroying them and unleashing their power. It had burned him. Othar wished with all his being that Dar had shared his torment. Yet she had stood in the king's spilled blood, and it had protected her. Dar had watched while Othar suffered. He recalled seeing his flesh bubble and blacken as his finger bones fell joint by joint to the floor. *Her death was too easy.*

With painful effort, the former royal mage raised his head. He was in a pit surrounded by the decaying bodies of paupers and criminals. The smell was nearly unbearable.

Lacking hands and feet, Othar wondered how he'd ever climb out. Then he heard voices.

"They dumped a new one this evenin'."

"And ye say guardsmen did it?"

"Aye. Could be someone wearin' more than rags."

Othar saw a hand extend a lantern over the pit. It illuminated the coarse faces of two men. The instant the mage glimpsed their eyes, he knew their thoughts. These weren't expressed in words, but he understood them nevertheless. *The one with the lantern will tell the other to take my clothes.* Othar was amazed, for he had never possessed this power before.

The mage sensed that his pain and rage had masked another sensation. It tingled in the way he imagined a lightning bolt would after it struck. But it was more than a feeling. It seemed like another self; one that was potent, restless, and ravenous.

A ladder was lowered into the pit. "Go down and get his robe," said the man holding the lantern. "'Tis good as new."

His companion hesitated. "That's Blood Crow. I won't touch him."

"Then my foot will touch yer arse! Climb down or fall down, take yer pick."

"I don't like the looks of him, Tug. He's all burnt, 'cept those eyes! By Karm, they give me shakes!"

"He's dead, Nuggle. Beyond harmin' anyone. Get to it! Quick done is quick over."

Nuggle slowly descended the ladder, and Othar sensed his reluctance as if it were his own. As he probed Nuggle's mind, Othar realized that he could ensnare it and bend it to his needs. "Help me," said Othar in a hoarse whisper.

Nuggle halted, and the sorcerer felt his shock and terror. Othar gazed up at Tug. "Come here."

Tug obeyed, and Othar spoke to both men. "Take me from here."

The men wanted to resist, and Othar sensed their fear and revulsion. These emotions were extinguished as he wrested the men's wills, pulling both to the edge of madness. Unable to do anything but obey, they meekly lifted the mage from the damp earth, dragged him up the ladder, and laid him on the ground. Othar's skin cracked from being handled, and his agony was excruciating. When it subsided, he spoke to Nuggle. "Steal a handcart. Bring it here." Nuggle hurried off.

Othar turned to Tug. "When he returns, take me to your home. I'm master now."

Tug nodded.

"Tell me news of the palace," said Othar.

"I only know what the criers say," replied Tug, his voice flat and lifeless. "The king's dead. Word is ye killed him and died yerself. Queen Girta rules in her son's name."

"And the one called the orc queen? The girl. What of her?"

"She went home to her piss eyes. Rode off last night with a guardsman."

"She lives?"

"Aye, that's what the criers say."

When Othar heard those words, his fury flared hot again and his thoughts focused on Dar's destruction. He envisioned torments of excruciating cruelty and longed to inflict them. His universe became rage, and nothing else existed except the object of his hatred. When his passion was finally spent, Othar spied Tug sprawled on the ground. His nails and fingers were bloody. Chunks of his face and throat were strewn about. It appeared that he had acted out the mage's fantasies by murdering himself using only his hands.

Nuggle had difficulty stealing a cart, and it was nearly morning when he returned to the pit. Othar's grip on him was so complete that he was oblivious of Tug's corpse.

He lifted the mage into the cart, then waited for further commands. "Take me to Tug's," said Othar.

Nuggle headed to where Taiben's poorest and most disreputable citizens lived, a squalid collection of makeshift buildings outside the city walls. As the cart's wheels bumped over rutted, frozen mud, Othar reflected on his downfall. Two mornings ago, he had been the feared and respected royal mage—the real power behind the throne. *Now I'm baggage in a stolen cart.* Yet, despite his blasted body and ruined fortunes, Othar had gained as well as lost. By some means he didn't understand, he had acquired the ability to read others' minds and rule them. *They'll become my instruments.*

Othar wondered what the full extent of his newfound powers was. Glancing about the dismal slum, he thought it the ideal place to find out. *No one here will be missed.* Nuggle halted the cart before a dilapidated shanty, interrupting Othar's thoughts. "We're here, Master."

Before Othar could reply, a slatternly woman burst out the door. "Nuggle, ye dog's waste, where's Tug?" She glanced at the load in the cart. "Why ye bringin' that shit here?" In the dim light, Othar's scorched face blended with his black robes and the woman jumped back when she noticed his eyes staring at her. "Karm's holy ass! What's *that*?"

"Your master," replied Othar in a low, raw voice. And with those words, it was true. "Tend me, Moli."

The woman seemed unperturbed that the grotesque stranger knew her name. She simply helped Nuggle get the mage off the cart and into the shanty, where a meager fire produced more smoke than heat. They eased Othar onto a filthy mattress. Moli brought over a loaf of hard bread and was about to give it to him when she saw that his hands were missing. Her dull eyes showed no surprise or any other emotion. Moli merely rose and grabbed a pot of cold, thin soup. Then she broke a piece from the loaf, which she softened in the soup before pushing it into Othar's mouth.

When Moli's fingers touched Othar lips, a sudden craving seized him. Like his power over minds, it was new. "Cut yourself," he whispered. "Bleed into the soup."

Moli pulled a knife from a pocket in her ragged shift and drew it across her wrist. Othar watched hungrily as a red stream colored the soup pink. Soaked in the bloody liquid, the next bite of bread was more to his liking. He would have enjoyed watching Moli bleed to death, but he needed her. "Bind your wound," he said, knowing that she lacked the will even to save her life.

Moli obeyed, then continued her ministrations. While she fed him, Othar leisurely probed her mind. A part was filled with terror and disgust, but that part was as helpless as someone bricked into a wall. Moli's memories were intact, but her thoughts were reduced to those Othar had given her. He realized that Moli would serve him until her mind snapped from the strain. The mage already sensed tears in her sanity, and he was curious what would happen when it tore asunder. *I'll find out soon enough*, he thought. *She can't last long.*

Othar decided to have Moli lure her replacement to the shack at dawn, for he had already discovered that he required eye contact to seize a mind. The mage was still puzzling on how he acquired the power, and he speculated that it either came from the bones or the entity behind them. The latter seemed most likely. Othar had felt its presence whenever he had used the bones to foretell events. It was malicious and bloodthirsty; his ravaged body was proof of that. *Then, why would it bestow this gift on me?* An answer came quickly. *So I can revenge myself on Dar!*

Two

♛

Dar awoke, both surprised and puzzled. "Mer lav?" *I live?*

A mother knelt before her. She bowed her head and replied in Orcish. "Muth la has preserved your life."

Why? thought Dar. She had returned to pass on Fathma, the Divine Mother's gift that bestowed sovereignty over the orcs. In her near-death state, she had been able to see it fluttering within the shell of her body, a thing of spirit like a second soul. That vision had departed. Dar could no longer see her spirit or any other's. The world was solid again. It was also unfamiliar. "Where am I?" she asked in Orcish.

"Your hanmuthi, Muth Mauk."

Dar realized that she was still queen. Muth Mauk—*Great Mother*—was not only her title; it had become her name. Dar tried to raise her head and look about, but found she couldn't. She recalled the mother's face, but not her name. After Dar had been reborn, every Yat clan member had formally introduced him or herself, and the parade of visitors had lasted days. "I know you," said Dar, "but I forget your name."

"I'm Deen-yat, clan healer."

"I thought I was dying."

"You were," said the healer.

Dar thought she should be relieved and joyful. Instead,

she felt daunted. *I returned to pass on the crown, not rule!* In her still-fragile state, that task seemed overwhelming. *I don't know what to do!*

Deen-yat smelled Dar's anxiety, but mistook its reason. "You'll live, Muth Mauk."

"Then I have your skill to thank."

"Your recovery is not my deed. That herb's magic is deadly."

"I was only scratched by blade."

"Such scratches have slain sons, and quickly, too. Your life is Muth la's gift."

Dar knew Deen-yat's words were meant to comfort, but they didn't. *Muth la has her own purposes.* While Dar thought she understood why she had become queen, she couldn't understand why she remained so.

"How long have I been here?"

"Sun has risen thrice since your return."

"I wish to see my muthuri and my sisters."

"And you will when you're better." Deen-yat smiled. "Even queens must obey healers."

The healer stayed by Dar's side and tended her throughout the day. Toward evening, Dar found the strength to sit up and gaze about. She was in one of the numerous sleeping chambers of the largest hanmuthi she had ever seen. Even the sleeping chambers had adjoining rooms of their own. *Many families could live here,* she thought. She peered through a carved stone archway into the spacious central room. As with all hanmuthis, it was circular and featured a hearth in its center. The room was empty, as were all the other chambers.

Dar's chamber was especially magnificent. There was a huge window glazed with panes of sand ice. The floor was a mosaic of a flowery meadow. The meadow extended to the stone walls, which were carved with a low relief that depicted a landscape. The foreground was filled with delicately rendered wildflowers. In the distance was an orcish city. "It that Tarathank?" asked Dar.

"Hai, Muth Mauk."

"I've visited its ruin," said Dar, recalling her night with Kovok-mah. Deen-yat's expression underwent a subtle change, and Dar realized that the healer had smelled atur—the scent of love. Good manners precluded Deen-yat from mentioning it, but orcs seldom hid their feelings.

"Washavoki brought me here on horse," said Dar, "but there was son who helped him. He gave me healing magic on way." Dar glanced down at the star-shaped incision beneath her breast. It was surrounded by dark, discolored flesh. "Did he come here also?"

"Do you mean your muthuri's brother's son?"

"Hai. Kovok-mah."

"He came here, but he has returned home."

Dar's heart sank. In her weakened state, she feared that she might start weeping. "I wish I could have seen him. He helped save my life."

"His muthuri forbade him to be with you," replied Deen-yat. "Once he learned you would live, he couldn't linger."

Dar's despair deepened. *So the word is out. Even Deen-yat knows.* "What of washavoki who brought me?"

"It has returned to its own kind."

So Sevren's gone, too, thought Dar. *At least I have my family.* "I'd like to see my muthuri soon. And my sisters, especially Nir-yat." Dar surveyed the empty rooms about her, already missing the lively atmosphere of Zor-yat's hanmuthi. "It's too quiet here."

"Perhaps tomorrow," said Deen-yat. She felt Dar's brow and sniffed her wound. "Hai, you should be well enough to see them." She gave Dar a sympathetic look. "It would do you good. It's lonely being great mother."

*   *   *

It was long after nightfall when Kovok-mah arrived at the hall where his parents lived. As he shook the snow from his cloak, his aunt greeted him. "Sister's son! I'm surprised to see you. Kath! Your son has returned from Taiben."

Kath-mah emerged from a sleeping chamber, still rubbing the drowsiness from her eyes. "Kovok? Why are you here? You were sent to kill for washavoki king."

"King is dead, Muthuri. Another rules washavokis now."

"Doesn't our queen wish you to kill for it also?"

"We have new queen."

"This is news indeed! How is that possible? Our queen lived apart."

"She found someone to receive Fathma. Before she died, queen passed it to that mother."

"But mothers no longer visit Taiben."

"This one did."

Kath-mah regarded her son irritably. "Who is she? Why don't you tell me?"

"She was Dargu-yat. But since Fathma changes spirit, she's Dargu-yat no more."

Kath-mah stared at her son, momentarily dumbfounded. Then her expression hardened. "And because I forbade you to be with Dargu-yat, perhaps you think I'll change my mind."

Kovok-mah bowed humbly to his muthuri. "That's my hope."

"When Dargu was reborn, magic transformed her spirit but not her body. She was still as ugly as any washavoki. Now that she's great mother, has that changed?"

"Thwa."

"Then her body won't bear me granddaughters."

"Although I wish for daughters, I think other things are more important."

"That's because you're young. Daughters give you

standing. Look at my sister and me. Who greeted you to her hanmuthi?"

"But Dargu is great mother!"

"And her hanmuthi—however grand—will always lack children."

"Then you won't change your mind?"

"Thwa."

"When I saw Dargu-yat in Taiben, she said you would bless us."

"Where would she get that strange notion?"

"Perhaps from her muthuri. Didn't you two speak together?"

"We did. And Zor-yat knew my mind in this matter. She sympathized and even warned me of Dargu-yat's power."

"What power?"

"Your attraction to her is unnatural. That's magic's doing."

"Dargu knows no magic, though Muth la sends her visions. My feelings come from Muth la."

"Don't speak foolishly. Sons don't understand such matters."

Kovok-mah summoned his courage, and for the first time in his life, he refused to submit passively. "My chest is strong in this."

"I know," said Kath-mah. "Air is heavy with your atur. Whether it is due to magic or Muth la, I remain firm and withhold my blessing. Do nothing rash. Our laws are strict, and even great mothers must bend to them. Heed my wisdom, or your feelings will destroy our queen."

Three

♛

Dar entered darkness with Muth-pah. As before, the Pah clan matriarch led the way through a narrow cave, which was dimly lit by the embers from a string of fires. As Muth-pah passed each glowing pile, she poured water on it. Steam from the extinguished embers filled the dark space, making it hot and damp. Unlike the last time Dar had entered darkness, they didn't arrive at a chamber. Instead, the piles of embers seemed to extend without end— a dotted line of faint orange lights in a black void.

Dar and Muth-pah continued to advance while the dark closed in behind them. Muth-pah's vessel never emptied and the steam grew ever thicker until the way was hard to see. The heat became oppressive. Dar spoke to Muth-pah. "When will this end?"

"How should I know, Muth Mauk? This is your journey." Muth-pah doused yet another fire, and when it went out, all light disappeared. Dar cried out, but there was no reply. She was utterly alone.

Dar sat up drenched in sweat and unsure if she was awake or dreaming. Since she had been stabbed, most of her existence seemed dreamlike. Dar recalled her arrival at the hall and wondered if she had truly viewed the spirits of everyone around her and judged their worth. *If I did, then there's one here who should be queen.* Yet that mother had vanished before Dar could bestow Fathma. Dar didn't know who she was, for spirits looked unlike bodies. Dar had recognized no one.

Dar gazed about the dark hanmuthi. For a moment, she thought she saw sleepers in the other chambers, sitting upright beneath sleeping cloaks. She rubbed her eyes, and the rooms were empty again. The only sleeper was Deen-yat, who sat in Dar's chamber. Dar rose from her mattress to stand and let the sweat dry from her torso. She resolved to bathe first thing in the morning, for she didn't want to greet her family "snoofa va washavoki"— *reeking like washavoki*. Dar suspected that the acceptance she had experienced upon her rebirth would be tested soon. She was no longer simply Zor-yat's daughter, and she'd be judged by a higher standard. Experience had taught her that mothers lacked the subservience of sons. Though she was queen, the obedience she had received in Taiben might not come so quickly in the Yat clan hall.

Dar walked over to the window on shaky legs. She scraped frost from a pane and peered through it. The mountains gleamed white in the moonlight. *The pastures are snow-covered*, she thought. *Kovok-mah's goats will be stabled for the winter, and he'll stay with his muthuri.* Dar reminded herself that it no longer made any difference where Kovok-mah stayed. He was unobtainable.

"Muth Mauk, why are you up?" asked Deen-yat.

"Dream woke me."

"Your flesh is bumpy. Are you chilled?"

"I'm fine," said Dar. "Air feels good."

Nevertheless, Deen-yat rose to stand close to her. "You're still weak. Evil magic lingers yet."

The healer guided Dar back to the mattress. When Dar lay down, Deen-yat covered her with a sleeping cloak. "Try to sleep, Muth Mauk."

Deen-yat's mention of Othar's magic evoked memories of the mage. Dar's last sight of him had been seared into her memory—a pair of eyes staring from a charred face. *He died*, Dar reminded herself. *And the bones, my greater enemy, were destroyed.* She had witnessed both events. *I've nothing to worry about.* Yet after her dream, a shadow of doubt arose.

It was late afternoon and Dar was seated in her hanmuthi, having bathed, blackened her teeth, and dressed in a new neva and new kefs. Following custom, she wore the pair of capelike kefs so her breasts were exposed, although that meant revealing her wound. Zor-yat's eyes fixed on it as soon as she entered the room. "Muth Mauk, my chest breaks to view your injury."

"Please call me 'daughter,' Muthuri. That name makes me most glad."

"Yet you're Muth Mauk now," said Zor-yat. "How can I forget? Where's your crown? You should be wearing it."

"There's no need for crown. My family visits."

"All urkzimmuthi are your family now. When my sister became great mother, everything changed. Dargu-yat is dead."

"Dead?"

"Dargu-yat's spirit is no more. Fathma changes everything."

Dar was about to say that she felt no different when she realized that wasn't true. Although she felt no wiser or mightier, she was imbued with a love for every orc. She also experienced vague, transient memories that she assumed belonged to former queens. "Hai, I've changed. But are you still my muthuri?"

Zor-yat smiled. "Of course, Muth Mauk."

"Then, I'm happy." Dar rose from her stool and embraced her muthuri though it made her wound ache.

Zor-yat smelled Dar's pain as she hugged her. "You must tell me all that happened in Taiben. We received tales from that washavoki that brought you here and my sister's son as well, but only you know everything. Why did my sister die?"

"Black Washavoki poisoned her long ago, then gave her healing magic to keep her alive. That magic clouded her mind so she spoke Black Washavoki's words."

"I thought magic was used on her," said Zor-yat. "So did Muth-yat. I'm glad Black One died."

"In order to clear her mind, your sister stopped taking healing magic, knowing it would cause her death. She'd been waiting for me."

"For you?"

"Hai. For mother to receive Fathma."

"So you could pass it to another?"

Dar recalled hovering on the edge of death and finding no one worthy to receive the divine gift. *Was Muthuri there?* It seemed likely, so Dar worded her reply carefully. "When I thought I was dying, I tried to bestow Fathma, but . . . but I lacked strength."

"Then we're lucky you lived." Zor-yat appeared to reflect for a moment. "Now that you have strength, you can do what you intended."

"Do you think another should be queen?"

"Crown is burden, even for those who are prepared to receive it. Look at my sister's fate."

Dar sighed. "Hai, but this burden is Muth la's gift. I shouldn't refuse it."

"Are you sure?"

"I'm sure of nothing." Dar thought how the Goddess Karm had temples with holy ones to guide the people. "Muthuri, is there someone among urkzimmuthi who understands Muth la best? Someone who offers guidance?"

"Hai, my daughter. She's called Muth Mauk."

Dar and her muthuri talked long. Dar recounted the events in Taiben as thoroughly as she could, knowing that

Muth-yat and many others would quickly hear them. Dar saved one item for last, and as she spoke, she watched Zor-yat carefully. "When I met Kovok-mah in Taiben, I told him his muthuri would bless us. I said this because you told me so. He called me foolish."

"And so you were, Daughter. I never said Kath-mah would bless you. I said I hoped she would."

Dar's recollection was distinctly different. *I never would have gone to Taiben if I'd known the truth.* As she gazed at her muthuri, she had the unsettling suspicion that she had been tricked.

"Love clouds judgment," said Zor-yat. "Your chest overruled your mind, and you heard what you wished to hear."

Dar wanted to believe her muthuri, but she didn't. Nevertheless, she felt it would be unwise to say so. "You speak wisdom," she said, inclining her head as a dutiful daughter. Zor-yat looked pleased and left soon afterward.

The visit had exhausted Dar, and she retired to the mattress in her sleeping chamber. Deen-yat was waiting there, so Dar feigned sleep. She felt both disappointed and disturbed. She had hoped that her reunion with her muthuri would be like her rebirth, when Zor-yat had cradled her and proclaimed to all that Dar was her child. That loving moment had not been repeated. Instead, Dar was certain that her muthuri had lied to her.

In light of that realization, Dar saw herself as Zor-yat and Muth-yat's pawn. Both had understood her visions. They knew Othar was Dar's enemy and didn't warn her. Dar concluded that Zor-yat had been right—feelings had clouded her judgment. Her desire to be a part of Zor-yat's family had blinded her. Dar wondered why Zor-yat had become her muthuri. She suspected it involved the crown.

If that's the case, who'll teach me how to rule? Dar

assumed Zor-yat's advice would be self-serving at best. *And Muth-yat's her sister. Does she want the crown, too?* It seemed likely. Dar knew that both mothers commanded obedience, and whatever she said—regardless to whom—would likely reach their ears. She could trust Zna-yat; his loyalty was absolute. But Zna-yat was a son, and sons knew little about wielding authority. Besides, he was in Taiben. Dar recalled her dream about entering darkness. It suddenly felt like a portent. *I'm lost, all right. And completely alone.*

"Don't visit your sister today," said Zor-yat to Nir-yat. "She's too ill to receive more visitors."

"Hai, Muthuri," said Nir-yat. "Your news saddens me."

"I understand. You two are close. I think she'll be better tomorrow."

"I hope so."

"I should warn you—that magic has gravely harmed her. You'll know that when you see her wound. Dargu isn't well. Neither is she prepared to rule."

"But I've heard . . ."

"Don't question my wisdom!"

Nir-yat bowed her head. "Hai, Muthuri."

"Tomorrow when you speak with your sister, encourage her to pass on Fathma. She intended to do so earlier, but her strength failed her. Now that's she's recovering, she should fulfill her intention. Dargu is newly reborn— a child really. Can you see her facing Council of Matriarchs?"

"She'd find it difficult," said Nir-yat.

"More than difficult. Catastrophic. Dargu received Fathma because she was only mother in Taiben. It was chance, not Muth la's will. If she remains great mother, it'll cause trouble. Another should rule."

Upon hearing those words, Nir-yat grew alarmed. "But afterward . . ."

"Dargu need not know about that. It would frighten her into making poor choice. I forbid you to tell her. Do you understand?"

Nir-yat bowed yet again. "I understand, Muthuri."

Four

♛

Dar received no further visitors for the remainder of the day. After she ate the evening meal, she called Deen-yat to her. "I feel much better. You needn't spend night with me."

Deen-yat bowed. "Shashav, Muth Mauk. It would please me to sleep in my own hanmuthi. But you must promise to do nothing foolish."

Dar smiled. "I'll try not to."

"Then I'll depart. There are always sons outside your hanmuthi. You need only clap and they'll attend to any need." Deen-yat bowed again.

"Go with my gratitude."

"I'll see you in morning. Sleep well, Muth Mauk."

After Deen-yat left, Dar rose and paced slowly about her grand but empty hanmuthi. It was far larger than Zor-yat's, which housed three generations. Dar gazed at the vacant sleeping chambers, feeling lonely. Again, she briefly saw sons and mothers in them. *Are these memories bestowed by Fathma? Ghosts? An effect of my poisoning?* All Dar knew for certain was that the images were growing more real and occurring more frequently. She thought of the generations that had lived within the space where she stood and felt like an interloper. She wondered if her muthuri was right and another should dwell in the han-muthi. Yet Dar couldn't imagine who.

When Nir-yat arrived the following morning and saw Dar's wound, she lost all decorum. She ran to Dar and embraced her, all the while making a keening sound deep in her throat. Dar's eyes teared when she realized her sister was crying. "I'm all right, Nir," she said, stroking Nir-yat's thick hair. "I'm healing. My wound looks worse than it feels."

Nir-yat calmed. When she drew back to examine Dar, her mood changed. She grinned to see the gold band upon Dar's head. "Baby sister's Muth Mauk!"

"Baby? I've twenty-five winters. That makes me older than you."

"Thwa. Those winters don't count. You were reborn this summer, so this is your first winter. You belong on Muthuri's teat."

"Next time I'm hungry, I'll tell her you said so."

The remark made Nir-yat hiss. Dar hissed also, as naturally as if she had laughed that way all her life. "It pleases me to see you, Nir. I missed you."

"I missed you, too. Thir does also." Nir-yat smiled. "She especially misses our room. Muthuri moved us from window chamber as soon as you left for Taiben."

Because she didn't expect me to return, thought Dar, who kept that assumption to herself. "Where is Thir? I thought she'd be coming with you."

"She's at Tok clan hall." Nir-yat grinned. "She has velazul there."

"Is it serious?" asked Dar, glad that her sister finally had a lover.

"She walked there in this weather. What do you think?"

"But he would be her first velazul!"

Dar's sister smiled. "I remember saying same thing to you about Kovok-mah." One glance at Dar's face made Nir-yat regret her words. "I'm sorry. I didn't know you still cared for him."

"I shouldn't," said Dar. "Kath-mah won't bless us."

"Yet head doesn't rule chest. I'm sad for you."

"Did Muthuri tell you of our speech together?" said

Dar, eager to speak of something else. "Do you know what happened in Taiben?"

"Hai. But speak of our brother. Why does he remain there?"

"Zna-yat's there to enforce my will. Sons will guard new washavoki queen, but they won't kill for her."

"Does that mean they'll no longer die in battles?"

"Hai."

"That's joyful news! You accomplished much!"

"You seemed surprised," said Dar. "Didn't Muthuri tell you?"

"Thwa. She thinks you're unfit to rule."

"Perhaps she's right. I know little about being great mother. Another may be more suited."

"I must tell you story," said Nir-yat. "Story about Grandmother."

Nir-yat's abrupt change of subject puzzled Dar, as did her note of urgency. "What is this story?"

"Grandmother was great mother before Zeta-yat. I was close to her. She visited old washavoki king often, and would have taught me washavoki speech had not Muthuri objected." Nir-yat gave Dar a meaningful look. "Muthuri dislikes washavokis." Then she resumed her story. "Five winters ago, Grandmother grew ill. Water filled her lungs, and Deen-yat said she would soon join Muth la. It's said that great mothers see with Muth la's eyes as death approaches, so they can know who should become next queen. Grandmother chose Zeta-yat, same great mother who chose you."

"She chose me because she had no other option," said Dar. "I was only urkzimmuthi mother there."

Nir-yat ignored Dar's comment. "What you should know is that Grandmother didn't join Muth la after bestowing Fathma. She lingered in this world."

"Did she recover?" asked Dar.

"How could she?" said Nir-yat. "She was dead."

"I'm confused."

"When mother receives Fathma, it and her spirit become one. When great mother passes Fathma to another, her spirit departs."

"So what happened?" asked Dar.

"Grandmother became ghost, and she was treated like one. No one talked to her. Everyone behaved as if she wasn't there."

"And if I pass on Fathma . . ."

"I'm not speaking about you," said Nir-yat quickly. "I'm forbidden to say what would happen."

"Forbidden by Muthuri?"

Nir-yat acted as though she hadn't heard Dar's question. "I'm speaking about Grandmother. My grandmother who watched me with lonely eyes while I . . ." Nir-yat looked on the verge of crying again. She paused to compose herself. "I was silent because it's unnatural to speak to those who are dead."

"Those were Muth Mauk's very words after she made me queen!" said Dar.

"Well, she should know," replied Nir-yat. "I hope she didn't linger like Grandmother."

"She didn't."

"Now, in obedience to Muthuri, I'll encourage you to give Fathma to another."

Dar grasped her sister's hand. "Say to Muthuri that I heard you speak about giving Fathma to another. Tell her this: I will consider what you said." Dar hoped those words would permit Nir-yat to answer truthfully when Zor-yat grilled her about their conversation. Daughters were required to obey their muthuris, and Nir-yat seemed distressed by her disobedience. It made Dar love her all the more.

After Nir-yat's cautionary tale, Dar immediately changed the conversation to Thir-yat's new velazul.

Nir-yat gave all the details of the romance, then filled Dar in on other gossip. The Yat clan hall was the size of a small town, so there was much to tell. Nir-yat was soon regaling Dar with a story about a mother with two velazuls. Neither knew about the other until both visited her on the same day. After Nir-yat described the calamitous meal that ensued, she concluded by saying, "So she learned having one velazul is better than having none."

Dar and Nir-yat talked into the afternoon before Dar returned to the subject of her sovereignty. "Nir, can you teach me how great mothers rule?"

Nir-yat instantly grew somber. "That's not my place."

"Who can I turn to? Muthuri? Muth-yat?"

"Muthuri will make me repeat every question you ask, so why not ask her yourself?"

Because, unlike you, she'll try to deceive me, thought Dar.

"Besides," Nir-yat added, "I was still young when Grandmother died. Soon after Zeta-yat became Muth Mauk, she went to Taiben and never returned."

Dar pondered her predicament, then replied. "Hai. I should ask Muthuri." She switched subjects and talked with her sister of other things before asking, "What was Grandmother's name before she became Muth Mauk?"

"We shared name."

"She was called Nir-yat?"

"Hai."

"Was her sister Dargu-yat?" asked Dar, trying to sound playful.

"Thwa," hissed Nir-yat. "Who would name their daughter Dargu?" *Weasel.* "Her name is Meera."

"So she still lives?"

"Hai, but she's so old that her daughter heads hanmuthi."

Having learned what she needed, Dar let the conversation wander where it would. But shortly after Nir-yat left,

Dar summoned one of the sons who stood outside her hanmuthi. He entered and bowed. "Hai, Muth Mauk."

"Do you know where mother named Meera-yat lives?"

"Hai. In her daughter's hanmuthi. It's in oldest part of hall, near court of black stone pool."

"Take me there, then speak of this to no one."

Five

When Coric heard pounding on his master's door, he approached it nervously. The sun was setting, and there had been a rash of robberies in Taiben. A rich merchant's house was a prime target. Coric slid open the peephole and saw a disreputable-looking man standing in the street. His coarse face had a vacant look. Coric noticed that his cheeks twitched uncontrollably and his chin was covered with drool. Beside the man was a handcart, its load covered by a beautiful tapestry. Coric assumed it was stolen, but he knew his master never questioned a bargain.

"I've somethin' fer yer master," said the man in a dead voice. "Open the door."

Coric smiled at the simpleminded ruse. "I think not."

"Then take a good look, and tell yer master what I bring."

Coric watched as the man lifted a corner of the tapestry to reveal a blackened face with staring eyes. "Obey me," said the face. Thought and will drained from Coric's mind. When he said, "Yes, Master," he spoke with the same lifeless tone of the man with the handcart.

Balten was annoyed by Coric's sudden appearance, and he let his servant know it. "You knock, you dog's spawn, afore you enter."

Coric seemed unfazed by his master's ire. "Come to

the entrance hall," he said in a flat tone Balten had never heard before. "There's someone you must meet."

"Must? Must indeed! I meet whom I please. Leave me and throw that arrogant intruder from my house."

Instead of complying, Coric grabbed Balten's arm and began pulling him toward the door. Balten struck his face repeatedly, but Coric didn't flinch as he dragged his master away. By the time the two reached the stairs, Balten had ceased struggling. When he arrived at the entrance hall, a bizarre sight confronted him. A dirty, unkempt man stood by an empty handcart. His face was animated by a constant twitch; otherwise it was blank. Two of Balten's house servants flanked him. Both their faces were equally vacant. A chair had been dragged into the hall and upon it sat the most grotesque member of the ensemble— a man with the aspect of a charred corpse. His lap was covered by an exquisite tapestry.

Despite his terror, Balten summoned up his outrage and addressed the blackened man. "How dare you trespass here? What have you done to my servants?"

"They're my servants now," replied the intruder. His voice, though low and hoarse, was commanding. He pointed with a handless sleeve at one of Balten's servants. "Slit your throat."

Without hesitation or hint of emotion, the man drew a small knife from his tunic and slashed his neck. Then he stood motionless until his life drained from him and he collapsed. Balten stared aghast.

"He would have slit your throat just as calmly," said the man in the chair. "Or I could enslave you like him and give the same command."

"Who . . . Who are you? What do you want?"

The charred man bared his teeth in a horrific grin. "You know me. I was the royal mage."

"Othar? They say you're dead."

"Not dead. Transformed. My body's suffered, but I've been compensated. I can seize minds with a glance and command total obedience."

Balten tried to swallow, but his throat was dry. "Are you going to rob me of my mind?"

"My slaves are useful," said Othar, "but they quickly end up like Nuggle here." He pointed to the drooling, twitching man. "He's lasted longest, but he's nearly spent. I want you intact."

Balten attempted a smile. "I'm gratified."

Othar smiled back. The effect was hideous. "You should be."

"Why are you doing this?"

"I can discern your thoughts, so I'll answer your true questions," replied the mage. "I want neither your wealth nor your life. Yes, you'll benefit. In fact, I'm going to make you wealthier. Much wealthier. And I'll settle that matter with Maltus. I need only a glance into his eyes."

"How did you learn about Maltus?"

"You have no secrets from me. I know you're tupping Coric's wife. Don't fret; Coric's past caring. You worry that your youngest is not of your seed. Bring forth your wife, and I'll find out the truth. This spring, you poisoned that Luvein cloth merchant for his goods. Need I go on?"

Balten silently stared at Othar.

"Good," said Othar. "I require a man to act as my agent. Someone familiar with the court, but inconspicuous. I'll stay in the shadows while you serve as my face and hands. In return, you'll prosper."

Before Balten could utter a word, Othar responded to what he was thinking. "Because wealth will make you more useful. You need only do as I say. Riches don't interest me, though I command many thieves. What surplus they bring, such as this tapestry, you may keep. Are you agreed to serve me?"

Balten started to reply, then realized his thoughts were laid bare. "Sire, you already know my answer."

Othar flashed another grotesque grin. "You learn quickly. That's good. Invite Maltus to this house tomorrow. Any pretext will do. To demonstrate my beneficence, I'll resolve your difficulties with him."

Balten thought it prudent to bow. "Thank you, sire. Will you tell me why you wish my aid? Since wealth disinterests you, what do you desire? Power?"

Without any gesture from the mage, Nuggle and the servant beside him turned to seize each other's throat. Othar watched the two men strangle each other until both expired. Then he chuckled hoarsely. "Power? I've power aplenty. I want the opportunity to use it against those I hate. You'll help with that. Revenge, bloody and merciless, is my desire."

The oldest part of the Yat clan hall was such a warren of hanmuthis, small rooms, and connecting passageways, Dar was glad that she had a guide. He halted before an antique doorway and bowed. "This is place, Muth Mauk."

Dar entered alone and was met by an elderly mother who looked surprised. After an awkward silence, the mother finally took the initiative and bowed. "Greetings. I'm Metha-yat, Muth Mauk."

Unsure how a queen should respond, Dar simply declined her head. "I wish to speak with Meera-yat. Is she here?"

"Hai. I'll show you to her chamber. You must speak loudly if she's to hear you."

Metha-yat's hanmuthi was so old-fashioned that it lacked windows and a chimney. The only daylight entered through the smoke hole above the hearth, and it was fading fast. Small oil lamps provided meager illumination, and in their dim light, Dar couldn't tell which of the adjoining sleeping chambers were occupied. Metha-yat took a lamp and walked over to one. Its light revealed an ancient mother sitting in the dark.

"Muthuri," shouted Metha-yat. "You have visitor."

"What?"

"Visitor. You have visitor."

Dar spoke quietly to Metha-yat. "My speech with your muthuri is for her ears only."

After Metha-yat bowed and left the hanmuthi, Dar stepped into the small sleeping chamber. Meera-yat had not turned to look at her, and Dar suddenly understood why. Meera-yat's yellow eyes were filmed over. She was blind.

"What's that strange smell?" asked Meera-yat.

Dar thought she had met every clan member after her rebirth, but she had no recollection of Meera-yat's distinctive face. *I hope she's heard of me.* She addressed the ancient mother in a loud voice. "I'm Zor-yat's new daughter. One who was reborn."

"No one tells me anything," muttered Meera-yat. She held out her hand. "Let me feel your face."

Dar guided the shaking fingers to her chin, so Meera-yat might touch her clan tattoo first. Meera-yat traced the raised lines of the Yat clan markings. "Your chin feels too round," she said. Her fingers brushed over Dar's lips, then halted when they reached her nose. Meera-yat's surprise and puzzlement were communicated by her touch. Her fingers traveled upward like startled spiders. "What's this? What's this?" Meera-yat's exploration ended at Dar's brow. "You're washavoki!"

"Thwa," shouted Dar. "I've been reborn. I'm urkzimmuthi."

"Reborn? Why didn't you say so?" said Meera-yat. "What's your name?"

"I was named Dargu. Now . . ."

Meera-yat grinned. "Who gives her daughter animal's name?"

"Zor-yat," said Dar loudly.

Meera-yat grinned again. "Hai, Zor-yat would do that."

"Dargu was my old name. Now I'm . . ."

Before Dar finished speaking, Meera-yat touched her crown. "What's this?"

"You know," yelled Dar. "Your sister wore it."

"Muth Mauk? You're Muth Mauk? How did this happen?"

"Same way it happened for Nir-yat." Dar gently grasped Meera-yat's hands and placed them on her chest, duplicating the act that had made her queen. "Fathma."

Meera-yat's hands lingered, and it seemed to Dar that a look of wonder settled on her wrinkled face. "My eyes no longer see," she said quietly, "so Muth la has enhanced other senses. I can feel my sister's spirit within you. It's mingled with many others." Meera-yat bowed as low as her old back would permit. "Forgive me, Muth Mauk, for calling you washavoki."

Rather than shout her reply, Dar gently grasped the old orc's hands.

"So you're Zor-yat's daughter." Meera-yat made a face. "Is she pleased you wear crown?"

"I think not," shouted Dar.

"I'm not surprised. Zor-yat was displeased when her sister, and not she, received Fathma. Now she's been passed over twice. So, Muth Mauk, why did you seek me out?"

"I'm queen, but I know little," yelled Dar. "I need guidance. What to do. How to behave."

"Is your muthuri no help?"

"She thinks another should rule."

"What?"

"Wants different queen," shouted Dar.

"Herself, no doubt. Probably Muth-yat is of like mind."

"Your sister was queen. You know as much as they do."

Meera-yat smiled. "I was by her side for many winters."

"Will you help me?"

"Hai, Muth Mauk."

"I must warn you," shouted Dar. "I think Muth-yat will be displeased."

"What do I care? I've nothing to lose. My line is cut. My granddaughters sickened in Taiben. My grandsons died in battles. Only Metha remains, consumed by grief." Meera-yat thought a moment, then asked, "Do you know of Muth la's Dome?"

"Hai," shouted Dar, recalling the place where she had undergone rebirth.

"That would be good place to talk. It's sacred space, and we'd be alone."

Dar liked the choice of meeting site. It was proof that Meera-yat recognized Dar's delicate position. "I'll send son to guide you there."

"I need not eyes to find way. When sun is highest, I'll go there and wait for you."

Dar bowed, though Meera-yat couldn't see the gesture. "Shashav."

"I deserve no thanks, for you honor me, Muth Mauk. I'll do my utmost. There is much I can teach you, but I can't find your path. That you must do yourself."

Dar had feared as much. Yet, she had one consolation, and she spoke it out loud. "At least I have Fathma. No one can take that."

"Council of Matriarchs can."

"How?"

"Haven't you heard of Muth la's Draught?"

"Thwa. What's that?"

"Test of worthiness. It's potion made from seeds of Muth la's sacred tree. Council can require queen to drink it if they think she's unfit."

"What does that prove?" asked Dar.

"If queen should rule, Muth la will preserve her life."

"Draught is poison?"

"Only if queen is unfit."

"And when she dies, Fathma goes to another?"

"Hai. It's Muth la's will."

This revelation stunned Dar, and her position suddenly seemed precarious. The "test" likened to an execution. "Has any queen ever passed this test?"

"Matriarchs are wise. When they think great mother is unfit, they've never been wrong."

Six

By the time Dar returned to the royal hanmuthi, her anxiety had grown. It had occurred to her that the clan matriarchs might oppose her, but she had no idea their opposition could prove fatal. It made her wonder if she had misjudged the intentions behind Zor-yat's advice to pass on the crown. Yet, while Dar felt threatened, she fought any impulse to surrender. She did so partly from stubbornness, but mostly owing to Fathma. It had continued to transform her in ways too subtle for her to precisely describe, so despite her ignorance, she felt ever more a queen.

Moreover, Dar hoped the matriarchs would appreciate the good she had accomplished already. No more sons would die in washavoki wars. Dar recalled the slaughter at the Vale of Pines, and the rage she had felt returned. *That must never happen again!* Her treaty with Queen Girta ensured it wouldn't. Dar assumed the orc regiments would disband, leaving only a small guard to protect the washavoki queen.

As soon as Dar thought about her treaty, she began to wonder how it was being implemented. Even as it was announced, she had been succumbing to the mage's poison. Her instructions to Zna-yat were simple: "Stay here and see my will is done." *Will he know what to do? He speaks only Orcish. Who will deal with Girta?* Dar had expected Kovok-mah to do that, but he had left Taiben to give her healing magic. Then he had returned home.

The more Dar considered the situation, the more precarious her accomplishment seemed. While she was recovering from her injury, it seemed that no one had followed events in Taiben. Dar had no idea what was happening there. All she knew was that the treaty was her responsibility. *This is what it means to rule.* Dar had a feeling that affairs in Taiben could easily slip into chaos. *If they do, it'll be my fault.*

Zna-yat stood in his rusty armor as one of the guards flanking the throne. He had been standing all afternoon, and he was bored. Washavokis came and went, babbling incomprehensibly to their great mother. Mingled with their reek, Zna-yat detected the scent of fear. He thought it was good that they were afraid; fear would make them less likely to attack the one he protected. As best as he could tell from overhearing the babble, she was either called "Quengirta" or "Yermajessy." Perhaps she had two names. Washavokis were strange like that.

Although Zna-yat disliked standing guard, as one who wore a leader's cape he had to provide an example. Dargu wanted Quengirta and her child protected, so his duty was clear. He would keep them safe, and obey Quengirta also. The last task was difficult because she didn't know the speech of mothers. Zna-yat had asked Gargatok to teach her a few basic commands such as "kill" and "help." *I wish Kovok-mah was here*, Zna-yat thought. *He speaks with washavokis skillfully.*

Zna-yat suspected Garga-tok's fluency was less than desired because Quengirta had yet to comply with most of his requests. The urkzimmuthi guards still lacked proper quarters within the palace. Their room was large enough, but it wasn't round. The washavokis had been displeased when sons had hacked the boundary of Muth la's Embrace into the wooden floor with their swords. Zna-yat had instructed Garga-tok to explain the importance of the sacred circle, but the washavokis had shaped their mouths in the sign of anger. They were even more displeased when sons built a hearth in the circle's center.

There was also the incident of the hairy-faced washavokis who tried to serve food. A son nearly killed the first one that stepped inside Muth la's Embrace. Zna-yat had prevented him from doing so, but trouble had ensued. When Garga-tok told Quengirta that sons must be served by mothers, she had replied that Dargu had sent them all away. That made little sense, for Dargu knew the proper way of doing things. Zna-yat could only conclude that the washavokis had misunderstood her. After much talk, woe mans were found to serve food. However, they smelled of fear and didn't know what words to say. Garga-tok had tried to teach them, but it had gone poorly.

Everything's gone poorly since Dargu departed, thought Zna-yat. His chest was heavy, for he felt certain that Dargu was dead. That didn't alter his obligations. Dargu had bitten his neck, which made his life hers. To Zna-yat's thinking, it would always be hers. As long as he lived, he must strive to carry out her wishes.

Zna-yat turned his attention to the washavoki babbling to Quengirta. Its ridiculous garments made it resemble a brightly colored bird. Even its sword had colored stones on its handle. Zna-yat wondered why washavokis made their weapons pretty and rudely wore them in their halls. He suspected it was because they liked killing. On impulse, Zna-yat bared his black teeth, exposing his fangs to the washavoki. Its neck jerked back, making it look even more like a bird. As the scent of its fear grew stronger, Zna-yat hissed softly. *I probably shouldn't scare it*, he thought. Still, it was amusing.

Zna-yat was glad when his watch finally ended and he could wash the reek of so many washavokis from his skin. Yet even bathing was a problem. Washavokis seldom bathed and lacked communal baths. Instead, they used vessels that fit only their small bodies. The sole basin large enough for a proper bath was in a hall where horses lived. Usually, its water bore a skin of ice. When Zna-yat returned to the urkzimmuthi living quarters, he shed his armor and his garments and headed for the basin.

His route took him through the palace, and as always, the washavokis he encountered acted strangely. The woe mans, especially, did peculiar things. They squeaked and covered their eyes as if the sight of his body hurt them. Zna-yat knew they behaved the same way when other sons went to the basin. He had sent Garga-tok to discover why, but Garga-tok came back with a silly reason. Sons without garments were called "nekked," and washavokis thought nekked was bad. That made little sense. Zna-yat wondered if the washavokis bathed with their garments on. If so, that explained why they did it so infrequently.

The icy water left Zna-yat refreshed. When he returned to Muth la's Embrace, he dressed in his tunic and cape, then sat close to the hearth. It was constructed of large stones laid upon the wooden floor, and the fire it contained was small. Used neither for heating nor cooking, its flame was mostly to remind the orcs of their homes. Nevertheless, smoke made the air hazy and had stained the ceiling.

"This room should have smoke hole," said a voice.

Zna-yat looked up and saw Magtha-jan. "Hai," said Zna-yat. "And round walls to mark Muth la's Embrace, and urkzimmuthi mothers to bestow Muth la's gifts."

"Muth Mauk said this would come to pass."

"Hai," replied Zna-yat. "But it'll take time. I appreciate your patience. I know you long for home, and I'm pleased you agreed to stay."

"It was hard choice," said Magtha-jan, "but I believe in wisdom of Muth Mauk's treaty."

"I hope washavokis do also."

"You think they don't?"

"Their queen fears us," said Zna-yat. "Her son does, too."

"I've smelled this also. Why should they fear us? We protect them."

"I'm not one to ask. I understand washavokis little. All I know is that most are strange and cruel."

"I think Muth la made Dargu-yat queen because she understands them," said Magtha-jan. "She's urkzimmuthi, yet washavokis don't fear her."

"You speak wisdom," said Zna-yat. Having received no announcement of Dargu's death, he kept his fears of it to himself. He was worried what would happen when the news arrived. The orc guards might choose to leave unless the new queen decreed they should stay. Zna-yat had no idea if she would.

The arrival of woe mans bearing food interrupted Zna-yat and Magtha-jan's conversation. Zna-yat was surprised to note that the woe man leading the procession had a branded forehead, which meant the woe man had served in the regiments. This was a change. Since sons had arrived at the washavoki great mother's hall, only unmarked woe mans had served. The branded woe man spoke the proper words. "Saf nak ur Muthz la." *Food is Muth la's gift.* This was also a change.

The orcs responded in unison. "Shashav, Muth la." *Thank you, Muth la.*

Afterward, the woe mans served. Unlike in the regiment, they brought the food on platters. As a woe man placed Zna-yat's meal before him, she attempted to say "Muth la urak tha saf la"—*Muth la gives you this food*—but her speech was barely intelligible. Nevertheless, Zna-yat was encouraged by the attempt at appropriate behavior.

The food was only a slight improvement over that

served in the regiment. As in the army, it was mainly porridge, though there were some boiled roots. The meal also
included meat, a rare item. Unfortunately, it was nearly
spoiled, a fact Zna-yat's keen nose detected despite the
dish's heavy spicing. He left the meat untouched.

The woe mans returned after the meal was over to retrieve the platters and depart for the night. Afterward, a
lone washavoki dressed in blue and scarlet entered the
hall. That was unusual. It halted outside Muth la's Embrace and did an unexpected thing: It spoke in the tongue
of mothers, albeit poorly. "Ma pahav Zna-yat." *I say
Zna-yat.*

Zna-yat rose, and approached the washavoki. It
seemed familiar, but most washavokis looked alike. It
bowed politely and spoke again. "Ma nav Sevren." *I am
Sevren.*

Zna-yat nodded and replied in Orcish. "I am Zna-yat."

The washavoki bowed again, and continued speaking
in the tongue of mothers. "I . . . take Dargu-yat . . ." It
imitated a galloping horse with its fingers. ". . . take her
to . . ." It seemed unsure what to say next.

"To hall?" said Zna-yat. "To healer?"

The washavoki made a puzzling gesture with its shoulders. "You hear? She live? She kill?"

It wants to know if Dargu lived or died, thought Zna-
yat. He replied as if he were speaking to an infant. "You
there. You see."

"I no see. Mother say go. Dargu-yat live? Dargu-yat
kill?"

"I do not know," replied Zna-yat. When the washavoki looked confused, he added, "Mothers no say. I no
hear."

"You no hear?"

"Hai."

The washavoki bowed low. "Shashav, Zna-yat."

Zna-yat watched the washavoki depart. It was a

strange encounter, and he didn't know what to make of it, other than the washavokis knew no more about Dargu's fate than he did. Zna-yat thought Quengirta might have sent the washavoki, since it wore the colors of her guard, but he suspected it acted on its own. Zna-yat's time with Dargu had taught him to recognize washavoki expressions. *It was sad*, he thought. His orcish sense of smell also detected another, more puzzling, emotion. *It was in love.*

A group of guardsmen waited for Sevren at a safe distance from the orcs' quarters. Valamar stood among them and grinned when he saw his friend returning. "Pay up, lads. He made it back in one piece."

As Sevren approached, the men paid Valamar their bets.

"What of the orc wench, Sevren?" asked one of the losers.

"Mind your tongue," he replied. "She's a queen now, or at least, she was."

"A queen of piss eyes," said the man. "Hardly royalty."

"More like their whore," said another.

Sevren knocked him to the floor. He was about to deal another blow when Valamar restrained him. "Calm down, Sevren. Thrashing Wulfar won't change anything. The whole army's named her orc wench. And worse. You can't fight them all."

Wulfar rose, trying to look menacing.

"Come, Sevren," said Valamar. "I'll stand you an ale at the Bloody Boar."

As the two headed for the tavern, Valamar spoke. "That woman's made you foolhardy, and tonight's a fine example. It's wise to avoid orcs. A few days ago, one nearly killed a serving man. Broke both his arms."

"He was sent by fools who should've known better. Orcs will na abide men serving food."

"Why should *we* change? If they're supposed to be guardsmen, let them act like guardsmen."

"They're na men, so they can na be guardsmen. Could you become an orc?"

"You claim Dar did," replied Valamar.

"Aye, and she thought it an improvement."

"Did you?"

" 'Tis unimportant now."

"So, what did the orcs say?"

"I'm still learning their tongue and lack skill in it, but it seems they know na more than we do. I fear she's dead. She seemed nearly so when I last saw her."

"Since you returned their queen, why wouldn't the orcs let you stay? That seems common courtesy."

"A queen's death is momentous. To them, I was only some washavoki."

"But to question you and turn you out? Your regard for them is overblown. They're called brutes for a reason."

"This summer, who used their own troops as bait? Who pillaged Karm's Temple? Mayhap orcs are brutes, but they're honest ones."

"I wouldn't trust an orc," said Valamar. "Dar addled your wits, and that's for certain. Still, I'm sorry she's gone. You were right—she had spirit."

Sevren sighed. "Aye, she did."

The two men entered the tavern, where Valamar purchased the ale. Sevren, having refused to touch plunder from the temple, was not a copper richer after the summer campaign. He thanked his friend, then raised his flagon. "To Dar, and what she wrought. To peaceful times."

Valamar touched his flagon to Sevren's. "I'll drink to your departed love, but peaceful times are lean times. No war means no plunder."

"Queen Girta has a treasury."

"Just a name for an empty chest. If there's no campaign, we'll be threadbare by summer's end. Men are already leaving. How about you?"

"I've na yet the price of a farm."

"Then why did you refuse your summer's share?"

" 'Twas obtained by sacrilege. You can na buy land with cursed gold. The curse lingers in the purchase."

Valamar grinned. "Then you're drinking cursed ale."

"Which I'll piss away afore sunrise."

Valamar's grin broadened. "That's the first wise thing you've said all evening."

Seven

♛

Dar pushed through snow and brown weed stalks to reach Muth la's Dome. It was not yet noon, but she wanted to ensure that Meera-yat could reach their meeting place easily. The small stone hemisphere stood in the center of an otherwise empty courtyard. No one had visited it recently, and the surrounding snow was deep and undisturbed. It formed a drift against the dome's ancient wooden door, which Dar struggled to pull open. In her weakened state, the effort left her panting.

The dome's single, circular room was ten paces across and partly below ground level. Dar descended a short set of stairs to reach its stone floor. A small opening in the apex of the ceiling admitted some dim light and an occasional snowflake. Dar gazed about the place that had been the site of her great ordeal and great joy. The room looked undisturbed since her rebirth, although the hole in the floor's center had been covered by a circular flagstone. Dar wondered if water still filled the hole. If it did, it was surely frozen. The floor about the flagstone bore a dusting of snow, and Dar's breath condensed each time she exhaled.

When Dar heard Meera-yat at the doorway, she rushed to help her down the stairs. "Greeting, Mother," she shouted. "You chose cold place for us to talk. Will you be warm enough?"

"My comfort is unimportant, Muth Mauk."

Dar led Meera-yat to where the floor was free of snow.

Meera-yat sat down and Dar huddled next to her. "What has Zor-yat told you about being great mother?" asked Meera-yat.

The dome's curved walls enhanced Dar's voice, so she didn't have to shout her reply. "Only that I should pass on Fathma."

"Did she speak of what would happen afterward?"

"Thwa, but Nir-yat did."

"Nir-yat has good chest. She's well named," said Meera-yat. "I assume you wish to keep your spirit."

"I've work that's unfinished. I can't die yet."

Meera-yat nodded. "Already, you think like queen. Muth la helped queen choose her successor wisely."

"I was only mother present. Queen had no other choice."

"Don't you think that was Muth la's doing?" asked Meera-yat.

"Muthuri doesn't."

"I won't speak ill of your muthuri, but . . . humph! Well, I'll tell you what you need to know. Great mother is muthuri to all urkzimmuthi. Remember this, and ruling comes naturally."

I've never had children, thought Dar. *How can I act like a muthuri?* She recalled how her human mother dutifully submitted to a man who crushed her spirit. That example provided no guidance. "Your advice sounds wise, but I've not lived among urkzimmuthi long," replied Dar, "and I've spent more time with sons than mothers."

"Yet you must know Muth la rules world through mothers. Muthuris are like Muth la in their own hanmuthis. Be like them. Show love, require obedience, and . . ." Meera-yat smiled. ". . . expect problems. Children aren't always tranquil, especially daughters. Some will be headstrong. You must be firm."

Dar imagined trying to be firm with Zor-yat and Muth-yat. "That won't be easy."

"Everyone expects queen to show path. If you're confident, they'll follow."

"But how will I show them this path?" asked Dar. Her own dealings with the late queen had been personal and direct. When she had led the orcs against King Kregant, she was surrounded by her troops. Dar had no idea how to rule subjects that lived in distant halls. King Kregant had officials to carry out his commands, which made her wonder if she'd have similar functionaries. "Who will aid me when I rule?"

"Clan matriarchs and your mintaris."

The latter word was unfamiliar. Dar broke it down into "sons" and "bitten." "I bit Zna-yat's neck, and his life became mine," she said. "Is it same with mintaris?"

"Hai. When son becomes your mintari, his first duty is to you. You come before his clan's matriarch or even his muthuri. Choosing your mintaris is major decision. It's best they come from all clans. Gather sons to you, but don't hurry to bite their necks. See if they're suitable first. This deed can't be undone."

"How do I gather them?"

"Ask each clan matriarch to send you unblessed sons to serve you. Two per clan is customary. You can ask for more later."

"Who chooses these sons? Matriarch? Or can I name them?"

"You can name them if you wish."

Dar immediately thought of Kovok-mah. "Can son's muthuri forbid him to go?"

"Thwa. Besides, it's honor to be asked."

Dar was glad that Meera-yat couldn't see her smile. *Kath-mah can't keep Kovok-mah from me!* "Should I do this soon?"

"Hai. It will let matriarchs know there is new queen. Then they will gather here for council meeting."

"What should I do at this meeting?"

"Impart what wisdom Muth la has given you."

Dar thought that advice was vague to the point of being useless. She envisioned a room full of matriarchs, all much older than she and accustomed to wielding authority. *They'll think I'm an upstart!* Dar grew anxious. She suspected Meera-yat smelled her fear, for the ancient mother grasped her hand and squeezed it. "Remember, you have Fathma."

"So did great mothers who drank Muth la's Draught and died."

"It's rare for Council of Matriarchs to question queen's fitness, and rarer still for them to call for Draught. Didn't you say you have unfinished work? I believe Muth la will permit you to complete it."

It occurred to Dar that her sole purpose might be to bring Fathma back to the orcs and someone with more experience should implement the treaty. *If that's the case, I'll be deemed unfit.* Dar wondered what would happen if she refused to drink Muth la's Draught. She suspected it would be futile.

"It'll take a while for matriarchs to arrive," said Meera-yat. "Muth-goth's hall is far away."

"Muth-pah's hall is even farther."

"Why do you speak of Muth-pah? Pah clan is lost."

"That's not so. I've stayed with Pah clan and met Muth-pah. Together, we entered darkness to receive visions."

Meera-yat didn't immediately reply, but her agitated expression made Dar uneasy. "You entered darkness? What happened afterward?"

"Muth-pah said world had changed."

"Oh my! And you're queen now! Oh my!"

"What's the matter?"

"Woe that I should live unto this time!"

"Won't you help me?" asked Dar, perplexed by Meera-yat's abrupt change.

"Help you? Never! How could I?"

Meera-yat struggled to her feet and began a shuffling search for the stairs. Dar rose to help her. "Please, Mother, tell me what's upset you."

"I must go. Help me to door, then let me be. I'll find my way."

Dar could do little more than comply, for the elderly mother refused to speak further. After Meera-yat left, Dar remained inside the dome, feeling alarmed and mystified. Zor-yat and Muth-yat had also learned about her visit to the Pah clan, and they had seemed undisturbed by the news. Dar pondered why it had upset Meera-yat. It was possible that she knew something Muth-yat and Zor-yat didn't. There seemed little hope of finding out what it was. It was also possible that circumstances had changed since Dar first told her story. One change was obvious. *I'm queen now.* Dar wondered for how long.

Dar was about to leave the room when she spotted someone sitting in its shadows. The discovery startled her, for she was certain that the dome had been empty when she entered it. Using her most authoritative tone, she addressed the stranger, who appeared as little more than a shadowy shape. "Reveal yourself. What are you doing here?"

The figure rose and advanced. The light revealed a frail old man with a long white beard. He was dressed in a tattered gray robe. Dar gazed at him, awestruck. "Velasa-pah?"

The wizard's deeply lined face was solemn. He bowed, then spoke in the human tongue. "Beware the bones."

"The bones were destroyed," said Dar.

Velasa-pah seemed about to reply when a stone block crashed onto the floor. Dar looked upward. The hole in the ceiling was no longer circular. Its edge had a gap like a missing tooth, and the sky beyond had an orange tinge. As Dar gazed at the ceiling, a second stone fell. Then the hole in the ceiling continued to enlarge as the stone blocks encircling it loosened and tumbled down. The entire dome threatened to collapse. Dar dashed out the door to avoid being crushed.

She emerged into a courtyard surrounded by fire. The entire clan hall was ablaze. Huge sheets of flame rose high into the sky, turning it black with smoke. The rumble of falling stones, but no voices, accompanied the fire's crackle and roar. The heat was searing. Already, the snow in the courtyard had melted and the weeds were smoldering. Dar heard a grinding noise behind her. She turned to see Muth la's Dome tumble down. The entire hall seemed in danger of doing the same.

"Muth Mauk!" called a voice. Dar turned toward the sound and saw Deen-yat emerging from the burning hall. She seemed calm. "You shouldn't be outside in cold," said the healer, her tone mildly scolding. "Come inside."

Dar was about to reply that the hall was on fire, when she realized it wasn't. *I'm having a vision*, she thought, hoping it would end. The flames faded, and the smoke-blackened sky turned gray. Without looking, Dar knew Muth la's Dome was still standing. *At least, for now,* she thought. Then, without a backward glance, she followed Deen-yat into the Yat clan hall.

Eight

♛

The flames had seemed so real that Dar's brow was flushed and sweaty. Deen-yat thought she had a fever. She escorted Dar back to the royal hanmuthi and directed her to rest. Dar didn't argue, but she insisted on being alone. She was deeply shaken and needed time to compose herself. Her meeting with Meera-yat, which had begun with such promise, had only compounded her insecurity. Dar feared that she had committed some error already and her vision was a glimpse of its consequences.

For a long while, Dar could think of nothing but the burning hall. She relived its destruction repeatedly until its horror gradually dulled. Only then did she ponder the vision's meaning. She assumed that it was somehow linked to her conversation with Meera-yat, who had been calm until Dar mentioned the Pah clan. Dar wondered if that was why she saw the vision of Velasa-pah and the hall's destruction immediately after Meera-yat's outburst. It seemed logical. Yet that assumption left Dar only more confused. She needed to discover what had alarmed Meera-yat. Direct questioning would yield no answers, though she didn't understand why.

Dar recalled the tale of Cymbe, the girl who ran off to live with a bear. Cymbe's naïveté had doomed her. *I'm equally doomed unless I discover what's going on.* As Dar considered her situation, it seemed hopeless. She needed a mother to guide her, but she didn't trust her muthuri or Muth-yat. Dar recalled the late queen's advice: "When you're Muth Mauk, just follow your chest." But an unsettled chest was an uncertain guide.

Queen Girta eyed Lokung with distaste. She distrusted the royal steward, but then she distrusted all of her late husband's courtiers. The fact that she needed Lokung made her like him even less. They were in her private chambers, away from the orc guards that made the steward nervous. Nevertheless, he kept glancing at the door, knowing they were stationed just outside it.

Lokung handed Girta a parchment. "A minor matter, Your Majesty. The Merchants' Guild needs a new master. If you approve, it'll be Balten."

"What happened to the old master?"

"Maltus took his own life yesterday afternoon. He stopped a guard on the city walls, handed him a note, then jumped to his death. The note was a confession. He'd been stealing from the guild treasury."

Girta recalled Maltus from court functions. "He had a reputation for honesty."

"Reputations can be deceptive, Your Highness."

"Who's this Balten?"

"You've seen him in court. He's guild treasurer."

"Since the treasury was looted, he seems a poor choice for master."

"The guilty party has confessed. Besides . . ." Lokung flashed a smile that Girta found patronizing. ". . . why concern yourself with the affairs of peddlers?"

"Affix my seal," said Girta. "They can have whoever they wish for master."

After marking the parchment with Girta's seal, Lokung brought up another subject. Girta had noted that he never spoke first about what concerned him most, so she was not fooled by his casual tone. "One of your guardsmen visited the orcs last night."

"So?"

"It was that traitor, Sevren."

"I pardoned Sevren, and with good cause. He helped to bring about peace."

"Every wolf is peaceful after it's supped. The orcs rebelled, and now they're sated. But for how long?"

"All they wanted was peace."

"They chose a strange manner to show it. Your husband's dead."

"Killed by his own mage."

"So they say. Yet no one saw him do it."

"Dar was witness."

"Who could have done the deed and murdered Othar as well."

"Then poisoned herself for good measure?" said Girta. "Your imagination's overripe."

"Still, Your Majesty, I'd closely watch the orcs and those that consort with them. Sevren's been seen with one who's notorious for orcish dealings."

"A glass merchant," replied Girta. "From whom would he purchase his wares if not from orcs? They first discovered the secret of its making and still do the finest work."

"How do you know this?" asked Lokung.

"Not through spies. Sevren told me."

"You've spoken to him?"

"Of course. He serves in my royal guard. He's the one who told me that women must serve orcs food. He also found a woman experienced with them. Since she entered my service, meals have gone smoother."

Lokung smiled. "I'm glad he knows what quiets orcs. Let's hope they stay appeased."

"'Appeased'? Why use that word?"

"So you believe the orcs want peace?"

"You speak as though you've heard otherwise."

"I don't credit rumors. Still, the orcs have revolted once already and now they dwell in the palace."

"They've sworn to guard me."

Lokung noted uncertainty in the queen's voice and seized his opportunity. "Aye, Your Highness, they're fearsome guards. Well you know my fear of them. In truth, I don't trust what I can't understand. Their yellow eyes liken to a beast's. Who can tell their thoughts . . . the nature of their lusts . . . what provokes them? When they stare at you, silent and grim, don't you feel uneasy?"

"They serve me," replied Girta. "As do you."

Lokung noted the fear in the queen's eyes. He gave a deep bow and departed, feeling the conversation had gone well. Balten had recruited him to drive a wedge between the queen and the orcs. Girta's apprehensions were making the job easy. All Lokung needed to do was fan them. The payment he had been offered was ample compared with the effort. If Lokung obtained more assignments, his gambling debts would cease to plague him. Betraying the queen's interests didn't bother him, but he worried that future tasks might be less easy. Furthermore, Balten's new associate unnerved him. Still, there was no turning back. The stranger was not one to cross. That was already evident. Balten had made dark hints about the man's powers. When he spoke of them, there had been fear in his eyes.

The royal steward's rooms lay within the palace, but Lokung did not return to them. Instead, he left the castle's safety to visit Balten's house. Taiben's narrow streets were dangerous after dusk, but Lokung went alone. He hurried, hoping to be done with his errand before sunset.

A frightened servant admitted Lokung into the merchant's house. When Balten arrived in the entrance hall, Lokung handed him the parchment. "The queen bestowed her seal. You're guild master now."

Balten smiled, but Lokung thought he looked almost as anxious as his servant. The merchant glanced nervously at a closed door. "He wants to speak with you."

A chill settled in Lokung's stomach. "Do you know why?"

Balten shook his head. "Don't keep him waiting."

Lokung gathered his courage and approached the door. Before he could knock, he heard a hoarse voice. "Enter."

Lokung obeyed. The room was cold, though there was a fire in its ornate fireplace. Candles provided light, for heavy curtains covered the windows. Despite exquisite tapestries on the walls and opulent furnishings, the chamber had an eerie atmosphere. Even the candlelight seemed pale and watery.

Balten's nameless associate sat in a huge chair of carved walnut. He was richly dressed in somber hues, but Lokung's eyes were drawn to his head. It was enclosed, both front and back, by a silver mask. A craftsman had formed its features so they appeared both noble and tranquil. The eyelids drooped in a languid manner and the parted lips were formed in a gentle half smile. There were small holes in the silver head at the ears and nostrils. The openings for the eyes and mouth were larger and hinted that a monstrosity lay beneath the metal. The eyes, in particular, countered the expression of the mask. They terrified Lokung.

He bowed. "I spoke with the queen, sire."

"And?"

The eyes behind the mask fixed on Lokung, who suspected they possessed supernatural perception. Thus, prudence made him honest. He gave his account, ending it by asking, "Are you pleased?"

"You still live," replied the man behind the mask.

"Sire, it's said our royal mage could read minds. Do you possess that power?"

"Speak of this mage. He interests me. Where is he now?"

"He's dead, sire."

"Do you mourn him?"

Staring at the bland, silver face, Lokung felt the chill of menace. "I . . . I feared him, sire."

"A wise answer. And true." The last comment seemed to confirm Lokung's suspicions. "I want the orcs estranged. Continue your efforts with the queen and spread mistrust throughout the court. Take your time. Be subtle. Do you have any thoughts on this matter?"

"Girta wants a man's guidance," replied Lokung. "The right one could easily sway her will."

"You're thinking of yourself, perhaps?"

Lokung thought he heard mockery in the low voice. "Nay, sire. She doesn't trust me. I think she trusts no man in court."

"Who then?"

"Someone from outside the court who has knowledge of orcs. The orc regiments have been disbanded, and their human officers have lost their commissions. Perhaps one of their number might aid you. If you find someone suitable, I could promote his cause in court."

The masked man nodded. "Your idea has merit, but only if we can find the right man. Let it about that I'm a rich merchant recruiting a commander for my personal guard. Tell all I'm generous." With a hand wrought from silver, he pointed to a small bag on a table. "You've served me well. That's for you."

Lokung took the bag and heard coins clink. Pleased by their weight, he bowed low. "Thank you, sire."

"Send me those officers you spoke of. When I find one that suits me, I'll let you know. Advance my interests, and you'll prosper. Now go."

Lokung left the room feeling relieved. Balten was absent from the entrance hall, but a stranger stood there. He was a young-faced man whose deep tan set off his light gray eyes. Those eyes regarded Lokung with contempt before they turned away. *Wait till you stand before Silver Face*, thought Lokung. *Then you'll be scared, too.*

*   *   *

The loud knock startled Othar. It also puzzled him, for he had not perceived another presence outside his door. He was even more surprised by who entered without his leave. "Gorm!"

Othar had not seen Gorm since he had come, unbidden, to peddle the magic bones. Despite his shabby, travel-worn clothes, Gorm had refused to haggle over their exorbitant price, and Othar had been hard put to convince the king to pay it. After receiving his gold, Gorm had disappeared as mysteriously as he arrived.

Trying to read Gorm's thoughts, Othar gazed into his eyes. As on the last occasion they met, the pale gray orbs struck Othar as too old for the face around them. They were impenetrable. Othar redoubled his efforts and attempted to seize Gorm's mind. The effort failed. Gorm's lips formed a sardonic smile. "Those powers won't avail you. If you want to know why I'm here, you must ask."

For the first time since he had been carried from the pit, Othar felt a twinge of fear. "I paid you for the bones. We've no further business."

"That's untrue. You allowed the bones to be destroyed."

"Aye, but they were mine, so that's not your concern."

"I received coins for them, that's true. Yet if you paid me for the sun, would it be yours?"

"You've come a long way to speak riddles."

"I've come to serve my master," replied Gorm.

"Do you mean me?" asked Othar.

Gorm flashed another mocking smile. "I serve the power behind the bones. Surely you've sensed it."

Othar recalled the malevolent presence that was always strongest when he consulted the bones. "Aye, I've sensed it. When the bones were burned, it nearly destroyed me."

"It entered you. It's the wellspring of your new powers. Now you embody my master."

"What double-tongued nonsense! Am I your master or not?"

"I'll serve not you, but what's within you."

"Then begone! What use is a servant who won't obey?"

"Oh, I'll be useful. You and my master are united by the same desire. You want revenge and my master requires blood. Purchased men shrink from vengeance's gruesome deeds. I won't. My devotion will spur me on, for my master thrives on slaughter."

"Who is this master?" asked Othar.

"It yet has no name. In time, it will. Each death brings that day closer—an era of black temples, splashed red from sacrifices."

"Do you speak of a god?"

"That word will do. Don't you feel godlike in your power and wrath?"

"Very like," replied Othar.

"In me, you've found an acolyte. Hold to your grim course, and no one will be more dedicated. Do you accept my service?"

"Since you're immune to my powers, I seem to have little choice. Have you much experience?"

Gorm grinned. "Many decades' worth."

"Decades? You look too young for that."

"I was once like you, a minor sorcerer. I had but one trick—my mind could roam the Dark Path to seek memories discarded by the dead. Memory lingers, even after the spirit journeys westward."

"So it's said," replied Othar.

"And 'tis true. Horrific deaths render especially potent memories, and on the Sunless Way I encountered a being those memories nourish. It's capable of rewarding living followers. As yet, it's confined to the netherworld. But that will change when it grows more powerful."

"And slaughter feeds it?"

"Aye. This summer's warfare fortified it. Your new powers are proof of that."

"How did you come to serve it?"

"I created the magic bones, which permit my master to sway events."

"The same bones you sold me?" asked Othar, recalling their bloodthirsty counsels.

"Aye."

Othar eyed the man before him, and envied his body. "Your master preserved your youth, yet I was blasted."

"I am but its servant. You are its vessel."

"You mean a new version of the bones," said Othar.

"As you once turned to them for guidance, so I will turn to you," replied Gorm. "Name your enemies, and I'll help seal their doom. Forget restraint. Realize your most violent urges. Don't let my young face fool you. I've honed my skills for ages."

Nine

♛

Dar spent an uneasy night. When she wasn't lying awake worrying, she had disturbing dreams. Their details faded quickly, but not their air of menace. This combined with Dar's vision of the hall's destruction to give her a sense of approaching danger.

Within Dar's mind warred two views of her circumstances. In one, she was queen by accident. That was what her muthuri believed, and if Zor-yat was right, Dar should abandon the crown. That course brought up new dilemmas. Dar had no idea who should succeed her, for she could no longer perceive worthiness. Then there was the question of what she would do afterward. *If I remain here, I'll be treated like a ghost.* Living in Taiben held no appeal.

The contrasting view was that Dar was destined to be queen. That could be the reason Muth la had preserved her life. Yet Dar had difficulty believing a branded peasant woman was meant to be queen of the orcs. Her visions seemed evidence of such a destiny, but they provided little guidance. *Will this hall burn if I remain queen or will my abdication doom it?*

Dar wrestled with the problem most of the day. The struggle wore her out without providing an answer. At last, she realized logic was useless. There was no way to determine which path was the correct one. *Velasa-pah said I should follow my chest. He said it wouldn't always be easy.* Once Dar ignored reason and fear, she knew she must remain queen. She couldn't forsake the orcs. She loved them too deeply, for Fathma had bound her to them. They were her family and her children. Dar resolved to reign as best she could and hope that would suffice.

With that resolution came a measure of calmness. Dar realized that she still needed guidance to succeed and considered to whom she might turn. Only one mother came to mind. In many ways, she was a poor choice. Yet this was the mother Dar wanted by her side. *She might refuse to help. I'd hardly blame her if she did.* That possibility made Dar anxious again, and she spent another uneasy night.

The following morning, Dar acted. When the daily work within the hall was well under way, she left her hanmuthi without an escort and made her way to the workshop where cloth was woven. The long room featured north-facing windows that filled it with natural light. The floor space was crammed with looms, each with a son or mother busy weaving. As Dar walked among them, no one noticed her at first. When she was spotted, work halted and the room grew quiet. All eyes fixed upon her, and once again, Dar was keenly aware that she didn't know how to behave.

At last, Dar spotted Nir-yat, who sat motionless with a shuttle in her hand. She bowed when Dar approached her. "I wish to speak with you," said Dar, in a low voice. "Will you come to my hanmuthi?"

Nir-yat bowed again. "Hai, Muth Mauk."

The two walked silently until they reached the royal chambers and Dar spoke. "Nir, I need help." She noted how her sister's expression turned uneasy. "I assume Muthuri has forbidden you to aid me." Knowing that Nir-yat was incapable of lying, she pushed the point. "It that so?"

"Hai."

"Daughters should be dutiful to their muthuri, and

your obedience is proper. Yet I fear it will doom me."
Dar saw distress in Nir-yat's face. It seemed a promising
sign. "Only one hope remains." Dar gazed into her sister's eyes to communicate her urgency. "Will you bend
your neck so I might bite it?"

Nir-yat's face paled at the enormity of Dar's request.
"Bite my neck! Why?"

"If your life is mine, you'll be free from Muthuri's
authority."

"She'll be angry, and she'll still have one hold on me.
Only muthuris can bless unions."

"Would she withhold her blessing to punish you?"
asked Dar, who hadn't foreseen that possibility.

"She might."

"I wouldn't ask this if my need weren't great."

"Why me? I'm too young to be wise."

There was no word for "trust" in Orcish, for that
would require an understanding of deception. Thus, Dar
had to explain her reason in another way. "Whenever I've
sought wisdom, I've been told to follow my chest. That's
what I'm doing now. I want advice that springs from love.
Even before I was reborn, you took my side."

"Because you saved brother's life."

"I think Muth la has sent me to save more than him.
Perhaps, to save all urkzimmuthi. I'm only living mother
who has witnessed war. If my reign fails, many others
may see it also."

"I know nothing of wars or matriarch councils," said
Nir-yat. "What use can I be?"

"I'm ignorant of royal duties and etiquette. Little mistakes make one seem foolish, and fools have few followers."

"If you bite my neck, Muthuri will make my life difficult."

"I know, so best you live with me."

"Forever?"

"If I succeed, I think Muthuri will forgive you. If I fail, I'll perish. Then you'll be released from your obligation."

Nir-yat thought a long while. Dar, sensing her inner struggle, waited patiently. At last, Nir-yat spoke. "Sister, I'll follow my chest." She sank to her knees, bent her head, and pushed her hair aside to expose her neck.

Dar knelt beside her sister. As tenderly as possible, she bit Nir-yat's neck hard enough to leave a mark. Then she embraced her.

Othar was surprised by how many officers visited him. He had already seen two sustolums and a tolum, and it was not yet noon. Karg was the second tolum he interviewed. There was a stigma attached to serving in the orc regiments, and the displaced officers were anxious for positions. Othar needed no special powers to perceive their desperation.

The sorcerer had questioned each officer, for spoken answers were more precise than the impressions he obtained through reading minds. Nevertheless, Othar usually based his judgments on the latter. He had already decided that Karg was as unsuitable as the others, perceiving he was unadept with women. Othar was about to take Karg's mind when he uncovered an interesting memory. "The orc queen served under you."

Karg looked surprised. "How did you know that?"

"I have my ways."

"Aye. She was in my shieldron. She was only the orc wench then. Once, I even had her whipped."

Othar smiled beneath his silver mask. "That must have been amusing."

"I didn't do it. Only gave the order."

Othar discovered another memory—one that was far more useful. "Too bad Murdant Kol didn't do the flogging." As soon as the name was uttered, Karg's thoughts

filled with images of a rugged man with piercing blue
eyes. *Karg feared him*, thought Othar, *as a cur fears a
wolf.*

Karg was unaware of the scrutiny. "Aye, if Kol had
his way, it would have been the end of her. Then things
wouldn't have gone to shit."

"Were they enemies?"

"She was the only woman Kol never tamed. He couldn't
abide that."

"Where is he now?"

"Who knows? The regiments have scattered." Then
Karg's face went blank as Othar seized his mind.

The sorcerer leisurely probed the memories of his latest victim, seeking additional information. The more he
learned, the more he was convinced that Kol would be
perfect for his plans. When Othar was finished with his
examination, he spoke. "Return to your lodging. Tomorrow, seek out a duel. Lose it."

After what remained of Tolum Karg departed, Othar
called for Gorm. The youthful-seeming man quickly appeared. "Aye, Master," he said without a trace of subservience.

"I'll see no more officers. Instead, find a man named
Kol. He was high murdant in the orc regiments. Persuade
him to see me."

"A promising candidate?"

"Very promising."

"Every hanmuthi is Muth Mauk's hanmuthi," said Nir-
yat.

"Does that mean I must give first greeting?" asked Dar.

"Hai. But don't state your name, for everyone knows
it. Instead, you bless ranking mother."

"May Muth la bless you?" said Dar.

"Hai, but you must bless her by name. That's important. Always learn it before you enter."

Dar recalled with embarrassment visiting Metha-yat's hanmuthi. "So I've been doing it wrong."

Nir-yat sighed. "You've been doing everything wrong. You should only wear green kefs and color your claws same shade. Your nipples, too."

Dar suppressed a smile. "My *nipples*?"

"Hai."

"Why green?"

"It's royal color."

"My predecessor did none of these things."

"She did before washavokis imprisoned her."

"Where do I get this green for my claws and nipples?"

"It called 'talmauki.' Jvar-yat provides it."

Dar recognized the name. "She's latath who gave me my tattoo."

"Hai," said Nir-yat. "And her lore includes secret of making talmauki."

Dar clapped her hands and a son entered the hanmuthi. "Tell Jvar-yat to bring talmauki."

After he departed, Nir-yat spoke. "You should send for Thorma-yat, next. You'll need to order proper clothes. Then have Gar-yat come to help plan your feasts."

"Feasts?"

"You must invite each hanmuthi here for feast, starting with most lowly."

"How will I know which one is that?"

"Yev-yat is lorekeeper. She'll help you."

Dar was starting to feel overwhelmed. "There's so much I don't know. Why didn't anyone tell me?"

"They were forbidden."

"By whom?"

"Muth-yat. She said it was test of fitness."

A test she took pains to ensure I'd fail, thought Dar.

Ten

♛

Nir-yat returned to her muthuri's hanmuthi late in the afternoon, accompanied by two sons who were to fetch her things. To her dismay, Zor-yat was waiting for her. "Why are these sons with you?"

"They're to carry my chest and sleeping mat," replied Nir-yat.

"To where?"

"Muth Mauk's hanmuthi."

"I thought as much," said Zor-yat. "Dargu takes you from your work, then suddenly Jvar-yat is preparing tal-mauki. I suppose you told Dargu about it."

"Hai, Muthuri."

"Then you disobeyed me! I told you not to help Dargu."

Nir-yat pulled her hair aside to reveal Dar's teeth marks on her neck. "She's Muth Mauk, not Dargu, and my life is hers now."

Zor-yat's face darkened. She glared about her hanmuthi and made a gesture that caused everyone to retreat. When the room was empty, Zor-yat scowled at Nir-yat. "Your foolishness has placed us all in peril."

"I followed my chest."

"Because your head's empty. You've no idea what you've done."

"I agreed to help my sister."

"Ask your sister about Velasa-pah. Then you'll regret your rashness." Zor-yat sighed with frustration. "Yet that bite can't be undone. Gather your things and leave. You're dead to me."

"Muthuri . . ."

Zor-yat turned her back to her daughter. "Go!"

Dar was unsettled by how distraught Nir-yat looked upon her return. "What happened?" she asked.

"Muthuri said I'm dead to her."

The news stunned Dar. "I'm sorry."

"She called me foolish, and told me to ask you about Velasa-pah."

Dar's stomach lurched at the mention of the wizard's name. It made her wonder if Zor-yat knew about her vision, though Dar couldn't imagine how that could be possible. "Did she say why?"

"Thwa. But she said I'd regret my rashness."

"I don't know why Muthuri would say that," said Dar. "You already know of my encounter with Velasa-pah. I told you all about it when I first arrived."

"Have you had visions of him since?"

Nir-yat's question came uncomfortably close to the mark. "I've had another vision of Velasa-pah," said Dar, "but I've no idea what that vision meant. None of my visions have been comforting; yet not all have come to pass. Some were only warnings."

"Are you sure?" asked Nir-yat.

Dar realized that she was not. She recalled the horrific vision that had prompted her to rescue Zna-yat. The figure burning at the stake could have been anyone. Her most recent vision renewed the terror of the earlier one. *I could be that burning figure!* Keeping those thoughts to herself, Dar replied, "It would be cruel of Muth la to send visions of things one can't change." Then Dar recalled her vision of Twea's death and the ambush at the Vale of Pines. *Both came to pass despite my efforts.*

Nir-yat smelled a whiff of fear. "I didn't mean to

frighten you, Sister. I was seeking reassurance." She sighed. "Muthuri has upset me. She thinks that by helping you I've placed everyone in peril."

"Are you sorry I bit your neck?"

"I don't understand Muthuri's thinking. You're Muth Mauk. What threatens you threatens us all."

Dar wondered if she should tell Nir-yat about her vision of the burning hall. She didn't want to upset her further, but she felt guilty about keeping secrets from someone who had given her everything. Dar was still wrestling with the matter when Jvar-yat entered the hanmuthi, providing a welcome interruption.

Using her newly acquired knowledge, Dar addressed the latath in the appropriate manner. "Muth la's blessing, Jvar-yat."

"Shashav, Muth Mauk." Jvar-yat bowed, then set a polished stone tray on the floor. "I've prepared talmauki as you requested."

"You have pleased me," replied Dar, using the correct formality.

After Jvar-yat left, Dar examined the tray. It held a little brush, a piece of cloth, and two small vessels. The latter were carved from the same dark stone as the tray. They gave the impression of being very old. Dar lifted the top of one. Inside was a paste that matched the blue-green of fir trees. "That's for your nipples," said Nir-yat.

Dar touched the paste. It felt like greasy clay. "When do I wear this?"

"Always," replied Nir-yat. Then she added, "Unless you're nursing."

Dar thought the last comment was irrelevant. She applied the paste, then wiped her fingers on the small cloth that accompanied the tray. Afterward, she opened the second vessel. It contained a thick liquid the same color as the paste. "That's for your claws," said Nir-yat. She gazed at Dar's fingernails, then took the brush from the tray. "Let me paint them."

Dar held out a hand and Nir painted a nail. Instead of coloring its entire surface, she painted only its center so it resembled an orcish claw. "What do you think?"

Dar smiled. "It looks more natural."

"I think so, too."

When Dar's fingernails were painted, Nir-yat painted her toenails in the same manner. Afterward, Thorma-yat was summoned to make Dar's royal wardrobe. The seamstress stated that kefs of the proper shade would require several days to make because the cloth was woven from specially dyed wool. Producing enough material to make a talmauki cloak would take even longer. Thorma-yat apologized for the delay. "It's been five winters since queen has lived here. I'll speak to dyer right away."

"You can make Muth Mauk's other garments," injected Nir-yat. "She need not wait for those."

"You're right, of course," said Thorma-yat, appearing flustered. She bowed to Dar. "I'll get my samples."

After Thorma-yat hurried off, Nir-yat spoke. "Sister, let me guide your choices. I'll praise many fabrics, but when I say, 'Does this one please you?,' that is cloth you should select."

"Why not just choose for me?"

"That would give wrong impression. Great mothers often receive counsel, but they decide."

Dar appreciated Nir-yat's subtlety, especially once Thorma-yat returned. When the seamstress had made Dar's first outfit of orcish clothing, she had brought a few dozen swatches. On this occasion, she was overburdened with all kinds of material. Dar had never seen such a variety of cloth. There was a wide range of colors and patterns, and the material also varied in many other ways. Besides the familiar wool, there was cloth that Dar had never encountered before. The samples ran from sheer to weighty, and the weaves differed greatly.

Thorma-yat presented the plethora of choices without expressing any opinions, but Nir-yat helped Dar without being obvious. She eschewed bright colors and strong patterns, steering Dar toward a rich but understated look. She preferred textured weaves, soft greens and blues, and warm earth tones. Toward the end of the fabric showing, Dar perceived that Nir-yat's recommendations fit together to create a harmonious look. Having grown up wearing a single homespun shift until it became a rag, the idea of coordinating outfits was novel to her. If it hadn't been for Nir-yat, Dar would have selected only a few fabrics. Instead, she chose dozens. When the selection was over, Thorma-yat surveyed the pile of cloth. "What garments shall I make from these?"

Dar thought quickly and answered. "I wish to look at them awhile. We'll speak tomorrow." As the seamstress gathered up the rejected fabrics, Dar said, "You have pleased me, Thorma-yat."

After Thorma-yat bowed and departed, Dar turned to her sister. "Why don't you like red?"

Nir-yat made a face. "Only sons wear that color. You're Muth Mauk now, not some pashi farmer."

"Queen Girta has red robes."

"And she's washavoki. It proves my point."

Dar recalled the gaudy fashions she had seen in King Kregant's court. Their bright, contrasting colors and gold embroidery differed markedly from the fabrics destined for her wardrobe. *My clothes will look plain in comparison.*

Nir-yat spoke as though she had read Dar's thoughts. "You're everyone's muthuri," she said. "You should appear serene." She held up a piece of cloth, the color of willows in a fog. "Look at this weaving. Three different threads were twisted to make this color. This is elegant work. Discerning eyes are mark of wisdom."

"Among washavokis, only powerful ones could wear bright colors."

"Here, every mother can choose anything from Thorma-yat's stores, as long as it's not talmauki. She can have her neva made from this or that ghastly blue-and-yellow pattern you fancied." Nir-yat grinned. "You thought I didn't notice, but I did."

"I like butterflies," said Dar.

"Then let them fly on your sleeping cloak, not on your neva. Speaking of nevas, we'll discuss them next. You should be prepared when Thorma-yat returns."

The concept of fashion was new to Dar, and Nir-yat's discussion of clothes seemed in another language. Dar knew the skirtlike garment was called a "neva," and the paired capes "kefs," but the rest of the terms were new to her. Dar found the topic dull, but calming. The immediacy of deciding on the cut and hem length for a neva kept darker matters at bay. Moreover, it cheered up Nir-yat, who was clearly interested in the subject and quite opinionated. The two planned Dar's royal wardrobe until time for the evening meal. Dar sent sons to fetch it, glad that she would not eat alone.

Murdant Kol had forgotten when he had eaten last or whether it was day or night. Racked by fever, he was delirious. His entire body ached and burned, but the festering wound below his shoulder hurt the worst. It felt as though a hot poker were pushing into his flesh. He no longer knew where he was. Instead of a dingy room in a shabby inn, he thought he was astride Thunder, whirling his whip as he galloped toward Dar.

He relived the moment again and again, each time thinking it would end differently. He saw the orc queen by Dar's side, too feeble to flee. He watched Sevren fighting the soldiers, outnumbered and preoccupied. Everything happened at a slowed pace. Dar turned, looking panicked.

She groped for the dagger slung at her waist. *Where did she get a weapon?* Dar turned the dagger in her hand, grasping it by the blade. Then she threw it. The dagger moved through the air so slowly that Kol could watch it gracefully flip so its point was forward. His horse traveled just as slowly. *I need only move and it'll miss me.* It didn't, and Kol was just as shocked—and enraged—as he was the first time. The events that followed were a haze to the murdant's fever-stricken brain. *Something about orcs.* There were muddled impressions of an escape and a growing pain. Then Kol was astride Thunder again, galloping toward Dar.

Two men sat on the room's other bed, strangers as disreputable as their surroundings. They watched Kol, waiting for him to die. "Can't be long, now," said one. "He's out of his head."

"His stink's more tellin'," said the other. "Like rotten meat."

"Maybe we could hurry him along."

His companion eyed a recent bloodstain on the dirty wooden floor. "And get what that other fella got? That's a hard one there, dyin' or not. Let's bide our time."

"Hope it's worth the wait."

"Well, he sold that horse."

The other man laughed. "To a cheatin' bastard."

"Aye, the innkeep's a sharp one, and this fella was half-dead when he came."

"From where, do you suppose?"

"Taiben, most like. It's all stirred up."

Kol was rolling on his sweat-soaked mattress, trying to dodge Dar's blade, when the door opened. The innkeeper, a rat-faced man, entered and spoke. "Clear out, the both of ye. This room's been let."

"To us!" said one of the men watching Kol.

"It's been let again. Ye can move to the stables, or best this man's offer."

The men regarded the gray-eyed stranger who had joined the innkeeper. He had an intimidating look, despite his youthful face. Moreover, his clothes marked him as someone with means. Rather than protest further, the men followed the innkeeper out of the room. As they entered the hallway, they noticed a Wise Woman standing there, clutching her bag of healing herbs. The stranger who had usurped their room spoke to her. "Come. This is the one." The Wise Woman entered the room and the door closed.

One of the men turned to the innkeeper. "Who was that fella?"

"Don't know. Don't care."

"Well, we had interests in that dyin' bloke. Interests ye pissed away."

His larger companion pushed the innkeeper against the wall. "Aye, pissed away. So, we'll have our money back."

The innkeeper attempted a nervous smile. "Why not take it back as drink and sleep in the stable for free?"

The two men grinned at each other. "We'll do that," said one.

"Seems our luck has changed," said his comrade. He glanced toward the closed door. "And not just ours."

Eleven

♛

Nir-yat renewed the discussion of Dar's wardrobe first thing next morning, picking up where she had left off the previous evening. By then, Dar had learned there were many other garments besides nevas, kefs, and cloaks. All of them had names, and all their parts had names also. Dar even remembered a few of them. She surveyed the carefully arranged piles of fabrics that covered the floor of her hanmuthi, each pile destined for a different garment. "Nir, this is never going to work. I can't remember what's supposed to be what."

"It's simple, really. Those gabaiuks are for your sukefas. They have two sides so they're paired with tuug that . . ."

"Enough, Nir! You'll have to tell Thorma-yat what to make."

"But . . ."

"Secret of wisdom is recognizing it in others. I can't do everything myself. Should I grow my own brak and pashi? If I cooked my feasts would you want to eat them?"

Nir-yat grinned, recalling Dar's ineptness in the kitchen. "Thwa."

"So I'll rely on your wisdom when it comes to clothes."

"You must tell Thorma-yat something."

"Then tell me what to say. Something brief."

"Tell her your nevas are to be long and fit tightly," said Nir-yat.

"For what reason?"

"Because you'll always sit on stool or throne, never on

cushion. Also tell Thorma-yat your kefs should taper to point below your waist. That's most elegant."

"I can manage that," said Dar. "I'll send for Thorma-yat. I'm as ready as I'll ever be."

After the seamstress arrived, she stayed most of the morning. Dar repeated what Nir-yat had told her, then asked her sister to describe how each item was to be made. While Thorma-yat and Nir-yat talked, Dar only half listened. Finally, the seamstress gathered up the fabric samples and bowed to Dar. "I know what must be done, Muth Mauk."

"You've pleased me, Thorma-yat." Dar waited until she was alone with Nir-yat before curling back her lips in a broad orcish grin. "Sister, you've pleased me also. I'm certain I'll look grand."

Nir-yat returned Dar's smile. "You will!"

Dar was encouraged by Nir-yat's self-assurance, for it was a sign that her sister hadn't been cowed by their muthuri. Nir-yat had handled ordering the clothes skillfully, and Dar expected she would be helpful in many other ways. *She learned more from her grandmother than she realizes*, thought Dar. *She knows how a queen's hanmuthi runs*. Indeed, Nir-yat's thoughts were already on the next task. "Before you speak to Gar-yat about feasts, we should get hanmuthi list from lorekeeper."

"One that says which families are high and which are humble?"

"Hai. It can be delicate matter." Nir-yat explained that, though many Yat clan members lived in the surrounding countryside, hanmuthis within the clan hall were coveted. There were only thirty-three. Since there was no room on the mountaintop to build more, deciding which families occupied them and which mother headed each hanmuthi was a complicated and often contentious matter. It was largely based on ancestry, but other factors came into play. Hanmuthis changed hands as the standing of families rose or fell, and the lorekeeper recorded all the changes. Thus, the order in which the hanmuthis were feasted would be carefully noted.

That afternoon, Nir-yat led Dar to the lorechamber. It was in the old part of the hall, and resembled a hanmuthi in its design, except that the adjoining rooms were not sleeping chambers. Instead, they were filled with shelves that were stacked with thin wooden boards, each approximately an arm's length and a palm's width. Dar had the impression that she had entered a carpenter's storeroom, not a repository of knowledge. The center chamber was filled with tables, and these were also piled with boards. The lorekeeper was seated on a stool next to the central hearth, like a muthuri in her hanmuthi. She was gazing intently at a board on her lap and was startled when Dar spoke. "May Muth la bless you, Yev-yat."

The mother immediately rose and bowed. "Shashav, Muth Mauk."

Dar was surprised that a mother who looked only slightly older than Nir-yat was the lorekeeper. Yev-yat had exotic features. Her thin face made her green eyes look especially large, and her thick hair was jet-black, an unusual color among orcs. Lightly built, she was only Dar's height. A brass object dangled from a cord about her neck. Dar, having never encountered a key before, assumed it was a pendant.

Yev-yat glanced approvingly at the talmauki on Dar's nails and nipples. "It's said that since you bit your sister's neck you've grown in understanding. Now I see that for myself."

"Nir-yat has been most helpful," replied Dar, who had ceased to be surprised by how rapidly news spread through the hall. "Yet I've much to learn."

"Then you've come to good place. Instructing queens

is one of my duties." Yev-yat walked over to a table and picked up a board. Unlike most of the others, its surface was painted with white clay so the dark markings on it stood out plainly. She handed the board to Dar. "I've already prepared list of clan families."

Dar examined the rows of marks on the board. They reminded her of those carved in the walls at Tarathank.

"Most humble family is written at top," said Yev-yat.

Nir-yat looked over Dar's shoulder, then turned the board in Dar's hand. Dar blushed when she realized that she had been holding the writing upside down. "I've seen such marks before," she said, "but I don't know their meaning."

"I'd be honored to teach you that skill," said Yev-yat.

Dar handed the board to Nir-yat. "Show this to Gar-yat so she might begin planning my feasts."

After her sister departed, Dar surveyed the room. "Does each board contain knowledge?"

"Hai, Muth Mauk. They're called deetpahis."

Dar broke down the word into "boards" and "speaking." Yev-yat handed her a deetpahi. It was different from the one that listed the families. Its wood was unpainted and the marks were burned into its surface. The entire deetpahi had been covered with wax, which had darkened with age. "How does this wood speak to you?" Dar asked.

"Each mark is picture of sound. There are forty different marks, one for each sound in our speech." Yev-yat touched a mark with a claw. "This one shows 'mmm.'" She moved her claw down the row of marks. "This says mmm-oo-th-oo-rr-ee, muthuri."

"This is useful knowledge," said Dar. She gazed at the thousands of boards. "There's much learning in this room."

"There is, Muth Mauk, and I study it every day. I still have much to learn, and this place is tiny compared to

Tarathank's great lorehall. It's said some of its deetpahis were made on first day of world."

"I was at Tarathank, but I saw no place like this."

"Washavokis burned that wisdom," said Yev-yat, her voice as mournful as if the deed had occurred yesterday.

"When Muth-yat spoke to me about rebirth, she said she had learned its secrets from ancient texts. Are those texts here?"

"Hai, but they're hard to understand. Their words sound strange to us."

"Did you help her understand them?"

"I did, but Muth-yat hears only when she wants to listen. I warned her that those reborn have strange fates."

"Like Velasa-pah?" When the lorekeeper failed to reply, Dar asked, "Has Muth-yat forbidden you to speak of him?"

"Deetpahis speak, not I. No matriarch can silence lorekeeper."

"Yet you grew silent."

"Tales of Velasa-pah are unsettling. When I spoke of him to Muth-yat, she grew angry."

"Why?"

"Each deetpahi has its own voice, and they don't always agree. Muth-yat wanted certainty, and I provided none. Perhaps you'll be angry also. Little is certain about Velasa-pah."

"Was he wizard?"

"Hai. That much is common knowledge. Muth la sometimes speaks to sons, and such sons become wizards. Wisdom she gives them is different from that she shares with mothers. To Val-hak, she taught magic of sand ice. To Fluuk-jan, spells for forging steel."

"What wisdom did Velasa-pah receive?"

"His gift was most unusual. He had knowledge of spirits. Washavokis called his skills 'deep magic' and feared him. He made stone that caused those who held it to relive memories of departed spirits. It's also said he could foretell events."

"What happened to him?"

"It's written that he died when Tarathank fell."

"Are there not other tales of his fate?"

Yev-yat's eyes lit up. "Hai. Known to very few. Where do you hear them?"

"No one told me. I met Velasa-pah on my journey, and he seemed alive. He cooked food and made magic with feathers."

Yev-yat looked alarmed, and for a moment Dar feared that the lorekeeper would behave like Meera-yat. "And Muth-yat knows this?"

"Hai," replied Dar. "She's known it for long time."

"But you're queen, now. That changes everything."

"How?"

"That is difficult question, Muth Mauk. Ancient voices often disagree, making it hard to tell where wisdom lies."

"Yet when I mention Velasa-pah, others are dismayed."

Yev-yat did not reply immediately. Instead, she entered one of the adjoining rooms. She searched among the stacked deetpahis awhile until she found the one she was looking for. "This is deetpahi of Tarma-goth. She fled destruction of Tarathank and speaks of its last days." Yev-yat placed the deetpahi on a table. Its wood had darkened so much that the marks burned into it were barely discernible. The lorekeeper ran her fingers along its surface, mumbling softly to herself. Then her fingers stopped. "Ah, here. . . . and on second moon, washa-vokis violated Muth la's Embrace . . . She's speaking of one enclosing Tarathank . . . and gave death to all they met. They slew queen and Fathma was lost. Then urk-zimmuthi . . . This section I cannot read . . . but Velasa-pah refused, saying it was his fate to greet new queen."

Yev-yat looked up. "Tarma-goth believed that Velasa-pah's life would be preserved until new great mother arrived."

The lorekeeper set the deetpahi carefully on a table. "In older deetpahis, this tale is called 'Velasa-pah's Promise' or 'Velasa-pah's Oath.' Only later was it named 'Velasa-pah's Doom.' When Tarma-goth wrote, most urkzimmuthi had fled to Blath Urkmuthi, but some still dwelled in ancient homeland. Because Velasa-pah remained behind, it was said that next great mother would arise from that place. Yet, as time passed, that hope faded. Our homeland filled with washavokis who brought only death with them. In time, urkzimmuthi no longer looked westward."

"Except Pah clan," said Dar.

"Where did you learn this?"

"I've seen this clan. They still live in western mountains. Until I came, they watched western heights."

Yev-yat's eyes grew wide. "You visited lost clan?"

"Hai. But Muth-pah said they are lost no longer."

"And Muth-yat knows this?"

"Hai."

Yev-yat frowned. "She has hidden much from me. You also, I suspect. Did she speak of Morah-pah's vision?"

"I've never heard of it."

"Many deetpahis describe visions, and Morah-pah's deetpahi records significant one. It was written after Yat clan child was born with Fathma. Original is lost, but I have copy."

Yev-yat went into another chamber. In addition to shelves, it contained a chest. The lorekeeper removed the object that Dar had assumed was a pendant, inserted it into a small, oddly shaped hole in the front of the chest, and twisted it. Dar heard a *click*. Then Yev-yat lifted the chest's lid and removed a deetpahi. It had darkened until it was nearly black. The lorekeeper treated it as though it was somehow dangerous. "This is lore that I may impart only to great mothers and their sisters. Thus few know it, and for good reason."

Dar felt uneasy. "And now that I'm queen, this is something I must know?"

"Hai, Muth Mauk, for I believe it speaks of you."

Twelve

♛

Murdant Kol opened his eyes and saw a man peering at him. The man smiled, but his gray eyes were calculating. "You were hard to find," said the stranger. "You're fortunate I succeeded."

Kol's jerkin was gone and a bandage encircled his bare chest where none had been before. It pressed pungent herbs against his wound, which still ached but no longer burned. Kol suspected that the man had been caring for him. He couldn't imagine why, and his wariness was stronger than his gratitude. He regarded the man again, and with a voice as forceful as his weakened state allowed, asked, "Who are you?"

"My name is Gorm."

"Why are you here?"

"My master desires your service."

"My service? For what? Someone's private guard? I'm a soldier, not a watchman."

"A soldier without an army."

"They're always wanting swords in Luvein."

"Proud words for one in your position," said Gorm. "You still need this woman's care." He gestured to the Wise Woman seated on the other bed. "I hired her. If I leave, she leaves."

"I'll take my chances."

"I've been to Luvein," said Gorm. "Its lords want soldiers, but their squabbles are scarcely wars. Do you wish to fight over cattle? To conquer vineyards?"

"With luck, I might rise high," replied Kol.

"No need to seek your fortune. Fortune has found you. My master is Othar the Mage."

Kol noted that Gorm's eyes appeared much older than his face. They seemed capable of more than ordinary perception, an idea he found unsettling. "I heard he's dead."

"Now you're privileged to know the truth. Very few do."

Kol suspected that knowledge put him in jeopardy. "And what service can a soldier provide a mage?"

"Lead a war against his enemy."

Kol was about to laugh when he saw that Gorm was completely serious. "How could I do that?"

"With powerful friends, ambitious men rise high. Commissions are easily bought. You've served under officers. They gave the orders, but who was the better soldier? You or them?"

"War's hard and bloody work," replied Murdant Kol. "And no man's harder than me."

"Othar agrees. A hard man is what the realm needs, especially now that it's ruled by a woman. Girta wants for a strong hand to guide her. You could become that hand and push for war."

"War against whom?"

"The orcs' new queen."

Again, Kol suppressed a laugh. "The piss eyes' queen?"

"Aye, and you know her. She's Dar."

"Dar! That's impossible!"

Gorm smiled. "Not for a conniving bitch. Who knows that better than you?" Gorm paused and his smile grew mocking. "Isn't she the one who wounded you?"

Kol only grunted.

"So, what will it be?" asked Gorm. "Slink off to Luvein or take on your foe?"

Yev-yat read from the deetpahi of Morah-pah. It spoke of an ominous vision. A queen who appeared in the west would usher in turbulent times. The deetpahi described a disaster that was chillingly similar to Dar's vision. In it, the royal hall was reduced to ruins. At first, Dar argued that the vision didn't apply to her. "I wasn't queen when I was in western mountains," she said. "I wasn't even urkzimmuthi."

"Velasa-pah appeared to you," Yev-yat replied. "He said he had been waiting."

"He might have been waiting for someone else." Yet even as Dar made that argument, she doubted it was true.

"Muth Mauk, I think Muth la placed your spirit in washavoki's body so no one would recognize you at first. That is reason you were welcomed in this hall. When Muth-yat and Zor-yat aided in your rebirth, they didn't foresee you becoming queen."

"If they had, would they have helped me?"

"Are they helping you now?"

Then the lorekeeper spoke of an old controversy that began when a child purporting to possess Fathma was born into the Yat clan. The child grew up to become the first queen of the urkzimmuthi since the fall of Tarathank. At that time, the Yat clan occupied the easternmost settlement. It consisted of only a few rude huts. Six generations had passed since the urkzimmuthi last had a ruler, and they were in disarray. Exiled from their ancestral lands and harried by the washavokis, they were a race on the edge of extinction.

After she was crowned by the Yat clan, the new queen spent the first years of her reign visiting the other orc settlements. In time, all the clans but one agreed that she possessed Fathma. The Pah clan—the former Queen Clan—resolved to wait for a sign from Velasa-pah. Until then, they would neither acknowledge nor disavow the sovereignty of the sitting queen.

Meanwhile, with the other clans' support, the queen found a way to end the washavoki raids. She bought peace by pledging sons to fight for the washavokis in their wars against one another. By wisely choosing which sides to support, the orc queen ended the washavoki forays. This policy was the precedent for all the treaties that followed, the one with King Kregant being only the latest.

Treaties with the washavokis appalled the Pah clan and exacerbated the schism between them and the other orcs. Their matriarch did not attend the royal councils and her clan remained in the western heights when the other clans moved eastward. In time, the Pah clan became known as the Lost Clan.

Morah-pah's vision was recorded as the schism was first forming. As word of it spread, the clan's isolation became more pronounced. "Velasa-pah's Promise" became "Velasa-pah's Doom," the epitome of a lost cause. The wizard came to be seen as an unfortunate figure from a tragic era, someone long dead and best forgotten.

Dar realized that her appearance as queen had stirred up those half-forgotten controversies. Having arrived from the west, Dar saw how she could be viewed as a harbinger of doom or even its instigator. Thus she was relieved when the lorekeeper didn't shun her as Meera-yat had. "You're to be queen in troubled times," Yev-yat said. "That's Muth la's will, not your fault."

After Yev-yat locked away the foreboding text, she spent the rest of the afternoon recounting how former queens had ruled. Dar listened attentively, hoping the past would offer lessons for the future. All the while, she felt as she had when she nearly drowned in the Turgen River— seized by currents beyond her control. In tales from her childhood, becoming queen was always a happy ending. That afternoon, it seemed just the opposite.

Murdant Kol suspected that Othar's "offer" would be fatal to refuse, but more than fear prompted him to accept it. Gorm promised an opportunity beyond Kol's wildest hopes—a chance to rise above his station. As high murdant, he had reported directly to the Queen's Man and his duties for General Tarkum occasionally had taken him to the court. There, the courtiers had treated him as little more than a servant. Though it had stung his pride, Kol always held his tongue, for an offended nobleman could ruin him. But with funds and patronage, his humble background wouldn't hold him back. Othar could provide both. With those advantages, "ambitious men rise high."

Pondering the task before him, Kol had no illusions it would be easy. *It wasn't easy to become high murdant, either*, he thought, recalling his rise. He knew that the brutality he had employed in the regiment wouldn't work in the court. Charm and cunning would be more useful. He had learned to read people while working in his father's inn, and the skill still served him. *After all, a court's only a glorified common room. I'll find a way to thrive.* Kol was confident because the monarch was a woman. He fancied himself good with women. Only one had ever eluded his wiles. *Dar!*

When Kol thought of his adversary, he reflected on the ironic turn of events. He became her enemy because she challenged his authority. With the orc regiments disbanded, his nemesis would become the means for him to regain power and rise to even greater heights. With Dar a queen, it would take a war to bring her down. Othar had promised to help him start one. If things worked out right, Kol would be a general soon. He smiled at the prospect of leading an army against the piss eyes. Commanding such might would be far sweeter than any vengeance he could inflict on Dar. *Let Othar have her!* Kol almost pitied Dar when he imagined what the mage would do. Compared with the sorcerer's revenge, a death by flogging would seem merciful.

Thirteen

♛

Muth-pah woke with a start. It was the middle of the night, and the fire in the hearth had died to embers. The smoke hole was partly covered to keep out blowing snow, so the hanmuthi was nearly black. A few snowflakes drifted down from the opening in the ceiling. Otherwise, the room was absolutely still. Despite the darkness, the matriarch immediately spied someone sitting on her stool. It had to be a stranger, and an oddly formed one at that. Muth-pah rose to confront the intruder, her cold joints aching from the effort.

Before Muth-pah could speak, the stranger greeted her. "Tava, Muth-pah. Ma nav Velasa-pah." *Greetings, Muth-pah. I am Velasa-pah.*

When the matriarch had entered darkness with Dargu, she had encountered the wizard's spirit. Then, his appearance had been youthful, his Pah clan tattoo prominent on his smooth chin. The chin of the figure before her was covered with a growth of long white hairs, something Muth-pah had never seen before. His clothes also looked strange, but with the understanding that sometimes comes with visions, the matriarch knew he was the legendary wizard.

Muth-pah bowed and waited. Velasa-pah continued to speak in Orcish. "New queen sits on throne," he said. "Queen from west."

"So soon?"

"Hai. She is in peril. You must go to her."

"Snow covers path," replied Muth-pah. "I'm old, and my bones hurt in winter."

Velasa-pah seemed not to have heard her. "Leave at dawn. Bring son for new queen's mintari." The wizard fixed his gaze on Muth-pah. Even in the murky dark, she saw his eyes were the color of the sky. They also seemed as deep, and the matriarch was drawn into them. A sense of urgency kindled in her chest even before Velasa-pah spoke again. "Think of moth in spider's web. All urkzimmuthi are that moth. Spider approaches. We must break free or perish. Do not wait single day. Before path is clear of snow, our fate will be decided."

Muth-pah started to reply, but the wizard grew as pale as smoke and as insubstantial. A gust of wind came through the smoke hole and blew his form into nothingness, leaving the matriarch staring at the empty dark.

Dar spent most of the night pondering if she should tell Nir about what she had learned. As sister to the queen, Nir-yat was permitted to know. Muth-yat and Zor-yat did. So did Meera-yat. Dar worried that Nir-yat might react as they had and see her as a threat to the clan. She dreaded what would happen if Nir-yat turned against her. The possibility kept her from sleeping.

As dawn approached, Dar decided that loyalty based on ignorance was worthless. Even if she kept silent, Nir-yat could learn the secret lore from someone else. Muth-yat and Zor-yat might tell her. *Muthuri has already made hints. It's best for Nir to learn the secrets from me.*

Having resolved to confide in Nir-yat did not make it any easier, and Dar kept postponing it throughout the morning. Instead, she and Nir-yat began planning the feasts that Dar must host. "You'll want to be properly attired," said Nir-yat after reviewing the list of families again. "You should wait until your talmauki kefs are ready."

"When will that be?" asked Dar.

"I asked Thorma-yat yesterday. Cloth will be ready tomorrow. Kefs should be done following day."

"Then I could have first feast that day. Are you permitted to attend?"

"Hai. But only you can serve. That's tradition. And first feast must be most lavish."

"Must I serve falfhissi?" asked Dar, recalling how the liquor had made her drunk at her welcoming feast.

"Hai, but you need take only small sips," replied Nir-yat, her lips curling into a smile.

"Are you thinking how I confessed my love for Kovok-mah that night, then forgot I told you?"

"Hai."

"Yet you spoke of it to no one," said Dar. "I was grateful for that."

Nir-yat declined her head to acknowledge the compliment.

"Nir, I must tell you other secrets. Yev-yat spoke of frightening things yesterday. Things you should know. Things about me."

"What?"

"Ancient lore says Velasa-pah was doomed to live until queen arrived from west. Another tale speaks of this queen. It says her appearance marks dangerous times. Yev-yat thinks I'm that queen."

"What does she say will happen?"

"There is deetpahi that speaks of this hall's destruction. I've had similar vision."

Nir-yat grew pale. "One might say you drew this danger to us."

"They might," answered Dar in a quiet voice. For the first time ever, Dar detected a faint, sharp smell. She thought it might be the scent of her sister's fear.

Nir-yat silently surveyed the beautiful and ancient room around her, then sighed. "Such words would only increase your burden. They'll never come from my lips."

*   *   *

In the afternoon, Dar went to the lorechamber for her first lesson in the arts of reading and writing. She went alone, for she thought she knew the way. Dar made several wrong turns before reaching her destination because the passageways seemed different somehow. *They can't be different*, she told herself. *Stone hallways don't change overnight. I'm just tired.*

Yev-yat was waiting for her at a table that had several blank, clay-covered deetpahis. Beside them was another deetpahi with a set of symbols marked upon its white clay.

"May Muth la bless you, Yev-yat."

"Shashav, Muth Mauk. Today, I'll teach you all forty soundmarks." She gestured to a sticklike object and a small vessel of black liquid. "With these you can practice making them." She picked up a flat stone blade. "With this, you can scrape your mistakes away."

Dar smiled. "I think I'll be using it often."

"I doubt so, Muth Mauk. You've made these marks before."

"Never."

"Besides writing, I'll teach you another skill. Tell me, Muth Mauk, do you occasionally glimpse things that aren't there?"

"Sometimes."

"Are these episodes growing more vivid?"

"Hai."

"Look around. Does this room seem different?"

Dar gazed about; then her expression grew puzzled. "I recall different floor. One without patterns in stone. How can that be?"

"And my face. Does it remind you of someone?"

Dar stared at the lorekeeper. "Yes it does. You resemble Eva-yat. Is she your muthuri?"

"Thwa. Eva-yat was my grandmother. She died three

winters ago." Yev-yat smiled at Dar's confusion. "It's due to Fathma, Muth Mauk. Your spirit is mingled with those of your predecessors. Their memories linger. Long ago, this floor had no pattern."

"When I received Fathma, I felt love for all urkzimmuthi, nothing more." Dar reflected a moment. "Thwa. I also recall soft voices, like leaves in wind."

"Those were memories. They affect each great mother differently. No one knows why. Some scarcely notice them. For others, they become like visions. I suspect that, for you, they'll be particularly strong."

"Muth la help me! How will I know present from past?"

"Once you learn to handle them, you'll find these memories useful. Learning to write will help. Pick up writing stick." When Dar did so, Yev-yat smiled. "You already remember how to hold it properly. This is also exercise in memory. With some practice, your fingers will recall how to make soundmarks."

The lorekeeper's prediction proved accurate. With only a little practice, Dar could make all the Orcish letters, albeit sloppily. Still, she was amazed that she could do it at all. Dar also quickly identified the sound each mark represented. She wrote out four marks on the white clay and read them aloud. "Dee-Ar-G-oo. Dargu." Dar grinned. "That's my name."

"That *was* your name. It's now Muth Mauk."

"Of course," said Dar. "Fathma has merged me with all great mothers."

"Some deetpahis say there has been only one Muth Mauk, though her body changes."

"What of Pah clan mothers who became queen. Do I possess their spirits also?"

"Only you can answer that."

As an experiment, Dar turned her thoughts to Tarathank. At first, she recalled only the ruin she had visited, envisioning its fire-blackened stones overgrown with vines. Then the image in her mind began to waver like a distant vista on a hot day. She recalled standing on a tower. It rose from a city of white stone softened by numerous gardens. Tarathank was not only intact, it was alive and vibrant. Dar's memory of it was so immediate that she scarcely knew she was standing in the lorechamber. Instead, she was surrounded by the sights, sounds, and smells of a place she loved—her home in a former life.

Still in the reverie of memory, Dar gazed beyond the city to the green plain that surrounded it. The land was divided into lush fields that extended to the mountains. Then something out of place caught her eye. It seemed a spreading stain or a black cloud that hugged the ground. The queen whose memory this was had not yet comprehended what she was viewing, but Dar did. *Invading washavokis!* She could make out sunlight flashing off bare steel blades. The image wrenched her back to the present.

Dar looked about her. The room she was in seemed dark and close. Yev-yat was staring at her with consternation. Dar's face was wet, and she realized that she had been weeping.

Fourteen

♛

Murdant Kol was still weak when Gorm decided to take him back to Taiben. Gorm made all the arrangements. He acquired food, healing herbs, and bandages for the journey and paid the innkeeper's inflated price for Thunder. When everything was ready, the two men departed the inn, accompanied by the Wise Woman, who traveled on foot. They left late in the afternoon, an unusual departure time in Kol's judgment, and moved at a pace slowed to match the woman's.

Kol thought the Wise Woman would travel with them to the capital, but toward dusk she turned from the road and bowed to Gorm. "Sire, ye've been most generous, and I'm grateful for the escort home. Follow my instructions, and the wound should heal cleanly."

The Wise Woman bowed again, then headed down a dirt path that led into the woods. Kol watched her go, then spoke to Gorm in a low voice. "She knows that Othar lives."

Gorm grinned. "I planned for that." He waited until the woman was out of view, then slipped off his mount. Before heading down the path, he spoke to Kol. "Only her daughter lives with her. This shan't take long."

Kol waited, realizing the late departure had probably ensured that the Wise Woman's daughter was home. Soon, a column of smoke began to rise from the woods. It thickened rapidly, and experience told the murdant that a hut was on fire. A short while later, Gorm emerged from the trees. "No tongues will wag back there," he said.

The two men journeyed until it was too dark to travel, then camped in a sheltered spot. Gorm built a large fire and by its light changed Kol's dressings. Afterward, they supped on wine, bread, and cheese. "I expect you're more used to these accommodations than those you'll find in court," said Gorm.

"Is that where we're headed? Court?"

"Not yet. You'll stay awhile where Othar lodges. It's the House of Balten, a merchant's dwelling."

"Why would he live with a tradesman?"

"Balten has his uses, and a hidden hand moves freely. When you see Othar, you'll find him much changed."

"How?"

"A force was unleashed on him. He's maimed and disfigured, but his power has increased manyfold. He can seize minds now."

"Is he still a man?" asked Kol.

"He's become more than that."

"Why would such a one need soldiers?"

"Slaughter feeds his power. He thirsts for the blood that only war can bring."

"Before, you said he wanted vengeance. Now it seems he craves something else. Will victory satisfy him?"

"If it's accomplished by extermination."

As a soldier, Kol thought killing was the means to an end, not an end itself. He reflected that excessive slaughter squandered resources and was the mark of a poor commander.

Gorm gazed at Kol sharply, as if he had read Kol's thoughts. "I know of your reputation with a whip. It's said you once flogged a woman half a day. Wasn't that overmuch?"

"An example heightens discipline."

"Then the flogging wasn't excessive. Othar's aims

aren't either. It's not your place to question his goals, only to fulfill them."

"I never said I wouldn't," replied Kol. "You found the right man."

"Even if Dar wasn't the orcs' queen, a war against them makes sense. They're ripe for conquest. They lost their experienced fighters in this summer's campaign, their halls are unfortified, and their slaughter will disturb no one."

"I see your point. Why spill human blood when piss eye blood will do?"

"Why indeed."

Kol took another swig from the wine skin, then wrapped himself against the cold. He relaxed, feeling that he could handle whatever loomed ahead. Accustomed to ruthlessness, Kol thought Othar's objective was extreme, but not extraordinary. *The Queen's Man sacrificed six regiments and lost no sleep over it.*

The following morning, the two men resumed their ride to Taiben. Gorm set a leisurely pace and related everything that had happened in the capital. Much of it was news to Kol. After the orcs revolted, he had been isolated from events. By the time he had stopped fleeing, he was already succumbing to infection. Afterward, Kol had heard only muddled rumors. Thus, Gorm's news often surprised him. He didn't know the Queen's Man was dead, or that orcs formed Queen Girta's personal guard. Kol was certain that some of the news had been obtained by supernatural means, for Gorm knew that Dar had recovered from her poisoned wound, though no messages had come from the orcs.

The travelers spent the night at an inn, where they kept their conversation superficial. Gorm waited until they were on the road again to brief Kol on the situation at court. "The royal steward's our man, and he knows all the ins and outs. Be aware that Girta doesn't trust him. It won't do to seem his friend. Have you heard of General Voltar?"

"Yes, he's infantry."

"In exchange for certain favors, he's going to make you his aide. You'll be a tolum."

"Tolums don't lead wars," said Kol.

"Then don't remain one. Gain the queen's favor."

"You talk as if that will be easy. I've never even met her."

"You live only because we think you're useful," said Gorm, giving his voice a menacing tone.

Kol laughed in his face. "And I'll die if I prove otherwise? Save your threats for cravens. A soldier makes that bargain before every battle. Do you think that death by magic is worse than an arrow in the throat?"

"I'm glad you know the stakes."

"I've always known them," replied Kol. "So let's speak plainly and save innuendo for the court. First, I must regain my health. I can't be seen as weak. While I do that, gather intelligence. I want to launch my campaign knowing my adversaries."

Gorm smiled, seeming to approve of Kol's boldness. "I'm joining the court myself as a manservant to a count. As such, I'll be nearly invisible."

Kol grinned. "But not blind. Every woman has a weakness. I need to know Queen Girta's."

Dar's new kefs arrived on schedule, but she didn't host a feast that night. The onset of the memories from past queens had disoriented her. Their frequency increased until they flooded Dar's consciousness. Some were little more than passing recollections—a name accompanied by a face, a long-ago event, or a glimpse of a place she had never visited. Others were more like hallucinations and had all their reality. Those left Dar reeling and confused. Although most were pleasant, a few were frightening or sad. Nir-yat stayed by Dar's side throughout, pulling her back to the present whenever necessary. Over time, the episodes grew less intrusive, and Dar learned to manage them as easily as her own recollections.

Even while the memories buffeted her, Dar realized their value. They proved to be a special kind of knowledge. They weren't instructions on how to do things or a chronology of events. The memories were random impressions that connected her to her subjects, and provided an understanding of their history that went beyond mere facts. She felt as though she had lived through those times, experiencing things that otherwise had passed beyond recall. Once, she saw her sister through the late Nir-yat's eyes—a toddler scampering naked through a field of yellow brak flowers. When the recollection faded, Dar affectionately grasped Nir-yat's hand. "Your grandmother loved you very much."

Four days after Dar received her new kefs, she felt settled enough to have her first feast. Traditionally, it was the most lavish, although it would be served to the humblest family within the hall. Each successive night, Dar would entertain another hanmuthi until the clan matriarch's family was feasted with a simple, everyday meal. After Dar reviewed the elaborate menu with Gar-yat, the head of the communal kitchen, she went over the guest list with Nir-yat. Already, Dar was able to read it, and she took care to memorize all the names. When that was accomplished, Nir-yat told her what she knew about each guest.

Dar learned that Tauma-yat's family occupied the smallest hanmuthi within the hall. Located in the oldest section, it housed forty-three individuals, for Tauma-yat lived with her three sisters and an unblessed brother. Tauma-yat had four daughters, three of whom were already blessed and had children of their own. She also had two grown sons, both unblessed. Tauma-yat's sisters were older, but they had only one daughter apiece. That was why the youngest sibling headed the hanmuthi. The complex rules of status had been incomprehensible to Dar until the memories began to arrive. Then, like reading and writing, they suddenly made sense to her.

As the feast approached, Dar bathed, colored her nails and nipples, blackened her teeth, and dressed in her new clothes. Her russet hair had grown long enough for Niryat to weave it into a single five-strand braid, which she tied with a talmauki ribbon. Dar placed the crown, a simple gold band, upon her head and nervously waited for her guests.

As soon as they arrived, Dar's nervousness transformed into affection. *These are my children*, Dar thought as she blessed each one by name. When they were seated on cushions in the royal hanmuthi, Dar sat upon the royal stool and a procession of sons brought in the food. The room instantly filled with rich aromas. The featured dish was tahweriti, small fowls that had been stuffed with dried fruits and brak, then slowly roasted over aromatic wood. There were skewers of spiced goat and mutton, five different stews, dried fruits, hard milk, vegetables fried in spiced oil, roasted pashi, sweets, and ewers of herbed water, both hot and cold. One of the stews was muthtufa, the same dish Velasa-pah had prepared in his lonely hut. Its aroma made Dar recall her first encounter with him.

When all the food was laid about the hearth, Dar rose from her stool. "Food is Muth la's gift," she said.

"Shashav, Muth la," said everyone in unison.

Then, like a muthuri, Dar personally served each diner the first dish. After Dar had given everyone a fowl, Taumayat and her sisters helped Dar serve the next round of dishes. Then, as in a family meal, their daughters joined the servers. When everyone's platter was heaped with food and every cup was filled, the feasting began. For a while, the room was quiet as the diners savored the elegant meal. It was custom to fast before a feast, and everyone was hungry.

Conversation began later. It was easy talk that lacked the pomp and formality Dar had observed in King Kregant's court. Instead, Dar felt she was at a family gathering, though her human family had never been so festive. It was the memories of the former queens—recollections that had become her own—that made Dar feel she was attending a joyful reunion, the latest in a series that spanned generations. At times, she glanced at Tauma-yat and recalled her guest's muthuri. Other times, she remembered Tauma-yat's grandmother. Dar was full of questions, wanting to know what everyone was doing and how they'd fared. Her interest was heartfelt, and the whole family sensed it.

Falfhissi arrived in a large silver urn. Custom called for Dar to take the first drink, and it was supposed to be a deep one. She grabbed the urn by both its handles and held it to her mouth a long while, though she took care to sip sparingly. She had experience with the spicy liquor, and didn't wish to overindulge again. Nevertheless, she soon began to feel its effects. As the company grew boisterous, Dar joined in, regaling them with tales of her ineptitude in the kitchen. Dar's comic imitation of Gar-yat tasting one of her efforts left everyone hissing with laughter.

When the feast was over, Dar blessed each guest as they departed, full and happy. Only Nir-yat remained. She seemed tipsy as she beamed at Dar. "I'm so pleased you're my sister," she said. "You were everyone's muthuri tonight. You reminded me of Grandmother."

The mention of that queen made Dar recall how she had died alone. Thinking of her fate brought Dar to the verge of tears. *Don't spoil a lovely evening*, she told herself. *I'm weepy because I drank too much.* Yet Dar's melancholy didn't feel like a drunk's maudlinness. Instead, it felt like a warning.

On the evening Dar threw her second feast, a dinner was held at Balten's house in Taiben. The purpose was to introduce General Voltar to his new aide. The general and Lokung, the royal steward, arrived at dusk and were greeted by Balten. Immediately afterward, a servant brought goblets of hot, spiced wine.

Voltar took a deep draught. "So where's this Kol fellow?" he asked.

"He's coming with Gorm," replied Balten.

"Gorm!" said the general, not bothering to hide his displeasure. "Will *he* be dining with us?"

"Yes. And his master."

At that news, the color drained from Lokung's face and even the general grew subdued. He took another gulp of wine, then muttered, "*That* should make for a festive evening."

"General," whispered Balten, "it's not . . ."

Gorm's arrival cut him short. He accompanied Kol, who was dressed appropriately for his new rank. He wore a finely made black leather jerkin, dark blue trousers in the military style, and high black boots. The sword and dagger that hung from his belt were new and adorned with touches of gold. Voltar gazed at him with disdain. "I know you! You were a murdant!"

"You'd best forget that, General," said Gorm. Then he smiled. "Tolum Kol's success will preserve your good fortune. Life's pleasant with a new, young wife, but it won't do to become complacent."

Voltar looked away.

"Come now, General," said Gorm. "We're all comrades here, and comrades help one another."

"I swore I'd do it," muttered Voltar, "and I will."

"Then no half measures," replied Gorm. "Those won't satisfy my master."

General Voltar forced a smile. "Tolum Kol, welcome to my staff. Rest assured you'll have my fullest backing."

Kol bowed, his lips bearing a hint of a smile.

"Supper is ready," announced Balten as though he dreaded it. Two servants opened the doors to the dining chamber.

Kol entered the room with the others. It was chilly despite a roaring fire in a large fireplace. At the head of the banquet table sat someone who wore a silver mask and had hands wrought from the same metal. Kol assumed it was Othar and bowed to him.

The mask declined slightly, but no voice issued from its half-smiling lips. The silence appeared to unnerve all of Kol's companions except Gorm. He seemed perfectly at ease. Kol tried to emulate his example, although he couldn't achieve Gorm's air of amusement.

Servants entered the room bearing food and wine. All appeared subdued and frightened, except one—a young woman. Her pretty face was vacant, and her wrists were wrapped in bloody bandages. She remained by Othar's side when the other servants departed.

A voice from behind the mask broke the room's silence. "All here have benefited due to me." The gleaming face turned to briefly gaze at everyone but Gorm. "Tonight you'll learn the repayment I require. What secrets I reveal will remain behind these doors. Yet before I speak of them, let us enjoy our repast."

Although the guests' plates were heaped with delicacies, only a covered tureen sat before the mage. Kol wondered how Othar would eat, for his hands looked strictly ornamental and the mouth in the mask appeared too small to admit food. His question was answered when the blank-faced woman removed pins in the sides of the mask. A hinge was hidden in its top, and with the pins gone, the front and the back of the head split apart. The woman removed it to reveal the face beneath.

It was as hideous as that of any corpse Kol had encountered, and he would have been far more comfortable if it weren't living. However, what surprised him more was Voltar and Lokung's reaction. They were surprised. "Othar?" said the general. "By Karm, is that you?"

Lokung blanched as he stared wide-eyed. "You . . . you're dead. I saw it with my own eyes."

"I did, too," said the general. "How is this possible?"

"My life was preserved so I might accomplish greatness. One day, they'll speak of Othar Orc-bane, the man who rid the world of piss eyes."

The woman lifted the cover from the tureen, exposing what looked like a dark red stew. Othar smiled, his teeth gleaming against his cinder-black flesh. "Eat . . . eat. We'll talk later." The woman lifted a spoon and began to feed him.

Kol forced himself to eat some of his meal, which was rapidly growing cold. Among the other guests, only Gorm possessed an appetite. The general pecked at his food, while Lokung and Balten merely stared at theirs. While Kol ate, he made a point of glancing at Othar, not wanting to appear too cowed to meet his gaze. The "stew" the mage devoured was chunks of meat in a red broth. The meat looked raw and the broth resembled blood. When Kol had this thought, Othar flashed him a knowing smile.

On closer examination, Kol concluded that no ordinary fire had burned the mage's flesh. Although the mage's nose and ears were gone and his skin resembled scorched crusts on a skillet, his flesh remained supple and capable of expression. *He's been transformed, not consumed*, Kol thought. Othar nodded as if he understood what Kol was thinking. *Can he read my thoughts?* Othar nodded again.

Did you enslave that woman through magic? Kol thought.

Othar grinned his reply.

The meal was over as soon as Othar finished eating. Balten rang a bell and servants returned to clear the table and refill the wine goblets. Kol wondered what price they'd pay for seeing Othar unmasked. Then Othar spoke, interrupting Kol's speculations. "Before dinner, I spoke of a war against the orcs. That enterprise is why you're here. To gaze upon me is to know why I hate their queen. My condition is her doing. Only war can repay my grievance." Othar gazed about the room. "You're here to aid in accomplishing that. Tolum Kol has the hardest task. He must make a woman see sense."

General Voltar forced a laugh at the remark.

Othar smiled before continuing. "You know of the treaty between our queen and the piss eyes. They're to be her guardians, and in exchange, they'll no longer fight our enemies. That pact alters everything. Without piss eye troops, war will be costly and its outcome unsure. Have no doubt—peace means disbanded regiments and an impoverished court. If the piss eyes won't plunder for us, then we should plunder them. Only a treaty stops us. Tolum Kol's job is to turn Girta against it."

"How can he do that?" asked Voltar. "Girta lacks a spine."

"I aim to give her one," said Kol.

"You can't change a ewe into a she-wolf," said the general.

"Then I'll try some other tactic," replied Kol. "I'll do anything as long as it results in war."

"And your obligations are to help him by whatever means necessary," said Othar. "Make sure you understand that. Otherwise, you'll share this girl's fate." He spoke to the blank-faced woman by his side and she fell screaming to the floor. There, she continued to shriek while she writhed and clawed her face bloody. As her self-mutilation drew out, Lokung and Balten became sick and even Voltar grew pale. The woman died when she tore out her throat, making Kol think that an arrow in the neck would have been a gentler death.

Othar looked pleased. "Gorm will advise you on your roles. Fulfill them and we need not meet again. Balten, ring the bell."

Balten obeyed and two vacant-faced men entered the room to lift Othar's chair and carry him out. Afterward, one returned to drag the woman's corpse away. After she was gone, Gorm smiled and glanced about the room. "My master likes a dramatic touch. As Tolum Kol says, an example heightens discipline."

Fifteen

♛

From her aborted conversation with Meera-yat, Dar knew a new queen had other duties besides throwing feasts. Most important among these was calling for unblessed sons to become mintaris. Not only would the sons she chose serve throughout her reign, the call for candidates would summon the clan matriarchs for a council. Dar worried it would be a difficult meeting. If Muthyat challenged her fitness, she would do it then. Postponing a call for sons would postpone the council, but Dar saw no advantage in that. Instead, she decided to face the matriarchs and be done with it.

Dar brought up the subject of mintaris with Nir-yat during dawnmeal. She related what Meera-yat had told her, then asked, "Can you add anything to what she said?"

"Not much," replied Nir-yat. "Except take your time in choosing. Meera-yat was wise to say don't bite son's neck unless you're certain you want him. Great mothers often take years to decide. Bear in mind that your mintaris will become like your children, except they'll live in your hanmuthi even after they're blessed."

Dar suddenly understood why the royal hanmuthi was so large. "Meera-yat said I should ask each matriarch for two candidates."

"Hai, but you need not accept them. Still, it's best to have at least one mintari from each clan. Keep asking for candidates until you get one who suits you."

"Meera said I could ask for sons by name."

"Hai, if you wish."

"Do you have any suggestions?"

"I'm only familiar with sons from Mah and Tok clans," said Nir-yat. "Consider Kazan-mah and Togu-mah. Kak-tok might be good choice also. You know our clan's sons, and you've already bitten brother's neck."

"What do you think of Nagtha-yat?"

Nir-yat looked surprised. "He's Grandmother's youngest son, he must be fifty winters old. Why would you consider him?"

"I met him when I lived among washavoki soldiers. He was Wise Son who called me mother and allowed me to sleep within Muth la's Embrace."

"I heard he went to fight," said Nir-yat, "but I don't know if he survived."

"Doesn't he live in this hall?"

"He lives in his daughter's hanmuthi. She's Jan clan."

"I thought he was unblessed, because only unblessed sons were sent to fight."

"His muthvashi died, but he remained with her clan."

"If he lives, I'd like to see him," said Dar. "Which Mah clan son is better, Kazan-mah or Togu-mah?"

"Why not ask to see both?"

"Because I'll ask for Kovok-mah."

"Kovok-mah!"

"Hai. I want him."

"He can't see you! His muthuri has forbidden it."

"She can't forbid him to become mintari."

"That's true, but he must withhold his love. That won't change. Why torment yourself?"

"I'm only being practical. He speaks washavoki tongue. That's rare skill among urkzimmuthi."

"Sister, others speak washavoki tongue. They'd be wiser choice."

"Do you think me unwise?"

"In this matter, I do. Please don't choose him."

"I was told to follow my chest."

"By who?"

Dar recalled that it was Velasa-pah who first had given her that advice. As soon as she had that thought, she knew she shouldn't voice it. "It's common wisdom."

"There are times when your head must overrule your chest. This is one of them."

"I'm queen, free to choose my mintari."

"You're not free from Muth la's laws. You're making dangerous choice."

"Dangerous?"

"You understand my meaning. We're sisters. I know your chest."

"Kovok-mah will be one of my mintaris," said Dar in a tone she hoped conveyed finality. "I'll send message to Muth-mah today."

Nir-yat sighed and bowed. "Then at least you should ask for Togu-mah also."

Later that morning, sons left the Yat clan hall bearing messages to the clan matriarchs. None went to the Lost Clan, so Muth-goth's hall was the most distant destination. Three sons left on that long journey, which took nearly a moon in the summertime. In winter, the way was too perilous for a solitary traveler. The other clans were less difficult to reach, and only one messenger was sent to each.

Muth-yat watched the messengers depart from the window of her hanmuthi, then turned to Zor-yat. "Nir-yat visited me earlier today with Muth Mauk's request for mintaris."

"Muth Mauk!" said Zor-yat in a bitter tone. "She'll always be Dargu to me!"

Muth-yat smiled at her sister's petulance. "Still, we must call her Muth Mauk. You should know that your son was on her list."

"That's no surprise. She's bitten Zna-yat's neck already."

"She also named Nagtha-yat."

"Strange choice."

"Wise choice," said Muth-yat. "Another was less wise."

"Who?"

Muth-yat grinned. "Kovok-mah."

Zor-yat's face lit up. "Kovok-mah! Are you sure?"

"Nir-yat told me only because Muth Mauk had not forbidden it."

"Why would she forbid it? Everyone will know soon enough." Zor-yat's grin broadened. "Kath-mah will be furious!"

"Perhaps Muth Mauk thinks Kovok-mah's muthuri will change her mind."

"Then she doesn't know Kath-mah! This is good news, Sister."

"It's as I hoped," said Muth-yat. "Muth Mauk's foolishness will quickly end her reign. Our hall will be saved."

"So Kovok-mah will dwell within royal hanmuthi. Every moment, Dargu will be tempted."

"Once before, she risked her life to be with him," added Muth-yat.

"Then, she had to journey to Taiben," said Zor-yat. She smiled. "This time, she'll need only to cross her hanmuthi."

"That won't happen if Nir-yat's there. Zor, you must forgive Nir-yat and make her welcome in your hanmuthi."

Zor-yat frowned. "She chose Dargu over me!"

"That doesn't matter. Make peace with Nir-yat. And for our hall's sake, you must make peace with Muth Mauk, too. If she feels secure, she'll be less cautious."

Sevren made his way along Taiben's darkening streets. They were nearly deserted, for the plague of thieves continued unabated. He kept a watchful eye, knowing that the robbers would attack even a guardsman. Word had it that they were unskilled assailants, but fearless and dogged. He arrived at the sand ice merchant's house without incident and knocked on its door. A peephole slid open. A moment later, the door was unlocked, and a gray-haired man bade him enter.

The modest house was both a home and shop, and the merchant's wares were everywhere. The sand ice vessels, all of orcish make, sparkled in the firelight. They seemed to Sevren like icicles made by magic. It was a sight that never failed to enchant him. "Tava, Sevren," said the man. *Hello, Sevren.* "Sutak fu ala keem suth?" *Have you come for more learning?*

"Hai, Thamus, tep pahav pi daku urksaam." *Yes, Thamus, and to speak of other things.*

"Atham?" *What?*

"Ma kramav . . ." *I fear . . .* Sevren halted. "Let's speak in our tongue tonight."

"You'll never learn Orcish that way."

"I know, but there's a matter that worries me, something too important to speak about unskillfully."

"I'm only a sand ice merchant, weighty matters aren't my province."

"But you know the urkzimmuthi," said Sevren. "You not only speak their tongue, you're welcome in their halls."

"Aye, they extend me that honor, but that doesn't make me wise."

"I think you know more about them than anyone in Taiben."

Thamus laughed. "That's saying little."

"It's about Queen Girta's urkzimmuthi guard. Would they revolt against her?"

"Didn't their queen pledge their loyalty?"

"Aye, but she was deathly ill."

"That makes no difference. The sons will remain true to her word."

"But what if they're pushed to revolt?"

"Treachery goes against their nature. All double-dealing does. When I'm in their halls, I've no need for locked chests. Only here . . ."

"I do na doubt their honesty," said Sevren. "I'm worried about their tolerance. They're na treated well. They're called Palace Piss Eyes and Girta's Goblins."

"Even if they understood those insults, it wouldn't sway them. Their loyalty is to their queen, not ours. Yet I take it things aren't going well."

"I think Queen Girta fears her guard. I know she neglects them. They were to be housed properly, so their own women could join them. Yet no steps have been taken."

"That's shortsighted. Has no one told our queen that?"

"I've tried, but she complains of the expense. Courtiers sway her from her true interests. I fear the cause is lost without Dar to speak to her, queen-to-queen."

"Any news of Dar?"

"None," said Sevren, his eyes mournful. "I fear the worst."

"She's the reason why you wanted to learn Orcish."

"Aye, but she wasn't a queen then. I still thought I had a chance with her."

"Even after your hopes were dashed, you've persisted with your lessons. Why?"

"With orcs living in the palace, it seems prudent to understand them." Sevren smiled. "And Thamus, I like your company. Court's a nest of vipers. It's good to talk with an honest man."

"Shashav, Sevren. Gu fwilak ma pahi ta tha." *Thank you, Sevren. It pleases me to speak with you.*

It was dark when Sevren left Thamus' house, and he carried his sword unsheathed while returning to the palace. Once, he heard furtive footsteps, but they faded into the distance. The unsafe streets seemed to him another sign that things were awry. There was something abroad that made Sevren uneasy, although he couldn't say what it was. He had hoped that the death of Kregant and his mage, coupled with the new treaty, would usher in better times. Instead, men grumbled and rumors abounded. It seemed likely that Dar's sacrifice had been for naught.

Thamus' assurance that the orcs would be steadfast should have encouraged Sevren, but he still worried. Queen Girta's orc guards were her best deterrent against usurpers; yet she shrank from them. *A woman beleaguered by rats should na shun cats.* But Girta did, and Sevren feared her enemies would thrive.

Things have gone sour, Sevren thought. *I should be moving on.* He couldn't imagine where. His purse remained short of the price for a farm, but he didn't wish to soldier in Luvein again. In truth, he still clung to the hope that Dar lived. His dream of taking her to Averen seemed utterly lost—sand ice dropped on a stone floor. Yet the memory of it bound him to Taiben until he knew Dar's fate.

Sixteen

♛

Despite her words to the contrary, Dar worried that Nir-yat was right, and it was foolish to call for Kovok-mah. Dar knew that, even as queen, she couldn't gainsay his muthuri. Dar could make Kovok-mah serve her, but only Kath-mah could bless their union. Dar wasn't even sure if he could touch her without his muthuri's permission. She thought he probably could, but further intimacies would be a major transgression. *So why torment myself?* Dar's reason was simple. She was tormented already.

Dar believed that she was urkzimmuthi because of Kovok-mah. Even when they first met, he knew she was different. He had taught her Orcish, healed her wounds, and protected her from the washavoki soldiers. When she incited the orcs to desert, he followed her leadership. He said she made him feel secure. And then, in Tarathank's ruins, he had given her love. It was his love that made Dar feel truly urkzimmuthi—more than her crown or even her rebirth—because it had preceded both. *No washavoki has ever received such love as I have.*

But Kovok-mah's love was denied her because his muthuri wanted granddaughters. Dar knew they would bring Kath-mah more status than a son's marriage to a queen. Though Dar felt a muthuri should care more about her son's happiness, Kath-mah didn't, and there was little Dar could do about it. That brought Dar back to her dilemma: She could keep Kovok-mah by her side, but he must stay aloof. Dar didn't know which would be worse—having him close or not having him at all. Her chest wanted him close. Her head told her that was fool-hardy.

The evening of her third feast, Dar was often distracted by thoughts of Kovok-mah. She had already calculated how long it would take her message to reach Muth-mah and how soon Kovok-mah might arrive. The hanmuthi Dar was hosting that night was headed by a muthuri who was scarcely older than she. Yet the muthuri already had three daughters, none of whom was old enough to serve. Her hanmuthi also included two elderly aunts and their families. Clearly discontented, they reminded Dar of Kath-mah.

Despite drinking too much falfhissi, Dar slept fitfully after the feast. The next morning, she woke with a headache. After chewing a washuthahi seed to ease her hangover, she went to see the lorekeeper. Dar was still taking lessons in reading and writing, but that wasn't the reason for her visit. Nevertheless, Dar practiced her writing awhile before asking what she wanted to know. "Can reborn mothers have children?"

Yev-yat responded by stroking the lines of her clan tattoo. "Interesting question," she said after a long pause. She continued stroking her chin awhile, then rose and began pulling deetpahis from the shelves. She returned with an armload and read through several before pointing to a passage. "Here's tale of washavoki son who was reborn as Hunda-pah. He and mother named Dir-tab were blessed. There is no Tab clan now."

"Is it lost like Pah clan?" asked Dar.

"Thwa, they're all dead. Before washavokis came, there were thirteen clans. Now there are only eight, nine if you count Pah clan. But I digress. Here." Yev-yat pointed to a passage. "Dir-tab bore son named Tak-tab." Yev-yat read silently a while. "It says he looked strange."

"How?" asked Dar.

"It doesn't say." Yev-yat read some more. "Later he was killed."

"By who?"

"Some washavoki that was kin to Hunda-yat's washa-voki parents."

"But Dir-tab was born urkzimmuthi," said Dar. "Does any deetpahi speak of reborn mothers who bore children?"

The question prompted another bout of reading and more visits to the stacks of deetpahis. Dar waited patiently as the lorekeeper sought the answer. At last, Yev-yat spoke again. "No one has been reborn for long time, and much wisdom has been lost. I've found tales of three reborn mothers, but only one was blessed. She was Deen-jan and she lived near Tarathank. Perhaps she had child, but that child may have been her sister. Tale is unclear about this." The lorekeeper gathered up the deetpahis. "Why did you ask that question?"

Dar's face reddened. "I hope to have daughters."

"What mother doesn't?"

Tolum Kol made his first appearance in court at one of its frequent banquets. Girta's feasts were neither as lavish nor as well attended as her late husband's, but the ambitious came. As they milled about, all noted the new officer on General Voltar's staff. Word was out that he was an expert on orcs, and that information spurred a round of speculation. Some thought the tolum was there to curb the orcs. Others believed he was their advocate. Many wondered if he was being groomed as the new Queen's Man.

The consensus among the ladies was that Tolum Kol cut a dashing figure. He was deemed handsome in a rugged way and many commented on his piercing blue eyes. The men who regarded him a likely rival took comfort in his lack of noble birth. They found his confident demeanor unsettling, despite his courtesy.

Prior to the formal seating, courtiers could approach Queen Girta with petitions and other business. Those that did found her distracted. She was worried about her son, who had been withdrawn since his father's death and prone to night terrors. Orc guards stood silently behind the queen, casting a pall over the entire gathering. Young Kregant III seemed terrified by them. He fidgeted anxiously by his mother's side while she listened to petitions with half an ear.

General Voltar waited for a lull, then approached the queen. "Your Majesty," he said with a bow. "May I introduce my new staff officer, Tolum Kol."

"Your Majesty," said Kol, bowing deeply, all the while keeping his gaze on Girta.

"He knows a thing or two about piss eyes," said General Voltar.

"That's useful," replied the queen in an absent manner.

The general seemed about to say something more when Kol touched his sleeve. Voltar bowed instead, and the two men departed to be replaced by a count with some grievance. Queen Girta didn't think of Tolum Kol again until the banquet was nearly over and her son slumbered fitfully on his miniature throne. Then all she could recall were his eyes and how assured they looked.

While Girta thought of Tolum Kol's eyes, Dar's feast was also winding down. She had arrived late from visiting the lorekeeper and had been barely ready when her guests arrived. The family she hosted that night was even larger than Tauma-yat's, and serving everyone was time-consuming. As on the previous night, Dar was distracted by thoughts of Kovok-mah, but she put on a good effort and thought the night had gone well.

After the falfhissi urn had made its way around the room several times, a son who was feeling its effects called Dar "Muth Velavash" and spoke of how she had blessed him before a battle. Dar didn't recognize him, but the orcs had been helmeted while waiting to attack. He bowed low to Dar, then commenced to sing the lament for the slain. Fortunately, a mother made him stop after the first thirteen verses. The feast ended shortly afterward.

When the guests had departed, Nir-yat spoke to Dar. "Thir's returning tomorrow. Muthuri told me."

Dar didn't know what pleased her more—that she would see her young sister again or that Zor-yat was speaking to Nir-yat. "Why didn't you tell me earlier?"

"You were busy," replied Nir-yat. "And, Sister—Muthuri's no longer mad at me. She called me wise because I foresaw you would be good queen."

"She said I was good queen?" said Dar.

"Hai," replied Nir-yat, beaming. "She said it's become common wisdom."

Dar wished she shared her sister's satisfaction, but she didn't. Like most orcs, Nir-yat didn't grasp deception, which made her incapable of cynicism. That wasn't the case with Dar, who was convinced that Zor-yat played loose with the truth. *Muthuri has worked against me up to now. Why this sudden change?* Dar didn't voice her doubts to her sister. She merely smiled, though inwardly she felt wary.

The following day, Tolum Kol entered Thamus' shop and was greeted by its owner. "Good morning, sir. May I help you?"

"I'm looking for a gift. Something for a lady."

"A special item? Perhaps something that speaks of romance?"

Kol smiled. "You guess rightly."

"Then you've come to the right place. I sell only orcish wares."

Kol acted surprised. "Orcish?"

"They do the finest work," said Thamus, holding up a delicate vase. "Note its clarity and the perfection of its form. This is true sand ice, not the cloudy and lumpy stuff we make."

"Is it expensive?"

"I must journey to their halls, no easy trip. And the road's not gentle to fragile wares."

Kol smiled amiably. "Which is to say they're dear."

"I've some pieces that cost only a few silvers." Thamus selected a tiny, stoppered vial from a shelf. "Rose sand ice. Perfect for perfume. Five silvers."

Same as the bounty for a branded woman's head, thought Kol. He held the piece near a window to examine its color and nodded appreciatively. "You trade directly with the orcs?"

"Aye."

"Do you speak their language and know their ways?"

"I do."

"Then this is a happy meeting. I've been posted to our queen's court, where ignorance abounds about her new orc guards."

"So I've heard."

"It's an ignorance that I regret I share. I fear provoking my orcish comrades through some misunderstanding. If I knew their speech and customs, I could avoid that. Perhaps you'd tutor me." Kol produced a gold coin. "I'd pay you."

Thamus eyed the gold. "That's a lot for a few lessons."

Kol smiled. "Not really. Peace is priceless."

Thamus accepted the coin, but insisted it also paid for the perfume vial. Afterward, he commenced with Kol's lessons. The two spent the entire day together, and by its end, Kol was aware of how little he had known about orcs. Throughout his years in the regiment, he had regarded them as talking cattle—bulls, and just as dangerous. As a murdant, he had known how to avoid provoking them and that was all. Dealing with the piss eyes was an officer's job. Kol had concentrated on mastering soldiers, horses, and women.

Tolum Kol had expected to learn a few useful Orcish phrases and some facts to bolster his claim of expertise. In addition to these things, he acquired far more valuable information. For the first time, he saw how Dar had bested him. *Piss eyes are ruled by their women, and Dar acted like a piss eye bitch.* Kol conceded it was a clever ploy. Thamus had also related how Dar had become the orcs' queen, for a guardsman in his acquaintance had witnessed the event. Kol remembered the guardsman's name and decided to keep an eye on him. When Thamus praised the orcs' honesty and their devotion to their ruler, Kol saw both as weaknesses. *Honest men are easier to trick,* he thought, *and devotion makes them vulnerable.* He reasoned the same was true with orcs.

When Kol departed the shop at dusk, he didn't look forward to his next lesson. He found that day's session tedious enough, and his tutor's admiration of orcs annoyed him. Thoughts of Thamus prompted Kol to remove the perfume vial from his jerkin and examine it in the dying light. It seemed too delicate to be made by brutes. Yet Kol had come to see that the brutes possessed similar fragility. He didn't understand Fathma, but he grasped its most crucial point: If Dar was captured, her realm would be imperiled. If she died in captivity, it was likely to collapse. Kol threw the vial against a wall, shattering it. Then he returned to court.

Seventeen

♕

Five days after messengers were sent to the clan matriarchs, one returned accompanied by two sons. Dar, who had spent the afternoon with the lorekeeper, was greeted by Nir-yat with the news. "Candidates for your mintari have arrived."

Dar tried to appear calm. "From which clan?"

"Mah clan. Their hall lies closest to ours."

Dar noticed that Nir-yat was watching her with a concerned expression. *She probably smells atur*, Dar thought. Though Dar seldom could detect the scent herself, she was certain that she smelled of love. Her sister's face confirmed it. Following custom, Dar didn't respond to her sister's expression. Besides, she had a more immediate problem. "How should I receive them?"

"I don't know," replied Nir-yat. "You should ask Muthuri."

"She's been no help before."

"She's changed, Sister. I'm certain of it. Send for her."

Dar was dubious, but her options were limited. Neither she nor her sister was versed in protocol, but Zor-yat was. Dar decided to send for her and dispatched a son on that errand. He returned with her shortly afterward. "Muth la's blessing, Muthuri," said Dar.

"Shashav, Muth Mauk," replied Zor-yat, bowing especially low. "I beg your forgiveness, Most Honored Daughter. I've been ill-mannered and foolish."

"Why do you say that?"

"I should have been by your side, helping you through difficult days. Instead, I stood apart, hoping you'd falter."

"Why?"

"I envied your place. I fought Muth la's will. My actions have been shameful."

"Then undo them by aiding me. Deeds are weightier than words."

"I'd be grateful for chance to help."

"Muth-mah has sent me two candidates for my mintari. How should I proceed?"

Zor-yat smiled as she bowed. "You should receive these sons in Great Chamber. Merely being there honors them. Speak of why they're being considered, then let them rest from their journey."

"Will they stay in my hanmuthi?"

"Only if you bite their necks. Until then, families within our hall will host them. I can make first two welcome, and Muth-yat can find places for others as they arrive."

"What will candidates do?"

"Whatever you tell them. For one thing, they'll replace those sons who have served you up to now. Their duties were only temporary."

"Your advice has been helpful," said Dar.

"I'm glad, Muth Mauk. I hope I can be equally useful in future."

Zor-yat left a short while later, after giving Dar some advice on managing the royal hanmuthi. She recommended that Nir-yat coordinate the candidates' schedules and mentioned other tasks that she might do for Dar. While Dar remained suspicious about her muthuri's change of mind, she was pleased to have the benefit of her experience. Moreover, the prospect of seeing Kovok-mah dominated her thoughts, making her other concerns seem trivial.

As soon as Zor-yat left, Dar prepared to receive Togu-mah and Kovok-mah. She bathed, dressed in her finest clothes, blackened her teeth, applied fresh talmauki, and had Nir-yat braid her hair. She took extra care to look regal, for while pretty by human standards, Dar judged herself by orcish ones. She lacked a prominent brow, a sharp chin, and a ridge along her nose, and she felt this made her unattractive. But her brown eyes disturbed her most. Dar thought they resembled a rat's. Only her black teeth and the clan tattoo on her chin were lovely in her estimation. Making matters worse, her forehead bore King Kregant's brand and the skin beneath her breast remained discolored from her wound. *At least the scars from my flogging are hidden.*

Dar recalled how Kovok-mah had treated those lashes with healing magic, and that memory evoked a cascade of others. *He sees my spirit, not my ugly face.* Dar placed the crown upon her head, then headed for the Great Chamber. As she passed the son assigned to serve her, she told him to bring the two candidates there.

The Great Chamber resembled a hanmuthi except that a high throne carved from a single block of marble replaced the hearth in its center and arched windows replaced the entrances to sleeping chambers. The throne, which had no back or arms, was a more elaborate version of the stool that matriarchs sat upon. Its seat was so high that steps were necessary to reach it. The windows provided a panoramic view of the surrounding mountains, which were white with snow. The stone floor was heated from beneath, so the chamber was comfortably warm, despite the frigid weather. Dar noted that the stool Muth-yat had sat upon was gone from beside the throne. She climbed into the royal seat, and waited for Kovok-mah and Togu-mah to arrive.

They entered the chamber soon after Dar and halted before the throne. From her elevated position, Dar gazed down at the two sons. The sight of Kovok-mah affected her even more than she expected. The last time she had looked into his green-gold eyes she was certain that she was dying. That moment came back to her, and she saw his gaze held the same expression as then—a mixture of grief and love. It took a while for her to find her voice. "Muth la's blessing, Togu-mah and Kovok-mah."

Both sons bowed low. "Shashav, Muth Mauk." Then Kovok-mah added in the human tongue, "Please don't choose me."

Dar responded in Orcish. "Kovok-mah, I'm pleased you still practice speaking washavoki tongue." Then she changed to human speech. "We'll talk later." Switching back to Orcish, she added, "Both of you can render me valuable service."

Dar regarded Togu-mah. He was shorter but more massively built than Kovok-mah. He had a likable face, lined by frequent smiles, and his eyes bespoke intelligence. Dar had met him while visiting Kath-mah, but she knew him mostly through Nir-yat's description. He had fought for the washavoki king three times, but not last summer. Like Kovok-mah, he herded goats. He was also skilled at healing their hurts and diseases. "Togu-mah, my sister, whose judgment I respect, spoke highly of your wisdom, strength, and tenacity. I've need of son with such qualities."

As Togu-mah bowed in recognition of her praise, Dar noted his puzzled expression. Dar was certain she had said nothing to provoke his response. She was wondering what had caused it when she detected a faint scent. It was almost imperceptible, but she recognized it immediately. *Atur! If I can smell it, the air must be thick with it. No wonder he's looking at me strangely.* Dar was unable to tell if the fragrance betrayed her feelings or Kovok-mah's, but her awareness of it increased her awkwardness. She stared at Kovok-mah awhile before remembering that she should address him also.

"Kovok-mah, you've shown skill in dealing with

washavokis. I'll need emissary who can speak with washa-voki great mother."

Kovok-mah bowed.

"Togu-mah, Zor-yat will welcome you into her han-muthi. Go rest from your journey. You have pleased me." As Togu-mah bowed, Dar addressed Kovok-mah. "Ko-vok-mah, we must speak further."

Both Dar and Kovok-mah fell silent until Togu-mah left the chamber. "Kovok, I've missed you."

"Muth Mauk, please . . ."

"Call me Dargu when we're alone."

"You're not Dargu. You're Muth Mauk now, and we can never be alone. Muthuri has forbidden it."

"Once you're my mintari, that won't matter."

"If you bite my neck, your authority will be greater than hers in all things but one: We must have her bless-ing to give love. Without it, you'll become thwada."

"I've been thwada before."

"That was different. You were thwada for sacred rea-sons. When you returned from darkness, you were no longer untouchable. Thwada I speak of lasts forever. It's like death."

"To be apart from you is like being thwada," said Dar.

"Before you speak like that, may I tell you tale?"

"What is this tale?"

"When I was youngling, I accompanied my father on journey. He brought she-goat with us that was too old to give milk. When we reached ridge that lay far from our halls, he made me chase goat away. Then we headed home. I was curious and asked why we had done that thing. Fa-ther said that goat was for ghost."

"Ghost?" said Dar.

"Hai. I was more puzzled than before, but Father would speak no further of it. Yet his words remained with me, for I had never seen ghost. Winter passed, and next spring I was deemed old enough to roam about alone. Then I thought again of that ghost and resolved to see it."

"Did you?"

"Not on my first trip to ridge. Three times I made journey. Last time was when leaves had fallen from trees. Then I saw her. Ghost was mother unlike any I had ever seen."

"How?"

"She resembled animal. She wore hides, not proper clothes. It was cold, yet she had no cloak or footwear. And she was as wary as any wild creature. When she saw me, she ran away."

Dar saw where the tale was heading. "And that mother was thwada."

"Hai. Muthuri told me when I spoke of her."

"What did she say?"

"Only that she was mother who had done forbidden thing with her velazul."

"You mean thing forbidden by her muthuri."

"Hai," said Kovok-mah. "She was cast out, to be forever nameless and dead to all her clan. No one could speak to her, or acknowledge her in any way."

"What of her velazul? Was he cast out also?"

"He was shamed, yet he remained among urkzimmuthi. Sons are weak. Mothers are not."

"Did you ever see her again?"

"Three winters later, while searching for lost goat, I came upon hole. Its sides were circular and lined with rocks. There were remains of roof. It had caved in. Bones were beneath it."

"Her bones?"

"I think so. They were of our kind."

"So she died alone."

"You will, too, if you make one mistake."

"Do you think me weak?"

"Thwa, yet I'm still afraid. I don't want to hurt you in any way."

"Our separation hurts me."

"But . . ."

"I need you by my side. I can't do everything alone."

"You'll find others more worthy than me."

"Who will speak to Girta if not you? Garga-tok? He'll frighten her. He lacks your gentleness and your skill with washavoki speech."

"But Muthuri will . . ."

"She'll change her mind."

"You don't know her as I do. She's resolute, and her word is law."

"I want you for my mintari," said Dar. "Would you refuse that honor?"

Kovok-mah gazed at Dar, his face betraying his inner struggle. With a pang of remorse, Dar thought he looked miserable. Then he lowered his head. "Sons are weak," he said in a low voice.

Dar climbed down from the throne, determined to take action before her reservations grew stronger. "Bend your neck."

Kovok-mah solemnly sank to his knees, then lowered himself further so his hands rested on the floor. As Dar knelt beside him, he stared downward, not at her. She pushed his hair aside, to expose his neck, and the moment she touched him she felt overwhelmed with yearning. His scent evoked memories of the courtyard in Tarathank, when she lay naked atop him, experiencing his body with all her senses. Dar knew she was doing something that she was likely to regret and understood Kovok-mah's struggle and misery.

Dar almost pulled away. Instead, she bent farther, until her lips rested on Kovok-mah's neck. His skin felt warm and soft. Fragrance filled her nostrils. "I smell atur," she whispered.

"Do you also smell my fear?"

Dar drew back and detected a sour note. Perhaps

Fathma had sharpened her washavoki sense of smell, or perhaps the memories of the former queens caused her to recognize the scent. Either way, she knew Kovok-mah was afraid. Regardless, she pressed her lips against his neck again. She kissed it in the orcish fashion, rubbing her tongue over his skin, savoring the taste of it.

Kovok-mah spoke in a husky voice. "Bite, not kiss!"

With sudden anger, Dar bit down until she tasted blood. Then she drew back, horrified and perplexed by what she had done.

Kovok-mah stayed motionless, as blood welled from Dar's teeth marks. "Now I'm marked," he said with resignation in his voice. "My life is yours."

After an awkward silence, Dar retreated to her throne. She told Kovok-mah to rise and he obeyed. Another awkward silence ensued. Eventually, Dar spoke again. "Now that you're my mintari, you'll stay in royal hanmuthi. You should place your things there."

"Hai. It will be my home for as long as you're queen."

"So you know about that."

"Everyone does."

Dar glanced at the chamber's entrance and noticed that Nir-yat was approaching. Her sister halted at the doorway and bowed. "Muth Mauk, your feast . . ."

Dar realized that the sun had set and the Great Chamber had grown dim. "Have my guests arrived?"

"Hai."

Dar jumped off the throne and hurried from the room. Kovok-mah remained put, clearly confused. He regarded Nir-yat. "Cousin, what should I do?"

"Go to Muthuri's. You'll stay there."

"But I'm to live in Muth Mauk's hanmuthi."

Nir-yat's face fell. "She bit your neck?"

Eighteen

♛

As a murdant, Kol had learned how to deal with those who considered themselves his superiors. He handled the nobles in the court as he had the officers in his regiment. Tolum Kol humored their presumptions, while exuding an air of polite competence. Both the royal steward and General Voltar nurtured his reputation as useful but unambitious, and Kol took care to make men easy in his company. He avoided close contact with the queen but ensured she saw him. All the while, he studied her and the prince.

Kol bided his time before he made his move. Formality always slackened as the court gathered for a banquet, and that was when Kol chose to act. He waited until courtiers pressed around the queen, then approached the prince. The boy was fidgeting as usual, ignored by the adults. Kol knelt down so he was at the child's eye level. "That's a big brute you got there," he said, nodding at the orc guard. "Does it make a good pet?"

"It's not a pet."

"Oh, they're just like dogs, only not as smart. Watch this." Kol curled back his lips in an orcish smile and bowed to the guard. "Pahat tha pah pi urkwashavoki?" *Speak you speech of washavokis?*

"Thwa," said the orc.

"Ma lo-tamav tha fleem washavoki," said Kol. *I will teach you washavoki courtesy.* He bowed again, then standing tiptoe, whispered in the guard's ear.

The guard bowed to the prince. "Ah eem Booger Nose."

"Tha pahat grut," said Kol. *You speak good.* He turned to the prince, who was beginning to smile. "Bow to it and say, 'Shashav, Booger Nose.'"

Young Kregant III did so with a giggle.

The sound of the prince's laughter caught Queen Girta's attention. She ignored the wheedling count before her, and turned her gaze toward her child. He and the man kneeling before him seemed to be enjoying a private joke. She had seen the man in court, and though she couldn't remember his name, she recalled his blue eyes. He seemed deferential but friendly to the prince, and her son appeared animated in his presence.

Queen Girta motioned to the royal steward, who hurried to her side. "Who is that man talking to the prince?"

Lokung curled his lips with disdain. "Tolum Kol. An officer of lowly birth. Shall I shoo him away?"

"No," said Girta, disliking the steward's haughtiness more than usual. "Seat him at the head table tonight. Next to the prince."

Lokung rolled his eyes. "As you wish, Your Majesty."

Girta watched her steward perform his errand and noted her son's delighted expression. Tolum Kol looked in her direction and graciously bowed before returning his attention to the prince.

The banquet began when Queen Girta and the prince were seated. Servants rushed food and drink to them before serving the other guests. Seats at the head table were coveted, with those closest to the queen deemed the most desirable because they provided access to her. Usually, whoever sat next to the prince ignored the boy and spoke with Girta. Tolum Kol acted differently. He entertained Girta's son with tales of army life that were so amusing that the queen found herself straining to hear them also.

The banquet ended when Girta rose to depart. Usually, her son was asleep by then, but Tolum Kol's attention had kept him wide awake. Kol had risen with the other guests, and the queen turned to speak to him. "Sir, the prince appears to enjoy your company."

Kol bowed. "He's a fine lad, Your Majesty."

"The rest of the company has failed to notice that. He's usually ignored."

"Perhaps they overlook him. A boy's easy to miss when the nose is held high."

Girta smiled. "Sir, I think you've hit the mark. Yet you didn't overlook him."

"I'm but a rooster in a pen of peacocks, more fit for a boy's company than the high and mighty."

"Yet a rooster has more uses than a peacock. Do you ride, sir?"

"I do, Your Majesty."

"Then, if the weather's fair tomorrow, come to the royal stables at noon. I take my air on horseback."

Tolum Kol bowed. "You honor me."

Kovok-mah needed no device or special clothing to mark him as a mintari. His presence in the royal hanmuthi did that. Throughout Dar's feast he felt conspicuous. He ate silently and attempted not to stare overmuch at Dar. That was difficult, for her transformation awed him. *She's truly our Muth Mauk*, he thought as she served her guests and spoke affably with them. He recalled the fierce, filthy washavoki he had forced to bathe and marveled at the change. *This is Muth la's work.*

Dar had been reborn urkzimmuthi and Fathma had made her queen, yet Kovok-mah was aware that she lacked his senses. She seemed blithely unaware of how her scent betrayed her feelings. Everyone in the room was conscious of them, and while they wouldn't speak of them to her, they would among themselves. *How can Dargu not know this?* Kovok-mah thought that she might but had chosen to defy convention. *Her will was always strong.* He worried where such defiance could lead.

Toward the end of the feast, the falfhissi urn made its rounds. By Kovok-mah's third draught, he was unable to take his eyes from Dar. The scent of his longing filled the air, but he no longer cared. He was caught up in reliving that night in Tarathank when Dar chose to acknowledge his feelings. He recalled standing in the pool, his skin wet and cool, when she first touched him. Kovok-mah could almost feel the warmth of her hands. *If she were to touch me again, could I deny her?* He felt weak, and doubted he could.

A hand touched Muth-goth's shoulder, rousing her from sleep. She opened her eyes. A mother bowed. "Matriarch, travelers have arrived."

Muth-goth blinked and fought to leave the world of dreams. Few traveled in winter and fewer still in the frigid night. Muth-goth could think of no traveler so important that she should be awakened. "Build up hearth fire. Then help me to my stool." Muth-goth thought of greeting the travelers in her sleeping cloak, but decided against it. When the mother returned from feeding the fire, Muth-goth asked her to fetch her kefs and day cloak. Old age made dressing an ordeal, and the elderly matriarch needed help with it and walking to her stool.

When the travelers were ushered in, they appeared to Muth-goth as frosted blurs. She rose with difficulty to greet them. "I am Muth-goth."

The foremost blur bowed. "I am Muth-pah."

"Muth-pah! I haven't seen you for dozen winters."

Muth-goth smiled wryly. "I can scarcely see you now. Come closer."

Muth-pah moved closer, and Muth-goth squinted at her face. "You've grown old, too. Why would you travel in midst of winter?"

"Queen from west sits on throne."

Muth-goth stared at her visitor, momentarily dumbfounded. When she spoke, her voice was filled with awe. "Are you certain? No messengers have come this way. How did you learn this news?"

"Velasa-pah himself was messenger."

"You've had vision?"

"Hai, and I've been journeying ever since. These are urgent times when hope and fear meet. Tomorrow we must leave for royal hall."

Muth-goth slowly lowered herself to her stool. "My body is failing me. I can barely journey across my hanmuthi."

"Then sons must carry you. Queen is in great peril. I have learned this in my vision."

"How can we do anything about that?"

"I don't know," replied Muth-pah. "Yet we must try."

Muth-goth sighed as if already wearied to the bone. "I think I will be traveling only eastward. This hall I will never see again."

"That is likely for both of us, old friend. I have foreseen our journey. We will reach royal hall. Beyond that, all is darkness."

Dar lay on her bed, her thoughts chaotic. Kovok-mah's tale of the mother who was thwada replayed through her mind. Imagining that mother's loneliness, Dar wondered about the nature of her transgression. She knew that only blessed couples were permitted intercourse, but unblessed sons and mothers were free to give love. The intimacies she had experienced with Kovok-mah were commonplace in orcish courtship. Mothers talked about them freely. *Both Nir and Thir have been given love.* Yet Kovok-mah's tale hinted that such acts could be forbidden also. *Where is the line drawn? Who draws it?*

Frost coated the panes on her window, rendering the moonlight soft and murky. Dar could barely see Kovok-mah sitting in his chamber across the room and had no idea if he was awake. Nir-yat slept close by, sitting upright like Kovok-mah. Dar was glad that she was there. If it were otherwise, Dar envisioned herself crossing the room. *He's so close. It would take but a moment.* Dar recalled Meera-yat's advice about choosing her mintari and how the deed couldn't be undone. *Kovok-mah would be here every night.* Dar wondered if, over time, it would become easier to remain in her bed. *Or harder.*

Nineteen

♛

The noon sun sailed in a clear blue sky, though the air was crisp. Thunder's breath smoked as he trotted toward the royal stables, which were apart from those used by the guards and courtiers. Six mounted guardsmen were stationed by its door. When it opened, Queen Girta emerged riding a dappled gray. Tolum Kol was pleased to note that no one else accompanied her. He spurred Thunder in her direction.

The queen, followed by her escort, met him in the middle of the courtyard. Kol reined in his mount and bowed from the saddle. "Your Majesty. A brisk day, but a fine one to be out."

"I'm thinking the same," said Girta. She headed her horse for the palace gates. "There's little snow on the windward plain. We'll ride there."

Tolum Kol rode alongside Girta through Taiben's cobbled streets. When they passed outside the city gates, the queen spurred her horse to a gallop. Kol kept Thunder apace, and the two rode over the dry, brown grass, which had only a dusting of snow. When Girta slowed her mare to a trot, Kol did the same with his stallion. "You ride well, sir," said Girta. "I would have thought you a cavalry officer had my son not told me you served with orcs."

"He repeated my tales?"

"Every one. They amused him greatly."

"I'm glad they entertained him."

Girta chuckled. "The one about the orc and the sow was especially merry."

"If the prince can laugh at orcs, he'll fear them less. That will benefit him. Orcs can smell fear."

"The same is said of dogs, though I don't credit it."

"It's no fable when it comes to orcs. They sniff out other feelings, too. Anger, pain, love. They're alert to any weakness."

Girta laughed. "Is love a weakness?"

"I've seen men undone by it. Orcs, too."

"An orc undone by love?"

"Perhaps lust is a better word."

Girta looked intrigued. "I hope that's one tale you didn't tell my son."

"It's not fit for young ears."

Girta smiled. "Or mine?"

"You know it in part already. How do you think a woman could become the orcs' queen?"

"Do you mean Dar?"

"The same."

"She's dead, so speak no ill of her."

"She's not dead. She's far too clever."

"I assure you she is," said Girta. "She was nearly so when I last saw her."

"I've heard that story. She was victim of a poisoned wound. But where's that deadly blade?"

"An orc took it."

Kol smiled. "That was convenient. Don't be surprised if you hear from Dar again."

"So you're saying she was false?"

"I knew her from the regiment. She was ever guileful. How else could she manage to get orcs inside the palace? They remain there still."

"They're there for my protection. Orcs honor women."

Kol looked surprised. "Who told you that?"

"Dar."

"Then why did they keep them as slaves?"

"It was the army, not the orcs, that conscripted them."

"Only because the orcs insisted, they refused to fight otherwise."

"I have a different understanding," said Girta.

"And it's not my place to change your mind. I'm only a tolum. You have nobles to advise you. If Dar's dead, my worries are groundless. I'll speak no more of them."

"Good, because I'm getting chilled." Girta turned her horse toward Taiben's gates. Kol and her guard followed her.

When the queen dismounted in the palace courtyard, she turned to Kol. "Join me for some hot spiced wine. A guardsman can care for your mount."

"You're very kind," said Kol.

"Come, I'm frozen."

Kol dismounted, handed Thunder's reins to a guardsman, and followed the queen into the palace. She led him to a large but private room with a window that overlooked the city. A fire blazed in the fireplace, and a servant was standing by with a ewer of spiced wine. He poured two goblets at Girta's command and heated the liquid with a hot poker from the fire. Girta warmed her hands on her goblet before sipping the steaming wine.

Tolum Kol took a warming drink and sighed contentedly. "This day was colder than it looked. Your Majesty has the hardiness of a seasoned trooper."

"I grew up on the western plains."

"I've campaigned in that region. They say its winters are harsh."

"And they speak true, yet I rode year-round."

"Then you must find Taiben confining."

"I do at times. I imagine the women you know lead more adventurous lives."

"I know no women," said Kol. "I have sisters, but I haven't seen them in years. A military man leads an unsettled life."

"But women served in your regiments."

"Those branded wretches! Honorable men avoided them."

"Why?" asked Girta. "Because they were unfortunate?"

"Their misfortune was their own doing. When we levied women, the villages sent their troublemakers. Slatterns, thieves, and worse. Still, I loathed branding them."

"Then why did you?"

"Our king's command. Unbranded women fled. Orcs are not gentle masters."

"Dar said differently."

"She knew how to please them."

"And how was that?" asked Girta.

"To say, I must violate your injunction."

"And speak ill of her?"

"Yes, and most indelicately."

Despite herself, Girta was intrigued. "Say your tale. I'll hear it."

"I'm told orc females look not unlike human ones. Though bull orcs think our women ugly, they're not repelled by them."

"Are you saying that . . . that . . ." Girta shuddered.

"I said it's an indelicate subject."

"How unnatural!"

"Unnatural, but not so uncommon. We've all heard of shepherds who take solace with their ewes. A woman can't fight off a lustful orc. But Dar was different. She didn't resist. Quite the opposite."

"I can't believe that."

"Ask any of your royal guards about the orc wench. They were there. That's what Dar was named. A title she bore proudly."

"Are you saying she whored her way to the crown?"

"I don't believe she did. Whoring may have gained her some advantage, but I think she offered them more than her favors."

"What?"

"Your realm."

Girta took a deep swallow of wine. "Can you explain your meaning?"

"Orcs are cruel and savage fighters, but they're not clever. We humans have always used our wits to best them. That's why they fight for us rather than against us. But don't doubt their resentment. I liken them to dogs. We're the masters, yet if we drop our guard they'll tear out our throats. I think Dar offered to betray her kind in exchange for the crown. Look how she fooled the Queen's Man and your husband. And that treaty she had you sign brought orcs inside the palace."

"How would that treaty benefit her?" asked Girta. "She was dying."

"If she truly was, it gained her naught. But I'd keep an eye on your orc guards."

"The same guards you're teaching the prince not to fear?"

"Fear encourages attack. You should be calm, but wary."

"I keep a wary eye on everyone. Men are dangerous, too. And as you've said, they're more treacherous than orcs."

"You're right about that," said Kol. "I trust your son can defend himself."

"He has a fencing master."

"Would he be safe against a cutthroat with a dirk? Assassins don't abide by fencers' rules."

"He's only eight."

"All the more reason to know a few tricks."

"Tricks you could teach him?" asked Girta.

"I've eluded death more than once. I'd gladly show the prince what I know."

"When he becomes king, I want him to know more than war."

"You're wise to hate it. I've seen too much to call war glorious or noble. The prince should fight only to save his life or his kingdom."

"Then we're like-minded in this," said Girta. "It would please me if you spent time with the prince."

"I'd be honored to instruct him."

Queen Girta called for Lokung after Tolum Kol departed, and asked him to fetch a guardsman, specifying that he be one who served on the summer campaign. The steward left and returned with a man named Wulfar. Girta sent Lokung outside the room before she spoke. "I'm told you fought for my husband this summer."

"I did, Yer Majesty."

"I'm curious about a woman who served in the regiments on that campaign. I'm told she was notorious. They called her the orc wench."

"Has Sevren complained to Yer Majesty?"

"Why do ask that?"

"I've heard he has yer ear."

"So?"

"He was sweet on her. Still is, I think. So if he's told tales against me . . ."

"He hasn't. I just want to know about the orc wench."

"Well, she tupped an orc. I know that. And it killed a man for her."

"I see," said Girta. "What happened to her?"

"She must have run off with her orc. Leastways, she was gone when the fighting stopped. I thought she was dead until she showed up here."

"Can you tell me any more about her?"

"Not really, Yer Majesty. The rest of the guard will tell ye much the same."

"You may leave. And send my steward to me as you depart."

As much as the queen disliked admitting it, she conceded that Lokung had been right in disparaging Sevren. *Even if Sevren isn't a traitor, his loyalties are divided.* Girta could see no reason for Wulfar to lie to her, and his assertion explained why Sevren had helped Dar. When Lokung entered the chamber, Girta instructed him to bar Sevren from further audiences. The steward bowed and departed, his expression neutral.

When the queen was alone again, she took stock of her situation. She had heard much that compounded her worries. Tolum Kol seemed right; her uneasiness with the orcs was justified. Girta realized that her belief in Dar's sincerity had convinced her to make a treaty with the orcs and solicit their protection. *What if she played me false?* Further questions followed. *Is Dar still alive? If so, what are her intentions?*

Though Girta had no way to check all of Tolum Kol's claims, her interview with the guardsman had verified a major one. It seemed certain that Dar had taken an orc for a lover. A woman capable of that was capable of anything. Yet despite its worrisome implications, Girta was glad to have confirmed Kol's story, for it proved his truthfulness. *And I sorely need someone I can trust.*

Twenty

♛

In the two days following Kovok-mah's arrival, Dar received seven more candidates for her mintaris in the Great Chamber. The sons from the Hak clan and the Jan clan had been selected by their clan's matriarchs. Although Dar knew their names, they were strangers to her. Nagtha-yat, whom she knew and had requested, accompanied the Jan clan sons. The Tok clan was also represented. Kak-tok had been recommended by Nir-yat. The other candidate proved a delightful surprise. He was Lama-tok. He grinned broadly as he bowed. "Dargu! One of your wolves has returned." Then he howled.

Dar laughed. "How good to see you again! How's Duth-tok?"

"My brother was blessed upon his return and now lives with his muthvashi in Smat clan hall."

Custom required Dar to bless each son by name, and she interrupted her conversation with her old traveling companion to do that. After the blessings were accomplished, she felt at a loss. The mixture of strange and familiar faces did not suggest a single course of action. The sons gazed at her expectantly. Dar's mind began to race, and for a moment, she feared she'd have nothing to say. Then the memories of a long line of queens came to her. Each had overcome similar awkwardness. Encouraged by their example, Dar grew calm and words came to her.

Dar gazed into the eyes of each son before she spoke. "I know some of you, and some I'll come to know. Yet all have been deemed worthy to stand before me, and I'm pleased you're here. For many generations, your clans have sent sons to serve great mothers. Yet there has never been great mother such as I. I'm not sure why Muth la set me on this throne. I didn't seek to become queen. I'm still surprised I'm here.

"Because I've been reborn, I look strange to you. My spirit is urzimmuthi, but my body still has its old form. Perhaps that's part of Muth la's plan, I don't know. What I do know is that Fathma unites me with all great mothers. Their spirits have mingled with mine, and my fate is same as theirs—to be muthuri to all urzimmuthi. When you serve me, it's our race you truly serve."

Dar saw affirmation in the sons' expressions. All seemed proud to be there, and their attitude was gratifying. It reminded her of how readily the orcs in the regiments had obeyed her when she led them against the king. Dar realized that sons were used to being led and not prone to question a mother's authority. *No wonder queens use mintaris to rule.* Dar was inclined to accept all the candidates on the spot, but decided it would be prudent to wait. Instead, she turned them over to Niryat, who arranged for their lodging.

Throughout the remainder of the day, she met with each candidate individually in order to get to know him better. Every son provided a detailed genealogy and spoke of his profession, which was often associated with his clan. The Jan clan was known as the Iron Clan and both its sons were metalworkers. One was skilled at foundry work, and the other fashioned armor. The Tok clan was the Stone Clan. Dar already knew that Lama-tok was a mason. Kak-tok, who was his third cousin, was a stone carver. As Dar expected, one of the Hak clan sons made sand ice, but the other grew crops.

Dar spoke with Nagtha-yat the longest, because he had been raised in a queen's hanmuthi. "It was bustling place," recalled Nagtha-yat. "Not only did my family live there, but also thirteen mintaris and their families. Sons live with their spouse's clan, except if they're mintaris."

"Does that cause problem for mothers?"

"Some mothers won't wed son whose neck is bitten," said Nagtha-yat. "That's why only unblessed sons or widowers are sent as candidates. Yet many mothers are pleased to live in queen's hanmuthi, for not all have prospect of heading hanmuthi of their own."

"My hanmuthi is nearly empty," said Dar. "Only my sister and one mintari share it with me."

"You have mintari already?"

"Hai. He is Kovok-mah."

"I remember him. You slept in his shelter."

"Hai. And we journeyed together after great battle," said Dar. Nagtha-yat's expression altered, and Dar suspected her scent was revealing her feelings. She quickly changed the subject. "I've spoken to your aunt, Meera-yat. She advised me briefly, then refused to speak further." When Nagtha-yat didn't ask why, Dar volunteered the reason. "She believes that I'm queen from west."

Nagtha-yat appeared undisturbed by the news. "Because you journeyed here from west?"

"Hai."

"What difference does that make?"

"There are tales about western queen. Have you heard them?"

"Thwa."

"I want you as one of my mintaris. Your experience would be valuable to me. But I must first warn you that Meera-yat fears my reign will bring destruction to this hall. To her, I'm ill-omened."

Nagtha-yat regarded Dar thoughtfully. "You warn me so I might decline to bend my neck?"

"I don't want you to regret your decision."

"Though Muth la seldom speaks to sons, I know this:

She often sends difficult choices. I'm speaking about you, not myself. Do you love this hall?"

"I do. I was reborn here. Within its walls I've found love and acceptance. Former queens have given me fond memories of this place."

"Hai," said Nagtha-yat softly. "My muthuri's memories are among them. Your eyes are strangely colored, but I see them there." He paused. "Perhaps Muth la will send you some terrible choice. If she does, I think you'll choose wisely. Believing that, I can serve you without reservations. If you wish, I'll bend my neck for you."

Tolum Kol had prepared in advance, so his gift was ready for the prince's first lesson. Kol gave it to the boy when they were alone. It was a sword, as well made and as deadly as the one he wore, but sized for the boy's stature. The prince seized the weapon and drew it from its scabbard, brandishing it gleefully. Kol smiled as the boy engaged in an imaginary sword fight, wildly slashing the air.

"That's no toy," said Kol. "It will slay as quickly as any blade." His voice took on a conspiratorial tone. "And if you slash it around, you'll alarm your mother."

The prince made a face. "Will she take it away?"

"I hope not. You'll be a man sooner than she thinks, and a man needs a sword. A dagger, too." Kol produced an adult-sized weapon, which the prince examined with the same enthusiasm he had the sword.

Afterward, Kol commenced his lessons. He combined practical tips for self-defense with stories of adventures with arms. His goal was less to teach the boy than to win him over. From his own observations and the intelligence from other conspirators, he had surmised that the prince pined for a father. By all accounts, Kregant II had been a distant parent who had left a void in his son's life even before his death. Kol aimed to fill that void, and he proceeded with the prince as if he were seducing a woman.

Kol's life fitted him well for the task. His father had been a brutal man who meted out curses and blows, but not affection. As a young boy, Kol longed for his father's love as a starving man dreams of banquets. Disappointment made him cynical. Kol's father owned an inn, and there Kol was taught to deal callously with people. By the time he ran away, he was a skilled manipulator. It was a talent that proved useful in the army, especially when augmented by ruthlessness. Those recollections of his boyhood guided Kol's dealings with the prince. He attempted to personify the caring father he never had. Kol was not only patient and kind; he cut a heroic figure who exuded adventure. He became the ideal companion for a boy, and he could do what Girta couldn't—introduce the prince to the world of men. There, he aimed to teach him the manly art of war.

While Tolum Kol showed the prince feints and attacks, he often disparaged women's timidity. By such means he hoped to separate the boy from his mother and initiate him into the fraternity of warriors. Kol knew that he had to do this slyly, for he didn't want to alienate the queen. At the moment, he wasn't sure whether the mother or the son would be more useful to his cause. Kol had decided to take a different tack with each. He would play on Girta's fears while encouraging the prince's bravado, and see which tactic proved more promising. Kol was aware that he couldn't pursue this double strategy too long. Sooner or later, he would have to choose mother or son and eliminate the other.

Kol ended the day's lesson by showing the prince how an upward thrust could slip between the plates of an orc's armored tunic. He had procured one for the purpose. "Just like sliding under fish scales," Kol said, demonstrating with his dagger. "Now you try it."

Kregant III attacked the tunic as if it were an orc, thrusting savagely. "Die, piss eye! Die! Die!"

Kol laughed. "Well struck! Well struck! That piss eye's dead for sure. Mind the blood now. Don't track it on your mother's floor."

The prince jumped up and down in the imaginary puddles. "Splash! Splash! Splash! Orc blood everywhere!"

Kol laughed more heartily. "By Karm, you're a lad after my own spirit."

Dar hosted her tenth feast with practiced graciousness, although the nightly dinners were beginning to wear on her. *Twenty-three more to go,* she thought, feeling fatigued by the prospect. The fare she served that night was ample and delicious, but less elaborate than earlier dinners. Tahweriti was no longer the main dish. It had been replaced by gatuub, a stew of mutton and dried fruit. As always, the meal ended with falfhissi.

The family Dar served that night was headed by an elderly muthuri, who had three blessed daughters. These also had daughters who had begun families of their own, so Dar's hanmuthi held four generations. Only Kovok-mah augmented that crowd, for Dar had not chosen additional mintaris yet and Nir-yat was spending the night with Thir-yat. When Dar's guests departed, Kovok-mah quickly retreated to his sleeping chamber.

Dar retired also. When she slept, she dreamed of Twea. It wasn't the first time her dreams included the girl, but upon this occasion the dream was especially vivid. Dar was watching Twea play on the Turgen's bank. Twea was shoeless and ragged, but happy. Sevren was there also, smiling at the sight. "She's a sunny child," he said, "though she has little cause. In Averen, we'd say she's 'faerie kissed.'"

In her dream, as on the day she dreamed of, Dar

replied, "She's just ignorant of her future." With those words, Dar awoke. Lying on her bed, she recalled the events that followed: Twea on the forced march, her thin body growing thinner still. Carrying Twea when the girl couldn't walk. Hiding her in the wagon before the battle. Their separation. Laying Twea's body within Muth la's Embrace and covering her bloody chest with wildflowers.

Regret and grief hit Dar hard. *She was like my daughter, and I failed her.* The dream had been so real it seemed that Twea had just left the room. Dar's sense of loss was equally immediate. It felt unbearable. Dar rose from her bed. Her bare feet made no noise as she crossed the dark hanmuthi.

Kovok-mah sat motionless on his sleeping mat. As Dar approached him, she whispered, "Are you awake?"

"Hai, Muth Mauk."

"I dreamed of Little Bird," said Dar, using Kovok-mah's name for the girl. "I miss her so."

"I, too."

"Only you and I remember her now." Dar sighed. "She looked so tiny next to you, but you never frightened her. I think she saw your gentleness right away. Do you recall that day when she stuck flowers in your armor?"

"I remember."

"And how happy she was to have some bread on morning of battle?"

"Battle you warned me about, though I lacked understanding. I found you standing over Little Bird . . . screaming curses at all washavokis . . . inviting death and . . ." Kovok-mah paused. "Muth Mauk, your face is wet."

Dar wiped her eyes. "I'm sad, Kovok. So sad. And I want to sleep. Sleep upright, like urkzimmuthi, not lying down like baby or one who is ill." Dar paused to sniffle. "And I can only do that if you hold me like you did on our journey."

Dar waited, but there was no reply. Taking Kovok-mah's silence for acquiescence, she climbed onto his lap and reclined her back against his broad chest. Kovok-mah's arms tenderly enveloped her. They trembled slightly as his lips softly brushed her ear. "Dargu," he whispered.

Twenty-one

♛

The cold, stony ground hurt Dar's bare feet with every stride. She ran regardless of the pain, driven by panic. *He mustn't see me!* There was a crevice between two boulders, and she scrambled into it. At first, she was panting too hard to hear footsteps, despite straining to detect them. When her breathing calmed, she heard the crunch of leather soles on flinty ground. The pace was unhurried. Dar was too tired to run anymore. Instead, she remained in her hiding place, hoping to be overlooked.

Wedged into the cramped space, she smelled her unwashed body. Its musky odor was that of a wild animal. Her skin, moist with sweat, was already beginning to chill. The hides she wore provided little warmth. Stiff with dirt, their matted fur was already falling out. *I'll freeze this winter, unless . . .* Dar could imagine no alternative.

The footsteps grew louder, then halted. A figure was outside the crevice. *A son!* His green-gold eyes glanced into the darkness between the boulders. As soon as they caught Dar's gaze, they shifted away, denying her presence. Dar's panic transformed into something worse—desolation. *I'm dead*, she reminded herself. *Thwada*.

Dar awoke in Kovok-mah's arms, and the panic returned. It was still night. Without a word, she scrambled from his embrace and retreated to her cold bed. Lying down, she relived her nightmare. There was no mistaking its warning. *I can never be weak again!* Dar knew that

Kovok-mah would do anything for her, but he was incapable of lying. Nir-yat was also. Secrets could not be kept. A simple question would uncover the truth, and Dar had no doubts there were those who would ask it.

Unable to sleep, Dar devised strategies to avoid temptation. She decided to bite Nagtha-yat's and Lama-tok's necks that day, reasoning that a more crowded hanmuthi would be more inhibiting. She also would send Kovok-mah to Taiben to report on how the treaty was faring. She felt she had neglected that matter far too long. *Girta probably thinks I'm dead. The sons who guard her probably do also.* Dar was pleased how Kovok-mah's journey would solve two problems at once. After coming up with the plan, she resolved to implement it in the morning.

When Tolum Kol arrived to give the prince his lesson, he was greeted by Lokung. The steward informed him that the queen wished to see him, then added in a low voice, "Beware. She's angry about the sword."

Forewarned, Kol entered the chamber. Girta stood gazing out the window, clutching his gifts to her son. When she heard his footsteps, she whirled to face him. "Tolum, what are *these*?" she asked, holding out the sword and dagger.

"In truth, Your Majesty, they're charms. Charms against fear. Charms against danger."

"They look more like weapons to me."

"Yet they serve as charms. Your son's in peril, and they'll make him safer."

Girta drew the child-sized sword. "How can this toy make him safer? You said you'd not teach him belligerence."

"That's not my intent. Let me ask you one thing: If an assassin were to approach, how would you alert your guards?"

"I'd shout 'tav.' That's the word Gargo-something taught me."

"And 'tav' means 'kill' in Orcish," said Kol. "Your Majesty, just who would the orcs kill?"

"Why . . . my assailant."

"They wouldn't stop there. They'd slaughter everyone who smelt of fear. I've seen it countless times. Men. Women. Children. Orcs make no distinction."

"You're saying they'd kill my son?"

"They'd be obeying your command—at least as they understood it. That's why your son must not smell like an enemy. If that sword makes him confident around them, it need not be unsheathed to save his life."

Girta pondered what Kol had said, then handed him the sword and dagger. "Sir, I misjudged you."

Kol bowed. "That's understandable. Few comprehend the twists of the orcish mind, so my actions seem counter to common sense. It feels unnatural that a sword could render a boy safe when weapons so frequently cause mischief."

"Yes, unnatural indeed," said Girta. She glanced at the closed door and envisioned her orc guards stationed beyond it. The idea of them made her hair rise.

Muth-mah came to the Yat clan hall on the morning Dar added Nagtha-yat and Lama-tok to her mintaris and sent Kovok-mah on his journey. Togu-mah brought Dar news of her arrival. Dar glanced to Nir-yat. "What I am I supposed to do?"

"I don't know," replied Nir-yat.

"Muth Mauk," said Nagtha-yat with a bow. "I can answer that question."

"Speak."

"Muth-mah will be arriving for Council of Matriarchs, and matriarchs prefer their own company. Muth-yat will host her, but Muth-mah should pay you courtesy."

"How will she do that?" asked Dar.

"Give her chance to rest awhile, then greet her in Great Chamber. When you're ready, send Togu-mah to her and she will come." Then Nagtha-yat spoke to Togu-mah. "Matriarchs are never fetched. You must say 'Muth Mauk is thinking of you. She sits in Great Chamber.'"

Dar took extra care in her preparations. Needing an ally against Muth-yat's opposition, she hoped to make a regal first impression. She was nervous when she went to the Great Chamber and ascended the throne. After she sent Togu-mah with her message, she expected the Mah clan matriarch to appear soon after, but that was not the case. Dar waited a long time before Muth-mah arrived. She was an imposing figure. A full head taller than Dar and in her middle years, Muth-mah appeared powerful and robust. Her eyes were golden, not yellow, and their gaze bore the assurance of one accustomed to obedience.

"May Muth la bless you, Muth-mah."

Muth-mah inclined her head instead of bowing. "Shashav, Muth Mauk."

"You're first matriarch to arrive."

"Way is short, and I was curious."

"About me?"

"Of course. Everyone has heard of reborn mother who is now queen." The matriarch regarded Dar with frank appraisal. "You're even uglier than I expected."

"My appearance is not urkzimmuthi, but my spirit is. It was even before I received Fathma."

"Hai, I've heard that tale. It's said you were only mother near dying queen."

"She was dying because she sacrificed her life," said Dar. "She did so only after deciding I was worthy."

"She wanted someone to return Fathma to urkzim-muthi, and you have. You couldn't have done that without becoming queen. Whether you're fit to remain one is different matter."

"You seem to speak as though you think I'm not."

Muth-mah gave the equivalent of a shrug. "I'm only one voice among seven."

"There are nine clan matriarchs," said Dar.

"Pah clan is lost, and Muth-goth has stopped coming to councils. She's very old, and way's too long and difficult for her, even in summer."

"I'll miss seeing Muth-goth," said Dar. "I met her when I traveled from west." She watched Muth-mah's face for a reaction, but detected none.

"I saw Togu-mah when I arrived, but not Kovok-mah," said Muth-mah. "Where is he?"

"I sent him to Taiben. Why do you take interest in my mintaris?"

"I don't. Only Kovok-mah interests me. His muthuri is concerned."

"Why?"

"You and her son were velazuls until she forbade it."

"Thus we are velazuls no longer."

"Though you're reborn, and I'm told you remain handicapped. It's said you see poorly in dark and have little sense of smell. You can't tell if someone's angry, fearful, or in love."

"There are other ways to know these things besides smell."

"Hai. Just as blind ones see with their hands and ears. Still, are you aware that you smell of atur?"

"That question is impolite."

"This matter is too important for politeness."

"I don't control how I smell, only how I act. I'm aware of our laws. How could I be otherwise?"

"Wise deeds should match wisdom." Muth-mah gave an abbreviated bow. "It's tradition for matriarchs and new queen to stay apart until council. We'll speak again at that time."

Dar declined to say, "You have pleased me." Instead, she nodded to Muth-mah. "I'll see you then."

Dar remained on her throne long after the matriarch had departed. She was shaken by Muth-mah's apparent hostility, for the upcoming council was a crucial one. The lorekeeper had told her so. It would be when the matriarchs affirmed her fitness to rule. Usually that affirmation was a formality, but not always. There had been three instances when a new queen had been required to drink Muth la's Draught to prove her fitness. On every occasion, the queen had died.

It wasn't hard to imagine how Fathma could go to an unworthy recipient, and Dar realized how some might see her crowning as an aberration. If a majority of the council felt that way, she was doomed. Dar was already calculating the votes. *Four can kill me.* So far, she feared two would go against her.

Twenty-two

♛

The route Kovok-mah took to Taiben was called the New Road, though it had been constructed generations ago as a quicker way to reach the washavoki capital. The road achieved this by ascending the mountains and cutting through a high ridge. Its elevation meant it was snow-choked in winter. After Kovok-mah left the Yat clan's valley, he encountered drifts upon the road. As he climbed higher, they became deeper until every step took effort. A man would have been forced back, but Kovok-mah persevered. He kept walking until he reached the pass. It was night by then, and he decided to camp.

The pass was the highest point on the road. Cut by hand through sheer rock, the passage provided protection from the wind and the drifts it created. Travelers often sheltered there, and the pass' vertical walls had been blackened by countless campfires. Kovok-mah entered the cut, walked to its center, where the snow was less deep, and set up his camp. He had carried wood for a fire, and soon he had one going. He cleared a spot for his sleeping skin, melted some snow to make herb water, and roasted some pashi roots to accompany the hard milk he had brought for dinner. He ate his simple meal wrapped in his traveling cloak and thought about the day ahead.

Kovok-mah was not looking forward to being in Taiben, though it would be good to see Zna-yat again. *He'll be overjoyed to learn Dargu lives.* Kovok-mah still thought of Dar as "Dargu," and he longed for the time when their love was uncomplicated. *Before Muthuri intervened. Before Dargu became Muth Mauk.* Holding her the previous night had stirred those feelings. His passion was so powerful that he was relieved when Dar had sent him away. He knew she was wise to do so. Yet Kovokmah's relief was balanced by despair. *How can I live like this?* He had no answer other than he must.

Kovok-mah tried to ease his torment by concentrating on the task ahead. Dar had asked him to observe the conditions in Taiben and send a report. That seemed easy enough. But she also wanted him to find out what the washavokis were thinking, and Kovok-mah felt unequal to that challenge. His relationship with Dar gave him little insight into ordinary washavokis, who he thought behaved in inexplicable ways. *Words are only sounds to them. Much that they say is meaningless.* Kovok-mah felt he could learn more by smelling washavokis than conversing with them. Yet Dargu wanted him to speak. So he would say the words she had given him and hope that would suffice.

Kovok-mah arrived at Taiben's gates at noon the following day. Although he wore no armor, he smelled the guards' fear as they barred his way. Kovok-mah kept his hand far from his sword hilt and recited Dar's message. "I come in peace with message from our queen to your queen. Will you tell her I am here?"

The guards seemed surprised that Kovok-mah had spoken to them, and they answered in the slow, simplistic speech used for half-wits and small children. "You stay here. We tell queen."

Kovok-mah waited patiently while one of the guards hurried to the palace. It was a while before he returned accompanied by armed washavokis in blue and scarlet. They escorted him through the city streets to the palace. Once inside it, they led him to the doorway of a large smoky room and halted. "Wait here," said one of the washavokis. "Queen will send for you. Understand?"

"I do," replied Kovok-mah, stepping inside. There were windows glazed with sand ice, but they had been so darkened by soot that the light was dim. That presented no problem to Kovok-mah's keen eyes, although they were beginning to smart. He saw that the smoke rose from a makeshift hearth in the room's center. He also noted that Muth la's Embrace had been carved into the wooden floor. Sons sat within it, and one rose when he spotted Kovok-mah. "Cousin Kovok?"

Before, Kovok-mah could respond, Zna-yat was bounding toward him. "My chest is filled by seeing you! Tell me your news, though I dread to hear it."

"My news is good. Dargu lives."

Zna-yat beamed. "Praise Muth la! Is she well?"

"Hai. She's recovered. She sent me here to learn how affairs are going."

"Then why did you call her Dargu?"

"I still think of her as Dargu."

"You should call her Muth Mauk, for that's who she is," said Zna-yat. "And how could she send you here? I thought your muthuri forbade you to see her. Has she changed her mind?"

"Muthuri remains unchanged, but Muth Mauk has made me one of her mintaris. You've been named one also."

"This news mixes sweet with bitter. Muth Mauk has honored me, but by choosing you she's placed herself in peril."

"I think she knows that, which is why she sent me here."

"Will you live here forever? Cousin, any wise nose can tell how you feel."

Kovok-mah sighed. "I know, but maybe Muthuri will relent. Dargu thinks she may."

"That seems unlikely. She craves granddaughters."

"Perhaps your muthuri could speak with mine."

"I think she already has," said Zna-yat. "I know her ways. Don't look to her for hope."

"I don't understand."

"You wouldn't, and that's your virtue."

Zna-yat's answer perplexed Kovok-mah, but he didn't pursue the matter. Instead, he asked him how things had fared since Dar's departure. Kovok-mah was unsurprised when Zna-yat complained that the washavokis showed little understanding—a quick survey of the room around him was evidence of that. It was minimally suitable, and Zna-yat told him that the washavokis had objected to every improvement. "If they had their way, we'd be sleeping outside sacred circle," said Zna-yat. "There's no proper bath. Our food is little better than when we marched with soldiers. They call us friends, yet this is how they treat us."

"Has no one spoken to washavoki queen?"

"Garga-tok has spoken to her, but little has changed. When I guard her, she smells of fear."

"How can this be?" asked Kovok-mah.

"Washavokis have no sense."

"Yet Darg . . . Muth Mauk made peace with them."

"She didn't want us to kill for them," said Zna-yat, "so she pledged we'd protect their queen instead. Muth Mauk was wise to make that treaty, but washavokis may lack wisdom to keep it."

A washavoki shouted in the human tongue from the doorway. "Messenger! Queen will see you. Come."

Kovok-mah headed toward the man, pausing only to remove his traveling cloak. He retained his sword, knowing that washavokis commonly wore weapons within their dwellings. He followed his escort into a huge room. Its entrance was guarded by two armored urkzimmuthi, but the room itself contained only washavoki sons, who were dressed in gaudy colors, and their great mother. She sat upon a wooden platform that was somewhat like a stool with a high wall in back and little walls to place her arms on. The platform was elaborately carved and covered in places with yellow iron. It seemed a place of honor, and Kovok-mah guessed it was a throne.

The washavoki great mother offered no blessing, but stared silently. Kovok-mah had the uncomfortable feeling that she was expecting him to do something, but he had no idea what it was. After an awkward silence, he acted as though he had been blessed, and bowed. "Thanks, Great Mother," he said in the washavoki tongue.

"I'm told you bear a message," said the queen.

"Hai, Muth Mauk sends you greeting."

"Moot Muck? Who's he?"

"It is name every queen takes."

"And who is Moot Muck now?"

"You know her. She made treaty with you."

"Dar? She said she was dying."

Kovok-mah noticed that the queen glanced at one of the washavoki sons who stood near the throne. Kovok-mah followed her gaze and was astonished by whom he saw. *Bah Simi!* he thought, "Blue Eye" being the orcs' name for Murdant Kol. Kovok-mah seized his sword hilt, but didn't draw the weapon. He noticed that Bah Simi seemed pleased by the action. Kovok-mah turned his gaze back to the queen and responded to her comment. "Muth la preserved Muth Mauk's life."

"I'm pleased to hear that," replied the queen.

Kovok-mah didn't think she looked pleased. *Words without meaning*, he thought. "Muth Mauk says she is pleased there is no killing. She hopes your urkzimmuthi guards satisfy you."

"They do, although they are slovenly guests."

"I do not know this word 'slovenly.' "

"I gave them a fine room to live in, and they ruined it. Also, they've behaved indecently."

"What does 'indecently' mean?"

Kovok-mah was surprised when Bah Simi spoke instead of the queen. "Your Majesty, it's futile to explain decency to an orc. The concept is beyond them."

The remark caused some of the sons to make their laughing noise, and Kovok-mah noted that the queen also fought against a smile. "It doesn't matter," she said. "It's more important that we're at peace."

Kovok-mah was perplexed by the queen's behavior. He was aware that he was being insulted, but he neither understood why nor knew how to respond. *None of them understands our speech, yet they mock me for not understanding one of their words. Worse, they won't explain it. If it weren't for Dargu, I'd forsake this ill-mannered queen.* He glared at Kol, whom he suspected had inspired his rude reception. *Bah Simi was always Dargu's enemy.* Knowing that he had to say something, Kovok-mah nodded and said, "Hai. Peace is good."

"Does Moot Muck have more to say?"

"I have spoken all her words, but she would like you and I to talk together."

"This is not a good time for that," replied the queen quickly. "Soon, perhaps."

Kovok-mah realized that he was being dismissed and bowed. "Shashav, Great Mother." Then he left the room.

Soon after the audience, Girta also left the throne room. She retreated to a private chamber, then sent for Tolum Kol. When he arrived she said, "You were right! Dar wasn't dying."

"Apparently not," replied Kol.

"I signed that treaty because I thought she was. She

said there was no time to waste. Now what should I do? Tear it up?"

Although pleased that Girta had turned to him for advice, Kol was alarmed by her question. Without the treaty, the orcs would depart into the mountains, and provoking a war would be nearly impossible. "I think that would be hasty," he replied.

"Why? It was based on deceit."

"Dar's deceit. The orcs lack her guile. Notice how clumsy her messenger was this afternoon."

"He acted pretty hostile for someone who likes peace," said Girta. "The way he looked at you! I thought for certain he was going to draw his sword."

Kol smiled wryly. "That's because I knew him. You see, he was Dar's lover."

Girta's face took on a look of appalled curiosity. "No!"

"When you see him, ask him if he slept with her. He'll admit it. He's proud of it."

"So why does he hate you?"

"Jealousy. Dar tried to seduce me before she seduced him."

"I don't know if I can abide such sordid creatures around the court."

"For the while, it's safer to leave matters rest and not tip our hand. Let Dar think we trust her. Without their mistress present, the orcs are much like guard dogs—vicious, but useful. They'll keep your other enemies at bay."

"But you say they're my enemy, too. Or, at least, Dar is."

"Yes. And we must deal with her eventually, but we need not be hasty."

"This sounds like a dangerous game," said Girta.

"It's always perilous to rule. But I know orcs, Your Majesty, and I'm always at your service."

"That service has proved invaluable so far. Only you saw through Dar's schemes. Does it not seem strange that in a court filled with nobles and generals I must turn to a tolum for sound advice?"

"If the advice is worthy, its source doesn't matter."

"You only say that because you're new to the ways of court. You're not respected because of your rank."

"It matters not to me."

"It does to me. I shall elevate you, if only to wipe the smirks from haughty faces."

"If you wish to honor me," said Kol, "why not name me Queen's Man? There are no orc regiments to command, so the rank's an honorable but empty title."

"The Queen's Man was a general!"

"And the late king's adviser on orcish matters. That service I can still fulfill."

"Such a rise will raise eyebrows, too."

Kol grinned. "Isn't that your intent?"

Girta thought on the idea and grew to like it. *What use have been my other generals?* She could think of none. "I'll do it, sir. I'll announce it at tonight's banquet."

Kol bowed most humbly, without a hint of triumph in his face.

Twenty-three

♛

While Queen Girta was announcing Kol's elevation to Queen's Man, Dar prepared to host her twelfth feast. She was still upset from her meeting with Muth-mah, and the arrival of another matriarch only increased her anxiety. Muth-tok had arrived at dusk, and Dar had used the feast as a pretext to postpone seeing her. The prospect of that meeting dampened Dar's spirits as she waited for her guests.

The family she entertained that night was headed by Thorma-yat, the seamstress. One of her two daughters had been recently blessed to a son named Duth-zut. When Dar served him, he bowed especially low. "Muth Mauk, you don't remember me, but I remember you. I fought washavokis at Taiben's gate."

"Then you saved my life," said Dar.

"Thwa, I think you saved mine. I had three brothers. Each was sent to kill for washavokis and never returned. When I left for Taiben, I expected to die also."

Duth-zut's muthvashi grasped Dar's hand. "Shashav, Muth Mauk, for your wisdom. When I have my first daughter, I'll name her Dargu."

"You honor me," said Dar. Then knowing "dargu" meant "weasel," she asked, "But will your daughter be pleased with that name?"

"When she knows your story, she'll be very pleased."

Dar's spirits lifted, and they remained that way for

the remainder of the evening. Her heartache over Kovok-mah's departure and her worries about tomorrow's meeting with Muth-tok were assuaged by the sight of Duth-zut and his muthvashi. *I'm walking Muth la's path*, she told herself. *All I can do is stay true to it and leave my fate to her.*

Kovok-mah spent the evening in the orcs' quarters. Dinner was served by woe mans, several of whom had foreheads that were marked like Dar's. They weren't ragged like the woe mans in the regiment, but the food they served was the same—porridge and boiled roots. He overheard one son complain that the queen had said true mothers would serve proper food. Kovok-mah didn't know if the complaint referred to Muth Mauk or the washavoki queen. As Kovok-mah recalled, the promise had been made jointly. He resolved to bring up the matter during his audience.

Night came without a summons to speak with Queen Girta. Kovok-mah was disappointed, for he had hoped to enlighten her on her orc guards' needs. The news of Dar's survival had lifted their spirits, and Kovok-mah wanted concrete improvements to follow. He was preparing to sleep when a washavoki approached Muth la's Embrace. He halted at its edge, and called out, "Nak Kovok-mah su?" *Is Kovok-mah here?*

"Hai, Ma nav su," replied Kovok-mah. *Yes, I am here.* He rose and regarded the washavoki. "Sevren?"

"Hai," said Sevren, who continued to speak in Orcish. "Can we speak?"

Kovok-mah replied in the same tongue. "Come inside Muth la's Embrace. We will talk."

Sevren bowed and entered the sacred circle. Kovok-mah sat down next to Zna-yat, who whispered to him, "That washavoki has come here before. Do you know him?"

"Hai. He is Sevren," said Kovok-mah. "He helped save Muth Mauk's life."

Sevren approached and bowed again. "Tava, Kovok-mah. Tava, Zna-yat."

"Sit," said Kovok-mah, continuing to speak Orcish for Zna-yat's benefit. "What do you wish to speak about?"

Sevren sat down. "Dargu-yat live?"

"Hai," said Kovok-mah. He was both surprised and puzzled when water flowed from Sevren's eyes. "Are you sad?"

Sevren smiled and replied in a voice that sounded strangely thick to the orc's ears. "Thwa. Very happy."

Kovok-mah gave an account of Dar's recovery, switching to the washavoki tongue whenever Sevren didn't understand. Then Sevren told him about conditions in court using his broken Orcish. "Queen Girta knows not wisdom. Washavoki sons give her bad words. She listen."

"I saw Bah Simi with her today," said Kovok-mah.

"Washavoki name is Kol. He is tolum now. He speaks bad words."

"I think this also," said Kovok-mah.

"Dargu-yat must hear this."

"Her name is Muth Mauk now," injected Zna-yat. "You serve Quengirta. Why are you here?"

"Muth Mauk is wise. Muth Mauk wants peace," replied Sevren.

Kovok-mah's nose informed him of another reason, probably the foremost one. *He still loves her.* Kovok-mah glanced at Zna-yat, certain that his cousin had detected the same scent. He saw a look of distaste on his face.

"Sevren," said Kovok-mah. "I wish to speak to washavoki great mother. This place is not good for us. She said we would have proper hall, place where urkzimmuthi mothers could live. If I tell her this, will she listen?"

"If you say, I think she speak good words, do nothing," replied Sevren. "I am sorry."

"Sev-ron speaks wisdom," said Zna-yat.

Kovok-mah feared that Zna-yat was right.

Kol's quarters within the palace were deemed suitable for a tolum. His room was small, with roughly plastered walls and only a tiny, unglazed window. Its sole furnishings were a simple bed and a chest. When Kol returned from the banquet, he expected to sleep there only one more night before obtaining grander accommodations. Upon opening the door, he spied a figure seated on the bed. "Good evening, General."

"Gorm! Why are you here?"

"To congratulate you, of course. It wouldn't do for me to approach you at the banquet. They think I'm only a manservant."

Kol said nothing as he waited to hear the true reason for Gorm's visit.

"You've risen high, Queen's Man. I hope your quick ascension hasn't left you dizzy."

"Dizzy?"

"Forgetful might be a better word. You're here for a reason, and my master sees little progress."

"He needs to be patient," said Kol.

"Patience doesn't fit his nature. He wants war. If you can't get him blood, you'll provide it yourself."

"You present me with a puzzle," replied Kol. "Why does a man with his powers need a war? You could carry him about the city and slaughter a battle's worth in an afternoon."

"You don't understand," said Gorm.

"But I *do* understand. Othar could destroy every soul in Taiben, but where would that leave him? Alone. You've told me he's no longer a man, and I suspect his appetites are both inhuman and bottomless. Am I right?"

Gorm didn't reply.

"Of course I'm right! Your master wants war because

it's like a conflagration. Spark it right, and a war can burn
on and on. Why slay all Taiben, when you can destroy
whole kingdoms? That's why Othar won't hurt me. I'll set
the blaze that feeds his cravings though I've only a timid
woman and a boy for tinder."

"Bravely said, General Kol. But my master wants acts,
not words."

"You can't slay a doe until she's in range. A wise
hunter waits until success is sure. A fool blunders into action and scares the game. You've seen the court. Who can
do this but me? Voltar and the other generals are fat and
lazy. Their wars were fought by orcs, not against them.
And what noble will sully his velvet gloves with blood?"

"I understand you," said Gorm. "Everything you say
is true, but you must understand this: It's not Othar I
truly serve, but that which possesses Othar. My master's
needs gnaw at him. Reason won't curb his hunger or his
wrath. Press for war as though a thousand demons were
at your back, for something very much their like is at
your heels."

A chill went down Kol's spine. Its cause was less what
Gorm said than the manner in which he said it. For all its
hardness, Gorm's voice held an edge of terror. *He's made
some infernal bargain*, thought Kol, *and glimpsed something no man was meant to see.* His own ambitions,
ruthless as they were, seemed benign in comparison. Yet
Kol needed Gorm to achieve them, just as Gorm needed
him.

"I know what you want," said Kol, "and I'm proceeding as fast as I can without losing the prize."

Gorm seemed reassured. "How can I speed things
along?"

"Obtain a woman and a child that look like Girta and
her son. Keep them safe and have them ready. Have
Lokung find them clothes that match the queen's and the
prince's attire."

"What do you need them for?"

"I'm playing this game as I go," said Kol, "but I think they may prove useful."

"Anything else?"

"Dar's key to my plans. When she finds out I'm Queen's Man, she won't be able to stay away. Othar must forbear his revenge until she's served her purpose. Can he do that?"

"If it leads to war, he can."

"Good," said Kol. "When I feed your master's hunger, Dar will be his dessert."

Twenty=four

♛

When dawn came, the first thing Kovok-mah wanted to do was bathe. The orcs still took their baths in a horse trough in the stables. Zna-yat offered to show him where it was. "Be warned," he said, "water will be icy."

"Yet I want to be clean when I speak with washavoki great mother."

"She won't notice," said Zna-yat. "She reeks like all washavokis."

"Regardless. I will bathe."

"Of course. We may live among washavokis, but we needn't sink to their level."

Kovok-mah undressed and followed Zna-yat out to the stables. As he walked through the palace, the claws of his feet clicking on stone floors, he noted that the washavoki mothers seemed agitated by his body. *Zna-yat was right*, he thought, *they squeak like mice*. Their behavior was amusing, but it also made him aware of how little he understood washavokis. *I wish Dargu were here. She could explain it.*

When Kovok-mah reached the "bath," he and Zna-yat had to break a layer of ice to reach the water. Kovok-mah washed quickly while horses watched, then dashed across the courtyard into the palace. Though accustomed to the cold, he resolved to ask the washavoki queen for a warmer bathing facility. Kovok-mah hoped that conversation would take place soon.

* * *

Though Dar dreaded seeing Muth-tok, she knew delay would only make matters worse. Thus she bathed and dressed in her finest. Afterward, she sent Lama-tok to tell his matriarch that Muth Mauk was thinking of her. Then Dar ascended the throne expecting another long wait. Muth-tok surprised her by arriving promptly.

The matriarch of the Stone Clan was older than Muth-mah but equally hearty. She had a large, muscular frame and the look of someone used to heavy work. Dar knew that many Tok clan mothers worked stone, and she assumed this was true of their matriarch. "May Muth la bless you, Muth-tok."

Muth-tok bowed low. "Shashav, Muth Mauk."

"One son you sent me has already joined my mintaris."

"I'm pleased you found Lama-tok worthy, but not surprised. I hope you'll find Kak-tok also deserving of honor."

"He's made good impression."

"As you have," said Muth-tok. "For long time, Lama-tok spoke little of his journey. Only recently have I learned its entire tale. I'm much amazed. Rarely is Muth la's will so plainly revealed." Muth-tok pressed her hand against her chest in the sign of the Tree. "These are wondrous times."

"I think some matriarchs would disagree," said Dar.

"Wondrous times are not easy times. I think hardship lies ahead. Why else would Muth la send you for our queen?"

"Some believe hardship could be avoided if I'm not queen."

Muth-tok's face darkened. "Bears vanish when you shut your eyes, but they still bite."

Dar smiled. "I believe I've found friend on council."

Muth-tok returned the smile. "After council, there is feast. There, I hope you'll honor me with tales of your travels. By custom, I must keep this greeting short;

otherwise I would beg to spend this day with you. Lama tells me that you saw Tarathank, visited Pah clan, and had many other adventures. Your visions particularly interest me." She gave Dar a meaningful look. "Lama mentioned Velasa-pah."

"That encounter is much on my mind," said Dar, not wishing to reveal too much.

"I shouldn't stay overlong, Muth Mauk. I'd rather not have Muth-yat and Muth-mah understand my mind as yet."

"You have pleased me, Muth-tok."

The Tok clan matriarch thanked Dar, bowed, and departed.

Kol made a brief visit to Balten's house to obtain funds, then went to a tailor's shop. There, he ordered clothes suitable for his new rank. He eschewed the bright colors worn by Voltar and the other generals in favor of a severe look. He ordered long-sleeved doublets of fine black wool trimmed with just enough gold to mark his new station without flaunting it. The trousers he ordered were also black with thin gold piping down their sides. He kept his old boots and sword.

Kol saw his situation in military terms. He had just taken favorable ground that also rendered him more visible. The crucial point was not to advance unprepared. He planned to consolidate his position and test the resistance first. For the time being, he would keep a low profile and be a paragon of humility.

Meanwhile, Kol would use others to advance his plans. He had already come up with a list of enemies in court, and he expected his promotion would reveal a few more. *Gorm can arrange for their elimination.* Othar's ability to seize minds would make it simple. Kol envisioned a rash of murders. *Deranged servants . . . jealous*

*lovers . . . robbers. Death can come so suddenly. And
I'll be blameless every time.*

While Gorm cleared the opposition, Kol planned to use
Lokung for double duty. First, he would have the steward
feed Girta's fears with rumors of intrigues against her.
*Nothing clear enough to act upon, just enough to keep
her insecure.* Second, he wanted Lokung to find recruits
for a new guard. *They'll be called the Queen's Men.
They'll wear black to set them apart.* Kol would be their
commander, and despite the guard's name, it would swear
loyalty to him.

Kol's primary concern was time. Despite Othar's impatience, he could not afford to move too quickly and alarm
Girta. The creation of the Queen's Men must not be seen
as a power grab. He had to continue to win the queen's
trust while wooing the prince. Kol was beginning to believe that the boy—though currently powerless—might
prove the means to achieve his goal. He planned to give
him a black uniform when the Queen's Men were created.
What boy doesn't want to protect his mother? When Kol
was the prince's age, he had hoped to do the same. He
smiled sadly at the thought of his boyish naïveté. Then Kol
grimly recalled his father's most brutal lesson, a lesson he
was prepared to give the prince if necessary.

Winter tightened its grip on Taiben. The city became
like a frozen lake, its still surface hiding currents in the
dark below. The queen grew ever more afraid. All the
while, Kovok-mah waited for a summons that didn't
come.

Meanwhile in the Yat clan hall, Dar continued to hold
her nightly feasts and wait for Kovok-mah's report. As the
days passed, she began to grow concerned that events had
gone ill in Taiben. There was little she could do about it,
for the round of feasts and the upcoming council occupied

her. Muth-hak arrived on the day she held her seventeenth feast. The Hak clan matriarch was a wiry mother, with bright yellow eyes and an animated manner. She was cordial during her brief meeting, and Dar counted her as an ally.

By the time Muth-jan came to the Yat clan hall, Dar had added three more sons to her mintaris—Tatfa-jan, Dil-hak, and Kak-tok—and was about to hold her twenty-first feast. The matriarch of the Iron Clan was shorter than Dar, barrel-chested, and quick to smile. Dar felt comfortable with her immediately. The matriarch ignored custom and spent the entire afternoon talking with her. Muth-jan proved to be the aunt of Magtha-jan, whom Dar had met in the garrison outside of Taiben. Dar told the matriarch about the queen's rescue and death, the orcs' revolt, and the treaty it produced. By the time Muth-jan left, Dar tallied three allies on the council.

Two days later, sons from the Smat clan arrived and presented themselves as candidates for Dar's mintaris. They had been sent by their matriarch, and their attitude was disquieting. Although outwardly respectful, they were clearly displeased to have been chosen. Dar thought their discontent boded ill. It seemed a sign that the Smat clan matriarch had given little thought to the candidates' selection, expecting their service to be brief. The following day, candidates from the Zut clan arrived. They were equally unsuitable.

Muth-zut and Muth-smat arrived together as Dar was preparing for her twenty-seventh feast. She postponed seeing them until the following day, and spent the evening dreading the encounter. Her dread proved well-founded when she met the pair. Muth-smat was elderly and dour. She spoke little and stared stone-faced at Dar throughout their meeting. Muth-zut, who was younger, bluntly questioned Dar's suitability to reign. After the brief meeting was over, Dar feared that the Zut clan matriarch's attitude reflected her companion's. In five days, Dar would host her final feast. Then the Council of Matriarchs would meet. By Dar's count, four of its seven members would oppose her.

"Tanath dovat," said Sevren in a low voice. *Something happen.*

Kovok-mah woke. It was night, and the only light within the orcs' quarters came from the embers on the central hearth. He was surprised that Sevren had been able to find him in the dark. "Atham?" asked Kovok-mah. *What?*

Sevren replied in Orcish. "See you washavokis in black?"

"Your queen has not yet summoned me," replied Kovok-mah in the Speech of Mothers. "I have only left this room to bathe."

"They are new guards."

"Like washavokis in blue and red and urkzimmuthi?"

"Like, but not like. Queen's Man leads them."

"Queen's Man is dead."

"Bah Simi is now Queen's Man."

"Why have you not told me this before?" asked Kovok-mah.

"It is danger for me see urkzimmuthi. Washavokis watch. I think that . . . that . . ." Sevren switched to the human tongue. "I think Kol's planning something. The royal guard has been disbanded. You're either one of the Queen's Men, or demoted to the city garrison. Word came out today. This is probably the last time I can get into the palace. As of tomorrow, only the orcs and the Queen's Men will guard Girta. That doesn't make sense. I know most of the guards who became Queen's Men. They all hate orcs."

"Many washavokis do."

"There's more to this than meets the eye. Why have two sets of guards? Especially two sets that are at odds.

It looks look a power play to me." Sevren paused, for even in the darkness he could tell that Kovok-mah was bewildered. *Such intrigue is alien to him.* Then Sevren tried to explain his concerns more simply. "Bah Simi is Muth Mauk's enemy," he said in Orcish. "He gathers friends. He grows strong. This is bad for Muth Mauk."

"I understand," said Kovok-mah. "When I speak to washavoki great mother, I will ask her why she has done this."

Sevren thought Kovok-mah's forthright approach was pointless, but he doubted he could explain why. It troubled him that the queen would replace the royal guard with Kol's men, while retaining her orc guards. He suspected Kol was behind that decision. If the rumors were true, he was her principal adviser. Sevren was puzzled why Kol would want the orcs to remain. He suspected the reason involved Dar. "Muth Mauk should hear this," he said.

"I cannot leave until I speak with your great mother," said Kovok-mah.

"I could go."

Kovok-mah considered the suggestion. "You should not go alone." He rose, then walked among the sleeping orcs, woke one, and returned with him. "Zna-yat serves Muth Mauk. Speak to him."

With Kovok-mah translating occasionally, Sevren repeated his story to Zna-yat, who seemed to grasp its implications better than Kovok-mah. "I should tell Sev-ronz tale to Muth Mauk," said Zna-yat. "But there is no need for it to come."

"He sees things that we don't," said Kovok-mah.

Zna-yat regarded Sevren. "Tell them to me and avoid long journey."

"I want to go," said Sevren.

"Why?"

Thamus had cautioned Sevren against lying to orcs, and he heeded that advice. "I wish to see Muth Mauk again."

Zna-yat gave Kovok-mah a meaningful look. "Should it?"

"Sevren understands washavokis better than you or I. He may be helpful."

"You may come," said Zna-yat. "I will leave tomorrow."

"I see you on road. Not inside city," replied Sevren. "I go now."

As Sevren slipped away, Kovok-mah turned to Zna-yat. "What's happening?"

"I'm not sure, but I know this: Washavokis are cruel. Expect some new outrage."

Zna-yat left Taiben the following morning, and soon afterward, Kovok-mah received the long-awaited summons to talk with the washavoki queen. He wondered if the two events were connected. Zna-yat guarded the queen. Perhaps his departure had displeased her. If it did, Kovok-mah didn't care. He was tired of washavoki rudeness.

Kovok-mah noted that the washavokis that escorted him to the queen all wore black. They took him to the large room he had visited before. The queen was seated on the object Kovok-mah assumed was a throne. Only sons dressed in black stood about her. Bah Simi was among them.

"I regret it has been so long since we last spoke," said the queen.

Unfamiliar with polite falsehoods, Kovok-mah found Girta's explanation puzzling, for a queen could do as she pleased. "I regret it also. Now that we speak, need others be present?"

Kovok-mah noted that the queen's face grew paler and the scent of fear wafted into the air. "These are the Queen's Men. They protect me."

"So do urkzimmuthi."

"Queen's Men also serve me."

Her mintaris, thought Kovok-mah. "I understand now. Great Mother, after you and Muth Mauk spoke together, you promised to house us according to our custom so urkzimmuthi mothers could live with us. This has not happened."

"I gave you a fine room to use."

"It was not suitable."

"The Queen's Man has told me so," said the queen, glancing at Bah Simi. Kovok-mah noticed that his black clothes were colored with yellow iron. "He has found better place for you."

Bah Simi showed his dog-white teeth and spoke. "There are halls nearby. Round, so each is Zum Muthz la." *Muth la's Embrace.* Evidently pleased to show off his Orcish, he continued. "Each has teemhani." *Hearth.* "We have also built proper spluf." *Bath.*

"Where are these buildings?"

"You stayed there when you fought for Great Washavoki."

Kovok-mah realized that Bah Simi was speaking of the orcs' former barracks. "I know these halls. They lie outside the city. How can we protect your great mother from there?"

"You'll only live there," said the queen. "You'll still come into the city to guard me."

"Muth Mauk said we were to live close to you. It is wise to have protectors near."

Bah Simi spoke. "And you will be close when we build proper rooms inside the palace. That will take time. Until then, Great Mother wishes to honor your customs."

Kovok-mah looked to the washavoki queen, puzzled

that she would let a son speak for her. Yet she didn't seem upset by his presumption. "It's only for a little while," she said.

Kovok-mah pondered his options. While he thought that Dargu would be displeased with the arrangement, he felt he lacked the authority to refuse it. "When must we move to these halls?"

"This afternoon," said the queen.

Twenty-five

👑

As latath for the Yat clan, Jvar-yat tattooed the chins of its members with the clan mark. She also prepared the black coloring used to create that mark, and her skills didn't end there. She distilled fermented pashi, steeping washuthahi seeds and honey in the burning water to make falfhissi. She prepared ink for the lorekeeper and talmauki for the great mother. She also mixed dyes and made healing extracts. She did all this in a special chamber, which was where Muth-yat found her.

Jvar-yat set aside the mineral that she was pulverizing into powder and rose when Muth-yat entered. "Greetings, Matriarch."

Muth-yat bowed, for the chamber was the latath's domain. "You must make something for Council of Matriarchs."

"What is it?"

"Muth la's Draught."

Jvar-yat's expression reflected her shock, but she replied calmly. "When do you require it?"

"In five days."

"Five days! This draught is brewed from yew seeds. It's winter, and most have fallen."

"Have you none stored?"

"I've never made Muth la's Draught. Neither did latath before me. Yew seeds have no use except to make this brew."

"Yet we need it and need it soon," said Muth-yat. "Go into forest and find what you require. I'll also need small stones. Seven green. Seven black."

Jvar bowed. "Hai, Matriarch. I'll leave this morning."

"Good," said Muth-yat as she departed.

The latath regarded the flat stone on her worktable. Its surface was covered with a grayish green powder from the mineral she had been pulverizing. Using a feather, she carefully brushed the powder onto another flat stone with a finer surface. Jvar-yat added a little mutton fat to the powder and used a flat-faced pestle to grind the two into a green paste.

Jvar-yat regarded the result of her effort. The tiny batch of talmauki would only last eight days. She recalled needling the clan mark on Dargu-yat's chin just that summer and sighed. It had been a joyous occasion. *Giving tattoos is always happy work. How unlike making poison.* As she carefully scraped the talmauki into a stone vessel, Jvar-yat sighed again. *Eight days' worth will be more than enough.*

Sevren rode out of Taiben, wearing clothes he had borrowed from Thamus. A scarf shielded his lower face from the winter winds and the eyes of the black-garbed men who manned the gates. Sevren kept Skymere at a trot until they reached the orc road. Then he spurred him to a gallop, assuming that Zna-yat was already traveling toward the pass. The empty road was mostly clear of snow and the former royal guardsman had little difficulty catching up with the walking orc. When Sevren spied him, he called out, "Geenat! Geenat!" *Wait! Wait!*

Zna-yat halted. When Sevren pulled up beside him, Zna-yat said, "Ga da-sutat." *You came.*

As usual, Zna-yat used the genderless pronoun that referred to animals, rather than the masculine one. The habit had always bothered Sevren, and he decided it was time to speak up. "Kam pahak 'ga'?" *Why say "it"?* "Ma nav thwa 'ga.'" *I am not "it."*

Zna-yat regarded Sevren. "Ga nat washavoki." *You are washavoki.*

Sevren replied in Orcish, the only language Zna-yat spoke. "Your queen is also washavoki."

"Muth Mauk is not! She only appears washavoki to those who know not her spirit."

"And you know it?"

"Hai. Muth Mauk is possessed by Muth la. Even when she was Dargu, she followed Muth la's path."

"I know her spirit also."

"I think not," said Zna-yat. "Tell me, Sev-ron, is she pretty?"

"Hai."

"That is why she fills your chest. You desire her washavoki body."

"Does not Kovok-mah?"

"He finds her ugly. As do I."

"Yet he wants her," said Sevren. "Why?"

"I cannot speak for him. I am drawn by her goodness."

"*You* love her, too?"

"You will sniff no atur about me. Mine is not that kind of love." Zna-yat paused and reflected. "Dargu has been touched by divinity. That is why she repaid my wickedness with sacrifice. Her deeds inspire reverence, and I have given her my life."

Sevren was unable to follow everything that Zna-yat said, but the orc's face bespoke his devotion. "I see more in Dargu than her pretty," said Sevren. "I have not words to say it. Big spirit, maybe."

"Sev-ron, she is above you."

"I know. Still, I want to see her. Can you understand?"

Zna-yat gazed at Sevren as if he were some unexpected curiosity. "Hai," he said finally.

Zna-yat walked silently awhile, lost in reflection, before he spoke again. "Sev-ron, I once hated Dargu. I called Kovok-mah foolish for naming her 'she' and not 'it.' I will not call you 'it' again."

"Shashav, Zna-yat."

Queen Girta stood by a large window that overlooked the palace courtyard to watch the orcs depart for their new quarters. Wrapped in rusty iron, they marched in an orderly rectangle of massive bodies. To Girta, it seemed as if a patch of earth had upped and was walking away. She felt relieved by their departure, but vaguely disquieted also. Girta tried to dismiss her ambivalence as foolish, yet it remained.

The Queen's Man moved to her side. "That room they occupied will need a thorough scrubbing," he said. "It's black from soot. And the floor's beyond saving, hacked with that circle and scored by foot claws."

"Are the women who serve the orcs moving out also?"

"Yes," said Kol. "It'll be more convenient for them to live in the garrison."

"I want them housed comfortably. Dar may have lied about most things, but not how the regiments treated women."

"They'll fare nicely. I've seen to it."

"The orcs won't . . ." Girta blushed. ". . . you know . . . take liberties with them, now that they're out of sight?"

"I've thought of that," said Kol. "The women will bolt their door at night and I've stationed Queen's Men in the old garrison, too. The orcs will cause no mischief."

"I'm pleased you've been so thorough," said the queen.

She was just about to leave the window when she saw a formation of black-garbed men enter the courtyard. There were two dozen of them, marching two abreast in a column. It wasn't the men who caught her eye, but the small figure dressed in black and gold marching beside them. He seemed to be directing their movements. "Is that my son?"

"Yes, Your Majesty. The prince is drilling your guard."

"When did he start doing that?"

"He'll be king someday. He should grow accustomed to commanding men."

Girta watched the pale winter sunlight glint off the abundant gold on the prince's uniform. "I don't want him playing soldier."

"The Queen's Men aren't troops. They're your protectors. It's natural for your son to want you safe. After all, his father was murdered."

"Don't explain the prince to me. I'm his mother."

Kol's face reddened, but his expression remained calm and humble. He bowed. "I'm sorry if I indulged the lad. He was so keen to learn. It won't happen again."

Girta glanced out the window. The column changed direction, bending like an angular snake. She faintly heard her son shout, and the column changed direction again. "No, no, he needn't stop," she said. "If it gives him pleasure, what's the harm?"

"As you wish, Your Majesty."

General Kol's always compliant, thought Girta, *so why don't I feel in control?* She watched as the last of the orcs passed through the gates. She had wished them to dwell outside the palace, and henceforth they would. She thought she should feel safer, but she didn't.

The snow upon the road grew deeper as Zna-yat and Sevren ascended toward the pass. Their goal was visible but distant, a narrow cut in a nearly vertical ridge. "Urk-zimmuthi made that?" asked Sevren in an attempt to engage Zna-yat in conversation.

"Hai."

"Why?"

"Because they were foolish."

Sevren rode in silence a while before he asked. "How were they foolish?"

"They thought washavokis had changed."

"In what way?"

"They believed washavokis had grown tired of killing. Great Washavoki wanted sand ice, yellow iron, wood, and even pashi. It would trade copper, iron, and milkstone for them."

"Heavy goods," said Sevren. "So you built road?"

"Hai. Some washavokis helped."

"Then what happened? This road is used little."

"Great Washavoki died and its son became Great Washavoki. That son was good. When it died, its son was bad."

"Kregant the Second."

"I do not know its name, only that it liked to take, not trade. Then no wagons traveled road. Only sons to kill for Great Washavoki."

"I wished to serve his father," said Sevren. "When I come, father dead."

"I think Kreegan-tesekun was like most of its kind. Washavokis like killing."

Sevren saw little point in arguing. *What has Zna-yat seen except our wars?*

The two reached the pass by late afternoon. Beyond the ridge, the road headed downward, but the snow upon it was much deeper. Sevren was forced to dismount and lead Skymere along the trail that Zna-yat broke. The snow reached Sevren's waist and the drifts were frequently taller than his head. Without the orc in front, he probably would have turned back.

Progress was slow, and the travelers were still far from the Yat clan hall when darkness fell. Sevren suspected that Zna-yat would have continued walking were it not for him. Yet it was the orc who suggested that they halt for the night. They found a sheltered spot on the wooded mountain and set up a camp. Zna-yat snapped off tree limbs for firewood while Sevren tended to his horse. Soon they had a fire going. When Sevren saw that Zna-yat planned to dine on cold leftover roots, he insisted that the orc share the bread and cheese he had brought. They melted snow for herb water, which Sevren augmented with brandy. Zna-yat took a tentative sip. "This is like falfhissi." He smiled. "Feast food. It warms you."

"We will need it this night," said Sevren, pulling his cloak tighter. He gazed at the dark mountain. "I was here with Muth Mauk. I thought she was dying. I was very sad."

Zna-yat took another gulp of brandy, then regarded Sevren, whose scent of atur had grown stronger.

"She looked at me like she saw my spirit," continued Sevren. "Could she do that?"

"Perhaps. She is no ordinary mother."

"Hai." Sevren took another swig of brandy and stared into the flames awhile. "Zna-yat, you were wrong. I love not her body. I mean, not only. We never . . ." Sevren didn't know the word. "Just . . ." He made a kissing sound. "And not many. I love her big good spirit."

"I understand. You should see Muth Mauk. But it will be hard for you."

"Hai. I think this also."

The following morning, Sevren and Zna-yat rose at dawn and continued their journey. They reached the Yat clan hall early in the afternoon. Once there, Zna-yat left his companion in a chamber close to the hall's entrance, for he thought Dar would want some warning of Sevren's arrival. Then Zna-yat went to the royal hanmuthi, where he was greeted by Nir-yat. "Brother, it pleases me to see you!"

"Your sight fills my chest, Sister. It'll be good to sit and talk, but first I must see Muth Mauk."

"She's with lorekeeper," replied Nir-yat, her expression growing somber. "She wishes to write her tale before council meets."

"I've news from Taiben, and Sev-ron came with me."

"I'll tell her you're here," said Nir-yat. Then she hurried from the room.

Dar returned with Nir-yat soon afterward. She smiled when she saw Zna-yat, but he thought she looked troubled. "May Muth la bless you, Zna-yat. I hear that you have news. And where's Sevren?"

"He waits nearby. Perhaps you will wish to greet him in Great Chamber, so he might see what you've become."

Dar smiled, appreciating Zna-yat's shrewdness. "That's good idea." Then she impulsively hugged Zna-yat. "I've missed you, Brother."

"I've missed you also." When Dar released him, Zna-yat noticed that her eyes had filled with water.

"So what news?" asked Dar. "How's treaty going?"

"Bah Simi is Queen's Man."

"What!" Zna-yat watched Dar's face grow red as the scent of her anger turned the air pungent. "That stupid . . ." Dar began to speak in the washavoki tongue. Although Zna-yat didn't understand the words, they were said in a hard, wrathful way. Then Dar switched back to Orcish. "How could Girta be so foolish? There should be no Queen's Man. No washavoki can speak for me. Do sons obey him?"

"Thwa, only washavokis who wear black. Red-and-blue washavokis are no more. Queen's Man has cast them out. Sev-ron can explain it."

"Are urkzimmuthi treated with honor?"

"Very little. Woe mans serve us, but food is poor. Our chamber is barely suitable."

"Do sons still guard washavoki great mother?"

"Hai. But I'm told black washavokis will guard her also."

"What's your impression of Taiben?" asked Dar.

"I think we aren't welcome. Quengirta fears us."

"It's Bah Simi she should fear," said Dar. "She doesn't understand him."

"But you do," said Zna-yat. "Perhaps you can give her wisdom."

"Thwa," replied Dar. "In four days, I think urkzimmuthi will have different queen. It'll be her task to deal with washavokis."

Dar was enthroned when Sevren was brought to the Great Chamber. His escort departed immediately, leaving him alone with Dar. He stood gaping at her until she said "May Muth la bless you" in the human tongue.

Sevren suddenly remembered that he should bow. "Shashav, Muth Mauk."

"Pahav tha Pahmuthi dup?" *Do you speak Orcish now?*

"Ke." *Little.* "I do much better in our tongue."

"Your tongue," said Dar. "Merz pah nak Pahmuthi." *My tongue is Orcish.*

"Of course. I meant your former tongue."

Having grown accustomed to the orcish manner of dress, Dar was unprepared for its effect on Sevren. She was annoyed that he stared at her green-painted nipples, and her tone reflected it when she asked, "Why are you here?"

"There's trouble in Taiben."

"I know."

"And Dar . . . I had to see you."

"So now you have, breasts and all."

Sevren's face reddened. "I . . . I . . ."

"You used to be more eloquent."

"My heart has overcome my wits. I thought you'd died."

Dar recalled her last ride with Sevren. Near death, she had been able to peer at his spirit and understand its secrets. Her annoyance melted as she realized he was still burdened with love. "I'm too harsh," she said in a softer voice. "You've come a long way for so poor a welcome." Dar adjusted her kefs so that one covered her chest, then descended from the throne. "Zna-yat says that Kol is Queen's Man now. What does Girta think she's doing?"

"Whatever it is, I do na know. The royal guard has been disbanded, replaced by the Queen's Men. I'm only a watchman now."

"I had hoped that you'd returned to Averen and become a farmer."

"That dream's still beyond my means. And less sweet now that you won't . . ."

"Don't speak of it," said Dar quickly.

"Aye, there's na point."

"No, there isn't."

"Since Queen Girta does na require my service, I'd like to offer it to you," said Sevren. "Your orcs keep to themselves and know little of what stirs in Taiben. I could prove useful."

Dar sighed and walked over to the window. Sevren followed her, but she kept her gaze fixed on the snow-covered mountains. "Your offer's untimely," she said in a quiet voice.

"Why?"

"I won't be queen much longer. A few days at most."

"You're abdicating?" asked Sevren, feeling hopeful but confused.

"Not exactly. The Council of Matriarchs will meet soon, and I'm certain they'll make me drink Muth la's Draught. It's a test of fitness. The queen drinks poison, and if she lives, she's meant to rule. But no queen has ever lived."

"They plan to murder you?"

"I don't think they see it that way. They believe that Muth la will save me if they've made a mistake. Of course, they don't think they have."

"If Muth la would save anyone, it'd be you."

"She doesn't work that way. Did she save Twea? Or the orcs in the ambush? Muth la doesn't change the world for our sake; she expects us to change it for hers."

"Then leave with me."

"I can't."

"Why? You're na docile. I can na see you just waiting to die."

"I belong here."

"The orcs do na seem to think so."

"You're wrong about that."

"Well, if their matriarchs will na have you, there's na point in staying."

"Fathma holds me here. The urkzimmuthi are my children, and their queens' memories have become mine."

"That makes na sense."

"I wouldn't expect you to understand."

"So you're just going to sacrifice yourself for the sake of a few memories?"

"They're my memories, too, and the next queen shall have them."

"For Karm's sake, Dar. Come away with me."

"For Muth la's sake, I won't. Fathma was her gift, and

I must pass it on. The last queen died so I might receive it. Can I do anything less?"

"You're right; I do na understand. 'Tis daft to throw your life away. Zna-yat said it would be hard to see you, but this is worse than anything I imagined."

"I'm sorry for you, Sevren. But it's Muth la's will."

"I've learned about Muth la. I thought she was compassionate."

"We can't always see her ends. I don't want to die, Sevren. But I won't run away."

Sevren shook his head sadly. "Nay, 'tis na your nature." He sighed. "I can na stay."

"You just arrived. You need food and rest."

"I'd be glad for some food for the journey. There is na rest to be had. Na here. Na in Taiben. Na place."

"Besides food, is there nothing I can give you?"

"Since you've inquired, I'll make bold and ask for a kiss. I've treasured every one, for they're great rarities."

Dar was about to refuse, but smiled sadly and relented. She grasped Sevren's shoulders and brought her lips to his. They lingered there longer than she intended.

When Dar pulled away, Sevren gazed at her with shining eyes. He was silent, and Dar found his silence unbearable. "I must go," she said, backing away. "I'll send Zna-yat with food." Then she fled the room.

Twenty-six

♛

Soon after receiving food from Zna-yat, Sevren headed back to Taiben alone. He felt angry, sorrowful, and completely helpless. As he saw it, Dar was set on sacrificing her life needlessly and there was nothing that he could do to prevent her. Sevren was glad that the road was a hard one. He attacked the snowdrifts, hoping to gain a small measure of peace through exhaustion.

As Sevren struggled, Dar finished writing down her story on clay-whitened wood. Yev-yat promised to produce a permanent copy of Dar's account by burning the words into a board and waxing it. Dar was glad it would be preserved. She not only recorded her history, but her insights and visions as well.

Dar thought her insights were important because no orc truly understood washavokis. Her experience in the regiment showed how easily orcs fell victim to human guile. She hoped her deetpahi would serve as a warning. Yet when she recalled her predecessor's fate, she despaired. *Othar kept her ensnared for years, and Kol's just as crafty.*

After recording her warning, Dar set down her visions. Most were easy to interpret, having come to pass. The mysterious "woman" by the hedge was a glimpse of the former queen waiting for her successor. The lights winking out in the valley were the orcs dying in the ambush at the Vale of Pines. The hole within Dar's chest was the poisoned wound and the precious thing inside her had been Fathma. Only one vision remained mysterious and unfulfilled—Velasa-pah's appearance in the burning hall. Dar hesitated to record it, knowing that Yev-yat would read her account. She pondered the consequences, then decided to go ahead. Convinced that she was doomed, she saw no benefit in concealing what Muth la had shown her.

Dar finished writing in ample time to prepare for her feast. It was a modest affair, for as the families she hosted rose in status, the food became more ordinary. The evening's feast would be Dar's thirtieth. The meal she would serve Jvar-yat and her family would differ from an everyday one principally because falfhissi would be served at its end.

As a lamp wick burns brightest when the oil is almost gone, Dar was incandescent that evening. She bestowed her fullest measure of warmth and grace upon her guests. Yet Dar's charm only increased their unease, for they knew her fate. Jvar-yat had spent two days searching the snow beneath yew trees for their poisonous seeds. Tomorrow she would steep them in burningwater to prepare Muth la's Draught. When Jvar-yat witnessed Dar's composure, she felt her chest would burst from sorrow. Being an orc, she was unable to disguise her feelings. Neither were her family members, who were aware of what Jvar-yat had been asked to do.

When the falfhissi urn made its rounds, Dar drank sparingly. Jvar-yat did not. After her fourth time with the urn, she rose shakily and bowed deeply to Dar. "Muth Mauk," she said in a slightly slurred voice, "you honor me and mine."

"It's you who honor me," replied Dar.

"Your chest is so, so big," said Jvar-yat. "Yet there's no cowardice within it. Not any. I . . . I don't understand." The latath slumped down and began to make the keening sound that Dar so rarely heard—the mournful cry of orcish weeping.

Jvar-yat's display of emotion silenced the room. Everyone knew its cause, but no one seemed capable of addressing it. Then Dar spoke. "Muth la's greatest gift is love, not life. Her creation lasts forever, and against eternity even long lives seem brief. Yet brief lives are full, if they encounter love. Shashav, Jvar-yat, for my full life."

Sevren did not reach Taiben until dusk the following day, and he barely made it inside the city before its gates were closed for the night. He went to the barracks of the municipal guard to discover if he still had a place with them. Companions from the royal guard had covered his absence, so he still had a cot for himself and a stall for Skymere. Sevren's dark mood kept everyone at a distance, except Valamar. He approached his friend with a flask of spirits. "This will warm you, Sevren, though that's its only virtue."

Sevren took a long gulp and winced. "A brew befitting our new station."

"Did you see Dar?" asked Valamar.

"Aye."

"And?"

"She'll die soon."

"I'm sorry. So the mage succeeded with his poison."

"Nay, and that's what I can na abide. It's some orcish business I can na fathom." Sevren stared at his friend, his face screwed up in anguish. "They're going to kill her, Valamar, and she's just going to let them."

"Piss eyes! They're worse than brutes!"

"Dar does na think so. Even now."

"Well, she was daft to stick with them. And you were daft to stick with her. I warned you on the day you met. You've always been drawn to reckless women. This is Cynda all over again."

Sevren sighed. "Only this time it's poison, na the noose." He took another long swig from Valamar's flask.

* * *

Dar had three more feasts to host before the Council of Matriarchs met, and she dreaded each one for a different reason. Her thirty-first dinner would include Meera-yat, who had fled from her in panic. The next night, Dar would host her own family, an awkward situation at best. Word was out that the council had requested that Muth la's Draught be prepared, and Dar anticipated a mournful evening. *Muthuri might not be upset*, thought Dar, *but she'll pretend to be.* Zor-yat and her sister were the only orcs that Dar knew who were capable of duplicity. She did not look forward to seeing her muthuri. Dar's final feast would be for Muth-yat's hanmuthi, and that meal promised to be the most strained of all.

Dar spent her days roaming the Yat clan hall, as if saying good-bye to it. She found that if she let her thoughts flow freely almost every sight evoked some memory from a former queen. Thus she saw the building through many different eyes that viewed it from the vantage point of earlier times. She gazed at Muth la's Dome and saw it as a rude hut on a nearly empty mountaintop. She peered through bricked-up doorways into vanished rooms. She ventured onto snow-covered terraces and saw brak blooms swaying in spring breezes.

Occasionally, Dar encountered someone who spoke to her, thus pulling her back to the present. The round of feasts had served their function well. Everyone knew her. It was also apparent that everyone knew what she was about to face. Some were certain that Dar would pass the test. Most were apprehensive. Others were deeply troubled. No one spoke what he or she was thinking, for that would be discourteous. Yet Dar had little difficulty discerning their emotions. While it was heartening to sense the outpouring of sympathy and concern, it also increased Dar's sense of doom. It drove her to seek the loneliest corners of the hall. Most of those were in the oldest part, where many of the rooms and hallways were used for storage.

The last three feasts proved to be the ordeals that Dar anticipated. Meera-yat refused to come to hers, so only her daughter showed, embarrassed by her muthuri's rudeness. Dar's feast for her own family had the gaiety of a funeral. The meal for Muth-yat was the worst of all.

Muth-yat once had three daughters. While visiting the late queen in Taiben, they had contracted her mysterious "illness." Othar pretended to treat them, but he provided no antidote for his poison. So, unlike the queen, all of Muth-yat's daughters had died. Her hanmuthi was diminished to herself, her husband, and a youngling grandson, the only child of her eldest daughter. Dar blessed each as they entered the royal hanmuthi. When they were seated, a son brought forth the evening's repast, which Dar had ordered specially. It consisted of a single dish, a traditional stew called muthtufa. After Dar served everyone, she looked Muth-yat squarely in the eye and said, "This is same dish Velasa-pah prepared for me and my companions when we journeyed from west."

Muth-pah calmly returned Dar's gaze. "Gar-yat prepares it well."

"Hai," said Dar. "But Velasa-pah's stew tasted different. I suppose it's because his recipe was older."

"Very likely," said Muth-yat.

"When I saw him in this hall, I should have asked for his recipe."

Muth-yat dropped the pretense of unconcern. "You saw him in our hall?"

"Hai," replied Dar. "This time, it was vision. Haven't you read those deetpahis in lorekeeper's locked box? Velasa-pah was allowed to die after he greeted me."

"That is secret lore," said Muth-yat, "and there are sons present."

"I'm aware of that," said Dar. "But when time grows short, it should not be wasted."

Only Dar, Muth-yat, and Nir-yat fully understood the conversation, but the others sensed its import from the tenseness in the air.

"Visions are warnings of trouble," said Muth-yat, "*and* troublemakers."

"Muth la sends us trials," replied Dar. "We flee them at our peril."

"I intend to face danger," said Muth-yat, "and eliminate it."

"Do you question my fitness to rule?"

Muth-yat smiled. "I'm only one of seven."

There was a long span of awkward silence before Dar spoke again. "Did you ever forgive Zeta-yat for becoming queen?" She smiled as Muth-yat's face grew pale. "I possess Fathma, so I have your sister's memories. You were enraged that she was deemed more worthy than you. She backed you for clan matriarch in hopes of winning back your love, but she never knew if she did."

Muth-yat looked away.

"You might as well speak up," said Dar, satisfied that she had struck a nerve. "Next queen will have my memories, and silence speaks loudly."

"Zeta's spirit doesn't belong in you!" said Muth-yat.

"Do you think you'll be comfortable with her memories? Or *mine*?" countered Dar. "Crown is burden. I know that all too well. Think upon what you seek."

"You're most discourteous!" said Muth-yat.

"Families sometimes bicker, Auntie," said Dar. "Yet I have hope that all can be mended. I was reborn in this hall. I love it deeply. Trust in love rather than fear."

Muth-yat refused to meet Dar's gaze. "All I can do," she said, "is what I think best."

Twenty-seven

♛

Dar bathed on the morning of the Council of Matriarchs, hoping to scrub away the scent of fear. Nir-yat
braided her hair and painted talmauki on her nails.
When Dar finished her preparations, she went to the
Great Chamber. She ascended the throne and sent Zna-
yat to inform the matriarchs that Muth Mauk was thinking of them.

Dar prepared to face the matriarchs and attempt to
persuade them of her fitness. She wouldn't surrender
without a fight. Nevertheless, Dar felt as she had on the
dawn when soldiers spilled from a barn to assault her.
She had been prepared on that day also, though a ladle
was her only weapon. *This time, Kovok-mah can't save
me. All I have is my wits.*

The matriarchs arrived, and Dar blessed each by name.
Dar knew what to say next, for the lorekeeper had
coached her. "Today we honor tradition with this first
meeting of great mother and foremost Clan Mothers. It's
our duty to protect Muth la's children and show them her
path."

Muth-yat stepped forward. "Today we must affirm
that Fathma was bestowed in accordance to Muth la's
will."

"Hai," said Dar. "Upon that matter I shall speak first."
She gazed at the faces before her and easily discerned each
matriarch's mood. She counted three friends and four

foes. *I only need to change one mind*, she thought. Then Dar began her attempt.

"Muth la gave me two lives," said Dar. "I was born washavoki. That life was hard beyond your imagining. Yet I knew of no other until Muth la set me among urk-zimmuthi. Then she sent me both visions and trials. I came to believe that urkzimmuthi should not fight for washavokis. I resolved to lead sons home. Muth la guided me as I journeyed eastward. I encountered Velasa-pah. I lived in Tarathank. I found Lost Clan. I returned sons to their muthuris' hearths.

"After I arrived here, Muth-yat came to me and spoke of her vision. She said I appeared to her to ask why I was not yet born. Then she told me of magic for rebirth. That magic was hard to endure and dangerous, but I gladly shed my old life. My spirit was transformed, and Zor-yat counted me among her daughters.

"Because my form was unaltered, Muth-yat wished me to go to Taiben. There, our queen dwelled. Black Washavoki said he was healing her sickness. Those words had no meaning. His magic was evil. He gave our queen his words to speak. That's why she called for so many sons to kill for Great Washavoki.

"When I freed our queen from Black Washavoki's magic, she agreed to flee with me. She did not say that this would kill her. She was willing to die because she deemed me worthy to receive Fathma. When I became Muth Mauk, I returned to Taiben to face Great Washavoki and Black Washavoki. Now they are dead. Sons no longer kill for washavokis. Instead, they protect washavoki great mother. All this was Muth la's will, which I fulfilled."

When Dar finished speaking, Muth-yat stepped forward. "I agree with everything Muth Mauk has said. Without her, Fathma would be lost to urkzimmuthi.

When my sister was dying, Dargu-yat was only urkzim-muthi mother present. That was why Dargu-yat received Fathma.

"If you are lost and thirsty, is it not wise to cup hands and drink water when you find it? Of course it is. But it is foolish to store water in one's palm. Enduring vessel is needed for that. Dargu-yat received Fathma and brought it to us. That was good. But is she fit to keep it?

"Dargu-yat was reborn this summer. Should infant be our queen? Her urkzimmuthi spirit dwells in ugly washa-voki body. Her nose is not wise. How can she tell what others feel? She smells neither fear nor anger nor love nor pain. These are dangerous times. We need experienced queen, not some crippled newborn."

"I agree," said Muth-zut. "We must test Muth Mauk's fitness. It's our responsibility."

"That test is rarely done," said Muth-tok, "and I see no need to do it now."

"Hai," said Muth-jan. "Seldom has Muth la's will been so clearly revealed. Muth Mauk has received many visions. How many have you received, Muth-yat? Only one I've heard of, and it revealed that Dargu should be reborn."

Muth-smat spoke up. "When sickness comes, we use healing magic. Sometimes it works, sometimes not. Sometimes, its cure is only partial. Is magic of rebirth any more reliable? I see no certain sign that Muth Mauk is urkzimmuthi. Perhaps she's only partly so."

"Or not at all," said Muth-zut. "I smell washavoki stink."

"Are you saying washavokis can receive Fathma?" asked Muth-tok.

"Thwa. I suppose they can't," replied Muth-zut.

"Then why did you speak so quickly?" asked Muth-tok. "We need wisdom here."

"I spoke my chest," said Muth-zut. "I don't like her looks."

"Indeed, I am unsightly," said Dar. "Strange, also. Why would Muth la choose one as strange as me to be your queen? I think it's because I understand something you don't—our enemy. Who among you understands washavokis' minds? Urkzimmuthi are strong and wise, yet washavokis possess our ancient lands. Why? I know, but our tongue doesn't even have words to explain. Washavokis say 'lies,' 'treachery,' 'betrayal,' and 'deceit.' These words are only meaningless sounds to us, with no translations. This summer, two thousand sons died because they didn't understand my warning. As Muth Mauk, I need not explain, only command."

"Are we to obey you without understanding?" asked Muth-smat. "I won't."

"When Muth-yat's sister was queen," said Muth-jan, "she commanded us to send sons to kill for Great Washavoki. We understood and obeyed. How many of those sons have returned to our halls?"

"Perhaps Muth Mauk understands washavokis," said Muth-mah, "but does she understand urkzimmuthi ways? Among us, muthuris are honored and their words are obeyed. Sons look to their muthuris to guide their chests. Yet I think Muth Mauk would have it otherwise and take some son for herself without his muthuri's consent."

"Why do you say that?" asked Muth-yat, as if she didn't know.

"Kath-mah came to me," replied Muth-mah. "She was much troubled over her son, Kovok-mah. Muth Mauk wanted him as her velazul. When Kath-mah forbade it, Muth Mauk bit his neck. Is this how she upholds our traditions?"

Muth-smat glared at Dar with disgust. "She should be thwada, not queen."

"Kovok-mah serves me," said Dar, "but he serves me in Taiben. Few speak washavoki tongue, but he does. I have honored his muthuri's commands."

"Are you not his velazul?" asked Muth-mah.

"We were velazuls until his muthuri forbade it."

"Did he give you love?" asked Muth-mah.

"We behaved properly."

Muth-mah pressed on. "Do you wish he would give you daughters?"

"We must be blessed first," replied Dar. "If that doesn't happen, my wishes are of no consequence."

Muth-mah ceased her questioning, but it had had its effect. The look of disgust on Muth-smat's face had deepened.

Muth-yat spoke up. "There is disagreement. Some among us think that we should test Muth Mauk's fitness, while others think it's unnecessary. This matter seems to require stones. Muth Mauk, will you call for them?"

Courtesy required that the call for stones be phrased as a question, but only one answer was permissible. "Hai," said Dar. "Muth-yat, will you open door?"

Muth-yat bowed and opened the double doors to the Great Chamber, which were closed only when the council was in session. Zna-yat stood outside them. "Bring stones," Dar commanded.

Zna-yat returned a short while later bearing a black, wide-mouthed pottery vessel. He set it by the throne, bowed, and departed, closing the doors behind him. Muth-yat reached into the vessel and removed the stones it contained. She handed two to each matriarch, one green and one black. Afterward, she spoke. "Muth Mauk, we are uncertain where wisdom lies. Should we give you Muth la's Draught? Is this test unneeded? These stones will guide us. Do you wish to speak before they decide?"

"Hai," said Dar. "Muth la has given me many visions.

They have guided me. Yet not all have come to pass. This means I still have more tasks to fulfill."

"If it's Muth la's will," said Muth-yat, "you shall drink and live."

"Muth la's Draught is poison," replied Dar. "Anyone who drinks it dies. Muth la prevents death by calling us to avoid killing."

"Stones will answer this question," said Muth-yat. "Black means Muth Mauk is tested. Green means she is not."

Each matriarch moved apart from the others and turned away so none could see what color she chose. Then each placed her hand in the vessel and dropped a stone. The click of them hitting the pottery was the only sound in the chamber. Muth-yat lifted the vessel and presented it to Dar. "Muth Mauk, will you count the stones?"

Dar reached into the black vessel.

"Green.

"Black.

"Black.

"Green.

"Black.

"Green.

"Black.

"Four black. Three green," said Dar.

"Stones say Muth Mauk should be tested," said Muth-yat. "Does this council accept their judgment?"

"Hai," replied the matriarchs together.

"Then I will submit to your wisdom," said Dar. "Muth-yat, will you open chamber doors?" Muth-yat did so. Zna-yat was outside. Dar spoke to him. "Zna-yat, have Jvar-yat bring Muth la's Draught to us."

As Dar waited to die, memories from the queens who had taken Muth la's Draught came to her unbidden. *It tastes of honey, but bitter. It acts quickly. I'll be nauseous and gasp for air. When I start to tremble, someone will step forward to receive Fathma.* Dar was certain that it would be Muth-yat. Before, when Dar had been near death, she had seen the worthiness of everyone's spirit. *It'll make no difference this time. I won't be given a choice.*

Jvar-yat entered the Great Chamber, interrupting Dar's thoughts. She bowed very low. "Forgive me, Muth Mauk, Muth la's Draught is not yet ready. It's my fault. I drank too much falfhissi at my feast and began steeping seeds too late. More time is required."

"When will it be ready?" asked Dar.

"Tomorrow morning."

Dar regarded the matriarchs, whose faces betrayed their mixed reactions. "We'll meet again then."

Jvar-yat bowed and departed. Then the matriarchs did the same, leaving Dar alone in the Great Chamber. She gazed through its windows at the surrounding mountains. Falling snow made them fade, so they seemed more like memories of mountains than real. *This time tomorrow, all that will remain of me will be memories.*

Twenty-eight

Dar remained in the Great Chamber waiting for her turmoil to subside. Any relief at her reprieve was spoiled by its temporary nature, and she wanted to be calm when she returned to her hanmuthi. Nir-yat and her mintaris would be waiting for her, doubtlessly aware of what had transpired. *The whole hall probably knows by now.*

Dar pushed dismal thoughts aside to ponder how to best use her remaining time. She concluded that the next queen must be warned about Kol. If he followed form, he would present himself as a friend. Dar did not want her successor to be fooled into voiding the treaty and resurrecting the orc regiments.

Despite her concerns, Dar saw no point in speaking to Muth-yat. Instead, she decided to give that task to Nir-yat. There seemed a chance that, once Dar was gone, Muth-yat would listen to her. The principal problem would be explaining the nature of the threat to Nir-yat. Dar feared her sister would not easily grasp how Kol would use deception. Dar was thinking about how to coach Nir-yat when Zna-yat rushed into the chamber, too excited even to bow. "Muth Mauk! More matriarchs have arrived! Muth-pah and Muth-goth!"

"How is that possible? Muth-goth doesn't travel, and I didn't summon Muth-pah."

"I don't know," replied Zna-yat. "All I've heard is that they're here and both are suffering from their journey.

Muth-goth arrived on litter. They've gone to Muth-yat's hanmuthi."

Dar grinned. "I doubt Muth-yat was pleased to receive these guests."

"I think this also," said Zna-yat.

"I wish to see lorekeeper right away."

"I'll bring her," said Zna-yat.

Dar waited anxiously, for she was uncertain if a decision made by stones could be reversed. When Yev-yat arrived, Dar put the question to her. The lorekeeper's answer was not reassuring. "It's never happened."

"But today's circumstances are unique."

"One can argue that," said Yev-yat. "I would, but I'm no clan matriarch. They'll decide this matter, not you or I."

"Then I must wait on their decision."

"I hope it goes your way, Muth Mauk."

Dar spoke with the lorekeeper at length about the relations between queens and matriarchs. Not surprisingly, they were often contentious. Nevertheless, the stones were seldom used to resolve disputes. The council ruled by consensus, and when it couldn't be reached, disputed actions were postponed. Unfortunately, deciding whether a new queen was fit to rule could not be put off. Hence, the stones were employed, and the resulting vote was called the stones' decision, not the matriarchs'.

Despite Yev-yat's uncertainty over whether a second vote would be permitted, Dar returned to her hanmuthi feeling hopeful for the first time in days. The arrival of the two matriarchs seemed like Muth la's intervention. Dar could think of no other explanation, and that changed her outlook. She began to see the next day's meeting as another chance to win the matriarchs' support. Dar sensed their support would be needed beyond the upcoming meeting, for she suspected another trial would soon be upon her. Her latest vision quickly came to mind. She felt that if she were spared, it would be for Muth la's purposes. *But before I worry what they are, I have to survive tomorrow's meeting.*

Dar returned to her hanmuthi, which was abuzz. The arrival of the two matriarchs seemed good news, and everyone had tried to learn as much as they could about it. It had not been easy, for the new visitors were sequestered with the other matriarchs. Nagtha-yat had spoken to Muth-yat, who had informed him that Muth-pah and Muth-goth were too exhausted to see Dar before the council met. Nir-yat had found out that Deen-yat had been called to the hanmuthi. The healer had remained there, leaving only briefly to procure some herbs. Nir-yat had questioned her when she did, but Deen-yat had been closemouthed, as was her custom concerning patients. Zna-yat had located the sons who journeyed with the matriarchs and spoken to them. "Three among them are candidates for your mintaris—Treen-pah, Ven-goth, and Auk-goth—so their duty is to you. Do you wish to speak with them?"

"Hai," said Dar. "I'll go now to Great Chamber. Send Treen-pah to me first."

Soon afterward, Dar greeted the Pah clan son. They recognized each other immediately, and Treen-pah was so astounded that he almost forgot to bow after Dar blessed him. Then, when he did bow, his head nearly touched the floor.

"I remember you, Treen-pah," said Dar. "You were with those sons who captured me and my companions."

"Forgive me, Muth Mauk. I was only obeying our law."

"You behaved properly. I was still washavoki then, for I had yet to be reborn."

"Until I arrived here, I didn't know rebirth still happened. And I had no idea it was you who had been reborn," said Treen-pah. "This journey has brought many surprises. None of my clan has stood before queen since Tarathank fell."

"That's because your clan was lost," said Dar. "It's lost no more. I'm queen Velasa-pah foretold."

"If I had wisdom, I might have known that, for everything changed after you came our way."

"Have you improved your hall?"

"Hai. We're adding more hanmuthis so sons and mothers can eat together. And because sons no longer patrol mountains, I think more children will soon arrive."

"Such news gladdens my chest," said Dar. "But, tell me—why did Muth-pah journey here?"

"She had vision. That's all I know. We've been traveling ever since, except for brief rest at Goth clan hall. We traveled thirty days through deep snow, encountering many storms. Then six days ago, Muth-goth had vision. Since then, we've traveled night and day, seldom resting."

"How have matriarchs fared?" asked Dar.

"Our matriarch is much worn by her journey, but Muth-goth is worse. Everyone fears she's dying."

"She has healer now. Her vision has saved her."

"Perhaps, Muth Mauk, but Muth-goth said her vision was meant to save you."

Six days ago, I met Muth-smat and Muth-zut, thought Dar. *That vision was no coincidence! But if the poison had been ready this morning* . . . Dar's hair rose at the thought.

After Dar sent Treen-pah for some well-deserved rest, she saw Ven-goth and Auk-goth. Auk-goth she knew, for he had guided Dar and her companions part of their way homeward. Exceptionally large and strong, he appeared little wearied by his difficult journey. After Dar blessed him, she grinned. "My old sapaha has returned."

"Hai, Muth Mauk. Yet if you bite my neck, it will be you who'll guide me."

Dar had never met Ven-goth, but she knew of him.

After she blessed him, she asked, "Were you not Fre-pah's velazul?"

"Hai, Muth Mauk, until my muthuri withheld her blessing."

"She wanted to keep you close, and Pah clan hall was far from hers."

"That was her reason."

"Yet my hanmuthi is farther still, and if I bite your neck, it will become your home."

"Muth-goth told me that, but I was willing to come."

"Becoming mintari doesn't mean you can't be blessed. Do you think Fre-pah would be willing to live in this hall?"

Ven-goth's face lit up, and he was unable to control his grin. "Hai, hai, Muth Mauk! She would be most pleased."

Dar smiled. "It's rare to hear son speak for mother."

"Fre-pah's chest and mine are one, Muth Mauk. Ask anyone."

"Then I'll speak of this to Muth-pah and Muth-goth. But remember, I have yet to bite your neck."

Ven-goth bowed low. "I hope you will, Muth Mauk, for I would be honored to serve one so wise."

After speaking with the Goth clan candidates, Dar headed for her hanmuthi. The evening's meal would be her first in thirty-three days that wasn't a feast, and Dar looked forward to a quiet dinner. It had been a tumultuous day, and the entire hall was affected. As Dar passed through its corridors, she sensed the tenseness in the air. Every son and mother appeared to know something momentous was in the offing. *There are few secrets here*, Dar thought, suddenly realizing that she must tell Yev-yat not to reveal her latest vision. Before Muth-pah and Muth-goth arrived, Dar had felt the clan should be aware of its danger, but circumstances seemed to be changing. *There'll be panic if everyone knows what I've seen.*

*   *   *

As a new member of the municipal guard, Sevren got undesirable duties. Night watch was one of them, for the plague of thieves had turned evenings dangerous. Midway through his third straight night of patrolling Taiben's dark streets, Sevren heard a low voice. "Psst! Guardsman!"

Sevren drew his sword, then looked about. He was in a poor section of town, where all the windows were shuttered tight. His watchman's torch cast the only light. Beyond its pale circle lay only shadows and vague, inky shapes. "Who calls me?"

"I do," replied the voice.

Sevren looked in its direction and saw a shadow move at the base of a wall. Wrapped in layers of rags, the man looked like a lump of refuse. Sevren advanced toward him.

"I mean ye no harm," said the man, "and could give none even if I meant it. I'm blind and crippled."

"Then how did you know I was a guardsman?"

"Yer walk. A gait speaks tales if ye have ears fer it. I've heared yers three nights runnin'. I know ye walk yer rounds sober but not timid. It's a proper gait, and I judge ye a proper man. Not the kind to shake a beggar for his alms."

"A flattering description, but I have na coin for you."

"No guardsman ever does, but I have something for ye."

"What?"

"A warning. The Taker roams about this night."

Sevren thought the beggar must be mad, but he humored him. "What's the Taker? And what does it take?"

"Folks' spirits. It makes them thieves. And worse."

"Is it man, woman, or beast?"

"Two men, carryin' a third by the sounds of it."

"So why haven't you been taken?" asked Sevren in a joking tone.

"Ye walk by thrice each night. Have ye ever seen me?

Nay, I'm not worth takin'. But it took a guardsman where ye're standin' now, just six nights ago. Took a woman afore that."

"How?"

"Magic, I suppose. A voice speaks and people change. Their steps lose that spark, like somethin's missin'. I'd say it was their spirit."

Sevren's tone turned less frivolous. "How do you know they steal?"

"They all have the same step, the ones that go by night. They go by day, too, but mostly by night. I've heared them doin' thin's. Robbin'. Killin'. Grabbin' folk. They're men. They're women. Young. Old. But they all walk without that spark."

"This sounds like sorcery."

"What does a beggar know of that? But I heared the Taker goin' up this lane just a bit afore ye come along. So take care, guardsman, or ye'll be took."

"Thank you for your warning," said Sevren. "I'll sharpen my eyes and my ears also." Then he sheathed his sword and continued on his rounds.

Sevren's first thought was to dismiss the beggar's claims as delusions. Sorcerers were powerful men, the counselors of kings and nobles. None had cause to slink about procuring sneak thieves and thugs. Yet the beggar's earnestness made his warning hard to ignore, and Sevren went only a little way before he extinguished his torch. When he resumed advancing in the dark, he did so with a light tread and an alert ear. Farther up the street, Sevren heard a noise. He froze and listened. He thought he heard a pair of men walking, their shuffling tread made heavy by a burden they shared.

Sevren stared up the gloomy street. It appeared as a ribbon of dark gray between the even darker houses. If a dusting of snow hadn't lightened the frozen slush on the road, Sevren might not have seen the moving shape. He strained to make it out, and it seemed to be two men bearing someone in a litter. Sevren's skin crawled as it had when he entered the mage's tower, and that sensation overwhelmed all the arguments of reason. He turned and ran without a moment's hesitation. Sevren didn't stop running until he was on the far side of town.

Twenty-nine

♛

Worry made Dar's sleep fitful, and she was tired and tense as she prepared for the council's meeting. The session could not begin until Muth la's Draught was ready, and that didn't happen until it was approaching noon. As soon as Dar was told that the poison had been made, she went to the Great Chamber and sent word to the matriarchs.

The procession that arrived was much different from the previous day's. First came Muth-goth, carried by two sons on a stretcher. She breathed in gurgling gasps and was accompanied by Deen-yat, who stayed by the matriarch's side after the sons departed. Muth-pah entered next. Dressed in an antique manner, she gave the impression of some stern figure stepping out of ancient tales. The other matriarchs followed. They seemed subdued by Muth-pah's presence.

Dar blessed each matriarch, then said, "Custom permits a healer's presence if she swears to silence about what she hears. Deen-yat, do you so swear?"

"I do."

"Good," said Dar. "Then we must begin anew. Shall I call for stones?"

"There's no need," said Muth-yat, "for stones have already spoken. What needs to be called for is Muth la's Draught."

"There are two here who haven't cast their stones," said Dar.

"Each morning, golden eye rises and new day starts," replied Muth-yat. "Yet what is past remains unchanged. You can't alter history to suit your whims."

"What foolishness!" said Muth-tok. "Let stones decide again."

"If we allow that," replied Muth-yat, "stones' decision would never be final. I say Muth Mauk's fitness must be tested, for stones have decreed it. She must call for Muth la's Draught."

"If she's forced to drink without calling for stones again," said Muth-jan, "she mustn't drink overmuch. We'll need some Draught for her successor."

"I, for one, will question that successor's fitness," said Muth-tok, staring ominously at Muth-yat, "and I'm not alone. If you become queen, you won't cast stones. But you'll receive their judgment."

Muth-pah also regarded Muth-yat. "Since when did urkzimmuthi learn to talk like you? You use words as daggers. Yet they're for reasoning, not slaying. This council was incomplete when it consulted stones. Now it's not." She bowed to Dar. "Muth Mauk, will you call for stones?"

Dar regarded the matriarchs and sensed the shift in power among them. "Hai," she said. "Muth-yat, will you open door?"

Muth-yat bowed and meekly complied. Dar called for the stones to be brought. When they arrived, she addressed the council. "Before these stones are cast, I wish to know why Muth-pah and Muth-goth have come, for it wasn't I who called them."

"It was Mother of Visions who sent me forth," said Muth-pah. "I was loath to make that journey, but how could I disobey?"

"None from your clan has come here before," said Muth-smat. "Has Muth la been silent to you for all those generations?"

"Thwa, but doom was laid upon us to wait and watch. That task is over. Muth Mauk came from west as was foretold."

"Does that mean world will change?" asked Muth-tok.

"Very like," said Muth-pah, "in ways we don't yet know. All I know is this: Muth la sent us this queen. Those who have wisdom know this also."

Muth-goth struggled to sit upright with Deen-yat's aid. The aged matriarch spoke in a faint voice between breaths that came with effort. "On journey, I . . . also had vision . . . It said hurry . . . or hope dies."

"Muth la has spoken to these two mothers," said Muth-hak. "We should listen also."

"Muth Mauk," said Muth-tok, "we're uncertain where wisdom lies. Should you drink Muth la's Draught or not? These stones will guide us. Do you wish to speak before they decide?"

"It's unnecessary," replied Dar.

"Black stone means Muth Mauk is tested," said Muth-tok. "Green means she is not."

The stones were cast, and Dar counted them. Two were black and seven were green. Muth-yat stepped forward. "Does this council accept stone's decision?"

"Hai," said all the matriarchs.

"Then we matriarchs affirm that Dargu-yat was fit to receive Fathma and become our queen," said Muth-yat. She bowed to Dar. "I give my obedience, as Muth la wills it."

Each matriarch bowed and made the same declaration in turn. Afterward, Dar spoke the traditional words. "Muth la has given me this crown. You have made its burden light. Shashav." In her great relief, she nearly forgot to invite the matriarchs to the feast that custom required. After she had done that, she dismissed the council and all departed except for Muth-goth, who waved Deen-yat and the stretcher-bearers away. Then she motioned for Dar to come closer. Dar crouched beside the frail old matriarch.

"Pardon me, Muth Mauk," said Muth-goth in a faint whisper. "I won't come . . . to your feast."

"Get well, instead," said Dar.

"Breathing's hard work. I shall stop soon. This summer . . . we spoke of visions."

"I remember. You said they'd make sense when choices must be made."

"Hai. And . . . you chose well . . . my vision . . ." Muth-goth broke into a coughing spell that left her gasping. "There was more . . . to it. Enemy . . ." Another coughing spell left her wheezing and it took even longer before she had the breath to whisper again. "Bones."

Dar felt a chill as she recalled Velasa-pah's warning. "What about them?"

"Not gone. Changed." Muth-goth lay down, apparently satisfied that she had delivered her message.

Dar grasped Muth-goth's hand. Its wrinkled skin felt thin. "Shashav, Mother, for your sacrifice. Shashav for wisdom you gave me this summer."

Muth-goth smiled, then Deen-yat was by her side. "Muth-goth has accomplished what she desired. Now she should rest."

"Hai," whispered Muth-goth. "Rest with . . . Muth la. Vata . . . Dargu."

Deen-yat motioned for the stretcher-bearers to take the matriarch to her quarters. Before they bore Muth-goth away, Dar gazed into her eyes. They were fixed on a distant place, and they seemed to see it clearly.

In the light of day, the beggar's tale seemed less convincing, and Sevren felt foolish for having fled the men the previous night. He suspected a joke had been played on him and resolved to refute the beggar's tale. That seemed easy enough to do, for the man had said a guard had been taken. Sevren sought out a murdant and asked if any on night watch had gone missing. The murdant had a ready answer. "Well, there's Huckle, the dog's turd. He lit off six nights ago."

"Deserted?"

"Rather burgle than guard, it seems."

"He became a thief?"

"Aye," said the murdant. "And a poor one." He laughed. "A servant skewered him two nights past. Caught him in his master's storeroom." The murdant eyed Sevren. "Why ye ask? Thinkin' of followin' his footsteps?"

"Nay. Just someone spoke of him last night."

Sevren left the murdant, feeling puzzled and uneasy. *Could that beggar be right? Is someone turning folk into thieves?* It seemed absurd. What Sevren knew about the black arts came from tales, most of which he suspected were false. *If someone could force others to do his will, what need would there be for thievery?* Sevren had no answer. *And who in Taiben could do such a thing? The mage is dead. Dar slew him by destroying his magic bones.*

Throughout the remainder of the day, Sevren put the beggar's tale from his thoughts, but as time for the night watch neared, it reared up again. He told it to Valamar, who agreed it was daft. Then Valamar had second thoughts. "I've heard the other guards talking," he said. "All say there's something odd afoot. Why not walk our watches together tonight?"

"I'd be grateful for another pair of eyes and ears," said Sevren. "And I think another sword might come in handy."

"Not against magic," said Valamar.

Word came shortly after the council meeting that Muth-goth had died. Thus at sunset, Dar, the matriarchs, members of the Goth clan, and other mourners gathered in a courtyard in an older part of the hall. There, the deceased matriarch lay upon a pile of oiled wood. When the sun left the sky, the funeral pyre was lit. As its flames consumed Muth-goth's naked body, Dar reminded herself that the matriarch no longer needed it. Then she led the mourners in the opening refrain of the funeral lament:

> "Your scent lingers,
> And we think of you,
> Though you have wandered
> From sight and touch
> Into Our Mother's arms."

Everyone in the courtyard added at least one verse between refrains. Each recalled and celebrated Muth-goth's life. Some verses were reflective. Others expressed gratitude. Many related stories. Dar sang of how Muth-goth had instructed her in the purposes of visions and told her it was better to be wise than pretty.

Dar felt somewhat uncomfortable hosting a feast immediately after a funeral, but custom required one after a queen's affirmation. Dar was surprised by its lavishness, for having worked in the kitchen, she knew many of the meal's dishes involved lengthy preparation. The stuffed fowls required slow roasting overnight, and several of the stews needed to simmer from early morning. It was apparent that Gar-yat had been more confident of Dar's triumph than Dar herself.

What surprised Dar even more was the feast's harmonious atmosphere. Matriarchs who earlier had advocated the fatal test treated her cordially. If they had been human, Dar would have assumed they were merely insincere, but orcs didn't engage in social falsehoods. The stones reflected a divided vote, but their "decision" had been accepted unanimously. Dar was queen, and all the matriarchs seemed reconciled to that without lingering animosity. Even Muth-yat appeared relieved that the conflict was over.

As muthuri of all the urkzimmuthi, Dar served every dish. At first, there was little conversation, for the food was so delicious. Talk began in earnest only after appetites were dulled. Muth-tok questioned Dar about her travels, and all the matriarchs were spellbound by Dar's description of Tarathank. The city loomed large in orcish tales, though no orc had seen it for generations. The memories bestowed by Fathma increased Dar's knowledge of the places she had visited. Thus she called the courtyard where Kovok-mah first gave her love by its ancient name—"Singing Water"—though she was silent on what transpired there. The stonework that had so impressed Duth-tok and Lama-tok was in the ruins of the queen's palace. It was from one of the palace towers— only rubble when Dar had visited it—that the last Pah queen first spied the washavoki invaders. After describing Tarathank, Dar related the events in Taiben that led to the downfall of the king and his mage. That tale also fascinated the matriarchs.

As the evening wore on, Dar's confidence grew along with her assurance of her power. After the falfhissi urn made a few rounds, she was gripped by fierce exultation. She had passed another of Muth la's trials and become queen for certain. *Now I must use the might that's been given me*, Dar thought. She already knew where she would employ it first. *Taiben.*

Thirty

♛

As Sevren and Valamar patrolled Taiben's shadowy streets, they sometimes heard furtive footsteps but were unable to trace their source. It was well past midnight before they happened upon a crime. They were walking where the merchants lived when they heard a crash that sounded like dropped metal goods. The pair headed toward where the noise had originated. It was a narrow alleyway between two houses. When their torches illuminated the confined space, it revealed a girl dangling from the ledge of an open window. She dropped to the ground and retrieved a large sack lying close by.

"Halt!" shouted Valamar, drawing his sword.

The girl drew a kitchen knife from a pocket in her shift and charged the guardsman while still gripping the bag. It was an uneven contest. With one swing of his sword, Valamar struck the blade from his assailant's hand. It made no difference to her. She still lunged at Valamar, who struck the girl with his sword hilt instead of slaying her. The blow bloodied the girl's lip and knocked her down, but she was on her feet in an instant.

Sevren entered the fray by tackling the girl, who still clutched the bag, though it encumbered her. Her free hand clawed at Sevren's eyes, and he avoided injury only by seizing her wrist and holding fast. Then he gripped the wrist of the hand that clutched the bag. The girl continued to struggle, and as Sevren pinned her to the ground, he was amazed by her age and single-mindedness. His captive appeared only thirteen. She was slightly built, no match for him at all. Regardless, she showed no signs of surrender, despite the hopelessness of her situation.

"She's a real spitfire," said Valamar as he sheathed his sword. He held his torch closer to the struggling girl's face. It proved the opposite of a spitfire's, for it was bereft of passion. Sevren and Valamar saw neither anger nor desperation in the girl's features. She displayed no emotion at all. Blank eyes stared from a face that might have been stone if it hadn't been animated by a constant twitch. It was a disturbing sight.

"Karm protect us!" said Valamar. "What have we caught?"

"Take the bag from her," said Sevren, "and look inside."

Valamar managed to pry the bag from the girl's fingers only by exercising all his strength. It contained silver dishes and goblets. "She's a thief, no doubt about it."

"Speak, lass!" shouted Sevren. "Where were you taking this?"

The girl remained silent as she continued her futile struggle. Valamar raised his fist to strike, but she didn't react. "Do na hit her," said Sevren. "Someone's already done her more grievous harm."

"What?"

"Look at those dead eyes. Someone's worked a spell on her."

"Was that beggar right?" asked Valamar. "Is her spirit stolen?"

"Either that or overpowered."

"What should we do?"

"Bind the girl, and return these goods."

"Then what?"

"If we take her to the guardhouse, they'll flog her or worse," said Sevren. He regarded the girl's dirty, vacant face. "I suppose she's beyond caring, but I propose another course. I've a friend who could hold her awhile. Mayhap she'll recover."

It took both of the men to bind the girl, who resisted silently. After they returned the stolen silver, they dragged their young captive to Thamus' home. There, Sevren prevailed on his friend to hold the girl in a small storeroom and watch for signs of recovery. Afterward, he and Valamar resumed their rounds.

Valamar shivered, but not from the cold. "By Karm, this has been a most unnatural night!"

"Aye," said Sevren. "That girl's a victim of sorcery. I'm certain of it."

"But who could work such a spell? The mage is dead."

"Is he?" asked Sevren. "He looked dead enough, but now I wonder."

"He's dead. You're daft if you think otherwise. I dumped what was left of him in the pit myself. If you think he lives, go there and take a peek."

"Mayhap I will."

Dar didn't meet with the matriarchs again until the afternoon after the feast. Then she addressed her foremost concern. "When Fathma was first recovered by urkzimmuthi, queen made treaty with washavokis. Our sons killed for them, and they stopped raiding us. I think she acted wisely, for treaty brought peace to our halls. Yet sons bought that peace with their lives, and because washavokis are cruel, those sons were required to do cruel deeds. When washavokis see urkzimmuthi, they recall those deeds and think we're evil. Moreover, they say we eat washavokis and relish killing."

"How could they be so foolish?" asked Muth-mah.

"It's their nature," said Dar. "When I was washavoki, I believed those tales also. I know that's surprising, but I did."

"If washavokis think we're evil, why did they want sons to fight for them?"

"To make their enemies fear them. Father of Great Washavoki did not like killing, neither did his grandfather. During their reigns, our sons seldom killed. But things changed after last great washavoki was crowned. Then many sons were called to kill for him. Black Washavoki used magic upon our queen to get them."

"Hai," said Muth-tok. "But those two are dead. Great Washavoki's muthvashi rules now. You made treaty with her."

"She seemed to see wisdom in peace," said Dar. "Yet washavoki mothers are ruled by sons."

"Even washavoki great mothers?" asked Muth-smat.

"Hai. Moreover, I know what son counsels her. He's evil and likes killing."

"How can she lack wisdom and still rule?" asked Muth-smat.

"Washavokis are not like us. They have not Fathma. Crown passes from father to son regardless of son's worthiness. This muthuri rules only because her son is too young. When he gets older, she must give him crown."

"What nonsense!" said Muth-smat.

"Washavokis are full of nonsense," said Dar. "Our treaty with them is wise, for it brings peace. But I'm not certain they want peace. Thus I plan to go to Taiben."

"What will you do there?" asked Muth-tok.

"I'll attempt to show washavoki great mother that peace is wise. However, I think she may request that sons kill for washavokis again. I won't allow that. Too many sons have died already."

"If we deny washavokis our sons, they may start raiding again," said Muth-yat.

"I believe you're right," said Dar. "They'll use road between here and Taiben. We must think of ways to stop them."

"Stone Clan built that road," said Muth-tok. "My grandmother was matriarch then. She had vision that is part of Tok clan lore. Spirit of her grandmother appeared to her and asked, 'Why do you make door that you can't shut?' My grandmother knew her vision spoke of pass in ridge, for that narrow passageway resembles door. Now know this: We can close it."

"How?" asked Dar.

"In heights above pass, we drilled line of holes deep into rock. All these holes were sealed and covered. If covers are removed and holes are filled with water, that water will freeze and split rock. Then it can be pushed down to plug passageway."

"Isn't there another route between here and Taiben?" asked Dar.

"There is," said Muth-yat. "It's called Old Road, but no one uses it. Way is long and dangerous, especially in winter. Wagons can't travel it. That's why New Road was built."

"Muth-tok, I would like you to send for sons with skills to close pass if necessary. I want to be prepared."

"I will do this, Muth Mauk."

"Your journey to Taiben sounds perilous," said Muth-jan.

"I think it will be," said Dar. "Yet Muth la has preserved my life thus far, so I think I'll live until I've accomplished my task."

After a night spent on watch, Sevren slept until early afternoon. After he rose, he walked to Thamus' house to inquire about the girl. The sand ice merchant looked exhausted when he opened the door. "What demon did you leave with me?" he asked. "I've had no rest since you departed."

Sevren could hear pounding behind a closed door. "Didn't you leave her tied to the chair?"

"I did. She toppled it and has been pounding her head against the floor."

"Did you feed her?"

"She took no bite of food, only one of me."

"I suppose she said nothing."

"Not a word. The only change is her twitch is worse, and she's drooling now."

Sevren sighed. "Let's see her."

Thamus unbolted a door, to reveal a small storeroom. Sevren's captive was tied securely to a chair, her feet to its legs and her chest and hands to its back. As Thamus had said, she had toppled the chair, which permitted her to pound her head against the wooden floor. Thamus had tried to soften the floor with a quilt, but the girl's persistent blows had blooded it. Sevren gazed into her eyes and saw only chilling blankness.

"Whoever did that to her," said Thamus, "is guilty of an abomination."

"I thought the spell might pass," said Sevren. "It seems that hope was empty." He moved to set the chair upright.

"Don't bother," said Thamus. "She'll only topple it again and perhaps hurt herself further."

"I've an errand to do," said Sevren. "Afterward, I'll come back and take her from your hands."

"Leave her with me. The guards will not be kind. She's vexing, yet I grieve for her."

"Karm's blessing on you," said Sevren. "You're a good-hearted man."

Sevren left Thamus' house and went to the guards' stables. There, he obtained a coil of thick rope, saddled up Skymere, and rode to the corpse pit that lay outside the city. As he neared the place, he noted the lack of tracks in the snow. The frigid air bore only a faint hint of putrefaction. Thankful that it was not summer, when the dead ripen quickly, Sevren dismounted and walked to the pit's edge. He had hopes of spotting Othar's blackened body, but none of the frozen faces that peered from the snow were his. *Mayhap he's covered by snow or corpses.*

Though loath to enter the pit, Sevren had no choice if he was to ascertain whether the mage was dead. He tied the rope to Skymere's saddle and lowered himself among the frozen bodies. A gruesome search uncovered no black robes or charred flesh. The sorcerer was gone, though Sevren felt certain that no one would take his corpse or even willingly touch it. He used the rope to climb from the open grave. Even when Sevren was free of the pit, its odor still clung to him. He shuddered, not from the stench, but from knowledge far more loathsome. *Othar lives!*

The conclusion seemed to defy logic, but magic always defied logic. Othar was missing from the pit, and someone was practicing sorcery—someone who moved about in a litter. Valamar had told Sevren that Othar's body had no feet, so at least the litter made sense. Little else did. Sevren's conclusion gave him no clue as to what the mage was about. He also had no idea who to tell. *Dar's dead, and Queen Girta's dismissed me.* Dar's fate had left Sevren resentful toward the orcs, and disinclined to warn them. He supposed he could tell the municipal guard, but decided they would only ridicule him.

In the end, Sevren told no one beyond Valamar. His friend listened dubiously and counseled silence. It seemed like good advice.

Thirty-one

♛

After her meeting with the matriarchs, Dar returned to her hanmuthi to speak to Nir-yat. "Sister, will you go with me to Taiben?"

Nir-yat bowed. "I'll do whatever you command."

"I won't command it," said Dar. "I want you with me only if you're willing."

"I've never been to Taiben, or seen any washavokis before you . . ." Nir-yat stopped herself.

Dar grinned. "Before I came?"

"You're reborn. I shouldn't call you washavoki."

"I still look like one."

"I've also seen Sev-ron. Are all washavoki sons so small?"

"Most are," replied Dar. "Small but dangerous. This journey will be perilous. You should know that before you answer."

"Sister, I wish to be by your side."

Dar smiled. "Your words warm my chest. Fetch Thorma-yat, for we'll need new clothes for our visit."

When the seamstress arrived, Dar explained what she wanted. "There is washavoki garment they call 'shirt.' It covers torso and arms. Nir-yat and I will need several."

Thorma-yat looked puzzled. "Why would you wear this thing?"

"To cover breasts," said Dar.

"Don't washavoki mothers adjust their kefs when they're cold?" asked Nir-yat.

"They don't wear kefs," replied Dar, "and they don't cover breasts for warmth. They wish to hide them."

"Why?" asked Nir-yat.

Dar blushed as she explained. "Among washavokis, sons rule mothers. They feel free to take pleasure from their bodies, even if mothers are unwilling. When sons see breasts they aren't reminded of mother's dignity and authority. Instead, they feel encouraged to . . . to . . ."

"Give love?" asked Nir-yat a shocked tone. "Give love without permission?"

"I wouldn't call it giving love. And some sons do even more than that. They thrimuk without blessing. Washavokis call it 'rape.'"

Nir-yat's face expressed her outrage and horror. "I never imagined such things were possible!"

"Not all washavoki sons are like that," said Dar, "but some are. I've witnessed it. That's why we'll wear 'shirts' in Taiben." She turned to her shaken sister. "Do you still wish to accompany me?"

"Knowing this, how could I leave your side?"

Thorma-yat seemed as stunned as Nir-yat by Dar's revelations, but she also had a job to do. "I've never made garment so outlandish. How does one get into it?"

Dar took a thin, clay-whitened board and drew a picture of a collarless, long-sleeved shirt that fastened in the rear. The seamstress left and returned with some cloth and sewing gear, then attempted to fashion a shirt to Dar's liking. It took several tries before she came up with a satisfactory pattern.

Between fittings, Dar discussed another project with one of her mintaris, Tatfa-jan, and his clan's matriarch. The Jan clan was known as the Iron Clan, but its members did all kinds of metalwork. Dar spoke to the two about what she wanted. "Washavokis expect rulers to display their power in their apparel," she said. "Powerful sons and mothers dress like gaudy birds. I won't do that, but I'll need some sign of my authority and might. I can do that with something washavokis call 'jewelry.' It's object of yellow iron that's worn on clothing."

"What kind of object?" asked Muth-jan.

Dar pointed to the shallow reliefs carved into the stone walls of her hanmuthi. "Something like that. Flat and small enough to hang about neck. Washavokis call such jewelry 'necklace.' Since they prize yellow iron, it should be large."

Muth-jan examined the reliefs. "What should this 'naklas' portray?"

"Tree is Muth la," said Dar, "so tree would be appropriate."

"That choice seems wise to me," said Muth-jan. "Tatfa-jan is skilled in casting."

"Hai, Matriarch," said Tatfa-jan, "but another makes my molds."

"Muth-tok is stone carver," said Muth-jan. "She creates designs such as those on Muth Mauk's walls. Perhaps you two could work together."

Muth-tok was brought in and the four discussed the necklace. Dar wanted its pendant to be the size of a hand with its fingers outstretched, an impressive chunk of gold. Orcs did not especially value the metal, and procuring enough to fashion the pendant posed a problem. However, it was one that Muth-jan felt confident of solving. After the discussion was over, Muth-tok left with Tatfa-jan to work on tree designs while Muth-jan sought to obtain the gold for it.

When Thorma-yat returned with fabric samples for Dar's and Nir-yat's shirts, Dar gave her one more task. "I want band of talmauki cloth to wear about my forehead so it covers this mark." Dar pointed to the scar made by the king's brand. "I don't wish washavokis to see it."

"Will this band go beneath your crown?" asked Thorma-yat.

"Hai," replied Dar. "And it only need be thick about forehead."

The seamstress bowed. "I'll make one, so you may see if it suits."

Dar returned the bow. "You have pleased me, Thorma-yat."

When Dar served dinner in her hanmuthi, she felt satis-fied with what she had accomplished. It was dark when the dishes were cleared, and Dar was surprised when a son appeared with a message from Muth-pah. "She requests to see you in Great Chamber."

"Tonight?" asked Dar.

"Hai, Muth Mauk. She said it must be dark."

"Tell her I'll meet her."

After the messenger departed, Dar went alone to the Great Chamber. She extinguished her lamp when she reached it. The moon had risen and its soft, dim light il-luminated the room. She climbed upon the throne and waited for Muth-pah. The matriarch arrived shortly.

"May Muth la bless you, Muth-pah."

"Shashav, Muth Mauk."

"I'm glad for this chance to speak with you, for I've thought much about my visit with your clan. After we entered darkness together, did you know I'd be queen?"

"Perhaps I should have known," replied Muth-pah. "Yet I didn't. Visions are always vague. Besides, our clan had waited generations for your arrival. We expected someone glorious."

Dar smiled. "Not some barefoot washavoki?"

Muth-pah returned Dar's smile. "Certainly not. I thought you were queen's harbinger, not queen herself. Only when I arrived here, did I learn you were Muth Mauk."

"So you were surprised."

"Hai, but it made sense. But I didn't ask to see you to

speak about that," said Muth-pah. "I have gift for you. Heirloom of my clan. It was made by Velasa-pah himself."

"It must be precious."

"It is. There's only one in world."

"What is it?" asked Dar.

Muth-pah gave Dar a dark cloth pouch containing a heavy object the size of a woman's fist. Dar opened the pouch to reveal a smooth, black stone. The darkness permitted a faint glow to be seen within its depths. It moved like a luminescent fog, shifting in shape and color as Dar watched. "That is Velasa-pah's Trancing Stone," said Muth-pah.

The stone grew warmer as Dar held it, heating her hand instead of the reverse. "Is it magic?"

"Hai. Like you, Velasa-pah was once washavoki. Washavokis speak of Dark Path where spirits go upon death. Do you know of it?"

"I do."

"It's said spirits leave their memories behind as they journey upon this path, and I believe this is so. Velasa-pah's stone allows those who hold it to find those memories and relive them. He created this stone after Tarathank fell, so he might recall perished loved ones. Yet, be warned that such glimpses can be perilous."

"How?"

"They can disturb your chest. Some memories are stronger than others. Those of great fear or sorrow are especially potent. I don't know what Velasa-pah saw, but I know it brought him sorrow. He said that when he gave this stone to my ancestors. He also told them that this stone was meant for you."

"Me?"

"Queen from west."

Dar glazed at the stone, fascinated but wary. "How does it work?"

"Hold it in dark and think of one whose memories you seek. They will come."

"Have you ever used this stone?"

"Only once."

"What was it like?"

"I can't speak of it. Forgive me, Muth Mauk, it's too painful."

"Shashav for this gift."

Muth-pah bowed and departed.

Dar sat in the dark gazing at the mysterious stone. Its shifting colors fascinated her and also the idea that she might experience moments from departed lives. Her mother immediately came to mind, but the traumatic memory of her death in childbirth made Dar rethink the choice. Dar could easily see how reliving that night would open old wounds.

Dar also thought of Twea. *Her death was even more terrible.* But it was also mysterious. *Who killed her?* Dar didn't recall Muth-pah saying that the stone revealed only moments that were fearful or sorrowful. *Besides, my dreams of Twea are already painful. Could the stone's visions be any worse?* Dar imagined not and yielded to temptation. Holding the stone, she thought of Twea.

What happened next seemed less real than waking life, but more vivid than any dream or memory. She was staring down at two bare feet. They were small and dirty. One foot swung from side to side, its big toe marking a crescent in the dirt. Above the thin legs was a ragged, oversized shift. Dar realized those were Twea's feet, as seen from Twea's perspective.

"Look at me!" shouted a woman's voice.

The view changed to a hard-faced woman whom Dar had never seen before. Yet she knew the speaker. Twea called her Auntie. "Ye're garbage," said Auntie. "Yer mother threwed ye away. That's why ye can't sleep in the house."

The image faded to be replaced by another. Dar recognized the setting. It was one of the army's encampments in enemy territory. Dar saw Taren stirring the porridge pot, and then she spied herself. She was dusty from the day's march and burdened with a load of firewood. Then— since this was Twea's memory—she felt a surge of love. It was so intense that she dropped the stone.

Dar was alone in the Great Chamber, still experiencing Twea's love. *She believed I was her mother!* Seen from the child's perspective, it didn't seem impossible, and Dar understood how need and imagination had made it so. *She never told me.*

Dar held the stone again and was in a different place. It was dark. She was in a wagon bed, hidden under a coarse cloth. There were shouts and screams horrible to hear. Weapons clanged. She was anxious and terrified. *When's Dar coming? She said she'd get me.*

There were soft thumping sounds at the rear of the wagon. Someone moaned. Dar recognized the sounds, though Twea did not. They were arrows striking someone. *Taren's just been killed*, thought Dar, steeling herself for what she knew would follow. Still, she gripped the stone, reliving Twea's last memory.

The cloth is jerked aside. "Dar?"

Not Dar. Soldiers. She had served them porridge just that morning. One speaks. "Nay, birdie. Dar's been hurt. We're here to take ye to her. Where's she at?"

"I don't know! She said wait here!"

"Are ye sure, birdie? Dar's hurt real bad. She needs ye. Needs ye now."

"I don't know where she is! I don't know!"

Sobbing.

"She's useless," said a soldier. "Do we take her to Kol?"

"Nay," said the other. "He only wants Dar. He said do it here."

A sword blade flies out. It feels like burning. *It's sticking in my chest! Blood! My blood!* Burning. Growing darkness. Burning. Nothing.

.   The Trancing Stone fell from Dar's hand, yet pain lingered in her chest. Not the pain of a sword strike, but pain equally as hurtful. Dar wailed with grief and rage. Gradually, rage dominated. It colored the darkness red.

"Kol!" screamed Dar. "Kusk washavoki!" *Washavoki filth!* "Ga dava-tak fer!" *You killed her!*

Thirty-two

♛

Although Kovok-mah pined for Dar, he found life in the garrison an improvement over that in the palace. Two barracks had been refurbished for the orc guards. Their circular walls made them feel homier and each contained a proper hearth, which vented through a hole in the ceiling. Reed mats covered the dirt floors, the rough stone walls had been plastered, and wooden doors replaced the hide door flaps. Better yet, another barracks had been turned into a bath with a flagstone floor, a stone bathing pool, and means to heat the bathwater. Even the food had improved somewhat. It was still served by woe mans. They and the black-garbed Queen's Men were the only washavokis within the garrison, which was otherwise empty except for the thirty-six orc guards.

The gates of the garrison were always open, and sons went freely into Taiben to serve at the palace. Two orcs guarded the queen by day and another two by night. This number bothered Kovok-mah, for it seemed inadequate. While two armed and armored urkzimmuthi were formidable protectors, he knew they could be overwhelmed. Separating the queen from her troop of orcish guards seemed foolish to Kovok-mah, and he worried that Dar would be displeased by the change.

Kovok-mah had felt isolated ever since Zna-yat had left for the royal hall. He had received no news or instructions from Dar, and Sevren hadn't visited the garrison. Kovok-mah had yet to send his report to Dar. He wanted to deliver it personally, but feared that would jeopardize her. After vacillating for days, Kovok-mah acted. He wrote out his account and asked Garga-tok to provide a courier. Watching the messenger depart, Kovok-mah nearly ran after him to trade places. Instead, he returned to the barracks. He opened his pack and withdrew the tunic he had worn on the night Dargu slept in his arms. He had not washed or worn it since. Kovok-mah held the garment to his face, breathed in Dar's scent, and sighed.

Queen Girta gazed out the window at Taiben's rooftops. After the previous night's snowfall, the city appeared pristine under a cloudless sky. *I used to love winter*, she thought. That was before her late husband had taken to warfare. Then winter became a pause between campaigns, a time when drunken men caroused and boasted of bloody deeds. Girta had come to feel that cold weather transformed the palace into a kennel for vicious dogs. But worse than them was the mage, whose ominous presence oppressed the entire court.

The demise of her husband and his sorcerer should have ushered in more peaceful times, but Girta felt they hadn't. Instead of the mage, there were orcs, who seemed equally menacing. Rumors of plots bedeviled her, and a string of misfortunes had overcome her closest confidants. Lady Rowena, Girta's friend from childhood, had been strangled by a deranged servant. General Gotha's wife had committed suicide, and Lord Nothur's spouse had suffered a fatal fall. All three women had always provided support and useful insights. Others were gone as well. Military officers, noblemen, and counselors had perished by mischance or random acts of violence. All were good men. Even Girta's lady's maid had been murdered by a lover. It had been a trying winter.

The queen's bulwark against her fears and misfortunes was General Kol. He was always self-assured, and she had come to depend on him. Sometimes Girta felt that she depended on him too much. There was occasionally something in his manner that sparked her resentment, a condescension that appeared at unguarded moments. These usually occurred when she was speaking to the prince and took the form of a look on Kol's part. It seemed to say, "Ignore your mother's foolishness." *I shouldn't think like that*, Girta told herself. *General Kol's my protector. No wonder my son adores him.*

A knock interrupted Girta's musings, and the door opened before she could respond. General Kol entered and bowed. "Your Majesty, another orc has abandoned your guard. The Queen's Men saw him leave this morning."

"Did they find out why he left?"

"They just let him pass, as per orders."

"*Whose* orders?"

"Mine," replied Kol, his face bland. "It's part of our plan."

"Oh yes," said Girta, wondering what plan he was talking about.

"To lure out Dar. We won't know what she's plotting until she comes to Taiben."

"What makes you think she'll come?"

"She'll come because she's about to learn her scheme has fallen apart," said Kol. Girta shot him a puzzled look and he elaborated. "Moving the orcs outside the palace thwarted her chance for a surprise attack."

"There are still two of her fiends outside my door day and night!"

"We've been over this before," said Kol. "If we banished the orcs altogether, Dar would know we're wary. Instead, we've improved their accommodations, which happen to lie outside the city. Just you wait. Dar will betray her intentions. She'll arrive to persuade you to move her orcs back into the palace."

"It's a clever trap," said Girta, "but I feel like the bait."

"The Queen's Men spy on those two orcs from hidden places, ready to burst forth and cut them down at the first false move."

"Still, I abhor all this trickery."

"Would you rather go to war?" asked Kol. "Shouldn't we try to snare Dar in her own noose before it comes to that?"

"You're right, as usual," said Girta.

Kol moved to her side. "I only want to keep you safe." He lightly placed his fingers upon her hand, which rested on the windowsill. It was the first time he had ever presumed to touch her, and the contact was tentative. Girta didn't protest, so Kol's left his fingers where they were.

Kovok-mah's message arrived at the Yah clan hall the following day. When Dar read it, her anger toward Kol, which had simmered ever since she had used the Tracing Stone, flared hot again. It was clear that Kol was already unraveling her treaty. Dar agreed with Kovok-mah that two orc guards were insufficient protection. *Girta's a fool*, she thought. *Her orcs were unshakably loyal, and she's replaced them with Kol's minions.* Dar was irritated that the orcs had so passively submitted to the change. However, she forgave them, for it was their nature to obey mothers. The irony didn't escape her. They submitted to Girta as Girta submitted to Kol.

Kol's rise within the court still surprised and perplexed Dar. As far as she knew, murdants never became officers. She assumed he had some powerful friends, but she couldn't imagine who. The Queen's Man had been killed when the orcs attacked Taiben. *Who else could Kol have known?* It seemed a mystery that only she had hopes of solving. The orcs would be useless in unraveling such intrigue.

Dar wanted to go to Taiben immediately, but she restrained herself until everything was ready. Her and Nir-
yat's clothing were completed first. Nir-yat worked with
Thorma-yat on the final details of the shirts. They fit well
and looked good to Dar's eye. The design for the pendant
was a broad-crowned yew, the tree sacred to Muth la.
Once it was cast, a wide talmauki ribbon was specially
woven to suspend it. Dar consulted with the lorekeeper
about both the New and Old roads to Taiben and studied deetpahis that mapped their routes. She also ensured
that all her mintaris had arms, armor, and new woolen
robes, since she wanted them to accompany her. She ex-
panded their number by biting the necks of the two Goth
clan candidates and Treen-pah.

After those preparations were complete, Dar had to
delay leaving until sons from the Tok clan arrived. They
would stand ready to seal the pass if she gave the order.
They came, nearly fifty strong, burdened by their heavy
tools and accompanied by some Tok clan mothers. After
Dar saw to their accommodation, she announced that
she would depart for Taiben the following day. By then,
all the matriarchs except Muth-pah had left for their
halls.

The evening before departure, Dar spoke to her traveling party. She told them that she wanted to ensure that
the washavokis' queen desired peace. She didn't explain
her concerns, for she was certain only Zna-yat could possibly grasp them. What Dar feared most was Kol's treachery. Aware of his cunning, she thought it was likely that
he had a trap waiting for her. Nevertheless, she was resolved to face him. *I've beaten him twice before*, Dar told
herself. *I'll beat him this time, too.*

Kol's secret benefactor lay on a soft feather bed
within his darkened room, incapable of rest. Othar was

tormented. Though his charred flesh no longer pained
him, he was afflicted by the knowledge that his body
wasn't wholly his. Whatever had possessed the magic
bones possessed him. It gave him extraordinary powers,
but the price was dear.

Unnatural needs governed the sorcerer. He craved
bloodshed. He craved it with the same single-mindedness
that a parched man wants water and for the same
reason—he needed it to survive. Without slaughter to
sustain it, his possessor would shuck him like a soiled
glove. That terrified the mage, for he had an inkling of
what nightmare being would be waiting for him on the
Dark Path. Thus the sorcerer dedicated all his powers to
helping Kol provoke a war.

There were signs he was succeeding. Othar had acquired some of the bones' powers of premonition. He
sensed forces on the move, and knew events were approaching fruition. The mage had misty glimpses of
massed soldiers. Snow swirled about them, colored red
by sheets of billowing flame.

Thirty-three

♛

When Dar departed for Taiben, the morning sky was deep gray and snow was falling. Despite the weather, Dar chose to press ahead. She had eight sons with her, and while they were encumbered by arms and armor, she felt that they could easily overcome any storm. Dar was eager to finish the distasteful business that lay ahead. Also, she longed to see Kovok-mah.

When the party left the Yat clan's winding valley, they took the New Road, which began to ascend almost immediately. At first, the slope was gentle, but it quickly grew steeper as it followed a wooded ridgeline. As the road climbed higher, the woods became sparser and its trees grew stunted. The snowfall increased until it hid the surrounding mountains and caused the slopes on either side of the road to fade into formless white.

Progress slowed as the snow on the road deepened, though walking remained easy for Dar, who followed the trail created by the sons in front. When she called a halt for a quick midday meal, Zna-yat told her they were halfway to the pass. By the time they reached it, daylight was beginning to fade. The snowfall had reduced to an occasional flake, so Dar had a good view of the pass and the ridge it penetrated.

Through most of their range, the southernmost Urkheit Mountains were formidable obstacles, and the ridge ahead was no exception. It formed a long barrier of steep rock that marked the highest terrain before the plains beyond. Dar gazed at it from a tactical perspective. The pass was a deep cut that resembled an alleyway into a wall of nearly vertical rock. If it were sealed, there seemed no way to reach the other side.

Dar called Lama-tok to her. "Your clan carved that?" she said, her voice awed.

"Hai," replied Lama-tok. "We tell many tales about its making." He pointed to the piles of huge stone blocks that flanked the cut. "You can still see rock that we removed."

"And you scaled those cliffs to do it?"

"Hai." Lama-tok pointed to holds cut into the rock. "We used those to climb them."

"So washavokis could climb cliffs also?"

"Thwa. There are no holds on their side."

"How quickly could this pass be shut?"

"Not overnight, but I think it would take only one or two days. It's always easier to break than to build."

When the travelers reached the pass, they stopped for the night and camped within its narrow walls. There, they roasted pashi, then slept huddled together for warmth. Morning brought fairer weather. Journeying downhill, they arrived at Taiben in the afternoon.

Dar stopped briefly at the garrison to visit the orc guards before proceeding to the palace. Both the late king's father and grandfather had hosted orcish royalty there. Nagtha-yat had been to Taiben several times when his muthuri was great mother, and he had told Dar about those visits. Additionally, Dar possessed memories of sojourns made by former queens. Thus, knowing what to expect, she was surprised by her reception.

Lokung, the queen's steward, stood waiting in the snow beside the palace's shut gates. When Dar and her party approached, he bowed deeply. "Greetings, Your

Majesty. Your friend and ally, Queen Girta, has sent me to extend her welcome and inform you that she will feast you tomorrow night."

"That's most gracious of her," said Dar.

"Our Majesty also wishes that she had suitable accommodations for Your Majesty and Your Majesty's attendants. Unfortunately, her palace lacks rooms suitable for your kind. She has, however, seen to the construction of barracks fit for her orc guards and hopes these will please you."

Dar knew perfectly well that the palace had proper orcish accommodations; they had been built two generations ago. Nevertheless, she chose to appear oblivious of Girta's deceit. "A monarch is always comfortable among her subjects. Those accommodations will suit us well." With that, Dar returned to the garrison, quietly fuming all the way.

When Dar reached the garrison, the orcs welcomed her again, and she began to feel glad that she was staying with them rather than at the palace. She suspected that her greeting from the steward was only a foretaste of the slights she'd experience in the royal court. Already, she feared her visit was futile.

Zna-yat took her aside after she had settled in. "I smelled your anger when that washavoki spoke. What did it say?"

"Words without meaning. Washavokis call them 'lies.'"

"These 'lies' are cloaks, I think," said Zna-yat. "They're meant to hide meaning."

"You're right," said Dar. "Yet few urkzimmuthi understand this. Washavoki great mother had rooms for us in palace, yet her washavoki said she did not."

"So it spoke 'lie.' Yet you saw beneath that cloak."

"Hai. Washavoki great mother doesn't welcome us, yet wishes us to think she does."

"Hence, your anger."

"I believe she fears us because Bah Simi counsels her with 'lies.' Perhaps I can make her understand that."

"I think that will be difficult," said Zna-yat. "Every time I guarded her, I smelled fear. Even before Bah Simi came."

"Still, I must try. Not all washavokis are cruel."

Zna-yat said nothing, but he thought, *Most are.*

When women brought food to the barracks, Dar served it. The single course consisted of porridge, and Dar perceived another insult in the meager meal. She suspected that the orcs did not feel slighted, so she said nothing. As Dar ladled out the porridge, she recalled her terror on the first night she served orcs. It felt like lifetimes ago. *Now I'm their muthuri.* Dar spoke with motherly affection to every son she served, thanking him for his loyalty and sacrifice. She spoke at greater length to those she knew personally. When she saw Garga-tok she asked, "Where's your cape with washavoki ears?"

"I still have it," he replied, "but I wear it not. Zna-yat says it frightens washavokis."

Dar grinned. "My brother is wise."

When she saw Magtha-jan, she said, "Muth-jan sends her love." Then she showed him the golden pendant that Muth-jan had helped to make.

When she saw Kovok-mah, she said, "I haven't seen you until now." Dar refrained from asking where he'd been, for she suspected he'd been avoiding her and knew he could only speak truth. "After eating," she said, "we must speak again."

Kovok-mah bowed his head. "Hai, Muth Mauk."

When Dar had served everyone, she sat down to her meal. The porridge was bland, but the company was good, and she ate contentedly. Afterward, Dar approached

Kovok-mah. "Come walk with me. I wish to know more of your meeting with washavoki great mother."

Kovok-mah bowed and rose. Dar grabbed her cloak and headed for the door. Kovok-mah followed. Snowflakes drifted down on a dark garrison that appeared deserted. Dar and Kovok-mah walked between the rows of empty barracks as Dar made inquiries about Kovok-mah's impressions of Queen Girta, Bah Simi, and the Queen's Men. Kovok-mah's observations were precise, but they gave Dar few insights into the intrigues within the palace. Kovok-mah was as naive about conspiracies as any child.

When Dar had learned everything she could, she grasped Kovok-mah's hand and pulled him toward an empty barracks. He quietly followed her into the dark building. "Sit," she said. Kovok-mah sat cross-legged on the dirt floor and Dar knelt in his lap so they were face-to-face. She reached out and softly brushed her fingertips over his cheek. "You've been much in my thoughts," she whispered.

"You dwell in my chest," replied Kovok-mah, his voice quiet with longing.

"And you in mine." Dar threw her arms around him as her lips sought his. There was only a moment's hesitation before he returned her kiss.

Dar's head swam with pent-up passion. The fervent way Kovok-mah returned her embrace and kisses heightened her feeling. *I taught him how to kiss*, Dar thought, *and he taught me how to love*. Dar's ecstasy lasted only briefly. Then Kovok-mah gently pushed her away. He spoke in a pained, husky whisper. "Dargu, we mustn't."

Dar knew he was right. That realization was as bleak as any she had experienced. She also saw Kovok-mah's restraint as proof of his devotion.

"Just hold me, then," said Dar. "I'm queen. Don't I deserve some happiness?"

Kovok-mah tenderly enfolded Dar within his arms. "You deserve more than some, yet I can give you only sorrow."

"That sorrow isn't your gift. It's your muthuri's."

"I must obey her wisdom, though I understand it not."

"There's none to understand," said Dar, "but that doesn't alter our law." Tears welled in her eyes as she struggled not to cry.

Kovok-mah held Dar, all the while wondering if even that meager solace endangered her. The scent of their atur was thick in the cold, dark building. *Muth la must forgive us*, he thought. *We've struggled so hard to behave properly.* He gently wiped away Dar's tears, which still seemed novel to him. "We can't see how things will end," he whispered. "We may be together yet."

Dar attempted a smile, knowing that Kovok-mah could see it in the dark, and lightly kissed his forehead. "Then hope must make us happy."

The cold soon drove Dar from the abandoned barracks back to the warmth where her sister and mintaris waited. She had no doubt her scent betrayed her feelings, but she was equally certain everyone was already aware of them. She went to sleep soon after her return, calming herself with a fantasy in which Kath-mah changed heart and blessed Dar's union with her son.

A messenger arrived the following morning with an invitation to Queen Girta's feast, which would commence prior to sunset. Dar spent the morning with her mintaris and her sister, trying to prepare them for the evening ahead. Nagtha-yat was extremely helpful, for he understood what washavoki customs would seem most bizarre to the urkzimmuthi. He told them that washavokis prized their weapons and wearing a sword within a hall wasn't considered rude. Dar added that she wanted her mintaris to wear theirs. Nagtha-yat also warned that drink at the banquet would be like falfhissi, though it would taste different. "Washavokis seldom bathe," he cautioned. "Their stench will likely kill your appetites. Yet eat something. It's considered impolite not to do so."

Zna-yat bowed. "Muth Mauk, why do you wish us to come? Only Kovok-mah and Nagtha-yat will understand what is spoken."

"Queen Girta will surround herself with washavokis," replied Dar. "I want to be surrounded by my kind. I'm proud of you and wish to see you honored."

"Will washavokis honor us?" asked Zna-yat.

"They should," replied Dar. "If they don't, they'll reveal their hidden thoughts."

Zna-yat bowed. "I see your wisdom."

Dar and the others spent the afternoon preparing for the feast. First they bathed. Among orcs, both sexes usually bathed together, though the bathing pool was far too small to accommodate all Dar's party at once. Kovok-mah avoided washing while Dar was present. After bathing, Dar and Nir-yat braided each other's hair. They chewed washuthahi seeds to blacken their teeth. Dar applied talmauki to her nails. She also colored her nipples with it, even though her shirt would cover them. As the sun neared the horizon, Dar dressed in her royal raiment. She wore high boots beneath her long neva and a shirt beneath her talmauki kefs. It was dark green, a shade that complemented her kefs and set off the large golden pendant. The ornament was as heavy as it was impressive and Dar donned it only at the last moment. The headband that covered her brand and her crown, a simple gold circlet, completed Dar's outfit.

Nir-yat wore a rust-colored neva with matching kefs, high boots, and a deep maroon shirt. Dar's mintaris were all identically garbed in white wool robes that ended at the knees. Dar chose white to contrast with the Queen's

Men's black. The robes were sleeveless, and short capes covered the sons' bare arms. Their sword belts and scabbards, contrary to orcish custom, were not treated as mere tools but as articles of attire. Their leather was not only dyed a shade of burgundy, but polished as well. All the sons wore matching burgundy boots.

When everyone was ready, they donned their cloaks and followed Dar into the city. People gathered along the streets to watch Dar and her procession march to the palace gates. Her dignity and bearing made an impression, as did her costly pendant and her formidable escort. The onlookers gazed silently, and when Dar glanced into their eyes, she saw a range of emotions. There was awe and respect, but there was also an abundance of fear and hostility.

Queen Girta was informed of the nature of Dar's retinue and kept posted on its progress through the city. When Dar approached the palace gates, Girta sent Lokung to meet her. She gazed out a window and watched her steward cross the snowy courtyard. A short while later, he crossed it again, still alone. He soon arrived, out of breath from climbing stairs. "Where's Dar?" asked the queen.

"Your Majesty, I told her of your welcome and then stated that the banquet was for her alone."

"And?"

"She replied that she was unaware tonight's occasion was an intimate dinner between two monarchs."

"Did you tell her that it's indeed a feast?"

"Yes, Your Majesty," said Lokung. "She said, in that case, she would extend courtesy in kind and bid you journey to her hall to dine alone among her followers. After that, she stated that she expected royal treatment for both her and her retinue. Then she added that if she did not receive it, she would withdraw her guards and leave."

"How did you reply?"

"In truth, Your Majesty, I was dumbfounded by her insolence. Then she said that if none could speak the Orcish tongue, I should address your orc guards myself and say these words 'Futh Muth Mauk pahak sutuk. Kutuk ma,' and then lead them to her."

Girta turned to General Kol. "Do you understand that Orcish?"

"Not entirely," said Kol. " 'Muth Mauk' means Great Mother and 'sutuk' means 'come.' I think 'Kutuk ma' is 'Follow me.' "

Girta addressed her steward. "Then say those words to my orc guards, so I'll be rid of them."

"No!" said Kol a little too loudly, adding "Your Majesty" only as an afterthought. Apparently chagrined by his outburst, he bowed humbly to the queen. "Pardon my ferventness, but I fear that would play into Dar's hands. Wouldn't it be better to feast her and discover her mind?"

Girta sighed. "Even if that means receiving all her brutes?"

"The Queen's Men will keep a watchful eye. You'll be safe, I promise."

When the palace gates opened, Dar was uncertain who would appear—hostile soldiers, two dismissed orc guards, or Girta's mealymouthed steward. Though she would have preferred to avoid the banquet, she was relieved to see the steward rather than soldiers. *The game's still on*, she thought.

Lokung bowed low. "My humblest apologies, Your Majesty. Poor fool that I am, I misspoke my queen's words. Of course she wished to honor all your party. I will lead you and them to the banquet hall."

Dar suppressed a smile at the steward's blatant lie. "I'm pleased she caught your error. Lead the way."

While working in the palace kitchen, Dar had brought

food to the banquet hall, but she had reached it by the hidden servant passageway. She had never entered the large and opulent hall via its grand doorway. As she stepped through the carved and gilded portal, Lokung called out in a booming voice, "Muth Mauk, Queen of the Orcs, and Friend and Ally to Our Gracious Majesty!"

The room was filled with people, and all of them turned their eyes toward Dar. Dar returned their gaze and quickly spotted Girta standing in the most prominent spot. Next to her was a man dressed in black and gold. Dar recognized him. *Murdant Kol!* Then she corrected herself. *General Kol, the Queen's Man.*

Dar knew Kol would be at the banquet, but that didn't lessen her reaction. She felt a jolt of fear and rage. Her face flushed red as anger got the upper hand. All the orcs smelled it and glanced at her. Dar took a deep breath to compose herself. Only when she looked outwardly calm did she meet Kol's eyes. They were as inscrutable as ever. Dar headed toward Girta, walking gracefully and forcing herself to smile.

Girta smiled back even less sincerely than Dar. "Muth Mauk," she said. "You look miraculously well, considering you were dying when I saw you last."

"Such is the power of the World's Mother," replied Dar. "It seems she had more plans for me."

"I'm delighted by your recovery," said Girta. "As is General Kol. I believe you two have met."

"We have," replied Dar. "General, has your shoulder healed?"

Kol's face darkened, but his expression and voice remained calm. "It has. So kind of you to ask."

"Your Majesty," said Dar. "Let me introduce my sister, Nir-yat." She turned and said, "Sutat, Muthana, tep tavat washavoki nathmauki." *Come, Sister, and greet washavoki queen.*

Nir-yat advanced and bowed. "Grut-tinz, Grat Muther."

"Greetings," replied Girta. She gave Dar a puzzled look. "How did you acquire an orcish sister?"

"The urkzimmuthi know magic that transforms one's spirit. It's called 'theemuth,' which means 'rebirth.' A mother underwent this magic with me, making me her child. Her children became my siblings. I also have a brother here."

"So you changed yourself through sorcery?" asked Girta.

"Rebirth is unlike the magic once practiced here."

"Yet, as I recall, Othar was slain by magic," said Girta.

"That was his magic, not mine."

"So you don't practice sorcery yourself," said Girta. "You only benefit from it."

Dar chose not to respond, and instead introduced her mintaris. Each greeted the queen by reciting the phrase he had memorized, except for Kovok-mah and Nagtha-yat, who were fluent in the human tongue. Their greetings were more eloquent. Nagtha-yat told Girta that he had visited the palace during the reign of Kregant I and praised the old monarch's love for peace. Kovok-mah expressed a hope that friendship would follow understanding.

Girta didn't reciprocate by introducing members of her court. Dar feigned to be oblivious of the slight. An awkward silence followed until Dar decided to bait Kol. "So, Queen's Man, how does a murdant become a general in only three moons? That must be a tale worth hearing."

"The Queen's Man was a tolum when he first came to court," said Girta.

"A rise equally astonishing," answered Dar. "When I last knew him, he was but a murdant and meek as a mouse before Tolum Karg."

Kol glared at Dar, but said nothing.

"Oh don't be bashful, Murdant," said Dar. "You've cleaned up well. If only Loral and Neena could see you now! They'd feel honored that you had tupped them."

Kol's face reddened but he remained silent.

"You'll gain nothing by bringing up your past," said Girta. "General Kol has told me your history."

Dar laughed. "I'm sure he has, and I blush to imagine the nature of his lies. He once lied to me as well, saying his only wish was to protect me. Has he told you that, too?"

"I see a crown hasn't changed your slattern's nature," said Kol, his voice cold, yet clearly angry.

Dar grinned. "Why, Murdant, court life has made you soft. You used to hide your feelings better. I believed your claim that you spared your daughter. But perhaps drowning her didn't upset you."

"Don't malign my friend," said Girta.

"Friend?" replied Dar. "Your Majesty, beware of such friends. An adder charms the bird before it strikes."

Thirty-four

The rest of the evening was as dreadful as Dar had expected. Queen Girta interrupted Dar and Kol's sparring by taking her place at the head table. Dar was seated to the left of the queen, who ignored her throughout the meal to dote on her son. He sat to Girta's right. General Kol's place was next to the prince, obviously a position of honor. A military man, who introduced himself as General Voltar, sat to Dar's left. He seemed principally interested in getting drunk as quickly as possible, a feat he readily accomplished.

It had been a long time since Dar had dined among a crowd of humans, and she found their odor nauseating. Girta, resplendent in a gown of scarlet and gold, had a musky scent with fishy overtones. General Voltar reeked like spoiled meat. Nevertheless, Dar forced herself to eat. She drank sparingly of the wine, knowing that she'd better keep her wits about her. Being deprived of meaningful conversation, Dar used her powers of observation to learn what she could.

The first person who drew her attention was the prince. He was still a child—Dar guessed he was perhaps eight—but he seemed to be trying to act a man. Like General Kol, he was dressed in black and gold, though his attire had more gold in it. The similarity of the prince's and the general's apparel bothered Dar, for she thought it was intentional. Kol's closeness with the future monarch disturbed her more. Watching Kol and the boy chat easily together, it was evident they were on very good terms. In comparison, Girta seemed slighted by her son.

The queen impressed Dar as insecure. *I think I frighten her*, she thought. *I fear to think what Kol's been telling her.* Queen Girta's mood seemed reflected in her court. Dar had only glimpsed one royal banquet when she served in the palace, but she recalled it as different from the present feast. For one thing, it was better-attended and the diners were livelier. One aspect hadn't changed: Though the mage was gone, a black-garbed figure still sat at the head table. It seemed to Dar that Kol's personality influenced the court as much as Othar's had. *He has power. I can see it in the way others look at him.*

None of Dar's party had been seated at the head table. They sat together in isolation. It was another slight, but Dar suspected they were happier with the arrangement. She felt sorry for them as they stoically picked at their food, and she wished the "festivities" would soon be over. As the meal wound down, Dar waited until Kol was engaged with the prince, then gently grasped Girta's hand. The queen started, but Dar held firm.

"I fear this pomp-filled night has made a poor beginning to our relations," said Dar. "Yet know I long for peace and think your safety is its best assurance. Can I meet with you tomorrow? I wish to speak to you, woman-to-woman, without the General present. I'll open my heart so you might see my intentions."

Girta tried to pull her hand away. "Please!" said Dar. "I'll come alone."

"All right," said Girta, her voice betraying her reluctance. "Come at noon. Alone."

Dar bowed as she released Girta's hand. "Thank you, Your Majesty. You'll be glad you agreed."

                    *   *   *

The banquet ended soon after Dar spoke to Girta. There was a formal exchange of courtesies between the monarchs at the night's conclusion, but no further conversation. All Dar's hopes centered on the next day's meeting. When she departed the palace, she was as uncertain about the future as when she arrived.

Dar walked through Taiben's empty streets until she reached the town's gates. They were closed for the night, but the Queen's Men opened them to let her and the orcs pass. Once she was outside the city walls, Dar breathed in the clean air and sighed. "I'm glad that's over," she said.

"How were you received?" asked Zna-yat.

"Fearfully," replied Dar. "Queen's fear is what I must overcome."

"How?" asked Zna-yat.

"I'll meet alone with her."

"Is that safe?" asked Kovok-mah.

"You'll be alone," said Zna-yat, "but washavoki queen will not. Our last great mother was imprisoned in that palace."

"I sense timidity in washavoki queen," said Dar, "but not . . ." She paused; she wanted to say "treachery," but there was no Orcish word for it. ". . . not cruelty. I think I'll be safe."

It was a cold night, and Dar quickly focused on reaching the warmth of the barracks. She didn't notice the man standing outside the city walls. He remained motionless beneath his cloak, but he was watching her intently. He did nothing until Dar and the orcs entered the garrison; then he hurried after them.

The orcs in the barracks were eager to hear how the evening had gone. Dar removed her boots, gold pendant, and shirt, then sat cross-legged near the hearth to recount the banquet. Her audience had a poor appreciation of innuendo, so she skipped over her sparring with Kol. She was relating how General Voltar had passed out during dinner when a knock on the door interrupted her. When an orc went to answer it, Dar noted that he took his ax.

Sevren stood outside. He had the look of one who couldn't quite believe what he was seeing, and Dar remembered that the last time they had spoken she said she'd been given poison. Sevren bowed deeply. "Tava, Muth Mauk. Ther lat." *Greetings, Great Mother. You live.*

"Fasak Muth la vashak tha, Sevren." *May Muth la bless you, Sevren.* "Hai, mer lav." *Yes, I live.*

Sevren continued to speak in Orcish. "May I come? I wish speaking."

"Please enter," said Dar.

Sevren bowed and stepped through the doorway, all the while resolutely keeping his gaze from Dar's breasts. "I thought urkzimmuthi kill you. I was very sad."

"I live because they are wise and good. You should not be surprised."

"You always surprise me."

"This washavoki is Sevren," said Dar to all present. "He saved my life and aided our former queen. He's our friend." Then she introduced her mintaris to Sevren before asking, "Why have you come?"

"I see thing you should know," replied Sevren.

"What?"

"Othar lives."

The orcs called the mage the Black Washavoki, not Othar, but they understood the news was grave by the scent of fear it evoked from Dar. She stared at Sevren, stunned. "Are you certain?"

"I wish politeness," replied Sevren. "But I speak more good Washavoki."

Dar switched to the human tongue. "How can he be

alive? You saw what happened to him. He was charred to a crisp."

"Someone in Taiben is practicing sorcery of the deepest kind. Folks' spirits are enslaved, so they're governed by another's will. They become heedless of their welfare or even their lives. I caught a lass so afflicted."

"But why do you think Othar's the sorcerer? Have you seen him?"

"Only a shadow. Yet the sorcerer seemed crippled and Othar lost both his hands and feet. Moreover, his body is missing from the pit."

"Does Girta know this?"

"Nay. From all I hear, she believes he's dead."

"So she's unaffected."

"I'm na so sure," said Sevren. "There've been strange happenings at court. I have a friend among the Queen's Men, and he says there's been a rash of deaths. Suicides, accidents, and murders—all seemingly unrelated. Yet they've cleared a path for one man."

"Kol?" asked Dar.

"Aye. 'Tis him."

Dar shook her head as if trying to break free from a nightmare. "But Othar can't be alive," she said. "When I threw those magic bones into the fire, he . . ."

"Changed," said Sevren.

Dar's hairs rose as she recalled Muth-goth's vision. *She said the bones were not gone, only changed. And Velasapah warned of the bones in Muth la's Dome.* "So what do you think happened?"

"I know little of magic," said Sevren, "but I recall Othar's sorcery turned on him once before. His face was blasted, yet he lived. Perhaps it was likewise when you burnt the bones."

"Those bones had power," said Dar. "I could feel it. Burning them might have only released it. But if their power went to Othar, why is he hiding? If he can take spirits, why hasn't he taken Girta's?"

"That girl I caught looked and acted strange," replied Sevren, "and the magic quickly killed her. A dead queen would be of little use."

"But you think he's the power behind Kol? That's a fearful thought. To what purpose?"

"I do na know," said Sevren. "And to tell the truth, until I learned you were alive, I did na care. I only questioned my friend this morning."

Dar remembered that only Kovok-mah and Nagthayat could follow her conversation with Sevren, so she spoke to the orcs in their language. "Sevren thinks Black Washavoki didn't die and is still working against us."

"Then you shouldn't go alone into Taiben," said Zna-yat.

"Brother," said Dar in a gentle voice, "since when do sons tell mothers what to do? Especially great mothers?"

"I'm sorry, Muth Mauk, but I had to speak my chest. What good are wisdom and bravery against magic? I'm frightened for you."

"I'm frightened also," said Dar. "Yet what use is great mother who can't face our enemies? Washavoki queen must be warned, for her danger will quickly become ours."

"I understood all Sevren said," said Kovok-mah, "yet I'm not certain Black Washavoki lives."

Dar turned to Sevren and spoke in the human tongue. "He has a point. You have no proof that Othar's alive. I doubt Girta will believe me."

"I'll find that proof. I offered you my service once before, and I offer it again. Let me be your agent inside Taiben."

"Sorcerers are dangerous quarry," said Dar. "Your offer's gallant."

"And sincere." Sevren smiled. "Even if it's from a washavoki."

"And I accept it."

"I think Zna-yat's right about visiting the palace," said Sevren. "It's too perilous, especially if Kol's Othar's man."

"I'm still going. It seems worth the risk to talk privately with Girta."

"And what if Othar's waiting for you?"

Dar had to admit it was a possibility. *Othar has good reason to seek revenge.* Nevertheless, Dar suspected that the mage—if he was indeed alive—would be involved in more grandiose schemes than mere vengeance. *If that's true, he won't reveal himself by attacking me. At least, not yet.* "I think I'm safe awhile. It's your job to warn me if I'm not."

"How will I do that?"

"I'm supposed to meet Girta at noon. Find me on the road to the palace if I shouldn't."

"You're not giving me a lot of time."

"I'm giving you all I have."

Sevren made his way to the sally port in the city's wall and knocked on its stout ironclad door. "Open up, Valamar, it's me."

There was the sound of a bolt sliding, and then the door swung open, revealing a short, dark tunnel. Sevren stepped inside it, and his friend closed and bolted the door. "Well," said Valamar, "did you see her?"

"Aye."

"And did she believe your daft story?"

"She wants more proof."

"And how in Karm's name will you get that? Supposing you're right; the moment you get near that man, he'll take your spirit."

"That beggar knew something was going on. I bet

others do, too. This town ignores its poor, but I suspect they've been hard hit. Those thieves aren't courtiers. Think of that unfortunate girl."

"It sounds like stirring up trouble to me," said Valamar.

"It's been stirred already. Best look to the pot afore it boils over."

Thirty-five

♛

As soon as the city's gates opened, Sevren headed for the squalid dwellings outside Taiben's walls. He didn't expect to be welcomed, and he wasn't. His sword and official standing marked him as an outsider and an enemy. Though his inquiries received hostile evasions, Sevren noted a disquiet that wasn't provoked by his presence. He glimpsed fear in people's eyes, and many of the shanties appeared recently abandoned.

After numerous fruitless encounters, Sevren knocked on yet another door. It was unbarred and swung open with the blow from his fist. Sevren peeked inside, expecting to find an empty room. Instead, he spied a worn-looking woman, bundled in rags, shivering in the dark interior. "Mother, are you all right?" he asked.

"Nothin' the Dark Path won't fix."

"You want for a fire. 'Tis a cold morn. Can I help start one?"

"I want fer a son, but mine's been took. Can ye get me 'nother?"

"Nay, but . . ."

"Then fire won't help. It's all Tug's fault. Nuggle's, too."

Sevren decided to play the fool. "Did they take your son?"

"Robbed the dead, they did. Stirred up somethin' best let be."

"What did they stir up?"

The old woman glanced about fearfully. "Don't know. If ye see it, ye're took."

"See what?"

"Nuggle brought it here. Took my Thom, it did."

"He brought it from the corpse pit?"

"Aye."

"Is it still here?"

"Nay. 'Tis gone. They say to town."

"Is Nuggle here?"

"Dead. So's my Thom. Ye don't last long, once ye're took."

"Thank you, Mother. I'll be back."

"Why? There's no point."

Sevren went to pull some wood from an abandoned shack so he could make a fire for the woman. He realized the futility of his effort, but he did it anyway. When he had a small blaze going, with some extra wood to feed it, he thanked the woman again before departing. She said nothing, and seemed no happier than when he had found her.

Sevren headed back to town, reviewing what he had learned. The sorcerer had come from the corpse pit, so it had to be Othar. He had stayed awhile in the shantytown, seizing spirits, before moving to Taiben. Sevren realized that most would dismiss the old woman's talk as madness. *I still lack proof.* He wondered if any was obtainable. The nature of Othar's power seemed to eliminate eyewitnesses. Sevren briefly imagined his fate if he had encountered the mage inside one of the shacks. The thought made him shiver.

Sevren wondered where Othar had gone. The palace was a possibility, but its gates were always guarded. That would prevent Othar from coming and going without notice. It seemed more likely that the mage was staying outside the royal walls. It occurred to Sevren that the sorcerer wouldn't seize the spirit of whoever sheltered him, for that would quickly kill his host. That meant Othar was someone's guest. Sevren speculated on why anyone would shelter the mage. Fear was a likely reason, but Sevren suspected Othar provided inducements as well. With loot from his thieves and the power to eliminate a man's enemies, he had plenty of those.

Sevren reasoned that Othar was most likely staying with someone rich and powerful. *But who?* Sevren thought of a man who might provide a clue and headed for the municipal barracks. The chief of the municipal guard was a genial man who knew all the wealthy men who funded the force. He was also a gossip and fond of a morning ale. Sevren sought him out and found him in the guards' common room.

"Well met, Furtag," said Sevren. "Just the man I want to see. I have woman trouble. Mayhap you can help me."

Furtag chuckled. "There's no cure for that kind o' trouble short o' gelding."

"I hope you know a gentler physic. Let me stand you for a mug as we talk it over."

Furtag readily agreed and went with Sevren to a nearby tavern. There, Sevren told him that he was seeing a wench with a son she wished to become a servant. "She wants him a master with rising fortunes," said Sevren. He flashed a bawdy smile. "She says she'll please me if I please her."

"Well, Balten's star is surely rising. He became master o' the Merchants' Guild after Maltus jumped from the wall." Then Furtag lowered his voice. "But tell the lad to keep away."

"Why?"

"Balten goes through help too quick."

"They leave because he's harsh?"

Furtag spoke in a whisper. "They die." Then he added,

"Ye didn't hear that from me." Sevren shot him a puzzled look, and Furtag responded with a shrug. "Things happen, but they happen often." Then he spoke in a normal voice. "Tumbar's a good master, and I heard he's looking for some help. He dwells on the Street o' Woodshapers."

Sevren grinned. "Thank you, Furtag. I'm sure my wench will be well pleased."

Furtag returned his grin. "Then I hope she pleases well."

Zna-yat pleaded to accompany Dar to the palace gates. Initially, she resisted the idea, thinking it would make a better impression if she came without an escort. But after she relented, Dar was glad she did. The idea of the mage lurking somewhere terrified her, and she was certain Zna-yat smelled her fear as they walked the winding streets. Dar kept a sharp eye out for Sevren, but he didn't show.

The palace gates were shut and guarded when Dar arrived. After Zna-yat left, she spoke to one of the Queen's Men. "I have a private audience with Queen Girta. Take me to her."

"I've had no word of this," replied the man.

"That's because it's a privy meeting. Your queen will confirm this."

The man looked dubious, but escorted Dar through the gates and into the palace. There, he spoke to Lokung, who seemed equally surprised. The steward led Dar to a closed doorway and bade her wait while he entered it alone. He returned shortly. "Our Majesty will see you."

Dar entered a room that featured a large window overlooking the courtyard. She bowed. "Queen Girta, thank you for seeing me. I'm glad for this meeting. We have much in common."

"We do?"

"Mothers prize peace, while men often favor war."

"First you became an orc. Are you now a mother also?"

"The urkzimmuthi consider all women mothers," said Dar.

"A quaint idea."

"Quaint or not, it's true. And because mothers bring forth life, they're loath to take it."

"That's very high-sounding, but why are you here?"

"I fear for your safety."

"I feel safe enough," said Girta.

"Feeling safe can be safety's opposite. An unwary victim is easily slain."

"I know what you're going to say. You're here to warn me of General Kol. He told me you would."

"I know he's your friend, but if you value peace, why take advice from a general? War's his profession. And why let him mold your son into the late king's image?"

Girta's face reddened. "Leave the prince out of this!"

"I don't wish to upset you, but when I saw your son, I was struck by his sword and military attire. It also seemed the General was overclose with him."

"The boy's lost his father."

"A bloodthirsty father who taunted me by saying 'Women lack the stomach for war.' Does General Kol think differently?"

"He does. The General wants only to protect me and my son."

"Once, he promised me protection."

"And you betrayed him for an orc."

Sensing the futility of her argument, Dar chose another tack. "Before Kol arrived, did you have other confidants? Men and women whose judgment you trusted?"

"I did."

"What happened to them?"

"It's been a hard winter," replied Queen Girta. "There have been many tragedies."

"All random—or so it *seems*."

Girta regarded Dar suspiciously. "What are you trying to say?"

"Don't all those deaths have one thing in common? Weren't all who died special friends to you?"

"No," replied Girta. "General Zam and I weren't close, and Lord Targ was no friend."

"Did they oppose Kol?"

"Surely you can't believe that . . ."

"I believe there's a hidden hand at work. I don't have . . ." The door opened, halting Dar in midsentence.

Girta smiled. "General Kol, you should listen to this."

Dar's face flushed. "You said we'd talk privately."

"This is just coincidence," replied Girta. "I kept this meeting to myself, not knowing its purpose. Yet now that I do, I'm glad for this happenstance. The General is entitled to defend himself." She turned to Kol. "Dar claims you inspire accidents and suicides."

Kol grinned. "She does? I must be quite a fellow—soldier by day and mage by night."

"Well," Girta said to Dar. "Continue."

"There's no point," replied Dar. "You won't believe me, so I won't risk my life."

Kol's grin broadened. "Risk your life? Does Your Majesty believe I'll run you through? My skin's thicker than you think. It's true we're not fond, but I won't harm you."

Dar sighed dramatically. "I'm leaving, though I do so reluctantly. Girta, one day you'll see this meeting as a lost chance. I fear it'll be a bitter insight."

"I doubt it," said Girta.

After Dar departed, Kol gave Girta a puzzled look. "What was that about?"

"You were wrong about Dar," said Girta.

"How so?"

"She's not as clever as you think. She told me that you

want war so badly that you've killed everyone who stood in its way."

Kol put on an amused expression. "And how, pray tell, did I do that?"

"Oh, she left that part out. She also said you're turning the prince into his father."

"I wouldn't besmirch the dead, but my feelings about your husband mirror yours."

"Oh well, I'm pleased Dar's gone," said Girta. "Now that we know her ploy, can we get rid of those dreadful orcs?"

"My guess is Dar will recall them herself, now that you've outsmarted her." Kol gazed out the window to watch Dar cross the courtyard. "I almost feel sorry for her. A lifetime among orcs!"

Girta shuddered. "What a dreary prospect!"

"I should have a Queen's Man see her safely to the garrison," said Kol. "Her crown is gold, and we wouldn't want her to meet with some mischance."

"You're a good man, General. Too bad Dar doesn't see that."

Thirty-six

♕

Dar strode down Taiben's streets in a black mood. *That woman's a simpleton!* she thought. *Kol has her completely fooled.* Dar resolved to revoke the treaty, withdraw the orc guards, and seal the pass. *If washavokis come raiding, we'll make them pay! Better for sons to defend their halls, than some ingrate!* Dar was considering pulling out that very afternoon, when she heard someone running. She turned and spied a Queen's Man dashing after her. Before Dar could run, her pursuer halted and bowed. "Your Majesty," he said between gasping breaths, "I've a message for you."

"What it is?"

" 'Tis a privy matter."

Dar suspected a trap. "Yet I'll hear it in this public place. Whisper it."

The black-garbed man bowed again and approached to whisper in Dar's ear. "My queen bids me tell you that she spoke as she did only from fear of spies. She knows you're a true friend. General Kol oppresses her, and she's desperate."

"I'm relieved she knows her danger," whispered Dar. "How can I help?"

"She'd like to discuss that in a secure place."

"Where?"

"She has one remaining trusted friend, the master of the Merchants' Guild. His name is Balten. You can meet safely in his house."

"When?"

"At morrow noon."

"Tell her I'll be there," whispered Dar. "And say she shouldn't abandon hope. Kol is clever, but I've bested him before."

"May Karm bless Your Majesty. This news will bring joy." Then the messenger turned and hurried away. Dar headed for the garrison, her hope rekindled.

After his man reported Dar's reply, Kol turned to Gorm. "Soon, your master will have the war he desires and revenge as well. When Dar arrives at Balten's house, he need only seize her mind and force her to slay the queen at tomorrow's banquet."

Gorm nodded approvingly. "Afterward, we want Dar captured, not slain."

"Naturally. Why spoil the fun?"

"When she's done the murder, I'll withdraw Othar's spell."

"You can do that?" asked Kol.

"I can't enslave minds," replied Gorm, "but I can free them. Dar will awake and find herself standing bloody-handed over Girta's corpse. She'll have no idea how she got there."

"That should make things interesting."

"Interesting indeed," replied Gorm. "She'll be fully aware when she's executed."

"Burning's the penalty for treason," said Kol. "Othar will appreciate that."

"Especially if it's done slowly."

"I'll see that it is." Kol grinned malevolently. "*Very* slowly. Mayhap, we can burn some piss eyes first. I'd love to roast that green-eyed one and the piss eye bitch that Dar calls sister. It'd warm the soldiers' blood for the invasion."

"And the prince? Any problems there?"

"None. He already yearns for glory, and soon he'll have his mother to avenge. Restraint's not for the young; he'll make a bloody king. And I'll play his obedient general."

"Until you succeed him."

Kol smiled. "I have my ambitions."

"We'll want the kingdom continually at war."

"You can rely on it."

Gorm returned Kol's smile. "We always have."

When Dar arrived at the garrison, Sevren was already there. She could tell that he had news, but he patiently waited while she spoke with her mintaris. He listened in, following her Orcish as best he could. Afterward, he asked in the human tongue, "Who's Bah Simi?"

"That's our name for Kol."

"And Girta knows he's her enemy?"

"Yes. That's why she couldn't speak freely. Tomorrow, we'll meet in a safer place."

"Where?"

"Outside the palace in the House of Balten."

"Nay!" said Sevren. "That's where Othar's hiding."

Dar grew pale. "Then the meeting's a trap?"

"Aye, for certain. From what I've learned, one glimpse from Othar will seal your doom," said Sevren. "Your spirit will be his."

Dar shuddered. "What else have you learned?"

"The sorcerer came from the corpse pit, so it has to be Othar. Grave robbers brought him out, most likely after he had taken their spirits. Later, Othar moved into town. I'm certain Balten's sheltering him. I've made inquiries. Balten benefited from a suicide and has prospered ever since. Yet his servants drop like autumn flies."

"I wonder who laid this trap?" said Dar, thinking out loud. "Girta or Kol? Either one could have sent that message."

"You can na go either way, so it makes na difference."

"It *does* make a difference. If Kol sent that message, he's playing with Girta like he played with me. He'll pounce when he's ready."

"Seems to me, it'll serve her right."

"No it won't," Dar said, envisioning Girta being driven into Kol's clutches as Othar killed off her friends, one by one. The image persuaded her of the queen's innocence. *The trap is Kol's doing. Girta's his prey, just as I once was.* Dar's pique toward the queen turned to sympathy. "We must save her."

"How? Mayhap, she does na want saving."

"I can't go to Girta, so she must come to me."

"She will na do that," said Sevren.

"Not willingly," said Dar. "But if I'm right, she'll thank me in the end."

"You do na mean to kidnap her!"

"Why not?"

"It'll start a war if things go wrong."

"If Kol gets his way, then war's inevitable. This is our only hope of stopping it."

" 'Tis a daft idea."

"You asked to be my agent, not my counselor. Will you help or not?"

Sevren sighed. "What do you need?"

"Women's clothes. Warm ones—a gown, boots, and a cloak. When we grab Girta tonight, we won't have time to dress her."

"Both the town and palace gates will be shut and guarded. How will you get her out?"

"By the same ways we used when the orc queen escaped."

"The Queen's Men watch them now. You'll be trapped in Taiben."

Dar thought for a moment. "We'll get her out," she said. "You just do your part."

Sevren gave an exaggerated bow. "Hai, Muth Mauk. I'll return at dawn." With that, he departed on his errand.

Dar told her mintaris they must get the washavoki queen away from Bah Simi. Then she discussed how to achieve that goal. Two shifts of orcs guarded Girta. A daytime pair stood watch while the city gates were open and were relieved just before they closed. Dar decided that one of the night guards would take the queen from her bedchamber before the palace rose at dawn.

Zna-yat raised the first problem. "We stand alone outside queen's door, but somehow washavokis watch us. They're close, for I hear and smell them."

"I have also," said one of the orc guards. "Wood covers wall opposite washavoki queen's door. There is much carving in it, but there is also small hole in its pattern. Eye peers from it."

"Is there just one looking-hole in wall?" asked Dar.

"Hai, only one," replied the guard.

"Then if one son stands in front of it, washavoki can't see queen's door," said Dar. "Other son might enter it."

"Then what?" asked Kovok-mah.

"Queen must be taken from room. Remember hidden way we took to reach Black Washavoki's tower?" asked Dar, referring to the passageway that allowed servants to move about unseen.

"I remember it," said Kovok-mah.

"At night, washavokis don't use it," said Dar.

"I don't think Quengirta will be willing to go," said Zna-yat. "She fears us."

The orcs had no word for "kidnap," and the idea was alien to them. Dar had difficulty conveying how a mother could be taken against her will. She described in detail how Girta would have to be gagged, bound, bundled up, and carried away. When Dar finished, she could see that the orcs were uneasy with the idea. Regardless, she never doubted they would obey her.

After Girta was secured, one of her abductors would have to carry her through the servant passageway to the palace kitchen, which had exits to the courtyard. Under the cover of darkness, the queen would be taken to the stables. Zna-yat suggested placing her in the latrine set aside for orcs, since washavokis never used it. Dar agreed that Girta should be hidden there until the city gates opened and the orc guards were changed. The departing orcs would retrieve Girta. One orc would strap her to the other's back. Then, hiding her beneath his cloak, he would sneak her through the gates.

Every step involved risks that could easily result in disaster. Dar gambled that Girta could be quickly enlightened about Kol and Othar's schemes and returned to the palace before she was discovered missing. If that could happen, the outcome would be worth the perils it required.

Having determined the basic plan, Dar and the orcs refined its details. Dar described the servant passageway that she had used while serving in the palace. Zna-yat and Kovok-mah volunteered to take the queen. Though reluctant to choose them for the task, Dar did so because they were the most logical choice. Both had used the servant passageway. Also, Zna-yat had experience as a guard and Kovok-mah could communicate with Girta. After that was decided, bindings and a gag were made. Two cloaks were sewn together to make a wrapping in which to bundle the queen. A means to secure her to Kovok-mah's back was also devised.

In both its broad outline and details, the plan was essentially Dar's. Accustomed to obeying, the sons didn't question its soundness. No one said the scheme was hastily conceived or overly complicated. Although based on sketchy information, its assumptions went unchallenged. If Dar wanted the washavoki queen, Kovok-mah and Zna-yat would get her. Or they'd die trying.

Thirty-seven

♛

Taiben's gates closed at sunset, so Kovok-mah and Zna-yat arrived there well before then. A storm threatened, and blowing snow caused the Queen's Men at the gate to huddle around a small fire, where they paid little attention to the orcs. The guards at the palace gates also admitted them without question.

Because evening came early in the winter, the two orcs had to stand guard through dinner. The banquet wasn't a formal one, and fewer people were present than when Dar was hosted. Still, as Kovok-mah and Zna-yat stood to the rear of Queen Girta, they found the company odorous and loud. The two orcs remained motionless throughout the meal, and the diners treated them as a pair of grotesque statues.

When the banquet was over, the queen retired to her private apartments. Kovok-mah and Zna-yat followed her and stationed themselves outside her door. It was located in the middle of a long hallway on the fourth floor of the palace. The corridor was wood-paneled, and along its length ran a wide band of decorative carvings. The two orcs scanned its wooden leaves, birds, and fruit for the peephole. In the dim hallway, even their keen eyes had trouble spotting it. When Zna-yat found it, he left his post flanking the queen's door, and stood in front of it awhile.

"What are you doing?" asked Kovok-mah, confident no listening washavoki understood Orcish. "It's too early for that."

"They must grow accustomed to me doing this," replied Zna-yat. "That way, they won't think it's unusual when I block their view at proper time."

Kovok-mah tried to make sense of Zna-yat's reply, but lacking his cousin's grasp of deception, he failed to see its logic. Nevertheless, Kovok-mah accepted his explanation. *Zna-yat thinks like Dargu*, he thought. *He understands her plans better than I.*

The palace gradually grew quieter as its occupants retired. Girta's attendants left her apartments for their quarters. The traffic in and out of the doorway to the servant passageway diminished, then ceased altogether. Three of the oil lamps illuminating the corridor went out, but no one relit them. The orcs' keen ears occasionally heard soft noises made by the spies hidden behind the wooden paneling. In time, they were the only sounds of human activity. Otherwise, the palace was deathly quiet except for the creaks and groans of an old building on a chill night. Zna-yat periodically moved to block the peephole. When the night was old, he did it again and motioned that it was time to act.

Kovok-mah quietly entered the queen's apartments. Speed was essential, but he had never been there before, and he had no idea where the queen slept. The entrance chamber had five doors within it, and he cautiously opened each to peer into the room beyond. None was for sleeping, and all the rooms contained additional doors. *I must search further*, he thought.

"It's doin' it again," said one of the Queen's Men.

"Doin' what?" asked his companion.

"Standin' in front of the other spy hole."

"So, what else is new?"

"Nothin'. Most like, it's as bored as . . . Nay, wait! The other piss eye just entered the queen's door."

"Let me see," said the second Queen's Man. He put his

eye to the spy hole and peered down the length of the hallway. There was only one orc visible. "Well suck Karm's
tits," swore the man. "And I thought piss eyes weren't
sly." He turned when he heard his companion draw his
sword. "Sheath that! We're to do nothin' without the
Queen's Man's say."

"Nothin'?"

"Aye, nothin', 'cept to report what's happenin'. So, go
tell him."

"You mean wake him?"

"Aye, ye stupid arse, and be quick about it. I'll keep
an eye on the piss eyes."

Girta woke with a start as a huge hand clamped over
her mouth. She opened her eyes and saw a nightmare shape
bent over her. It spoke in a low whisper. "I will not hurt
you. You will be safe."

Girta didn't believe a word. The hand lifted for an instant, but before she could scream, clawed fingers forced a
wad of cloth into her mouth. She was flipped over. A cloth
band was wrapped around her lower face to hold the gag
in place. Girta tried to tear it loose, but the orc grabbed
her wrists and bound them behind her back. She felt as
helpless as a trussed chicken. *Where are the Queen's Men?
The orcs were supposed to be watched.* A terrible thought
came to her. *The orcs slew them!*

When the orc pulled off the bedcovers to expose Girta's
legs, she realized that she was naked beneath her nightgown. She recalled horrific tales of orcs ravishing women
and tried to kick the brute, but it snatched her ankles
and bound them. Then, to Girta's terror, it lifted her and
placed her on the floor. Despite the fact that the orc had
just tied her legs together, she felt certain it would rape
her. Instead, it rolled her so that she was wrapped in thick
cloth.

Girta felt her captor binding her further, as if she were

a rolled carpet. When that was done, it lifted her and started walking. Girta wondered where she was being taken. *Will it throw me from the palace walls or will my death be crueler?* In her panic and despair, Girta had only one certainty: *This is Dar's doing!*

Kol entered the hidden observation chamber and found his man peering out the peephole. "What's happened so far?"

The man continued to observe while he explained. "One of the piss eyes carried a bundle into the servant passageway. From the looks of it, I'd say someone was inside it."

"It has to be the queen," said Kol. "Did you follow my orders?"

"Aye, sir. The piss eyes don't know we're onto them."

"Good," said Kol. He considered the situation. *It seems Dar smelled out my trap.* Kol didn't try to figure out how. Instead, he considered ways he might turn his setback to his advantage. Rescuing Girta seemed unpromising. He couldn't see her declaring war, no matter how provoked. She was more likely to banish the orcs, which would make sparking a conflict much harder. Though Kol's original plan was useless, one part was still salvageable. *Drastic measures are necessary*, he decided, *but these two aren't up for the task*. He turned to the man who had brought him. "Rouse Wulfar, then come back," he said. "Tell him to come here, but say he must gather iron first."

The man looked puzzled. "Did ye say 'gather iron,' sir?"

"Aye. Now go!"

After the man left, Kol addressed the other Queen's Man, who was still peering through the peephole. "Any changes?"

"Nay, sir. One piss eye's still gone and t'other hasn't

moved. Probably thinks no one sees what's goin' on." He chuckled. "Simpleminded brute."

"Aye," said Kol, silently drawing his dagger. "Piss eyes lack guile." Then he slit the man's throat.

Meanwhile, Kovok-mah carried Girta through the servant passageway. All the torches there had been extinguished and even he was blind in the total darkness. He had removed his boots upon entering it to feel his way with his feet as well as his hands. Dar had told him no washavoki would use the narrow corridor and stairs without a torch; thus light would warn him of anyone's approach. Yet negotiating the pitch-black passageway was difficult, and Kovok-mah did it slowly. The washavoki queen continued to make muffled noises and struggle feebly. Kovok-mah could smell her fear and felt sorry for her. *When she understands Dargu's goodness, she won't be afraid.* He hoped that she would reach that understanding soon.

Kovok-mah was relieved when he reached the palace kitchen and could see again. His keen ears heard someone sleeping in a corner, but he was quiet and quick as he made his way to the courtyard. There, he dashed to the stables with his burden. Since Dar had forgotten to caution him to hide his tracks, he was mindless of his footprints in the snowy courtyard. He entered the stables and made his way to the orcs' enclosed latrine. Its stone floor was cold, and Kovok-mah felt bad about leaving his captive on it. Nevertheless, he did and hurried back to his post.

The "iron" Wulfar gathered before reporting to the observation chamber consisted of the members of a secret brotherhood within the Queen's Men. Kol had created it and named it the Iron Circle. Only its men were privy to his true ambitions. Over a dozen in number, they were as hardened as the general, who killed the man he had sent to summon Wulfar upon his return. When the Iron Circle arrived, two corpses lay at its leader's feet.

"Piss eyes have kidnapped Girta," said General Kol. He glanced meaningfully at the two bodies. "Now, only we know it."

"What 'bout those at the other peephole?" asked Wulfar.

"They can't see," said Kol. "A piss eye blocks their view."

"What are yer orders, sir? Should we get the queen back?"

"I've been pondering that," said Kol. "I believe Dar got wind of my plan. Otherwise, this abduction makes no sense. It's a foolhardy move, but it forces my hand." He turned to one of the men. "Wake Lokung and escort him to the House of Balten. Tell him to fetch Girta's double and bring her here."

As the man departed, one of his comrades asked, "What about the piss eyes? They have the queen."

"I'm certain they'll try to sneak her to the garrison, so I want every way out of the palace and the city watched."

"Should we stop them?"

"Nay, let them pass, then report to me. I need to know when the queen reaches the garrison. Before she does, I want our men out of there." Kol turned to Wulfar. "Take three men to the garrison. Give my order for an immediate withdrawal. After the men are gone, kill all the serving women. Do it quietly. Then hack their bodies to make it look like orcs did it."

Kol could tell the men didn't understand the purpose of his orders, so he elaborated. "Having the queen out of Taiben serves my purpose, but only if no one knows she's missing." That was all he said, choosing to keep the rest of his stratagem secret until the time came to put it into action.

After the men departed on their missions, Kol took another look through the peephole. There were two orc guards flanking the queen's door again. *They've secreted Girta somewhere*, he thought. Kol felt certain that Dar wouldn't harm the queen, only talk to her. He wondered how much Dar knew and whether she'd be able to convince Girta of its truth. *It won't make any difference if she does.* Kol smiled, glad that the plotting was over. *I can act at last!* All that was left was to wait for dawn.

Thirty-eight

♛

Dar spent the night too nervous to sleep. Soon after Kovok-mah and Zna-yat had departed for Taiben, she began to see flaws in her plan. By then, it was too late for second thoughts; the arrow had been loosed. All that remained was to find out where it struck. Toward dawn, an orc informed her that all the black-garbed washavokis were leaving the garrison. Dar peered out the door, but snow was falling heavily, and she could neither see nor hear the withdrawal. Nevertheless, she didn't doubt the orc's keener senses. The development heightened her concern, for she feared it was a sign that something had gone wrong.

By the time first light appeared in the sky, Dar was in a state approaching panic. Still, she tried to appear calm as Magtha-jan and Nagtha-yat prepared to relieve Kovok-mah and Zna-yat from guard duty. Magtha-jan was chosen because he was an experienced guard, while Nagtha-yat could understand what the washavokis were saying. Both knew their mission was dangerous. Girta's orc guards said she usually slept late, and Dar hoped to return the queen—enlightened to her peril—to the palace before she was discovered missing. If that plan failed, Dar feared the consequences. Thus, it was with a heavy heart and many reservations that she sent the two orcs off as dawn approached.

The blizzard that had arisen during the night continued unabated, and Taiben was invisible in the storm. Dar received no report of whether the orcs had entered its gates. She waited anxiously for news. At last, two figures were spotted. It was all Dar could do to keep from running to them. Instead, she and Nir-yat donned shirts in hopes of receiving a royal guest. Dar's heart was pounding wildly by the time the door opened and Kovok-mah and her brother entered the barracks.

"Do you have her?" asked Dar in Orcish.

"Hai, Muth Mauk," replied Kovok-mah.

There was something about Kovok-mah's voice that disquieted Dar. When she glanced into his eyes, he seemed ashamed. "Release her quickly."

Beneath Kovok-mah's snow-covered cloak was a lump so conspicuous that Dar was amazed that he had managed to get past the guards at the gates. The cloak was removed to reveal Girta's body strapped to his back. It was wrapped in cloth that was further wrapped with rope. Zna-yat worked quickly to free the bundle. Then he gently lowered it to the floor, where he removed the bindings around the cloth wrapping and unrolled it to expose the captive inside.

With a single glance, Dar realized the magnitude of her blunder. Queen Girta sat up amid the cloth that had imprisoned her, still gagged and bound. She was shivering in her thin nightgown and her bare feet were blue from cold. Unable to speak, she glared about with wild eyes, resembling a snared animal in her terror and rage.

What have I done? thought Dar, understanding the cause of Kovok-mah's shame. She spoke to him in the human tongue so Girta might understand. "Free her and see to her comfort."

Kovok-mah undid the gag first, and Girta spoke as he untied her hands and feet. "How *dare* you!" she said in a shrill voice.

"I did it for your welfare," said Dar.

"Don't lie to me! At least, spare me that."

"I had to talk to you, and I couldn't do it around Kol."

"So you sent your brutes to . . . to . . ."

"Listen to me, Girta! Othar's alive. He's helping Kol."

"Liar! Liar! Filthy lying whore."

Girta's hysteria convinced Dar there was little point in reasoning with her. Kindness seemed a more promising approach. Dar brought her thick wool cloak over to Girta. "Warm clothing will soon arrive. Until then, wear this."

As Dar bent over to wrap Girta's shoulders, the queen struck out and raked her nails across Dar's cheeks. The orcs reacted immediately and lunged to seize Girta. Dar cried out "Gav!"—*Stop!*—before they grabbed the queen. The orcs froze, then slowly settled down. Dar touched her face and withdrew bloody fingers. "I've hurt this mother," said Dar in Orcish. "She's justly angry."

The orcs' reaction had further terrified Girta. She cowered, clutching Dar's cloak around her. The queen still shivered, but Dar doubted it was from cold. "I'm sorry, Girta."

Girta said nothing.

"I'd let you go right now," said Dar. "But if I do that, I fear Kol will harm you. I know his secret, and if he thinks you know it, too, he'll . . ." Dar could tell her words were having no effect. *Does she even hear me?*

Dar knew that time was quickly running out. The longer she held the queen, the greater the danger for Nagtha-yat and Magtha-jan. She knelt before Girta, taking care to keep out of striking distance. "I'll do anything you want."

"No you won't," said Girta in a flat voice.

"I will," said Dar. "Just tell me."

"Let me go. Right now."

"You're in a nightgown, and you can't walk barefoot in the snow!"

"I will if you let me."

"You'll have clothes and boots soon," said Dar, wondering why Sevren hadn't arrived. "Then you can go. Until then listen to me."

"Liar!" said Girta, stopping her ears with her hands.

As Dar stared at the queen with a mixture of frustration and remorse, she saw that the situation was hopeless. For the first time, she imagined the abduction from Girta's viewpoint. *It had to be her worst nightmare. I've been so stupid! She'll never trust me now.* Dar gloomily pondered her options and could envision none with a happy outcome. She decided that all she could do was free Girta when Sevren arrived with clothing, apologize profusely, and leave with the orcs immediately. That course would surely doom Girta and lead to war, but both results seemed unavoidable. It was clear that Kol had outsmarted her.

Having decided to free Girta, Dar wanted to do it quickly. For that, she needed Sevren, and her impatience grew as she waited for him. *It's well past dawn. He's late!* It was midmorning before the barracks door opened and Sevren entered. He was snow-covered, and his expression was both surprised and disturbed. Dar didn't hold back her anger. "Where are those clothes? I've been waiting far too long!"

"Clothes? What need have you for them?"

"For Girta, fool!"

"Girta? Your orcs killed her. All Taiben's in an uproar. The gates were closed. It wasn't easy getting out."

"The queen's not dead," said Dar. "She's right here!"

Sevren followed Dar's gesture and spied Girta slumped on the floor, wrapped in Dar's cloak. He walked over to her and bowed. "Your Majesty, all the criers say you're slain."

Girta looked up. "Slain?"

"Aye, Your Majesty. They say your orc guards did it."

"What happened to them?" asked Dar, her voice urgent.

"Killed in a bloody fight."

The news confirmed Dar's worst fears. Remorse and grief left her stunned. *It's my fault they're dead*, she thought, fighting back tears.

"What of the prince?" asked Girta, her face animated for the first time.

"He'll be crowned king this afternoon," said Sevren. "Rumor says he'll declare war." He turned to Dar. "I came here to make sure you knew, though I hoped you'd already fled."

"How can this be?" asked Girta. "How can this be?"

"I'm na a royal guardsman anymore. I hear my news from criers, like everyone else."

"But I'm alive! How can they say I'm dead?"

"I suspect that's the Queen's Man's doing," replied Sevren.

"No," said Girta. "It's all a mistake."

"How can you say that?" asked Dar.

"Yes, a mistake," said Girta. "But one that's easily corrected." She turned to Dar. "Let me go to Taiben."

"That won't be safe."

"My son's there! He thinks I'm dead."

"Because Kol told him so," said Dar. "He won't let you prove him false."

"You're wrong."

"You're not talking sense," said Dar. "Stay. You must."

"She will na be safe here," said Sevren. "Neither will you."

Dar suddenly understood why Kovok-mah had been

able to sneak Girta past the guards: Kol had given orders to let him pass. With a chill, she realized he planned to attack two queens at once. She spoke to Girta. "If the gates are closed, they'll be manned by Kol's men."

"They're called the Queen's Men," said Girta. "Their loyalty is to me."

"I'm na so sure of that," said Sevren. "I know some of those men."

"I won't abandon my son," said Girta. She spoke to Dar. "Lend me your boots. I think they'll fit me."

Dar thought the matter over, weighing hope against pessimism. There was a chance the queen's appearance would unravel Kol's plans, but only if Girta received the reception that she expected. Dar doubted she would. Then Dar envisioned trying to drag Girta away from her child, who had fallen into Othar's clutches. She sighed and acquiesced to Girta's plea. "You shouldn't go alone. I'll provide an escort."

Girta objected, but when Dar made it clear that the escort wasn't optional, she grudgingly agreed to it. Afterward, Kovok-mah approached Dar. "Muth Mauk, I brought this mother here. If she's harmed, it'll be my fault. Please let me protect her."

Dar wanted to say that he bore no guilt for her decision, but seeing his need to atone, she agreed to his request. It pained her to do so, for she knew she was endangering him. *I've endangered everyone*, she thought, once again fighting back tears. *Two have already paid for my foolishness.*

Dar chose four other orcs to complete the escort. As they donned their armor, Girta dressed in Dar's boots and extra clothes. When the orcs were ready, Dar spoke to them. "Washavoki great mother wishes to return, but I'm unsure how she'll be greeted. Evil ones may try to harm her. She's our friend, and you must protect her." Then Dar stood in the open doorway to watch the orcs and

Girta depart. The falling snow transformed them into ghostly shapes that soon disappeared altogether. Only then did Dar shut the door and retreat to the warmth of the hearth.

Waiting was agony. Only the slender possibility that Girta could undo Kol's treachery allowed Dar to stave off despair. But she had little confidence in that scenario, and her fears grew the longer she waited. When a sentry announced at last that orcs were approaching, Dar ran barefoot into the snow to meet them.

Although she could see only gray shapes initially, Dar knew something was wrong. The orcs were running and there were fewer than five. As they approached, their forms became clearer. One orc was carrying Girta. Two orcs were carrying a third. Another orc was missing. Dar called out, "What happened?"

"Washavokis shot many arrows," shouted an orc as he ran. "Washavoki queen is wounded. So is Togu-mah. Garga-tok is slain."

Stunned, Dar followed the party into the barracks. Kovok-mah carried Girta, who had an arrow protruding from her shoulder. Its feathered end had been snapped off, but the rest remained, surrounded by a growing bloodstain. The queen stared at Dar with wide eyes, her pale face marked by shock and pain. "They knew me! They made certain I was their queen. But when the gate opened, there were archers and they . . . they . . ." Girta shuddered and glanced at the shaft jutting from her shoulder. "But an orc stepped in front of me. A living shield. He died for my sake."

Dar looked to Kovok-mah, who was bleeding from a gash in his cheek. "Garga-tok?"

"Hai. It's like she said. He took her arrows until one struck his eye and killed him." Kovok-mah made the sign of the Tree.

At that moment, Dar felt the full weight of sovereignty. *My decisions caused all today's tragedies.* They had sealed the fates of Nagtha-yat, Magtha-jan, and Garga-tok. Dar wished with all her heart that she could alter her choices, but that was impossible. She also knew that she must continue making decisions. There was no other option; she was Muth Mauk.

Dar spoke to Kovok-mah. "Can you give healing magic to Queen Girta and Togu-mah?"

"Togu-mah will join Muth la soon," replied Kovok-mah. "No herb can cure his hurt."

"Then treat queen. Will you give her leaf that makes her sleep?"

"Hai. Removing arrowhead will be painful."

Dar spoke to Girta in the human tongue. "Girta, we'll give you healing magic for your wound. It will make you sleep. When you awake, we'll be far from here."

"But my son!"

"He'll be king by this afternoon. Take hope from that. He's been deceived, but we may yet undo Kol's treachery."

"How?"

"I'm not sure. All I know is you must stay alive to do it and this place isn't safe."

"Oh Dar, I've been a fool!"

"But you don't remain one. Both of us must learn from this day and make better choices in the future."

Kovok-mah, having retrieved his bag of healing herbs, knelt beside Girta. Dar grasped her hand. "An orc died so you might live. Will you trust Kovok-mah to heal you?"

"Yes."

"Then I'll leave you in his care. I must see Togu-mah." Dar caught a hint of panic in Girta's face, but she had other pressing concerns. She rushed to Togu-mah's side. He was lying on the floor. Lama-tok knelt beside him holding cloths to the front and back of his neck. They were soaked with blood, as was the front of Togu-mah's armored tunic. The sight made Dar queasy. She ignored her uneasy stomach to kneel beside her dying mintari. The orc's face was pale gray and his eyes were half-closed, but he spoke when he saw her. "Muth Mauk," he whispered. "You honor me."

"Thwa. It's you who honors me." Dar wanted to say something that gave meaning to his sacrifice, but she lacked words to convey her feelings. They were too intense and confused. She felt horror, love, grief, regret, and gratitude all at once. All she could do was stroke his cheek and say, "Shashav, Togu."

Togu-mah smiled.

Dar wanted to remain by Togu-mah's side, but there were other demands upon her. She went over to where Kovok-mah was treating Girta. The queen had chewed the sedative leaf and was already unconscious. Kovok-mah exposed where the arrow's broad head had pierced the queen. "Will she live?" asked Dar.

"I think so," replied Kovok-mah, "if her wound doesn't fester."

Then Dar turned to Sevren and addressed her next concern. "Why hasn't Kol attacked?"

"My guess is he lacks the men for an assault. His Queen's Men are a smaller force than the old royal guard, and he must spread it thin. He'll need the king's warrant to call soldiers to Taiben."

"He'll get that soon enough, no doubt," said Dar. "He probably already has it. We must leave before the soldiers arrive."

"Aye. Everyone believes you've murdered our queen. It's war for certain."

Though Dar knew she had to act quickly, she had to avoid acting rashly. Her first impulse was to flee. *I can't wait for an attack.* She had less than forty orcs, and her foe could summon regiments of men. *I have to flee, and Kol knows it. So what will he do while he's waiting for troops?* The answer was apparent. "Kol will take the pass," said Dar, "to cut off our retreat."

"Aye, that makes sense," said Sevren. "He'll na need many men to hold such a narrow way."

"I know of another road home. It's longer and more difficult but . . ." Dar stopped, realizing that by the time she returned home by the Old Road, Kol could take the New Road and be waiting for her.

"But what?" asked Sevren.

"The pass. Kol will use the pass."

"Aye, there's na way to stop him."

"But there is," said Dar. "I can seal that pass forever, but only if I get a message through it."

"A handful of archers would stop you cold."

"Only if they get there first," said Dar. She was on the verge of telling the orcs that they must leave immediately when she checked herself. If Kol's men beat them to the pass, disaster would ensue. *The urkzimmuthi would have no queen and no warning of Kol's invasion.* Dar tried to assess the chance that the way remained unguarded. Since Kol knew about the kidnapping, he could have pulled the Queen's Men from the garrison and sent them to the pass. It seemed possible, but there was no way to be sure. The only thing that Dar was certain about was that Kol always planned ahead.

Dar was forced to make a decision, and she did so with a heavy heart. A chance to seal the pass, however slim, couldn't be forsaken. She called out in Orcish, "Lamatok! Ven-goth! I need you." The two orcs hurried to her side. "You must get message to Yat clan hall as quickly as possible. Warn them washavokis plan to attack. Tell Tok clan sons I want pass sealed immediately."

The two orcs bowed.

"What I ask of you is dangerous. I think washavokis

are also headed for pass. If they get there first, they'll be waiting with arrows."

"Then we'll leave right away, Muth Mauk," said Lamatok.

Then Dar spoke to them as if she were their muthuri and not their queen. "Lama and Ven, you're dear to me. Take care. If you encounter washavokis, don't throw your lives away."

The two bowed, donned their cloaks, and headed for the door.

"Wait!" cried Dar. "Shouldn't you wear your armor?"

"We'll run much faster without it."

"Hai," replied Dar. "That seems wise." She watched them depart with a heavy heart. When the door closed, she noticed Kovok-mah standing beside her.

He bowed. "Muth Mauk, Togu-mah is dead."

Thirty-nine

♛

There was no time to grieve. Soldiers might arrive any moment, and Dar had to organize a hasty retreat. She told the orcs to don their armor, fashion a stretcher to carry Girta, and procure food from the garrison's kitchen. A few reed shelters remained from the summer campaign, and she sent some orcs to search for more in the abandoned barracks. As they left, Sevren approached Dar. "What can I do?" he asked. "I want to help."

"Are you sure? This could end up like the Vale of Pines."

"The new king's army will be Othar's army in truth. I will na serve such an evil cause."

"Then I'd be glad for your aid," said Dar. "Girta needs boots and warm clothes. And I must know what's going on in Taiben."

"I'll do my best. If you're na headed for the pass, how can I find your trail?"

"The Old Road goes west along the base of the foothills, then follows a river into the mountains. On horseback, you should catch up easily."

"Then I'll see you as soon as I can," said Sevren, "with clothes and news. Leave quickly. Karm's grace on you, Dar."

"Fasak Muth la vashak tha, Sevren." *May Muth la bless you, Sevren.*

Sevren left. Lama-tok and Ven-goth were already gone. The orcs were strapping reed shelters and packs onto their

backs when Zna-yat approached Dar. He held her golden
pendant. "Muth Mauk, should I pack this heavy thing?"

Dar eyed the necklace with distaste, for she felt it sym-
bolized the pointlessness of her mission. She was about to
tell him to leave it behind when she thought of the plunder-
ing soldiers. "Hai," she said. "Washavokis treasure yellow
iron. It would please them greatly to have it."

Zna-yat grinned. "Then it'll please me greatly to carry
it away."

As Zna-yat stowed the necklace in his pack, news arrived that the serving women had been slain. To Dar, it
was a foretaste of Kol's savagery and another tragedy to
add to a growing list. Her instincts warned her that something foul and malign had been loosed. At the moment,
she could only flee it, but Dar understood flight wouldn't
bring safety. *I must confront this evil. That's why Muth la
preserved my life.*

General Kol entered the prince's apartments. The boy
sat on his bed, still dressed in his nightclothes. Tears
streaked his face, as the prince shuddered from the effort
of suppressing sobs. As Kol gazed at the grief-stricken
boy, he briefly saw himself as a lad. Then he hardened his
heart and put on a mask of compassion. When the prince
looked up, he saw a face possessing the perfect mixture
of grief and sympathy.

"Your Majesty," said Kol. "Such a terrible day." He
walked over to the bedside and placed his hand on the
boy's shoulder. "What strength I have is yours."

"Why?" asked the prince in a quavering voice. "Why
did they kill my mother?"

"Because it's their nature to kill. She was good, and
they don't understand goodness. To them, it's weakness."

The prince began to shake.

"It's not unmanly to cry," said Kol, his voice gentle
and sad. He watched the boy sob, all the while rubbing

his shoulder. When he thought the prince had cried long enough, he spoke. "There's something you can do for your mother."

The prince ceased sobbing and straightened. "What?"

"It will be hard, but she deserves this," said Kol. "A sword's steel is soft until it's tempered. So you must face this trial to become a man. And have no doubt; this day will make you one."

"What must I do?" asked young Kregant, sounding timid.

"Visit your mother's chamber and view the orcs' handiwork. It won't be easy, but I'll be there. You owe this to her memory."

"Why?"

"So you will know your enemy. That knowledge will sustain you when doubt arises. It will allow you to do what's necessary."

The prince looked dubious, but Kol knew that he would come. *He wants so much to be a man.* Kol snapped his fingers, and servants appeared. "Dress His Majesty."

Though servants attired the prince in black and gold, it was General Kol who strapped on his sword. Then he led the boy through the palace to Girta's apartments. Queen's Men barred the hallway, but admitted the prince and his general. Even before they reached the queen's doorway, a bloody tableau was visible. The two men Kol had murdered lay in the corridor, their wounds gruesomely enhanced. They appeared to have been slain in a ferocious struggle. Nor were they alone. A severed arm lay on the floor. Nearby was a hacked and headless torso.

Kol pretended to be oblivious of the boy's trembling as he marched him toward the bloody scene. He wanted the prince to receive its full effect. The two skirted the corpses and entered the apartment. Inside lay Nagtha-yat and Magtha-jan. The poison arrows that had taken their lives had been pulled out and replaced by wounds that spoke of a more gallant assault. The men who had manned the other observation post lay near them. Slaughtered for silence and dramatic effect, they added to the carnage.

The prince scarcely noticed them. His eyes were drawn to the two women who lay nearby. One was his mother's lady's maid, her head nearly severed. She still clung to a woman who wore the queen's nightgown and favorite dressing robe as if attempting to shield her. The prince saw his mother's golden hair. It was soaked with blood. The face below the tresses was smashed beyond recognition. He felt that he should run and embrace the body, but he retched instead.

"This is how orcs repay goodness," said General Kol, his voice choked with outrage. "This is how they honor treaties." He took the prince's hand. "Come from this awful place, wiser about your foe. Your mother will be interred with solemn splendor. Those men who fell here will receive full honors. Songs and tales will recount their bravery. We'll burn the orcs like garbage."

Kol led the prince to another room with a wide window that overlooked the city. In the storm, Taiben seemed a phantom realm. Kol had a servant bring the boy a goblet of hot spiced wine, sweetened with honey. He watched the prince drink and waited for color to return to his face. When it did, Kol spoke. "The orcs are fleeing in that storm, thinking they'll be safe in their warm halls. War's hard in the winter. The weather's harsh, and the roads are slippery. But it'll be even harder on the orcs. When we drive them from their halls, they'll have no refuge. They can't eat snow, nor dwell in it."

The prince's eyes widened. "War?"

"Aye, Your Majesty. Were not the orcs' deeds war? Would you have them go unpunished?"

"Never!"

"Your mother spoke of your ancestor, Theodric Goblin

Slayer. She said he was your age when he guided men to a nest of orcs. They slew them all—bulls, sows, and whelps—and helped bring peace to a ravaged land. Theodric's blood flows in your veins. I sense his courage in you."

Kol suddenly knelt before the prince. "Soon you'll be my king, and all the realm will kneel as I do now. When they do, think how Theodric would repay your mother's death. All true men share your grief and anger. Say the word, and they'll fight for you. Call for war! We'll ride together and rid the realm of orcs."

"And their queen, too?"

"Aye, Your Majesty. She'll burn for her treachery."

The first troops reached Taiben by early afternoon. Kol ordered them to march into the palace courtyard, where they stood in ranks to be addressed by the newly crowned Kregant III. The child king's voice was swallowed by the storm, and the soldiers didn't know they were going to war until officers told them and ordered them to cheer. Having been promised brandy, the men cheered loudly. Then they marched to the empty garrison outside the city.

Dar was right about Kol's habit of planning in advance. He had begun gathering men and supplies for an invasion as soon as he was made a general. Since troops were not stationed within the capital, the buildup had been easy to hide from Queen Girta. Most of the units had assembled in far-flung garrisons. General Voltar had issued the orders, to disguise Kol's involvement. The men in the snowy square had known something was afoot for weeks. They had not known when they were going to war, but few were surprised that they were.

At the coronation feast, General Kol presented King Kregant III with a suit of armor. Its black helmet was embellished with gold and the chain mail fit his small frame perfectly. By then, Kol was no longer the Queen's Man, but Commander of His Majesty's Army. The black-garbed guardsmen were renamed the King's Men, but their duties remained the same. Within their ranks, the Iron Circle was gratified by Kol's rise and the prospect of plunder and advancement. All agreed, as they toasted their new king, that their night's labors had paid off handsomely.

While Kol feasted, Dar led the orcs through the storm. She was exhausted and miserable, but she grimly slogged through the calf-high snow, too anxious to stop. Zna-yat walked in front of her to make a path, and after it grew dark, Dar relied on her brother's eyes to help find the way. Neither he nor any of the other orcs had ever traveled the Old Road. Zna-yat relied on Dar's description of the route, a description she had obtained from the lorekeeper.

Snow hid most traces of the abandoned roadway, and visibility was poor. The foothills seemed more like vague presences than features of earth and stone. However, since the road would intersect a river and follow it into the mountains, Dar didn't worry about losing the way. She was more concerned about being overtaken by soldiers. Accordingly, she had the orcs walk single file and drag pine boughs to obscure their tracks. With luck, snow and wind would obliterate them entirely.

Sevren had not caught up with them, so Dar had no idea what was going on elsewhere. *Where's Kol?* she wondered. *Has the invasion started? Did Lama-tok and Ven-goth make it through the pass, or will we be fleeing to Kol's waiting army?* Each question spawned more until Dar was overwhelmed by all the dire possibilities. She forced herself to focus on the immediate future. That seemed daunting enough. They would have to stop soon, and Dar weighed risking a fire. Being spotted was a danger, but so was freezing.

Dar spoke to Zna-yat. "We must find campsite, somewhere our fire cannot be seen."

Zna-yat peered about the darkness. "I see no such place."

"Then we must continue onward until you do."

Zna-yat kept walking until Dar feared she would drop in her tracks. At last he said, "I see likely spot."

"Then we'll rest there," said Dar, who could see little more than falling snow, its flakes gray in the darkness.

Zna-yat veered sharply to the right. Soon, Dar could see snow-laden trees on either side of a fold in a foothill. When the fold became a winding ravine, Zna-yat halted. "Muth Mauk, is this good place?"

"Hai, it's perfect," said Dar. She called out, "We'll stay here tonight. Gather wood for fire. Set up shelters."

The orcs found a spot of level ground to erect their shelters, which resembled conical haystacks. They were just large enough to accommodate a son sitting cross-legged. Though orcs slept sitting up, Girta could not, and Dar wondered how she would rest. She walked over to the stretcher to see how the queen was faring. She was still bundled up, and Kovok-mah was beside her. "How is washavoki queen?" Dar asked.

"I gave her large nayimgat leaf to chew," replied Kovok-mah. "She'll sleep until tomorrow. When sun rises, I'll have better idea how she's healing."

"She can't sleep outside in this cold."

"Your sister spoke with me. She said queen will rest in your brother's shelter."

"Poor Zna," said Dar. "Does he know how bad this washavoki smells?"

Kovok-mah made a wry face. "Everyone does."

"Muth Mauk," said Zna-yat. "We'll soon be making porridge. How should we ration it?"

"For five more days of travel," replied Dar. Just saying those words disheartened her. *Where will our foes be in five days? Inside my clan's hall?* As she had all day, Dar tried to push that thought from her mind. She found it impossible. She recalled her vision of the burning hall with distressing vividness. It had haunted her most of the march. Pushed to her limits, Dar felt crushed by foreboding. Without another word, she wandered away from camp until she rounded a bend and was out of sight.

When she was alone, Dar surrendered to her grief. She didn't permit herself to cry, but hot tears flowed down her frigid cheeks. Then she heard quiet footsteps and turned to see Nir-yat approach. Dar hastily wiped her eyes. Nir-yat said nothing; she simply embraced Dar. Wrapped in her sister's arms, Dar began to sob.

The two stood together for a long while. Eventually, Dar cried herself out with a shuddering sigh. "Muthuri was right," she said. "I should have passed Fathma to another."

"Then no urkzimmuthi would suffer on this cold night," replied Nir-yat. "We would be content, like fattened lambs before feast. We would have different great mother, but Black Washavoki wouldn't be different, and we'd be doomed."

"I think it's my deeds that have doomed us."

"So you're responsible for all evil in this world?" said Nir-yat. "Should I blame you for this storm? Was it you who made washavokis cruel?"

"I haven't made things better. I've made them worse."

"I think not. At least now, we're aware of our danger. And so is washavoki queen."

"I'm afraid our foe is too great for me."

"This has been terrible day for us all, but especially for you," said Nir-yat. "I know you didn't sleep last night. Now you're exhausted, cold, and hungry. Will you do something for me?"

"What?"

"Share Kovok-mah's shelter."

"I can't. You know why."

"I know you need rest," said Nir-yat. "How will you get it lying alone on ground?"

"But . . ."

"I've already told my cousin he must shelter you. Would you have him disobey me?"

"Nir, is it wise?"

"Hai. Very wise. I'll challenge anyone who questions my judgment." She gave Dar an understanding look. "Even if she were great mother. Come, Sister. There's fire, and soon there'll be food. Afterward, you must rest."

The road leading to the pass dropped off steeply on either side. This exposed it to the wind, which blew so hard that the snow often flew horizontally. It obliterated Lama-tok's and Ven-goth's footprints almost as soon as they were made. The orcs' windward sides were crusted with snow by the time they neared the narrow passage through the ridge. Though it promised shelter from the storm, the two orcs halted and peered at it cautiously. In the dark, it resembled a thick black line painted on the wall of icy rock. Even the orcs' keen eyes couldn't penetrate its dark interior. Snow was mounded against its entrance in a drift that the wind reshaped as they watched.

"Washavokis are no match for this weather," said Ven-goth. "Come. Let's get out of it awhile."

Lama-tok didn't move. "Do you smell smoke?"

Ven-goth sniffed the turbulent air. "Thwa."

"I thought I did, but now I don't. I guess it's safe."

The two orcs slogged through the deep snow toward the pass. They were only a few paces from its entrance when an arch of arrows streamed from its dark interior. Both orcs were hit. Lama-tok was pierced through his thigh and dropped to the ground. Ven-goth stood a little longer, then he fell also.

Without rising, Lama-tok groped behind his leg until

he felt the arrowhead protruding from it. He snapped it off, then grabbed the feathered shaft that jutted from the front of his thigh and pulled it out. Blood warmed both sides of his leg. Arrows still flew overhead, but the deep snow hid him, and the washavokis seemed to be shooting blindly. They remained hidden within the dark pass, apparently afraid to venture into sight. Lama-tok slithered on his belly toward Ven-goth. "Are you badly wounded?"

"I'm not sure. I think so."

Ven-goth had rolled on his back. Three arrows protruded from his torso. "Lie still," said Lama-tok. "I'll pull you to safety." He grabbed Ven-goth's ankles, and crawling on his elbows and knees, dragged him backward. It was difficult and slow work. Excruciating pains shot through Lama-tok's thigh every time he moved it. Nevertheless, he made progress. It became easier when he reached the road's sloping side. After a while, he was able to slide downward with little effort, pulling Ven-goth behind him.

When he decided it was safe, Lama-tok stood to examine his companion. Ven-goth was breathing with gurgling gasps. A bloody froth issued from his lips.

"Lama?" said Ven-goth. "I can't see you."

"I'm here, Ven."

"Ask Muth Mauk ... let Fre-pah know ... last thoughts of her."

"When I get through pass, I will."

"Too many ... washavokis!"

"There were many arrows. Perhaps not so many washavokis. I'll wait awhile, then approach unseen. They can't surprise me twice."

"But ... if you fail ..."

"Speak of Fre-pah. Is she pretty?"

"Hai. And wise."

"She was wise to love you, Ven."

"Thwa. I was wise ... to love her."

Ven-goth breathed a while longer, but he lacked the breath to speak again. After he died, Lama-tok honored him. He carried his body away from the pass until he found a tree clinging to the steep hillside. He marked Muth la's Embrace beneath it. Then Lama-tok removed his friend's clothing so he might leave the world as he had entered it. Lastly, he placed Ven-goth within the sacred circle.

After this was done, Lama-tok limped slowly toward the pass, taking care to keep out of view. He was in no hurry. *Let washavokis think I'm dead*, he thought. He smiled, recalling it was Dar who had taught him how to think like a wolf. Tonight he would apply her lessons. He hoped his body was up to it. His blood-soaked leggings had frozen, and his thigh was stiffening also. Hugging the ridge, Lama-tok made his way to the passageway that his clan had cut into its face. It was well past midnight when he finally reached it. He paused to rest and gather his courage. Then he drew his sword and charged into the dark opening.

Forty

♛

General Kol awoke and bolted upright, his dagger drawn and ready. A shadowed figure stood in his bed-chamber, just beyond striking distance. "Good reflexes, General."

"Gorm! How'd you get in here?"

"Don't blame your guards. Few intruders possess my skills."

Kol uneasily speculated on what those skills might be, and Gorm answered as if he had read the general's thoughts. "They're unharmed. I'll revive them when I leave."

"So you sneaked in to congratulate me?" asked Kol in a sarcastic tone.

"Congratulate you? Why would I do that?"

"I got Othar his war. He should be satisfied."

"You presume too much," replied Gorm in a cold voice. "My master is far from satisfied. Declarations don't spill blood. Swords do. When they reap a harvest, you may rest easier, not until then."

"That will happen soon enough."

"When?"

"As soon as all my troops gather. They're dispersed, and travel's slow."

"Delay! Always delay!"

"Does Othar want me to deliver a slap or an ax stroke? I can harass the orcs or I can massacre them. Slaughter requires overwhelming numbers, and I must marshal them.

Can you fly troops here by magic or must they march through deep snow?"

"You grow overproud, General."

"I'm smart, not proud. Your bloody harvest requires blades. I'm gathering them as fast as I can."

"So we won't march until they all arrive," said Gorm, clearly unhappy with the news.

"What do you mean by *we*?"

"My master and I will accompany you."

"And how will I explain his presence to the king?"

"You needn't alarm the boy. We'll follow behind. Before you march, send nine men to Balten's residence. They need only be strong and healthy. Otherwise, they can be dregs and malcontents." Gorm smiled grimly. "Othar will render them obedient."

"Why would Othar suffer campaigning in the winter?" asked Kol, not relishing the idea of the mage accompanying him, even at a distance.

"The nearer he is to slaughter, the more he benefits. My master has fasted far too long. He's ravenous."

As before, Kol thought he caught an edge of fear in Gorm's voice. "You'll get your men," he said, "and Othar will get his carnage."

"Don't fail," replied Gorm. "There's a force abroad more powerful than one man's sorcery. Provoke it, and even death won't save you from its malice."

"Dar provoked your master, not I. And I'll soon deliver her to him."

Dar awoke warm within Kovok-mah's arms. She heard the wind blowing outside the reed shelter, but covered by her cloak, she was snug against Kovok-mah's chest. Reluctantly, she reached out and parted the reeds just enough to glimpse the light of early dawn. She withdrew her arm back under the cloak. Dar sighed and began groping for her boots. Then the arm about her waist tightened ever so slightly. "Dargu," whispered Kovok-mah.

"Hai?"

"Is it wrong that I wish you to stay?"

"Thwa," Dar whispered back. *Not wise, but not wrong.* She sighed again. "I wish to stay also."

"But you think it'll cause trouble."

Dar reflected that it could. *So what?* she thought. *What's this transgression compared to the calamities ahead?* "My sister was wise to say you must shelter me and to send me to you. I'm at peace this morning."

"I am, too. You give me strength, Dargu. You always have."

Dar surrendered to her heart's desire, and rested a while longer in Kovok-mah's arms. She rose only when she heard others stirring about the camp. Emerging from the shelter, she found it half buried in snow. Nir-yat was up and directing activities. There was a fire burning, and a son tended a kettle on it. "Heat it slowly," said Nir-yat. "I want that porridge thawed, not burned." When she spied Dar, she spoke to another son. "Have Zna-yat take washavoki queen to Kovok-mah." As the son went on his errand, Nir-yat smiled at Dar. "You looked rested."

Dar's principal recollections of the previous evening were of discouragement and exhaustion. She remembered crying, eating, and falling asleep in Kovok-mah's shelter; the rest was hazy. Dar realized that her sister must have organized everything. From the appearance of the camp, she had done it well. Nir-yat bowed to Dar, then approached her. "Sentries have spotted no washavokis."

"You posted sentries?"

"Hai, Muth Mauk. There were not enough shelters, so I had sons sleep in rotation."

"But not Kovok-mah."

"He was busy healing."

"Healing?"

"Hai," replied Nir-yat. "Not only flesh can be wounded. Spirits can be injured as well." She scrutinized Dar. "You look better, but I think you'll need further healing."

Dar smiled. "Since when have you become healer?"

"Since you bit my neck, I've discovered many skills."

Zna-yat walked by carrying an unconscious Girta, and Dar followed him to Kovok-mah's shelter. Nir-yat came also and stayed as Kovok-mah examined the queen. The arrowhead had been a broad one, and the wound it made had required stitches. Kovok-mah looked at the su-tured gash and sniffed it. Then he removed some dried herbs from his healer's pouch, chewed them, and spit herb-laced saliva on the wound. Afterward, he spit out the herbs and made a face. "Water!"

By the time Zna-yat brought a water skin, Girta was bundled up. Kovok-mah rinsed his mouth thoroughly before speaking again. "I had forgotten how vile that magic tastes."

"How's washavoki queen?" asked Dar.

"I'd be more pleased if her wound was less swollen. When she wakes, I'll brew some magic water."

"But she'll live?" asked Dar.

"I think so. She'll be in pain awhile."

Dar turned to Nir-yat. "We should resume our jour-ney as soon as possible."

When the leftover porridge thawed, the party had a quick meal accompanied by hot herb water. Afterward, they resumed their march. It was still snowing but not as heavily as the previous day. The wind, however, was just as harsh. The road was invisible beneath drifts, and Dar let Zna-yat pick out the route as she scanned ahead for some sign of the river that would take them into the mountains.

The sun was hidden by clouds, so Dar could only

assume that it was afternoon when Girta finally awoke and shrieked. Dar rushed to her side, as did Kovok-mah. "Girta! Are you all right?"

Girta struggled for a moment on her stretcher, then the wild look left her face and she relaxed. "I remember now," she said in a weak voice. "You saved me."

"We're fleeing Kol," said Dar. "He's far behind us." *At least I hope so*, she thought.

"My son!"

"He's king by now and safe awhile."

"I must see him."

"And you will in good time," said Dar. "Then you'll undo Kol's evil deeds."

"You said something about Othar. That he lives."

"He does, but he's too crippled to pursue us. Forget your worries and rest."

"That's easier said than done."

Despite agreeing, Dar said, "You must. Build your strength before you face your foes."

The march halted to allow Kovok-mah to brew some healing magic. Zna-yat roasted three pashi roots on the same fire, half of their entire store. He gave the food to Dar so she might serve it.

"Saf nak ur Muthz la," said Dar. In response to Girta's puzzled look, she said, "It's our custom to thank the World's Mother for our food. I just said food is her gift." Dar handed the queen the roasted roots. "Muth la urak ther saf la. That's the serving phrase. It means 'World's Mother gives you this food.' The appropriate response is 'Shashav, Muth la.' It means 'Thank you, Muth la.'"

"Muth la?"

"That's the World's Mother's name. She guides mothers and loves all her children, even washavokis."

Girta regarded the roasted pashi. "Shashav, Muth la." She bit into the warm root. "I've never had these before."

"They came from your storerooms. I used to cook them in the royal kitchen."

Girta gave Dar a puzzled look. "You serve me food, yet you possess more power than I ever had."

"That power comes from Muth la, and we believe she gives a measure to every mother."

"My courtiers disdained my womanhood, counting it as weakness."

"We believe just the opposite."

"So my orc guards were loyal to me."

"Absolutely."

"I feared them." Girta looked ashamed. "Yet one died for me."

"Two died," said Dar. "The wounded orc did not survive. I wish we could have had this conversation much earlier. Things would have turned out better."

"You tried, but I wouldn't listen. You said orcs honored mothers when we made our treaty, but General Kol claimed you lied."

"It's too bad you listened. But then, he's a skilled and practiced liar."

"He lied to you, also?"

"He called me his woman, and said he only wanted to protect me."

"What did he really want?"

"To tup me." Dar smiled wryly. "He was a murdant then and less ambitious."

"Do you mean he cared for you?"

"I was only sport to him. All he cared about was power."

"He hasn't changed, but I've just learned that," said Girta. "Now that I've made him a general, I suspect his ambitions include the crown."

"Most like."

"Then we have an enemy in common."

"Two, counting Othar."

Girta shivered at the sound of the mage's name and hoped Dar was wrong.

The chaos in Taiben both hindered and helped Sevren's mission. In the panic preceding hostilities, prices rose and goods became scarcer. The clothes and boots that he procured had been costly, but not new. Sevren spent more of his savings than he wished, making the dream of a farm even more distant. The military was almost as unsettled as the merchants. Rumors were abundant, but reliable information was rare. No soldier knew when they'd march, though every one had an opinion.

Sevren used the general confusion to move about freely. Armed and mounted, he assumed a purposeful appearance that discouraged interference. Whenever an officer or murdant questioned him, he said his unit had just arrived. Eventually, he found a few men he knew and trusted. From them, he learned some useful things. When he felt sufficiently informed, he casually rode off into the blizzard.

Sevren didn't follow the foothills in case someone tracked him as a deserter. Instead, he took a southwest route until he reached the river. It was a small and shallow waterway, and winter had reduced its flow. When Sevren urged Skymere into it, the water seldom reached the horse's knees. He rode upstream a distance in order to leave no trail. Then he crossed to the other side and rode a greater distance before crossing back. Satisfied that he had thrown off any possible pursuers, he followed the river into the mountains, looking for Dar and the orcs.

Sevren found a faint trace of footprints along the riverbank as the sun neared the horizon. Noting approvingly that Dar had taken care to obscure the tracks, he urged his steed onward. It was near dusk when he spotted a single line of marchers. Aware that his weapons and leather armor gave him the appearance of a common soldier, he called out, "Muth Mauk! Ma nav Sevren!" The marchers slowed and Sevren caught up with them.

Yev-yat had told Dar that the urkzimmuthi never used the Old Road in winter, even when it was the only route to Taiben. Dar had spent the afternoon learning why. The way was more a path than a road. In good weather, it was probably narrow and difficult. Covered with snow, it was hidden and treacherous. What appeared to be solid ground sometimes proved to be snow-covered ice. Zna-yat had fallen through five times. Caution slowed their progress, and Dar feared the journey would take more than five days. Yet, despite her sense of urgency, Sevren's appearance gave her a welcome chance to slacken the pace for a spell. He dismounted when he reached the line of marchers and let Skymere trail behind the column. Ever since the horse had borne Dar to the Yat clan hall, he had lost his fear of orcs. Then Sevren hurried his pace until he reached Dar.

"Tava, Sevren."

"Tava, Muth Mauk. Ma fwilak ther sav." *Greetings, Great Mother. I pleased you see.*

"What news have you from Taiben?" asked Dar in Orcish.

Sevren attempted to respond in the same tongue. "Girtaz son new great washavoki. Kol no go yet. Many washavokis came."

Dar switched to the human tongue. "When do you think they'll march?"

"When I left, more units were still arriving," said Sevren, relieved to express himself more easily. "I think Kol won't make a move until all his troops assemble. Nobody is certain when that will be. A day or two, at least."

"What about the pass? Any word of it?"

"I didn't hear a thing."

"Even if Lama-tok and Ven-goth got through, the Tok clan wouldn't have sealed it yet," said Dar, more to herself than Sevren. "Have you learned anything else?"

"Aye, something useful. All the soldiers will carry their own rations. Each was issued two days' worth. I saw no supply wagons, which means Kol plans to feed his men with plunder."

"Two days' rations will be enough to get them to the Yat clan hall."

"An army moves slowly. I suspect hunger will spur the men by the time they attack."

"The road may hinder their assault," said Dar, "but not our hall."

"Aye. 'Tis na fortress," said Sevren. "Kol's na preparing for a siege."

"He has no need," said Dar, thinking of the hall's lightly built doors and numerous windows. "How many men will Kol have?"

"When I left, troops overflowed the garrison. I'd say there were nine regiments on foot, and more coming. Nearly two thousand men."

Sevren's talk of logistics and tactics made the imminent attack seem more concrete. *How many sons remain to protect the hall? Do they have weapons? Armor?* As Dar thought these matters over, she feared any defense would be futile. "The pass must be sealed at all costs," she said, unconsciously picking up the pace.

"I brought Queen Girta boots and winter riding garments," said Sevren. "That way, she can ride Skymere when she's able."

"And what of you?"

"I'll walk with the rest."

"You've done enough. There's no reason to stay."

"Remember how I spoke of leaving home with only a sword to earn my way?"

"I remember."

"I was just a lad, with a boy's understanding of the world. I thought I'd protect the weak. Right wrongs." Sevren shook his head over his naïveté. "I quickly learned the nature of my patrons and my trade. But this time is different."

"Because it's hopeless?"

"Na hopeless. Do na say that."

"If the pass isn't sealed, what chance will we have?"

"What chance did you have when you last faced the mage? Worthy causes need na be lost ones. I want to fight for you. I need to."

"Then you may. And thanks," said Dar. She smiled somewhat sadly. "I keep sending you away, then thanking you for remaining."

"Aye, that's the pattern to our dance."

Dar lapsed into silence, and Sevren fell in step behind her. It grew dark. Since Zna-yat led the column, that wasn't a problem, and Dar intended to keep marching a while longer. Yet when the river turned a bend, she suddenly shouted, "Gat!" *Stop!*

Zna-yat halted immediately, asking in Orcish, "What is it, Muth Mauk?"

"Someone's coming."

Zna-yat said nothing. He simply moved behind Dar. As he did so, Dar saw by his expression that he was unable to see what she did. She gazed at the figure limping on the snow-choked pathway. In the dim light, she could see only a vague outline. It appeared to be a son. Dar began walking toward him, leaving the others behind.

The son stopped walking, and as Dar approached him, his form grew more distinct. He was unclothed. His pale skin bore dark marks. Dar drew closer and saw the marks were bloody wounds. *That's why he was limping.* The son's translucency made him hard to recognize. Snowflakes remained visible as they drifted through his body, and his features intermingled with the landscape

behind them. Dar knew him only when they stood a few
paces apart. "Lama-tok?"

"Tava, Dargu."

Dar wasn't completely surprised, but that didn't lessen
her shock and grief.

Lama-tok seemed aware of Dar's feelings, and he regarded her with affection and concern. Then he smiled
slightly. "Dargu, I was wolf. I slew all those washavokis."

"But they also slew you."

"My life flowed out before I reached your hall. But I
nearly made it."

"And Ven-goth?"

"Washavokis were hidden inside pass, waiting with
arrows. His last thoughts were of Fre-pah. He'd like her
to know that."

"I'm sorry you and he died."

"Know we're embraced by Muth la. There's joy in
this." Lama-tok began to grow fainter. "And know this,
Dargu: It isn't always unwise to die."

With those words, Lama-tok faded entirely, leaving
Dar staring into the empty dark.

Forty-one

♛

Dar composed herself before returning to the waiting orcs, who stood quiet and expectant. "Lama-tok and Vengoth didn't survive their journey," she said, making the sign of the Tree. "Tok clan sons haven't learned they must seal pass. Now only I can tell them. We must make haste."

Zna-yat resumed marching immediately, as did the other orcs, but Dar stood still and waited for Nir-yat to reach her. When she did, the two let the others pass so they might walk rearmost in the column. There, Dar related her vision.

"So Muth la sent you warning," said Nir-yat after Dar finished.

"Hai. Pass won't be sealed in time. Washavoki soldiers will get through it."

"Couldn't you send Auk-goth ahead?" asked Nir-yat. "He's swift and hearty."

"I think he'll arrive too late."

"Shouldn't he try?"

"This is what worries me," said Dar. "Tok clan sons would obey my command, but such obedience has short-comings. If situation changes, wisest course might change also."

"And they won't have your wisdom to guide them."

"Hai. I feel I must be there, Nir. It's important."

Nir gazed at her sister awhile before she spoke in a quiet, sorrowful voice. "You say that because of Lama-tok's final words."

"Last great mother died so I might be here. I may be called to make sacrifice also."

Nir-yat grasped Dar's hand. "Sister, I have no counsel to offer, only love."

Dar smiled. "That's what I need most."

Sevren understood what Dar had said, but he remained baffled. After trailing behind Zna-yat awhile, he spoke to him. "Zna-yat, how Muth Mauk learn?" he asked in Orcish. "When we speak, she not learn pass."

"Muth Mauk has visions," replied Zna-yat.

"What this word 'visions'?"

"Muth la speaks to her. She has done this before. Sometimes Muth Mauk sees what will happen."

Dar's a seer? thought Sevren. Somehow, he wasn't surprised. "What does Muth la say her?"

"I don't know," replied Zna-yat. "Muth la speaks to mothers, not sons. Her counsels are not for us."

Sevren fell behind Zna-yat again, for it was easier walking in the orc's footsteps. He trudged along, pondering Dar's gift with a sense of awe. He walked a long way before Zna-yat spoke again. "Sev-ron?"

"Hai."

"Washavoki great mother spent last night in my shelter. She chewed leaf, so she waked not."

"Hai," replied Sevren.

"Tonight she will not chew leaf. If you say yes, I will ask my sister if washavoki can sleep with you. I think she will like that better."

Sevren got the gist of what Zna-yat had said and understood why he was making the request. *He thinks Queen Girta stinks.* He wondered what Girta would think of the arrangement. *She might prefer me to an orc.* "If mothers say is good, is good me."

"Shashav, Sev-ron."

                    *   *   *

Sometime around midnight, Dar called a halt when the march reached another bend in the river. There was an area of level ground sufficiently large enough to set up a camp. Trees and tangled brush grew upon it, but Nir-yat set sons to clearing the brush away. Sevren was surprised when she took charge. She did so with more competence and authority than any murdant Sevren had ever met. As he tended to Skymere, Nir-yat had other sons gather firewood. Soon there was a fire. Sons placed water-filled kettles on the blaze, marked Muth la's Embrace, and erected shelters within the sacred circle.

While all this was going on, Dar quietly sat on a fallen log. She looked so tired and melancholy, Sevren wondered if her vision had drained her. His heart went out to Dar, and he became aware that his feeling wasn't unique. All the orcs appeared as moved as he was; he could tell by their faces. At that moment, Dar seemed too weary to notice.

When the water in the pots boiled, porridge was made and herb water brewed. Dar rose to say that food was Muth la's gift, but Nir-yat served it. After Dar ate, she disappeared into Kovok-mah's shelter. Sevren was experiencing a twinge of jealousy when Nir-yat approached him. "Sev-ron," she said in Orcish, "we have few shelters. I think it best that you and other washavoki be together. Will you tell her this? I do not speak your tongue."

Sevren bowed politely and replied in Orcish, "Hai, Mother." He walked over to where Girta was sitting. Noticing that she had changed into the clothes he had brought her, he bowed and asked, "Your Majesty, do your boots and garments fit?"

"Very well, thank you."

"If you feel up to it, my horse is yours to ride tomorrow."

"I'd be pleased to ride. You are gracious, sir."

Then Sevren summoned his nerve and spoke his

message. "The orcs are short of shelters, Your Majesty.
They've asked us to share one."

Girta looked askance. "You mean sleep with you?"

"Orcs treat mothers with utmost respect. They expect
me to also, and I will."

"But the appearance of it!"

"Last night, you slept with an orc. Perhaps you'd prefer to do so again."

"No," said Girta quickly. "I'm confident in your propriety, and there are no courtiers' tongues to set wag-
ging." She smiled slightly. "Besides, I'm deceased."

"I know. I attended your funeral."

"Was it tasteful?"

"Haste spoiled its solemnity. Kol was anxious to be
off fighting."

"Did you see my son?"

"Only from a distance. He looked heartbroken."

Girta let out a sob, then stifled another. "The cruelty
of that man! To think I trusted him."

Sevren, recalling how Girta had distrusted his advice,
chose not to reply. He rose instead. "I assume Your Majesty
will retire soon, so I'll cut some fir boughs for our shelter's
floor. Because orcs sleep sitting up, they never think of
bedding."

"That sounds better than a cloak spread on the snow,"
said Girta. A smile crept onto her face. "I haven't camped
outdoors since I was a girl."

Sevren and his monarch slept huddled close together. In
the cold night, warmth was more important than decorum. Nir-yat woke them at first light. After a hurried
meal, the march resumed at dawn. Its quick pace was set
by Dar's sense of urgency. She and Zna-yat led the way,
and the rest followed. Girta rode, handling Skymere skillfully despite her injury.

Their route continued to follow the river, which flowed

between two mountains. The way was steep and rugged. The snow-covered slopes flanking either side were also steep, causing the orcs to speak quietly for fear of starting a "kokuum." Sevren assumed that "kokuum" was the Orcish word for "avalanche," for he saw evidence of several. Three times, they clambered over swatches of splintered and flattened trees. Once, a huge pile of snow partly dammed the river, forcing them to scale a mountain slope in a precarious detour.

Throughout the day, Dar walked silently and steady. She seemed absorbed by her thoughts. Sevren suspected that they were troubled, judging from her expression. He couldn't help worrying about the future she had glimpsed. *Not a happy one, I warrant.* Yet Dar's hurried pace seemed proof that she had some hope. *No one rushes to certain death.* Then Sevren recalled that Dar had expected to die once before and refused to flee. That caused him to worry anew.

Dar had no idea what she would encounter at their journey's end. The Yat clan hall might be in flames and the valley below it swarming with troops. Yet there still might be a chance to do something. Dar knew circumstances would determine what that something could be. Her current ignorance was maddening, and it goaded her to go faster. Unlike the orcs, she wore no armor nor carried any burden. Yet she knew that they could easily outpace her, even encumbered. *That's why I must push myself. I'm slowing everyone down.*

Dar led the march until late in the night, when fatigue forced her to halt. As before, Nir-yat took over. After she served the food, she joined Dar. "We traveled far, Muth Mauk. You must be weary."

"The farther I walk, the easier I rest," replied Dar.

"Will we see our hall soon?"

"Not tomorrow, but next day. According to those

deetpahis I studied, we'll soon leave this valley and start traveling east. Then way will be easier."

"It's hard not knowing what we'll find," said Nir-yat. "You have poor sense of smell, so I'll tell you—I'm afraid."

"You already smell my fear," said Dar. "Are sons fearful also?"

"Every one."

"They should be hopeful, too. Muth la doesn't send visions without reason."

Dar finished her porridge in silence, brooding upon the future. When she finished eating, she rose wearily. Kovok-mah rose also and headed for his shelter. He was already sitting cross-legged on his fur sleeping mat when Dar joined him. The shelter's interior was cramped, but that also made it cozy. Kovok-mah's body heat had already reduced its chill. Dar climbed onto his lap, which he had cushioned with an extra cloak, to remove her boots. Afterward, she didn't sit with her back against his chest. Instead, she knelt facing him. Then she grasped his hand and brushed it against the front of her kef.

The breast touching gesture was the decorous one that mothers used to initiate love-giving. But Kovok-mah was forbidden to love Dar, so she understood the gravity of what she wanted. For a moment, he remained absolutely still. Dar sensed his inner struggle. Then—as she had hoped—he defied his muthuri's injunction. "Dargu," he whispered with such love and longing that it raised goose bumps on her flesh.

They found one another's lips in the dark. Kovok-mah first kissed Dar in the way she had taught him. Then he began kissing her neck in the orcish fashion, his active tongue teasing and tasting. Dar removed her kefs and washavoki shirt. As Kovok-mah's lips sought her breasts, even she could smell the fragrance of atur.

For a while, pent-up passion obliterated the future.

There seemed only one chance for bliss, and Dar seized it, desperate and hungry. She took off her remaining clothes, pulling her cloak over her naked body. Kovok-mah's hands and lips moved under the garment in the tender, reverent way she remembered. He grasped her hips and slowly lifted them, so that as Dar rose up, his lips traveled downward. When she stood on his thighs, Kovok-mah's tongue reached her center. Dar felt a jolt of pleasure that heightened, then slowly spread throughout her body. The cloak slipped off, but Dar was oblivious of the cold. Only the ecstasy of the moment mattered. When Kovok-mah brought her to release, it took all her self-control not to cry out.

Spent and contented, Dar sank into Kovok-mah's lap. He covered her with the cloak and embraced her. She stayed like that until a draught found her warm skin. Then Dar dressed, and like the cold, the future began to seep into her thoughts. Her bliss faded. It had been a joyous moment, but it was over.

On the fourth morning of the flight from Taiben, Nir-yat roused everyone at first light. As usual, she studied her sister when she emerged from Kovok-mah's shelter. On that morning, Nir-yat made two discoveries. Dar smelled of atur—the fragrance was thick and heady—and her features were tranquil but melancholy. Nir-yat's chest burst to see that look, for it reminded her of when Dar expected to drink Muth la's Draught. Then, with the wisdom that sisters often have, Nir-yat said nothing. But when she served Dar warmed-up porridge, she embraced her.

The sky was clear when the march began. Dar instructed Zna-yat to set a brisk pace, then walked with Nir-yat at the end of the column. Sevren trailed behind Zna-yat, for he had come to enjoy his companionship, though Zna-yat rarely spoke. They marched wordlessly most of the morning. Toward noon, the trail became easier. They were higher into the mountains and the valley they traveled widened and inclined more gently. Snow had fallen less heavily there, and the road was more evident.

With the walking less taxing, Zna-yat struck up a conversation. "Sev-ron. What do you do when not killing for great washavoki?"

"I killing only."

"That is not proper living. I grow crops."

"I wish grow crops, but I have no dirt."

Zna-yat smiled. "I think you mean 'land.' Do your mothers lack wisdom? They should let you grow crops on their land. It is better than killing."

"Washavoki mothers seldom own land."

"Then who does?"

"Whoever . . ." Sevren tried to think of the Orcish words for "pay" or "buy" but he didn't know if they even existed. "Whoever gives gift for it."

"Gift to who?"

"To son who owns land," replied Sevren. "I have no gift, so I have no land. I kill and get little gifts. Someday have enough for land."

"Washavokis are strange and foolish."

"Hai, Zna-yat, I think also."

Zna-yat walked quietly awhile, seemingly puzzled by what Sevren had told him. At last, he asked, "Sev-ron, what gift is as good as land?"

Rather than explain, Sevren pulled out his purse and emptied the twelve gold coins it contained into his palm. It was his life savings. "These," he said.

Zna-yat grinned incredulously. "Bits of yellow iron? That worth land? Why?"

Sevren gazed at the coins and was infected by Zna-yat's sense of absurdity. He replied by saying the only thing that came to mind. "Yellow iron is pretty."

"Hai," replied Zna-yat, shifting the straps of his pack, "but heavy."

Sevren put the coins away. "I think urkzimmuthi have more wisdom. Land better than yellow iron. Food from land gives life."

"Mothers also give life. That's why they own land."

Sevren imagined what Kol would do with the land about the Yat clan hall. *Give it to a follower*, he surmised. *Some thug who'll have peasants till the earth and take most of what they grow.* He envisioned drunken feasts in the hall's Great Chamber feting Kol as its owner's patron and lord. The idea was infuriating. He noted that Zna-yat was looking at him. *He smells my anger.* "I thinking no washavoki should have urkzimmuthi land. They too evil to possess it."

"Hai, Sev-ron. We must prevent that."

Forty-two

♛

By late afternoon, the marchers headed eastward, having passed through the southernmost range of the Urkheit Mountains. They were in urkzimmuthi territory, separated from the washavoki realm by tall heights that were crested by a formidable ridge. Mountains extended in all directions, forming a landscape familiar to the orcs. Toward evening, the road merged with one Dar recognized. She had traveled it to reach Kovok-mah's muthuri's hall.

Dar left Nir-yat's side to catch up with her brother. "You must have traveled this road often," she said.

"Hai, many times," replied Zna-yat.

"If we didn't stop, when would we reach our hall?"

"Before dawn, but not much before."

"Then we shall stop to eat this night, but not to sleep. I wish to reach our hall as soon as possible."

Zna-yat bowed his head. "Hai, Muth Mauk. If you grow tired, I'll carry you."

"You're kind, but that will be unnecessary."

"Please, Sister, don't overtax yourself."

"I wear no armor and carry no burden. I'll be fine."

"Muth Mauk, I think you carry greatest burden of all."

Dar smiled sadly, but didn't reply. As she headed back to Nir-yat's side, Sevren spoke to her in the human tongue. "Your Majesty, a word."

"What is it?"

"Why na send scouts ahead? Your orcs can move

quickly, especially if they shed their armor. There's na point in marching blind."

"That's a good idea," said Dar. She called Auk-goth and Treen-pah over to her, judging them the fastest runners. "Leave your armor for others to carry," she said. "I want you to go ahead and discover what washavokis are doing. Don't fight them or let them see you. Auk-goth, go to pass. Do you know way from here to New Road?"

"Hai. We came this way with matriarchs."

"Good," said Dar. "Treen-pah, I want you to go to Yat clan hall."

"Hai, Muth Mauk. I know way."

"Come back and warn me if you spot danger. Otherwise, go to Yat clan hall. I'll arrive there before morning, and you can tell me what you've seen."

Both mintaris bowed. Soon, they were off. Dar watched them lope down the snowy road with long steady strides. Before long, they were only specks in the distance. She turned to Sevren. "This journey will be less fearful knowing we won't be surprised along the way."

"You should have another son walk sixty paces in advance of our column. Soldiers could take positions after your scouts have passed through. Having someone walk ahead could prevent an ambush."

"That sounds wise." Dar sighed. "I know so little about tactics."

"You can learn them easily enough," said Sevren. "I only regret that you must."

Dar and the orcs continued marching until well after dark. Then Dar called a halt to cook a quick meal before continuing onward. The stars were brilliant in the night sky, and when a crescent moon rose over the snowy mountains, it evoked a memory of a former queen. For a moment, Dar was Muth Mauk from many generations past. She was returning from having witnessed the birth of a granddaughter. The sky and the mountains looked as they had on that night, and after Dar relived the long-dead queen's joy and awe, she felt a part of something larger than herself. She was but one in a line of queens stretching through time. *It's the line that matters*, she thought. *As long as it continues, I continue.*

Sometime after midnight, a cloud bank moved in, blotting out the stars and moon. The night darkened, and the white mountains turned murky gray. Dar saw the orcs only as shadows. Barely seen snowflakes began to strike her face in ever-increasing numbers. The storm made walking mindless drudgery. One step followed another while darkness and snowfall obscured the surrounding landscape. There was no sense of progress, for nothing seemed to change. Existence shrank to taking the next step.

The march dragged on. Dar no longer thought of its end. When Zna-yat said something about a valley, it didn't register on her fatigue-numbed mind. Then they started climbing a steep road that switched back and forth between terraced fields. It dawned on Dar that they were climbing the road to the Yat clan hall. She gazed upward. Crowning the heights, the hall was shrouded in snow. Its dark windows made it seem abandoned. "We made it," said Dar, as if she couldn't believe it.

Climbing the steep road to the hall's entrance was the final test of Dar's endurance. Despite her exhaustion, apprehension brought her to wakefulness. Neither scout had contacted her. *That's either a good sign or some disaster's happened.* The unlit hall suddenly seemed menacing. *Perhaps it's filled with waiting soldiers.* Regardless of that thought, Dar continued treading toward its door.

She finally reached it. The door opened, and Treen-pah stood inside. He bowed. "Muth Mauk, you've arrived at last."

"Hai. What news?"

"There's none to tell. I saw no signs of washavokis."

"What did Auk-goth see?"

"He hasn't returned."

Sevren, who had followed the conversation, bowed low to Dar and spoke to her in the human tongue. "It might be prudent to send out more scouts on the New Road, in case Auk-goth had a mishap."

Dar nodded her agreement. She recalled that Tauma-yat had two unblessed sons who farmed in summer and hunted in winter. She asked that they be brought to her hanmuthi. Then she turned to Nir-yat. "Find room for Sevren and Queen Girta in my hanmuthi. They'll need something to lie upon. Sevren also will need place for his horse."

"I'll do this and also find places for sons who accompanied us. If I have bath sent to washavokis' room, would they use it?"

"Thwa. Among washavokis, sons and mothers bathe separately. Also Girta doesn't understand wisdom of cleanliness. I'll teach her tomorrow."

As Nir-yat made those arrangements, Dar headed for her hanmuthi. Her exhaustion returned, but she waited for Tauma-yat's sons to arrive. When they did, she explained that she wanted them to seek for washavokis on the New Road. "Approach them as if they were hares," she said. "They must not see you. If you find them, remember I want knowledge, not fighting. I wish to know their numbers, whether they are still or marching. If marching, how fast. Note their location and activities. Discover if more are arriving through pass. When you learn these things, return quickly. This hall is in peril, and I need this knowledge to decide what course to take."

After the sons departed, Dar took off her boots. Without undressing further, she collapsed into her bed. Within moments, she was asleep.

* * *

Elsewhere in the night, His Royal Majesty and Monarch of the Eastern Realm, King Kregant III, shivered beneath his sleeping furs as he sucked his thumb. Winds buffeted his dark tent, making its walls flap loudly. But it wasn't the noise that prevented sleep. The boy feared his cloth shelter might be blown off the ridge it straddled, sending him plummeting to his death. He had voiced this concern earlier, but General Kol had belittled it, making him feel stupid.

The king missed his mother terribly. He had already grown disenchanted with war, although his ride out of Taiben had been glorious. Mounted on a black mare and resplendent in his new armor, he had felt very much the warrior hero. Crowds had cheered him. Shouts of encouragement and praise had swelled his heart. But the long ride to the pass had eroded that feeling.

A bitter wind had blown throughout the day. The meager winter sunshine hadn't lessened the cold's misery, and wearing metal armor increased it. The heavy chain mail sucked warmth from his body, despite the woolen garments he wore beneath it. The helmet was worse. His breath froze on it until his head felt surrounded by ice. The snow made progress painfully slow. When the road began to climb, snow also made the way treacherous. A sustolum in the king's party had been crushed beneath his horse when it slipped and tumbled down a slope. An entire shieldron slid down the mountainside, triggering the avalanche that engulfed it.

As bad as these conditions were, others oppressed the boy king more. The soldiers grumbled and regarded him with resentment. Men who had cheered him in the courtyard began to call him "the brat" and "young snotnose" within his hearing. The general ignored their disrespect, for he had changed also. That was perhaps the greatest blow. Once out of Taiben and among soldiers, General Kol was no longer the king's solicitous friend. Instead, he acted as if he were the real ruler. He was still polite, but there was mockery in his formality. The king's wishes were disregarded by both the general and his soldiers. Soon, he had come to feel that he was little more than baggage.

Heaped on those affronts and humiliations was another oppression, one that afflicted more than the king. There was uneasiness among the soldiers, an undercurrent impossible to ignore. The king became aware of it through the hushed talk and nervous glances of the men. The glances were always rearward. The soldiers appeared less afraid of what lay ahead than what trailed behind.

Once, when the winding road doubled back as it neared the pass, Kregant III caught a glimpse of what followed the army. A group of men walked at a distance from the rearmost unit. They bore an enclosed litter. It was black, and the men were garbed in the same shade. They moved with a quality that evoked instinctive fear. The boy felt he was viewing walking corpses bearing an equally unnatural burden. The litter and its attendants terrified him, and he wasn't alone in his reaction. The soldiers appeared frightened, too. Even General Kol seemed uneasy. It was the one thing the king and his general still had in common.

Soft winter daylight illuminated the room when Dar opened her eyes. Outside, snow was still falling. Nir-yat sat close by, her face anxious. Dar moaned, still thick with sleep. "I need bath."

"I'll come with you, Sister. There's much to discuss. All our hall knows what you said to Tauma-yat's sons."

Dar jolted awake. *I didn't forbid them to speak!* "Have they or Auk-goth yet returned?"

"Thwa."

"Does our hall smell of fear?"

"That scent is thick."

"I was tired when I spoke to Tauma-yat's sons. This fear is my fault."

"Sometimes it's wise to be afraid. Fearless birds feed foxes."

Dar smiled slightly. "So my oversight showed wisdom?"

"Everyone's aware of our peril. I think that's good."

"It's good only if I can lead them to safety," said Dar. "I must decide what to do, then present my plan. But I'll not do it reeking from my journey. I must bathe." She sighed. "I suppose I should persuade Girta to join me."

Nir-yat smiled. "Sev-ron has shown wisdom and convinced her to wash. She has done so already."

"That's pleasing news." Dar rose. "Come, Sister, let us talk as I wash."

Dar avoided the communal bath by using a tub in a room off her hanmuthi. While she washed, she and Nir-yat discussed what to do. There was hope that Kol's army had not yet marched, but Dar thought it was unlikely. She decided to have Nir-yat determine how many sons could be gathered to defend the hall and what arms could be obtained for them. Meanwhile, Dar would meet with the Tok clan to find out if the pass could still be sealed.

Dar dressed. Then, accompanied by Sevren and her mintaris, she went to the Great Chamber and called for the Tok clan representatives. Two mothers and a son arrived. Dar had learned their names in advance, so she might greet them properly. Karam-tok was Muth-tok's younger sister, and she possessed the same large, muscular frame as the matriarch. Karam-tok was accompanied by the Tok clan lorekeeper, an elderly mother named Gra-tok. The son, Tar-tok, wore a cape signifying leadership. He was the largest orc Dar had ever seen. Extremely tall, with arms much thicker than a man's thighs, his body seemed shaped by working massive stones.

After the Tok clan members bowed and returned Dar's

greetings, Karam-tok spoke. "Muth Mauk, we know why you've called us. Washavokis will invade through pass."

"Now all can appreciate your grandmother's wisdom," said Dar. "That door must be shut. Lama-tok said it would take one or two days. Can it be done faster?"

"Sealing pass is complicated process," replied Karam-tok. "Lines of deep holes were drilled into rock. Afterward, they were plugged. If those holes are filled with water, that water will turn to ice, expand, and split rock. Only then will sons be able to push rocks into passageway. Winter will make water freeze quickly, but it will also make holes hard to reach."

"Water may split stones, but sons must still leverage them apart and push them into pass," said Tar-tok. "That is hard work. It will take one day at least. I think two is more likely."

Dar regarded the massive orc. "If you call that work hard, it must be hard indeed."

"There is way to speed that work," said Gra-tok, "but its outcome is less certain."

All eyes turned to the Tok clan lorekeeper as she continued. "Holes were also drilled in peak short distance from pass. Rocks split there could be sent tumbling to start kokuum. Instead of sons, it could push loosened rock into pass."

"Gra-tok is wise to say outcome is uncertain," said Tar-tok. "Kokuum could make matters worse."

"How?" asked Dar, who thought triggering an avalanche would be a perfect solution.

"It might miss pass or fill it only partly. Worse, it could stop short of pass and cover loosened rock. That could add many days to our work."

"Slower way is surer way," said Karam-tok.

Dar was pondering her choices when Nir-yat rushed into the chamber. "Muth Mauk! Auk-goth has returned!"

A moment later, Auk-goth staggered through the doorway, so out of breath he was unable to return Dar's greeting for a while. At last, Auk-goth had the breath to speak. "There are washavokis on New Road."

Dar's face fell. "On our side of pass?"

"Hai. When I came upon them, it was night and they were inside cloth shelters. There were many hundreds of them, encrusting ridge like second snowfall."

"Where were they?"

"Still high on ridge, just beyond pass."

"So we know they're coming," said Dar. "But that's about all we know."

"When I was returning, I met those two sons you sent. We spoke before they traveled on toward pass. Perhaps they'll learn more."

Karam-tok's face reflected her dismay. "There's no point in sealing pass now. Wolves are in sheep pen."

"Urkzimmuthi are not sheep," said Dar. "Nir-yat, how many sons can protect our hall?"

"There are seventy-two sons within our hall who can fight. Most have swords or axes, but none possesses armor. Not even helmets. Those who lack weapons can use tools or farm implements. Another hundred or so Yat clan sons live close enough to aid us. Your mintaris and guards from Taiben add forty-one to that number."

"We have fifty-six sons in our party," said Karam-tok. "All bear axes. I'll put them at your service."

Dar pondered the situation before she replied. "Even if Tok sons join fight, this hall will have less than three hundred defenders. Sevren told me they'll face two thousand soldiers, perhaps more." Dar let the dismal news sink in. "Karam-tok, I need your clan's sons elsewhere."

"Where?"

"At pass. Can they reach it if there are washavokis on road?"

"I know of way to pass other than New Road," said the Tok clan lorekeeper.

"Then there's yet hope," said Dar, "though Yat clan mothers may not see it as such. I must speak to them before you can proceed."

Forty-three

👑

Word went out for all muthuris to assemble in the Great Chamber. They came quickly, followed by all the hall's residents. The chamber grew crowded, but formalities were observed. Muth-yat stood closest to the throne. Beside her was Muth-pah. The heads of the hall's other hanmuthis stood slightly farther back. Beyond them were the rest of the muthuris. Dar was surprised to spot Meera-yat. The remaining space was occupied by mothers, blessed and unblessed, young and old. They overflowed the chamber, spilling into the corridors beyond, where sons mingled with them.

The room was so tightly packed that it grew unpleasantly warm. Despite the crowd, the chamber was deathly quiet. All eyes were on Dar. As she returned their gaze, she felt her chest would break with love and sorrow. Everyone was precious to her, and everyone was in deadly danger. For a moment, Dar didn't speak for fear her voice would tremble. Then by some grace, she grew calm.

"This rooms smells of fear," said Dar. "It's Muth la's gift, for she wants her children safe. Fear may oppress you, but it can also lead to wisdom.

"I journeyed to Taiben to learn if washavokis desire peace. They don't. All washavokis aren't evil, but they've been gripped by evil. Black Washavoki didn't die. Instead, he was transformed. Using magic, he's compelled others to do his bidding. Washavoki queen wanted peace, so she was forced to flee with us. Black Washavoki hates all urkzimmuthi. He has sent army to slay us. That army approaches. It's already in our land."

The room grew so pungent with fear that even Dar could smell it.

"Before I was reborn, I lived among washavoki soldiers and saw war's cruelty. I think Muth la wished me to witness it in preparation for this moment. Now hear my wisdom: Our sons are brave and strong. Yet superior numbers can and will overwhelm them. I've seen this before. We cannot stop washavokis' attack. It's unwise to try."

Despite the orcs' deference to their queen, a murmur arose among them. Dar waited for it to quiet.

"Our enemy's strength is also its weakness. Big armies cannot hide. They have many mouths to feed. Washavokis don't know this land, but they can follow New Road to our hall. They have no choice but to come. They need food. They need shelter. They want our goods and our lives. All these things they must take from us. But when they come, they won't find them. They'll find death instead. Why? Because we'll have sealed pass so they cannot leave, and we'll have departed after destroying this hall."

This time, the chamber rang with alarmed voices. Muth-yat's was the loudest. Eventually, the others quieted so Muth-yat could speak for them. "So this is your wisdom?" she cried. "To become cowards and abandon our home?"

"I say cling to life, not this hall," said Dar. "We can overcome these washavokis, but only if we act wisely. Mothers will flee, but sons will remain. With no food or shelter and nowhere to flee, washavokis will weaken. We'll attack them as small birds attack hawk. We'll dart in to peck our larger foe, then fly away. Each peck will injure it. Many small wounds can bring death."

"You brought this on us!" shouted Muth-yat, violating all propriety. "You should have tasted Muth la's Draught!"

"Have her taste it now!" cried Zor-yat. "If she's worthy to rule, let her prove it!"

"Muthuri!" shouted Nir-yat. "Have you forsaken wisdom? This hall's destruction was foretold! You know this."

"How dare you speak to me like that!" screamed Zor-yat in reply. "You're my daughter. Show respect."

"I follow your example, Muthuri. How dare you question Muth Mauk's wisdom?"

The exchange stunned the crowd into silence. That was when Muth-pah mounted the first step of the throne, drawing everyone's attention "I am Muth-pah. Hear my wisdom. My clan was once mightiest among urkzimmuthi. We were Queen Clan. Tarathank was our home. Yet now my entire clan fits into one hanmuthi, and we're called lost.

"Most believe washavokis did that to us, but we did it to ourselves. True, washavokis destroyed our city and killed many of our number. But that didn't make us Lost Clan. We became doomed when our thoughts fixed on past. We sent our sons to kill, hoping to take back what had been lost. When that failed, we lingered in west. There, our sons hunted washavoki skulls. We embraced death, not life. Thus we diminished.

"Do not let this lovely hall become your Tarathank. It's only wood and stone. Your lives and your children are your true treasures. Heed Muth Mauk's wisdom. Forsake this hall."

Then Dar spoke. "Muth la sends me visions, but she doesn't tell me what to do. I must choose my path. As your queen, I can command you. I will not. I cannot make you live. That must be your choice.

"If you choose to remain, I'll stay and die with you. If you choose to flee, I will guide you. Whatever you decide, be aware that this hall *will* burn. Muth la has shown me its destruction. Perhaps washavokis will set it on fire. Perhaps we will. I don't know."

Dar swept her glaze over the entire room. "Now choose."

For a moment, everyone stood frozen. Then Jvar-yat, the clan's latath, spoke out. "Guide me, Muth Mauk. I will follow you." She sank to her knees and made the sign of the Tree.

"I'll heed your wisdom," said Tauma-yat, kneeling and making the sign for Muth la.

Then other muthuris did the same. The room filled with their voices as they knelt. From where Dar sat, the mothers looked like grass bending before a wind. Eventually, only Muth-yat and Zor-yat remained standing. They glanced about, then fell to their knees also.

The room grew still and silent. Dar regarded the kneeling orcs with tear-brimmed eyes before she spoke. "We must flee in haste but not in panic. Gather warm clothes and those tools you'll need to start new life. Carry as much food as you possibly can. Pile everything you leave behind together so it might be burned after you depart. Stay in your hanmuthis to receive further guidance. When it's time to leave, Nir-yat will guide you. You should go now."

As the chamber emptied out, Dar began to think of all the things that must be done. *I must finish the plan for sealing the pass . . . tell sons how they must fight . . . plot our escape . . . send messages to the other clans . . . direct the destruction of this hall.* When she considered each task, the details seemed overwhelming. Dar's head was awhirl with all she had to accomplish, and it was a while before she noticed her sister gazing at her. Nir-yat looked distressed. "What is it?" Dar asked.

"*I'm* to guide our clan as we flee?"

"Hai. I'll see this hall is destroyed, then join you."

"But you're our queen."

"And you're my sister. I have confidence in you."

"But . . ."

"I need you, Nir. Who else can I turn to? Not Muth-yat."

Nir-yat bowed. "Then I'll do my best."

"Your best is all that's necessary. Make sure this goes calmly. Head for Mah clan halls but avoid New Road."

Nir-yat thought a moment. "We can take road to Smat clan halls," she said. "It goes north, but after three days' travel, it joins with road that heads south. That way will add at least five days to our journey."

"Your plan sounds wise," said Dar. "Gather those living in countryside as you go. They must flee also. Nothing can remain for washavokis."

"You'll need sons to help destroy this hall," said Nir-yat. "How many should I send you?"

"Send thirty. Also set out sentries to warn of washa-vokis' approach. All remaining sons should go with mothers and protect them."

After Nir-yat departed, Dar summoned the three Tok clan representatives. "We're going to destroy this hall," said Dar when they arrived, "so washavokis will have no food or shelter. If you seal pass, they cannot escape."

"Desperate foes are dangerous ones, Muth Mauk," said Karam-tok. "Are you sure you want them in our land?"

Dar briefly considered letting Kol depart without a fight. Without the prospect of plunder, he might lose interest in the orcs. On the face of it, that seemed less risky than trapping and fighting him. Then Dar recalled how she had bested Kol before, only to have him return even stronger. Dar's instincts told her that Kol wouldn't let matters rest. *And what of Othar?* Dar assumed he was still in Taiben. *If the army returns intact, he'll use it for another invasion.* With that reflection, Dar resolved on her course. "Hidden foes are most deadly," said Dar. "We can't avoid this fight. Best have it now."

Karam-tok bowed. "Then let us discuss how we'll seal pass."

"We know washavokis were camped on New Road just beyond pass," said Dar. "I assume they'll arrive here late today."

Sevren, who had been following the conversation as best he could, spoke up in Orcish. "Washavokis will not fight dark. Will wait morning."

"That's good to know," said Karam-tok. "We'll need that time."

Gar-tok pulled out what looked to Dar to be a bundle of sticks and string. She tugged at one of the strings and the bundle opened to become an intricate, three-dimensional construction. It was comprised of sticks, which differed in shape, length, thickness, and color, that were bound together by cords that also varied. "This is trafpaha. It shows ridge and rocks that make it," said the lorekeeper. The three Tok clan members studied the object, clearly understanding its complex symbology.

Tar-tok pointed to a knotted cord. "So we would ascend here?"

"Hai," replied Gar-tok. "It's two hills west of New Road and out of sight from it."

"Yellow means steep climb," said Tar-tok.

"Use ropes," said Karam-tok.

"Hai," said Tar-tok. He slowly traced a series of sticks that portrayed the ridgeline. "This way won't be easy." His fingers stopped at a protruding stick. "Is this peak you spoke of?"

"Hai. What do you think?"

Tar-tok studied the pattern of small twigs radiating

from the stick that represented the peak. "Kokuum might work here. What do you think, Karam-tok?"

The mother examined the trafpaha. "It looks promising." She bowed to Dar. "Muth Mauk, shall we risk using kokuum to seal pass? It would be faster, though less certain of success."

"Speed is necessary for success," said Dar. "Use kokuum." She thought a moment, then added. "How will I know if passage is closed?"

"Perhaps we could light signal fire," said Karam-tok.

But who would see it? wondered Dar. The pass was far away and visibility was unpredictable. She resigned herself to living with uncertainty. "You needn't bother," she said. "After you seal pass, head for Mah clan halls. When we meet there, I'll know you succeeded."

Karam-tok bowed. "We'll leave at once."

As the three departed, Dar turned to Kovok-mah. "Will those mothers go with Tar-tok?"

"Most certainly, Muth Mauk."

"Even Gar-tok? She looks too old to be climbing mountains."

"She'll go," replied Kovok-mah. "She's their lore-keeper, and Tok clan lore concerns mostly rocks and mountains. She knows that ridge like I knew my goats."

Dar recalled how Lama-tok had loved stonework. *He dragged me about Tarathank to show his favorite walls.* Thoughts of her slain friend renewed her grief. "Peril and haste have made me neglectful," she said. "If I live, I must honor dead properly."

Time was not on Dar's side and she knew it. That was her only certainty. Almost everything else was unknown and unpredictable. *When will Kol's army arrive? Will they attack at once? Will the pass be sealed? If it's sealed, what will Kol do? Can we fight so great a foe? Will this storm help* or *hurt us?* Dar tried not to waste time attempting to answer those questions; there was too much to do.

Dar's initial impulse was to pitch in and help. If Kol's army arrived before the hall was evacuated, everyone would be slaughtered. Yet as much as Dar wanted to lend a hand, she knew that wasn't her role. She was queen, and her task was to lead. Dar had much to do. She had to ensure the evacuation went swiftly, oversee the hall's destruction, and prepare for the fighting to follow. That meant remaining in the center of the storm, not flying about in it.

Her first step was to meet with the thirty sons Nir-yat had sent to help destroy the hall. Dar spoke with them after they gathered in the Great Chamber. "Walls of this hall are stone," she said, "but most of its ceilings are wooden. Gather everything that will burn into piles within largest rooms. When I give word, we'll break all windows to let in wind, and set those piles ablaze. Those fires must spread quickly. How can this be aided?"

A son bowed. "In kitchen, there are cooking oils that could help piles ignite."

"Wise thinking," said Dar. "Use lamp oil, too."

Another son bowed. "Cloth could be soaked in those oils. That would make it light quicker."

"Hai," said Dar. "Do that, but save all white cloth. Worn like cloaks, it will make you hard to see in snow." Dar could tell by the orcs' faces that many failed to grasp the idea of camouflage. It seemed a foretaste of the difficulties ahead. "Do this thing and trust in my wisdom. Is there anything else that can speed fire's spread?"

"Deetpahis are waxed wood," said a son. "They'll burn well."

"Good suggestion," said Dar, "but I must consult with lorekeeper first." She turned to Zna-yat. "You know this hall well. Decide which rooms should be set ablaze and direct sons in assembling piles. I think we'll be lighting them soon."

Dar spoke to her other mintaris. "Assist Zna-yat. Sevren, come with me." Then she addressed the assembled sons. "Zna-yat will tell you what to do." She rose to see the lorekeeper. "Remember, Zna, washavokis should find nothing they can use. Keep me informed. I'll return here soon." As Zna-yat bowed, Dar hurried out of the room with Sevren at her heels.

"Have you been following what I've said?" asked Dar in the human tongue.

"I understand Orcish better than I speak it," replied Sevren. "Having your fighters wear white capes was a clever idea."

"Which a lot of them don't grasp," said Dar. "Murdant Teeg was right. Orcs lack guile."

"Their queen doesn't."

"So talk to me about tactics," said Dar as she walked. "What will Kol do first?"

"That depends on what he wants. If it's just plunder, he'll camp and wait for dawn to attack. If it's slaughter, he'll surround the hall right away to cut off any escape."

"Othar's his master," said Dar. "I'm certain he'll want slaughter."

"Then get your folk out quick and have them hide their tracks as best they can."

"There are ways out from this hall other than the road," said Dar. "If Kol thinks we're in here, he won't go hunting for us."

"But as soon as you torch this place, he'll know you've fled."

"I'll wait until the last possible moment."

"We could end up trapped in a burning building."

"That's not your problem," said Dar. "You're going with Nir-yat. Those sons with her must learn how to fight."

"They won't listen to me."

"They'll listen to her."

"What if I can't explain things properly?"

"Kovok-mah will help you."

"You're sending both of us away, and staying in the hall?"

"Only until it's on fire."

"But . . ."

They reached the entrance to the lorechamber. "We'll finish talking after I speak to the lorekeeper."

Forty-four

♛

As Dar expected, Yev-yat was in the lorechamber, not her muthuri's hanmuthi. She was crying as she sorted the stacks of deetpahis. Dar understood her grief, and her voice was gentle when she called the lorekeeper's name. Yev-yat started, then bowed. "Muth Mauk, you told us to gather tools. These are mine."

"And how many can you carry?"

Yev-yat's face seemed to crumble with despair. Her mouth trembled, but she was unable to reply. Dar embraced her, and for a while, she simply held the shaking mother. Then she spoke. "I'll have everyone take one deetpahi with them when they depart."

"Two, Muth Mauk. Please, two. They're not heavy, and there's so much wisdom here."

Dar smiled. "Two, then. You must hurry and select them. We depart soon."

Yev-yat went over to a table. "I have your two already." She handed Dar an ancient deetpahi, its wax dark with age. "This is Deetpahi of Morah-pah. It foretold this hall's destruction." She grabbed another wooden slat. "This speaks of Taren-hak."

"That name is new to me."

"To me also," said Yev-yat. "I read it only few days ago. Since then, I've saved it for your return."

"Why?"

"Taren-hak was reborn mother, like yourself. She was

blessed to urkzimmuthi son. Afterward, she had three daughters."

Dar stood stunned, oblivious of everything except Yev-yat's news. "So I could bear children?"

"Hai, it seems so."

Dar hugged the lorekeeper. "Shashav, Yev-yat." Then her face turned grave. "Choose those deetpahis to be saved. I'll send sons to distribute them. What remains will burn. I'm sorry, Yev-yat. Fate's often hard."

Yev-yat smiled sadly as she bowed. "How could I be lorekeeper and not know that?"

Dar wondered only briefly if Sevren understood the significance of the lorekeeper's news. Then her thoughts turned back to tactics. "Tell me how to fight Kol's army," she said as they strode through the hallways.

"Never attack Kol head-on," said Sevren. "He has too many men. Pick little fights. Win them and retreat quickly."

"How do I do that?"

"He'll send out men to gather fuel and scouts to reconnoiter. Make sure they don't return."

"How?"

"Hide and lie in wait for them."

"What about the rest of the army?"

"Surprise them at night when darkness gives you the advantage. Kol's men will have to spread out. Attack isolated units. Avoid any fight where the odds don't favor you. When they do, hit fast and disappear. Remember, ten orcs can beat ten men."

"What if Kol starts moving?"

"Send word to the other clans and begin gathering an army. These same tactics work on a larger scale. Plan ambushes."

"Such tactics run counter to the way orcs fight," said Dar.

"If you command them, they'll obey."

"I want you to explain these tactics to Nir-yat. She'll have difficulty grasping them, but if you're persistent, she will."

Sevren looked at Dar suspiciously. "This sounds like you're grooming your successor. Do you na plan to leave this hall alive?"

"I must," said Dar. "I possess Fathma."

"What's that?"

"It's too complicated to explain now. Just know that I must survive in order to pass on the crown."

"Then why lag behind?"

"If I'm meant to live, I will."

As Dar headed for the Great Chamber, she sensed the emotions pervading the hall. She had seldom heard orcs weep, but many did as they discarded almost everything but the clothes on their backs. *How many treasured heirlooms will burn tonight?* As muthuris urged their children to hurry, Dar heard some voices raised in anger and others taut with fear. Sons and mothers were rushing through the hallways, bearing all sorts of burdens. Some looked purposeful. Others appeared bewildered. Courtesy was forgotten as orcs stopped Dar to ask what would happen. She always gave the same reply: "We'll flee to safety. We'll live." She hoped it was true.

When Dar reached the Great Chamber, she discovered a pile of combustibles. Smashed furniture, sleeping mats, and clothing formed a chest-high mound. A son was breaking apart an exquisitely carved chest and tossing its pieces on the pile. Dar gazed out a window at the nearest hilltop, but no signal fire blazed on its summit. As she watched, the swirling snow briefly made the hill fade into ghostly whiteness. Then the summit was visible again. *How will the Tok clan reach the pass in this weather?* She hoped the storm that hindered climbers would also slow Kol's advance and hide the tracks of his intended victims. *The sooner they flee, the better their trail will be hidden.*

Zna-yat entered. "Muth Mauk, did you speak with lorekeeper?"

"Hai," said Dar. "Everyone will carry two deetpahis. Send sons to lorechamber so they can distribute them. Remaining deetpahis will go into fire piles. When will those piles be ready?"

"They could be lit now, but there's still much to go into them. We won't be completely done until dusk."

"Then let's hope washavokis don't arrive before then."

Zna-yat hurried off to carry out Dar's instructions. While Dar waited for his return, Tauma-yat's sons entered the chamber, still dressed in their snow-caked cloaks. The two looked worried. Dar blessed them and asked what they had learned. At first, their observations were unsurprising. Kol's army was already on the march when the brothers encountered it. They had hidden to watch it pass. The washavokis traveled on foot, except for a few that rode horses. Dar assumed the mounted men were officers. One of the washavokis on horseback was so small that the brothers thought he might be a youngling. *Girta's son?* wondered Dar.

Tauma-yat's sons had tried to count the soldiers and thought there were more than two thousand invaders. "When do you think they'll reach here?" Dar asked.

"Before evening," said the younger brother.

"So soon?" said Dar. "I had hoped this storm would slow them."

"They marched more quickly than I expected," said the elder brother. "I fought for Great Washavoki once, and his soldiers never marched quickly. But then, they weren't fleeing."

"Fleeing?" said Dar. "What do you mean."

"Washavokis were fleeing black robes like sheep that see prowling wolf."

"Black robes? I don't understand. Who were they?"

"They looked like washavokis, but they didn't act like them."

"Hai," agreed his brother. "They moved strangely, as if their bodies had no feeling. They carried two poles that held large black box."

A litter! thought Dar. She glanced at Sevren, and his face mirrored her alarm. "Othar?"

"Did black robes walk like have no spirit?" asked Sevren.

"Only those who are dead lack spirits," replied the elder brother.

"In box is maybe Black Washavoki," said Sevren. "It take spirits. Make washavokis say yes, even if kill them."

"Those black-garbed ones seemed heedless of their persons," replied the orc. "Perhaps their wills had been subjugated."

Dar saw that Sevren didn't understand the reply. "He said they seemed possessed," she said in the human tongue.

"It has to be Othar," replied Sevren in the same language. "His presence changes everything. Torch this place and flee with the mothers."

"If the army finds a burnt hall, it'll start hunting us immediately."

"They'll start soon enough anyway. Get out of here quick!"

"No, Sevren. I won't trade my subjects' safety for my own."

Sevren sighed and bowed his head. Dar turned to the two bewildered orcs and spoke in their tongue. "Sevren fears for my safety. I told him these are dangerous times." She made the sign of the Tree. "Muth la will protect us.

Join your muthuri. Protect her and other mothers. You have pleased me."

Zna-yat returned a short while after the two brothers departed, and Dar told him what she had learned. Like Sevren, Zna-yat urged Dar to leave with the fleeing mothers. Again, Dar wouldn't think of it. Nir-yat arrived a while later. "Muth Mauk, families are ready to depart."

"Good," said Dar. "Are they carrying as much food as possible?"

"Hai. And each has received their deetpahis."

Dar turned to Zna-yat. "All remaining food must be destroyed. That's critical."

"Not one root will remain for washavokis," said Zna-yat.

"Good," said Dar. "Sister, families shouldn't use road. Instead, lead them down north slope of mountain using pathways between terraces. Try to cover your tracks as we did when we fled Taiben."

Nir-yat bowed. "Would you bless each family before they depart? It would bolster their spirits."

"Of course."

"And Sister, I'll lead this retreat if you command it, but . . ." Nir-yat hesitated, clearly uncomfortable. ". . . I think there is wisdom in another course."

"What course?"

"Our clan's matriarch . . ."

"Muth-yat opposed me!"

"Hai, but she knelt eventually. If you ask her to lead, it would restore her honor. That would put her in your debt."

"So I must humble myself and ask for her help?"

"That deed won't demean you," replied Nir-yat. "It's said that only big chests have room for forgiveness."

Dar made a wry face. "It's also said that Wise and Easy

seldom walk together." She sighed. "Let's go see Muth-yat. I suppose I should see Muthuri also."

Muth-yat stood in the middle of her hanmuthi beside a pile of its possessions. Her expression was so desolate, Dar's feelings softened. "May Muth la bless you, Muth-yat, and all your hanmuthi."

"Shashav, Muth Mauk," said Muth-yat, her voice cold and formal.

"These are hard times," said Dar. "And hard words have passed between us. Yet I know you're devoted to our clan. So am I. If we've disagreed, it hasn't been because of that."

Muth-yat nodded.

"Our clan needs you, Matriarch. Will you lead them to safety?"

"I thought you wished to supplant me with Nir-yat."

"Nir-yat accompanied me to Taiben and saw what Black Washavoki has wrought. She understands our peril. Since I must linger in this hall while others escape, I turned to Nir-yat to guide our clan to safety. In her wisdom, she now turns to you."

"Matriarch," said Nir-yat. "If you lead our flight, it will reassure everyone. Will you do it? We need you."

Some of the despair left Muth-yat's face. She straightened. "I won't forsake my clan."

"Shashav, Muth-yat," said Dar. "It's time to leave. Come with me as I give blessings. Nir-yat will tell you about route I've chosen."

Muth-yat bowed. "Hai, Muth Mauk." She turned to her family. "Come. Let's discover what fate Muth la has decreed for us."

The hanmuthi they entered next was Zor-yat's. Dar was unprepared for the nostalgia she felt when she gazed about the room. *Soon this will be a blackened ruin*, she thought with a pang of loss. Memories welled up: The night of her welcoming feast. The celebration of her re-birth. Her camaraderie with her sisters. *I experienced so much joy here.*

Zor-yat seemed surprised to see Muth-yat by Dar and Nir-yat's side. She seemed even more surprised when Dar embraced her after bestowing her blessing. "I love you, Muthuri," she said. Then Dar switched to the human tongue, in which Zor-yat was fluent. "I know you can think like washavokis, because you've lied to me in the past. You grasp the uses of deception. Use that ability to help Nir-yat understand our foes."

"You want my help?" asked Zor-yat in Orcish.

Dar suspected Zor-yat switched languages so everyone would understand Dar's reply. "Hai," she said. "It's Muth la's will." Then she switched back to human speech. "I'm queen because of you. My rebirth and my first journey to Taiben were your doing. This hall's destruction was foretold, and you played a part in it. Now help our clan survive."

Again, Zor-yat replied in Orcish. "I'd be honored to aid you and Nir-yat. How can I help?"

Dar responded in Orcish. "Help mothers hide from washavokis. Also, Sevren knows ways to defeat soldiers. Help sons understand his plans."

Zor-yat regarded Dar thoughtfully, then bowed very low. "Please forgive me, Daughter. I spoke foolishly in Great Chamber."

"Pain and sorrow caused you to speak that way," replied Dar. "I know you love me."

Zor-yat bowed again. "I do, Daughter."

Dar didn't know if Zor-yat was sincere. However, a reconciliation would unite the clan, and unity would help it to survive. As Zor-yat's family left their hanmuthi, Dar hurried off to bless the next family and send them on their way.

* * *

The hall spilled warm bodies into the storm. Mothers, children, and sons snaked down the snow-covered terraces. Their burdens were heavy and the way was slippery, steep, and narrow. The mothers were abandoning the only home they knew, the place they had expected to spend their lives. That frightened them almost as much as the hardships ahead and the threat of a brutal death. Dar watched Nir-yat depart with the last orc family. Girta and Kovok-mah accompanied her sister, along with Sevren, who led Skymere down the steep path. Nir-yat directed the sons trying to smooth the trampled snow using brooms made of bundled reeds. Dar hoped the storm would improve upon their efforts.

Soon, the fleeing figures disappeared into the swirling snow. Dar stood alone, staring at the empty whiteness. Then duty called, and she headed into the hall to wait for General Kol's army.

Forty-five

♛

Zna-yat was in the Great Chamber when Dar arrived. He was staring so intently at the nearest hilltop that, for a terrifying moment, Dar though he was gazing at a signal fire. When he didn't turn at the sound of her footsteps, she concluded he was not. "Families have departed," she said.

"I wish you had departed with them, Sister."

Dar changed the subject. "How is work proceeding?"

"Well. All food is on piles for burning. So are deet-pahis."

"Have sons smash all windows and throw their wooden frames on piles," said Dar. "Windows in Welcoming Chamber have best view of valley. We should go there to wait for washavokis."

Zna-yat bowed. "This will be done, Muth Mauk."

Dar went to her hanmuthi to put on her warmest clothes, then headed for the Welcoming Chamber. It was a large room that lay to one side of the hall's main entrance and featured three huge windows. Dar recalled her sisters waving from them the first time she departed for Taiben. By the time she arrived at the chamber, its windows already had been shattered. Shards of sand ice littered the floor and the smashed sashes lay atop a pile of other combustibles. Snow blew in through the empty windows. Dar clutched her cloak against the wind and peered out at the valley. *It'll be dusk soon*, she thought.

Perhaps Kol will camp on the road and arrive tomorrow.
Despite that hope, Dar watched nervously for the sentries'
signal fire.

Heavy clouds had made for a dark day, and when the
sun behind them sank close to the horizon, the light grew
even dimmer. Dar was glad when Zna-yat arrived; his
eyes could pierce the gloom much better than hers. She
noted that he had donned his armor. "Sons are finishing
up," he said. "It's sad work. When they're done, they'll
come here to watch and wait." Zna-yat gazed into the
storm. "You could go where it's warmer."

"Thwa, I'll watch also." Dar noted that Zna-yat carried his two deetpahis. To make conversation she asked,
"What lore do you carry?"

"I don't know. I haven't had time to read."

"I carry proof that I could bear Kath-mah's granddaughters."

Zna-yat regarded Dar with a look that seemed both
surprised and pleased. "Does Kovok-mah know this?"

"Thwa. We've had no time to speak."

"Such news will give him hope."

"Do you think his muthuri will bless us now?"

"I don't know her mind, but that deetpahi should improve your chances." Zna-yat returned his gaze to the
valley. "It seems strange to talk of blessings and children
as we watch for death's approach."

"Children are our only means to overcome death,"
said Dar. "It's fitting time to talk of them."

The valley grew darker and the wind deposited ever
more snow upon the floor. As sons finished preparing for
the hall's destruction, they joined Dar and Zna-yat in the
Welcoming Chamber. It was dusk when Zna-yat suddenly pointed at a distant hilltop. "Muth Mauk, do you
see that?"

Dar stared into the storm but saw nothing. Then she thought she detected a glow atop a nearer summit. "Is that signal fire?"

Before Zna-yat could answer, another fire blazed in the storm, then another. Finally, a fire glowed on the nearest hilltop. "Muth Mauk, should we light piles now?"

"Thwa. Let's wait and see what washavokis will do. Delay will help fleeing mothers."

For a long time, nothing happened. The signal fires burned out without any sign of the invaders. As the light failed, Dar could see less and less. When her view was reduced to little more than vague silhouettes, Zna-yat spoke. "Washavokis approach."

Dar peered into the gloom. It seemed that a black shadow was flowing between the hills. She couldn't distinguish individual soldiers, but their masses darkened the snow. They moved slowly and steadily toward the hall.

"Shall we light fires?" asked Zna-yat.

"Not yet. Perhaps they'll stop and camp for night." Dar waited for the dark wave to halt. It continued to advance. *Sevren said they wouldn't attack at night.* She hoped Kol wouldn't prove him wrong. Eventually, the army reached the mountain's base. The valley was filled with soldiers. There seemed to be many more than two thousand. Instead of halting or moving up the winding road to the hall's entrance, the mass split and began to encircle the base of the mountain.

"Muth Mauk," said Zna-yat. "Now?"

"Thwa. We wait."

"For what?"

Dar answered the question for everyone's benefit. "I think washavokis will surround our mountain, then wait for dawn. They are tired and cold, and they see poorly at night. Soon they will sleep. When they do, we'll light fires." Dar sent sons to observe from other windows and report back. When they did, she was relieved to learn that she had guessed right; the soldiers were settling in around the base of the mountain. Already, campfires were being lit on the lower terraces. After a while, the mountain was ringed with fires. It gratified Dar to think of the mothers safely fleeing. *But we won't escape unnoticed*, she thought. *We'll have to fight our way out.*

Dar retreated with the orcs into a hanmuthi in the innermost part of the hall. There, they made a small fire to roast some pashi. Dar, who hadn't eaten all day, was ravenous. The smell of the cooking roots made her stomach grumble. When the pashi was ready, she said that the food was Muth la's gift and served it. The meal was eaten in silence, for everyone seemed deep in thought. Dar relived a memory of the queen who had been Nir-yat's grandmother, and for a while, her mind's eye filled the room with happy feasters. Dar knew that some of the children who laughed on that long-ago night were now elderly mothers, trudging in the storm as she ate.

Dar spent the remainder of her meal reviewing her plan to torch the hall. A fire pile at the center of the building would be lit first, in hopes that the blaze would be well established before the enemy noticed any flames. Once the first fire took hold, sons would fan out toward the hall's outer walls, torching rooms as they went. After all the fires were lit, everyone would rendezvous on a terrace near the northeast side of the hall. White cloth, torn into cloak-sized pieces, had been placed there. Everyone would don their camouflage and descend the mountain by a route different from the one the mothers had taken. At some point, they would have to break through the enemy's line.

It was past midnight when Dar lit the first fire. She touched a torch to an oil-soaked cloth and it blossomed into blue and orange flames. These quickly ignited the shattered furniture, sleeping mats, clothes, foodstuffs, deetpahis, and other items piled above it. As Dar watched, wind blowing through shattered windows whipped the flames into a swirling column of orange. The column reached the ceiling's wooden beams. Soon they were ablaze. Dar stood transfixed as the fire spread, reliving her vision of the burning hall.

Then someone gently touched her shoulder. "Muth Mauk," said Zna-yat. "We should leave."

Dar realized that she and Zna-yat were the room's sole occupants. The others had left to set more fires. Dar and Zna-yat strode through hallways that were already beginning to fill with smoke. They reached the exit and stepped into the frigid night. As Dar made her way to the terrace, flames appeared above the hall. The falling snow took on a red tint and bright, rising sparks mingled with it. Dar smelled smoke and cooking food. She smiled slightly, imagining the scent's effect on hungry soldiers.

When Dar arrived at the terrace, several sons were already there, draped in white cloth. She wrapped herself in a piece, then waited with them. As her party slowly assembled, Dar worried that the flames would awaken the soldiers. She hoped they would be confused and slow to react. By the time everyone had returned, billowing flames rose above much of the hall. All its windows were alight, giving it a falsely festive look. Dar felt conspicuous in the firelight.

"Zna-yat, be my eyes and lead way. Stay in shadow whenever possible, and choose difficult path. There'll be fewer washavokis there."

Zna-yat strode off, and Dar followed close behind. The northeast side of the mountain was the steepest part and little farmed. The terraced fields were few and far between and the narrow, snow-covered paths that connected them were hard to follow. When shadowed from the fire's light, Dar could see very little. More than once, she lost her footing on the slippery incline and would have slid down the mountainside if Zna-yat had not grabbed her.

When, at last, the way grew less steep, Zna-yat halted abruptly. He whispered to Dar. "I hear washavokis ahead."

Dar strained her ears, but heard nothing. "Are there many?"

"It's hard to say. Two are walking. Others sleep."

"Take several sons. Keep close to ground and hide under white cloth so you look like snow. Choose sons who understand reason for this. Kill walking soldiers silently if you can. Then slay sleepers."

"Hai, Muth Mauk."

Zna-yat chose Auk-goth and another son. The three started down the slope, then seemed to vanish. Dar waited nervously. For a long while there was only silence. Then a loud voice, shrill with terror, broke the stillness. "Orcs! Orcs! Or . . ."

Dar heard heavy, running footsteps. "Come, Muth Mauk! Washavokis are dead, but more are coming."

Zna-yat appeared, sword unsheathed. "Follow me," he said.

Dar ran to him, and he headed down the slope, mindful that Dar was following. He reached a small terrace where Dar spied the crumpled forms of men. One was headless. His blood made the snow look black. Yet the alarm had gone out, and even Dar could hear the response. The noise came from the next terrace down the slope. It was broader, and Dar could make out dark shapes moving about it.

"Attack!" Dar said. "Strike quickly!"

As the orcs dashed down the slope, Dar knew she must follow them as best she could. A swift attack in the dark offered their best chance. Speed was crucial, and if Dar lagged behind she could easily be stranded among foes. She paused only to search a dead soldier for a dagger. Finding one, she rushed after the orcs.

Slipping and stumbling in the dark, Dar reached the terrace where a struggle was already in progress. The orcs were outnumbered, but their surprised opponents fought clumsily. They screamed and cursed as they died, and the cries brought more men to replace them. Dar heard footsteps and turned to see a soldier advancing toward her, sword drawn. His teeth grinned white in his shadowed face. "Ah ha! A runt!"

"I'm human!" shouted Dar. "A woman."

"What's a bitch doing with piss eyes?" asked the soldier, lowering his blade.

"They kept me for food."

"Then why aren't ye bound? Perhaps ye . . ."

Dar plunged her dagger deep into the man's eye. For a horrible moment, he simply stood shuddering as if seized by a bone-rattling chill. Then he twisted slightly and collapsed, nearly wrenching the blade from Dar's hand as he fell. Dar stared at his corpse, sickened by what she had done. Then she glimpsed another soldier bounding toward her, an ax raised high. Before she could react, an orc darted between them and severed the man in two at the waist. As the torso fell at Dar's feet, its arms reached out. A hand briefly grasped her ankle, then relaxed.

"Muth Mauk! Way is clear!" Dar recognized Zna-yat's voice. She dashed in its direction. Beyond the terrace wall was another slope. The orcs were already scampering down it, but Zna-yat stood waiting for her. When Dar reached him, he grabbed her waist and bounded down the steep slope. Dar could barely breathe, much less talk during the quick, jarring trip down the remainder of the mountainside. Zna-yat set her down only when they reached level ground. By then, Dar's ribs ached from pressing against Zna-yat's armor. She didn't complain, for she saw the dark shapes of running men against the snow.

A broad, snow-filled meadow lay between them and a wood. "Let's flee, not fight, if we can," Dar shouted. Zna-yat made a move to grab her waist again, but she said, "I'd rather run." The orcs took off and Dar raced behind them, following the trail they made. Glancing over her shoulder, she thought their pursuers were giving only a halfhearted chase. When she reached the tree line, she looked back again and saw they had stopped running altogether.

Dar and the orcs headed north, their number reduced by two. Both were sons who had fought without armor. *Two slain already!* thought Dar. She suspected that the orcs had killed dozens, but in the grim arithmetic of war, that didn't matter: Kol had thousands to attack fewer than three hundred defenders. Fleeing and hiding seemed the most prudent course, until a terrifying possibility came to Dar. Although the washavokis were in unfamiliar territory, Othar might employ magic to guide them. The Mah clan settlement lay within two days' march. If Kol captured their larders, the orcs would be doomed.

Dar brooded over their situation, but her ignorance about the enemy prevented forming a course of action. *I don't know if Othar's directing the army.* That information was vital, and it seemed foolhardy to base her strategy on speculation. After more consideration, Dar came to a conclusion. She halted the march and told all the sons without armor to join up with the fleeing mothers. After they departed, only Zna-yat and four other mintaris remained. "Muth Mauk," Zna-yat said, "where will you lead us?"

"Back to washavoki soldiers."

Forty-six

♛

The wind clawed at the sustolum's cloak as his horse plodded through the snow. The young officer was cold, hungry, and disappointed. The latter exacerbated the first two miseries. He gazed despondently at the burning hall atop the mountain. Its flames cast an eerie light, tinting the night red. *My share of the plunder's up there. My rations, too. All naught but ashes!*

It didn't help that the general was such an iron butt. *General Voltar never made his staff officers check encampments. That's a murdant's job*, thought the sustolum—not that he dared tell that to General Kol. As the most junior officer, it was his lot to make the rounds before dawn, when the night was coldest. He had just rounded the northern end of the mountain when he saw a figure emerge from the woods. In the dim light, he could just make out a dark, walking form. It looked too small to be an orc. The sustolum drew rein and watched.

The figure continued to advance across the meadow, its form conspicuous against the snow. It seemed to be staggering. Then it collapsed near some snow mounds and called out for the first time. "Please help me!"

The sustolum was astonished. *A girl's voice!* He'd heard tales of girls who disguised themselves as soldiers. *Some man's whore.* The officer grinned. *This one got more than she bargained for.*

The girl had risen to her feet, but remained in place, swaying slightly. "Please, sir! Help me."

The officer turned his horse toward the lone figure. He was more than a little intrigued. *If she's pretty, I might keep her for myself.* The girl stopped swaying and waited motionless. As the sustolum came nearer, he could see her a little better. She seemed well dressed against the cold, with a hooded cloak and a white scarf wrapped around her chin. When he was a few paces away, he noticed something odd about her forehead, but he didn't recognize the crown-shaped scar until he rode up next to her and she gazed upward. "Why, you're a branded girl!"

The girl shouted "Dup!" and the snow mounds shot upward, revealing orcs that had been hiding beneath snow-covered cloth. The sustolum grabbed at his sword hilt, but a massive hand seized his wrist. The next instant, he was sailing through the air. He hit the ground hard and orcs swarmed over him. A hand wrapped around his lower face, covering his mouth. A second orc disarmed him as another held him down while a fourth bound his wrists. Then the girl bent over him and held a dagger beneath his throat. "Make one sound," she said in a low voice that was anything but girlish, "and I'll let the orcs kill you. They won't do it gently. Nod if you understand."

The sustolum nodded as best he could with a hand clamping his mouth and a dagger pressing his chin.

"Don't say a word. Don't moan. Don't even breathe hard. Am I clear?"

The young officer nodded again. The woman spoke some strange words and the orcs released him. Then she walked over to his horse, speaking to it in calming tones before taking the reins. "Follow me," she said, and began walking toward the woods. Surrounded by orcs, the sustolum obeyed.

When they reached the trees, the woman spoke to the orcs again. They cut pine boughs, and when they resumed marching, they used them to brush snow over their tracks.

A short while later, the woman halted and asked, "What's your horse's name."

"Foeslayer."

His captor smiled mockingly. "Foeslayer?"

"Aye."

The woman stroked the horse's nose. "Foeslayer, you're a good boy, and I'm very tired. Will you let me ride you? Ah, good boy. Good boy."

Although the woman had a way with the horse, she mounted it clumsily. Afterward, she spoke to an orc, and he took the reins. As the woman slumped in the saddle, the march resumed. The sustolum knew they were headed north, but nothing else. He wondered if the woman could possibly be the orc queen; she certainly had a commanding air. He had never encountered such a forceful woman. In fact, the sustolum could think of only one man who was as equally forceful. *General Kol himself.*

Dar had Zna-yat guide the way as she tried to doze in the saddle. It wasn't easy or comfortable to nap that way. She drifted off several times only to feel hands saving her from falling. Mostly, she hovered on the dreary border between dreams and awareness. When the sky lightened, she gave up trying to sleep and gazed blearily at her captive. He didn't seem a seasoned soldier, more a lad whose parents could afford to purchase a commission. He stared back at her, not daring to speak. "I know your horse's name," Dar said. "I might as well know yours."

"Dedrik, Your Majesty."

Dar grinned. "So you figured out who I am."

"Aye. What do you want of me?"

"Tell me what I need to know, and you'll see more sunrises. Otherwise . . ." Dar was pleased when Dedrik paled. *He'll talk*, she thought.

"What do you want to know?"

"We'll speak later. For now, be silent."

It was still morning when Zna-yat suddenly halted. "I smell urkzimmuthi."

Dar gazed about. The snow-covered road looked untraveled and the woods surrounding it seemed empty of anything but trees. Then a snow mound rose to reveal Sevren and Kovok-mah. "Stay in place," said Kovok-mah, obviously speaking to other orcs, who remained hidden. Then he spoke to Dar. "We're waiting for any washavokis that follow mothers. This is Sevren's teaching."

"He taught you well," said Dar. "I didn't know you were there. Where are mothers?"

"They're resting not far from here. I'll have son show you way. I must stay here and talk for Sevren." Kovok-mah called a name, and a son appeared from beneath pine boughs mounded with snow. He bowed deeply. "Muth Mauk, your return gladdens us."

"And I'm glad to return," said Dar, "but most anxious to see mothers."

"I'll take you to them," said the son. The route he took impressed Dar by its indirectness. *Someone's instructed him in subterfuge*, she thought, wondering if it was Sevren, Zor-yat, or a combination of the two. At last, they entered a hollow and found great masses of mothers and children huddled together like hibernating animals. No fire burned, so they had only one another to provide warmth. Most seemed asleep.

Nir-yat rose from a clump of bodies, and ran to embrace Dar. "Sister! You've returned! My chest bursts with happiness!"

Dar returned Nir-yat's hug. "Our home's destroyed, so it will comfort no washavoki."

"And is pass sealed?"

"There's no way to tell," said Dar. "How was journey?"

"It was hard. Meera-yat has joined Muth la."

Due to Fathma, Dar possessed the memories of Meera-yat's sister. Thus she remembered Meera-yat not only as ancient, blind, and nearly deaf, but also as a vibrant and beloved sibling. This made the news of her death especially heartrending. "I have sad news also," said Dar. "Two perished leaving hall."

"So it begins," replied Nir-yat. "This likens to when our foremothers fled into Blath Urkmuthi."

"Hai. I fear in days to come last night's losses will seem light."

Nir-yat nodded, then cast Dedrik a baleful look. "What's *it* doing here?"

"We need information about our foe. He'll provide it."

Dar addressed her prisoner in the human tongue. "Dedrik, when did you last eat?"

"Night before last, Your Majesty."

The answer pleased Dar, for she figured if the officers were hungry, their men would be more so. She said to Nir-yat in Orcish, "Have someone give this washavoki root to eat. Make sure it's small."

"I will, Sister. Join us and rest. You look exhausted."

At those words, the nearest clump of mothers parted, opening a space in its warm interior. Dar saw that the snow had been cleared away and evergreen boughs covered the frozen ground, Dar walked to the space and sat down. The others pressed around her. Among them, snug and secure, she quickly drifted off to sleep.

It was late afternoon when Dar awoke. The mothers around her were afraid and their tense bodies wordlessly communicated that emotion. No one spoke, causing Dar to think some threat was near. She strained her ears and after a while heard distant shouts. They were men's voices. Dar couldn't make out any words, but the tone of the mingled cries was unmistakable. She had heard that blend of rage, agony, and terror before. The sound of metal striking metal punctuated it. A battle was in progress.

With that fearful realization, Dar had a second one: There was nothing she could do. She had no idea how the fight was going and no way to find out without drawing danger to the mothers. She could only hope the sons would prevail. If they didn't, the best chance for the mothers and their children lay in stillness and silence. *We're fawns among wolves. We must hope we're overlooked.* Dar rose and all eyes went to her. She made the signs for "be quiet" and "don't move," then sat down again.

Waiting was torture. The noise remained distant and diminished into silence, but that was no indication as to which side had won. *Soldiers might be searching for us right now*, thought Dar. *If they find us, it'll be bare hands against swords and axes.* After a long spell of silence, Dar felt the mothers tense and turn to look in one direction. Knowing that they heard something she couldn't, Dar followed their gaze into the snowy woods. At first she saw nothing. Then a man came into view. He was running and clutching a bloody sword. Dar's heart sank, but before she could shout for the orcs to flee, the man cried out, "Math tut guth!" *We killed them!* Then Dar realized it was Sevren.

Behind Sevren came Kovok-mah and several other sons. Unlike Sevren, there was no exuberance in their step, and Dar sensed they didn't share his feeling of triumph. She left the huddled mothers and walked toward Kovok-mah. She would have run, but felt it would be undignified. When Kovok-mah saw her, he picked up his pace. When they met, Dar asked, "What happened?"

"Many washavokis came up road."

"Two shieldrons," added Sevren, in the human tongue. "All foot, with three mounted officers."

"We did as Sevren told us," said Kovok-mah. "We were

still and quiet, looking like snow. Washavokis walked without understanding. When Sevren shouted, we jumped up, our swords and axes ready. Washavokis were only steps away. Many died quickly, but others fought."

"Did any washavokis escape?" asked Dar.

"All died," replied Kovok-mah.

"I had them go for the mounted officers first," said Sevren. "Kol won't know what happened."

"How many sons were hurt?" asked Dar.

"Seven were slain, and thirteen more were wounded," replied Kovok-mah. "I think four of them will soon join Muth la."

"Eleven dead," said Dar. The news was a weight in her chest. She would know each of the slain.

"But they wiped out two shieldrons," said Sevren. "Seven-five men!"

"Out of Kol's thousands," said Dar. "And will we always be so lucky? What if he sends a regiment next time?" She turned to Kovok-mah. "I wish to bless wounded and thank them for their sacrifice. Afterward, I must decide what to do."

Dar went directly to the ambush site. The scene was as wrenching as she expected. The four most gravely wounded lay against a tree surrounded by crimson snow. Their wounds were ghastly, but they suffered silently. One died while Dar was blessing him. As Dar spoke to the wounded, sons butchered the three slain horses and dragged the dead washavokis away. Dar tried to think of them solely as enemies, but death had rendered them harmless. Many were only lads.

When Dar returned to where the mothers hid, she assembled an unusual council. It was composed of two matriarchs, Muth-yat and Muth-pah; three mothers, Nir-yat, Zor-yat, and Yev-yat; two sons, Kovok-mah and Zna-yat;

and three washavokis, Sevren, Queen Girta, and Dedrik. The sustolum was there by compulsion. Dar expected him to be an unwilling source of information, but Queen Girta's arrival both astounded and confused the officer. "Your Majesty!" he blurted out. "You're alive!"

"Now you understand the depth of your general's treachery," said Dar.

"If it weren't for the orc queen, I'd be truly dead," said Girta. "Is it true my son rides with the army?"

"Aye."

"How fares he?"

"Not happily," said Dedrik. "It's hard campaigning in winter, and Kol's a harsh commander."

"But my son's the king!"

"That counts for little here. He's a boy and under the general's thumb."

Dar had let the exchange take place because she thought it would be fruitful, but she interrupted it to ask about what troubled her most. "Dedrik, what do you know about Othar?"

"The old king's mage? You killed him."

"Unfortunately not. I'm certain he's riding in that black litter. Is he advising General Kol?"

"*That's* who's dogging us? No wonder the men are spooked!"

"Answer my question!" said Dar.

"That cursed band stays apart, but one visits the general. Gorm. I've heard them talking."

Dar looked at Girta and Sevren. "Have you heard of him?"

Sevren shook his head.

"I thought he was someone's servant," said Girta. "A nobody."

"The general doesn't treat him like a nobody," said Dedrik. "Gorm's the only one who shakes him. He came visiting after the hall caught fire. I heard him through the tent. No yelling, mind you, but there was menace in his voice."

"Did you hear what he said?" asked Dar.

"Something about a master. That master was displeased."

"How did the general reply?"

"Well, he sounded meek, which is uncommon for him. Said he'd find them. I take it he meant the orcs."

Dar focused on her principal concern. "Did Gorm tell him where to find us?"

"Nay. Just that the general better do it. He said time was running out."

"Time for what?"

"I don't know, but Gorm sounded both angry and scared."

Dar paused in her interrogation to give the gist of it to the orcs. While she did, Zor-yat asked Dedrik a question of her own. "Would you say Gorm's master wanted our hall?"

"Nay."

"Then what did he want?"

"Your deaths."

"There's only one thing you can do, Your Majesty," said Sevren. "Send runners to all the clans. Gather an army of orcs and lure Kol into an ambush. Those two shieldrons were doing reconnaissance. When they don't return, he'll head north. Let the mothers lead him into a trap. We'll slaughter his men like we did today. Sorcery can na stop a sword."

"My son's with them!" cried out Girta.

"It's *his* army," said Dar. "*He* declared this war."

"He's only a boy, and Kol deceived him, just as he did me," said Girta, her voice urgent and pleading. "Spare him! You must spare him!"

"Chaos reigns in battle," said Dar. "I can't promise anything."

"Aye," said Sevren. "When the blood runs hot, Mercy's a stranger."

"He doesn't deserve to die," said Girta.

"Neither do we," said Dar, her face lit up by a sudden inspiration. "We can't stop this fight, but your son can. He thinks we've slain you. Show him otherwise, and he'll end this war."

"Kol will na let him see her," said Sevren. "He'll slay her first."

"He nearly killed me once before," said Girta, touching her wounded shoulder. "I . . . I can't . . ."

Dar saw the fear in Girta's face and despaired. *As much as she loves her son, she's terrified of Kol.* Dar tried to push her point. "Then there's no hope for your son," she said. "He'll die with the others."

As if on cue, Zor-yat reached out and gently patted Girta's hand. "We'll honor your son," she said, "if we can find his corpse."

The remark caused Girta to burst out weeping. Dar let her sob before offering her final inducement. "I'll go with you. We'll disguise ourselves as soldiers and find your son. Kol can't harm you before the king." She turned to Dedrik. "If the soldiers knew what you know, would they rather face orcs for Kol or obey their king and return home?"

"They're hungry, and there's no chance for plunder. They'll gladly obey the king."

"Have you the courage to save your son?" asked Dar.

"If you'll go with me, I'll find it."

"Then I will," said Dar. "I have no love for war."

"You can na go!" cried Sevren. "Girta's their queen, yet she fears for her life. You're their enemy!"

"It's worth the risk," said Dar. "If we succeed, this war will end tonight."

"Muth Mauk, you risk more than your life," said Zor-yat in Orcish. "If you perish, Fathma will be lost."

"Fathma lost again?" said Muth-pah, who had been unable to follow Dar's conversation. "What is this talk?"

When Dar explained her plan, the matriarch was shaken. "If you perish, disaster will follow. It would be as it was when Tarathank fell. We'll have no queen, and washavokis will hunt us. Your plan risks too much, Muth Mauk."

"I admit you've acted wisely so far," said Muth-yat. "If we had remained in hall, we'd all be dead. Yet I agree with Muth-pah. Trying times lie ahead. Without our queen, we're doomed."

"Sister, listen to these mothers' wisdom," said Nir-yat. "You have big chest, but blades can pierce it. We can't lose you."

Girta heard the orcs speak without understanding a word, but she readily perceived their opposition. "Dar, you promised to help me. I can't do this alone."

Dar felt the full weight of her sovereignty. *A wrong decision will be disastrous. But what's the wrong decision? Risk everything for peace? Engage in bloody war?* She knew she had to decide and decide quickly, but she couldn't see her path. "I must think upon this," she said after a while. "Sister, will you walk with me?"

Nir-yat bowed, then followed Dar into the woods. The two walked silently until they were a long way from the other orcs. Nir-yat gazed at her sister and saw water running from her eyes. "I'm sorry I lack wisdom," she said.

Dar wiped her eyes and gazed lovingly at Nir-yat. "You have it in abundance, and I've relied on it."

"Yet I can't advise you, for I don't know how future will unfold."

"Neither do I," said Dar, "so let's talk about past. Remember when I returned as queen?"

"How can I forget? You were nearly dead."

"Were you with me then?"

"I was by your side, but you couldn't see."

"I could see, Sister. But I saw spirits, not faces. Muth la gives dying queens that skill, so they might bestow Fathma wisely."

"But you lived," said Nir-yat.

"Still, I was dying. Were you by my side entire time?"

"Until Deen-yat gave you magic draught. Then Muth-yat and Muthuri made me leave."

Dar smiled for the first time. "Sister, I remember your spirit. When I had strength to bestow Fathma, none was worthy to receive it. Thus Muth la preserved my life. But earlier, my successor was by my side. She was you."

"Thwa! Thwa! You're mistaken."

"I'm not. I'm certain of it," said Dar. "Tonight, I'll go with Girta. I'll risk my life for peace, but I won't risk our welfare. Fathma will be safe, for you'll be queen."

Nir-yat paled. "Queen! I can't be queen."

"That's what I said. And I'll reply as great mother before me did. You must. It's Muth la's will."

Forty-seven

♛

"I don't know what future holds," said Dar, "so I don't know which path is best. This way, we can take both. I'll take chance for peace. If I fail, you can guide urkzimmuthi in battle. You'll possess my memories. They'll aid you, as will Sevren and our muthuri."

"But you'll be dead either way," said Nir-yat. "Queen who surrenders Fathma loses her spirit."

"That may be so," said Dar, "but my body will linger. I can take Girta to her son. Did not your grandmother linger after she passed on crown?"

"Hai, and I told you what happened to her. She became ghost."

"Now I understand my last vision," said Dar, her expression melancholy. "Lama-tok told me it isn't always unwise to die."

When Dar returned to the hollow, her expression was somber. Nir-yat's was sad, but resigned. The two took Queen Girta aside and Dar had a lengthy conversation with her, which she translated for Nir-yat's benefit. Afterward, the three spoke with Sevren. Then he departed on an errand.

The orcs watched all these things without comprehension, although they knew something was afoot. After Sevren left, Dar called them together. She and Nir-yat stood in the center of the throng, surrounded yet apart. Then Dar spoke in a loud, clear voice. "Fathma is Muth la's gift to urkzimmuthi. Mother who receives this spirit is closest to Muth la. Her words are wisdom and must be obeyed. Long have mothers of our clan received this gift, each queen passing it to next." Then Dar recounted all the queens' names, ending with her own. "Muth la has both entered my chest and sent me visions. Thus I know what path to take. Perhaps this path will end in peace. Perhaps it will end with my death. All I know is that it's perilous, too perilous to risk Muth la's gift. Thus Muth la has sent another mother to receive Fathma. That mother is Nir-yat."

With those words, Nir-yat cast off her cloak to stand bare-chested. Dar placed her hands above her sister's breasts. Immediately, her fingers began to tingle. "Let Fathma pass to Nir-yat."

Dar saw Nir-yat's eyes widen, and she recalled her own experience of receiving Fathma. There had been a sensation of warmth, accompanied by transforming energy and murmuring voices. Bestowing Fathma felt quite different. Dar was left drained and empty. The world seemed suddenly silent, and Dar experienced a sense of profound loss. She removed her crown and placed it on her sister's head. The mother who had been Nir-yat was no more. She had become Muth Mauk.

"My time is over," said Dar. The crowd silently parted, and Dar walked through it. As she did, custom required everyone to gaze away. Many did so reluctantly, desiring one last glimpse of one they had come to love. Yet, eventually, all eyes turned elsewhere, and Dar began to feel invisible. As she departed, the orcs bowed to their new queen and shouted, "Tava, Muth Mauk!"

Sevren and Girta stood apart. Dar walked over to them. Sevren looked solemn and sad. Girta appeared frightened. "I think I found soldier's clothes that will fit," said Sevren. "You should try them on here. The boots are big, but you can stuff rags in them."

Dar wrinkled her nose. "I'm sure that stuff stinks of washavoki."

"There's na helping that," replied Sevren. "You'll ride Skymere, so hopefully you'll na wear them long. The queen will take the prisoner's horse."

Sevren led the women through the woods to a stack of corpses. Nearby, he had assembled two sets of soldier's clothes, armor, and equipment. Dar stripped down to the shirt she had worn in Taiben and her undergarment, then donned the soldier's outfit. It was blood-splattered and smelled even worse than she feared. While every item was too large, none was overly so. There was a greasy, long-sleeved tunic made of wool, which fit under an armored tunic of stiff boiled leather. Metal plates were sewn on the shoulders and over the heart. The woolen leggings had thick slabs of leather on the front. They were far too long, but tucked into the heavy boots. These were so large that Dar had to wrap her feet in layers of cloth before she could walk in them. A leather helmet, reinforced with metal, hid her long hair and brand. A foulsmelling scarf covered her clan tattoo. A tattered cloak completed the outfit.

When Dar was dressed, she showed herself to Sevren. "You'll pass for a soldier at night. All you need is a sword."

"It'd be useless, but I'll take a dagger."

"I found you a good one," said Sevren, handing Dar the dagger. "The sword is just for show. Every soldier must carry one."

Dar strapped on the weapons and walked about a bit. She felt clumsy in the heavy armor. Girta looked equally awkward in her outfit. "Dar, this isn't going to work. We look ridiculous."

"Don't even think of backing down," said Dar, casting Girta a hard look. "Not after what I've sacrificed!"

Dar's anger cowed Girta, and she seemed to sink into her oversized outfit.

"The guards will be looking for orcs, na women," said Sevren quickly. "Many a lad's marched off in his father's gear. The fit will na betray you."

"Think of your son," said Dar in a conciliatory tone. "You'll be seeing him soon."

"Yes," said Girta, "I must think of him."

The two women had a bit to eat, then rode off without an escort. Dar had not told Girta that she felt success was too uncertain to risk other lives. If they obtained peace, Girta would send messengers bearing signs of truce. If they failed, knowledge of the orcs' location would die with them. Nevertheless, Girta suspected Dar was pessimistic about their chances. It heightened her fear and kept her quiet.

Dar was quiet for another reason. She felt a part of her had died. She wondered how great a part. *Am I still Dargu-yat? Am I even urkzimmuthi?* Enveloped by a washavoki's scent, she feared she had become one again. Dar realized that her teeth remained black and she must take care not to reveal them. She looked down at her nails. Talmauki was still painted on them. She used her thumbnail to scrape it off. The effort brought tears to her eyes. The more the color flaked away, the more diminished she felt.

Dar could keep grief at bay only by thinking about what lay ahead. She was fearful, but also angry. Both emotions were preferable to emptiness. The idea that Kol could be exposed and die a traitor's death spurred her on. She thought of Twea and Loral and Frey. Each deserved justice. *And when Kol's gone, Othar will lose his protector. A mage can't stand against an army.* At least, Dar hoped so.

Dar and Girta reached the Yat clan's mountain before dusk. A blackened ruin crowned it. Troops no longer camped around its base, and Dar assumed that the army had consolidated in the valley. They rode around the eastern side of the mountain, keeping within the cover of a wood, until they spotted smoke from the army's encampment. Dar said they should dismount and view the encampment before darkness fell. Girta resisted the idea.

"We must scout the enemy's camp," said Dar, not bothering to hide her exasperation. "Otherwise, how in Karm's name do you expect to find your son in the dark among thousands of soldiers?"

Girta gave in and sneaked through the woods with Dar until they reached its edge. Tents filled the valley before the mountain, and they were far more orderly than Dar expected. *Kol must be a stickler for discipline*, she thought, recalling that Dedrik had called him "harsh." There was no separate royal compound, but Dar saw a cluster of blue-and-scarlet tents within the plain ones. "The king will be there," she said. She looked for the black uniforms of the former Queen's Men. Though she saw none, she suspected the men were there, dressed as common soldiers.

As the women were about to retreat into the woods, they heard a low, distant rumble. Dar glanced at the mountain ridge to the south, which was just visible above the hilltops. The setting sun illuminated a spreading dust cloud, making it glow orange. Dar grinned. "An avalanche! A big one!"

"Why are you happy?"

"Because it means the Tok clan sealed the pass. Kol can't retreat. He doesn't know the way."

"Are you sure?"

"No one's traveled the Old Road for fifty winters. The lorekeeper said so."

The way Girta sighed, Dar assumed the queen was thinking of her son. *Good!* she thought. *She needs to.*

The storm had spent itself, and the night was clear when Dar and Girta headed for the camp. A waxing moon lit the valley's floor, and Dar's impulse was to creep toward the soldiers. Knowing that would give the wrong impression, she did not. "We have to look like we belong here," she whispered to Girta. The queen straightened.

Dar's heart raced as they neared the camp's perimeter, for she was aware their women's voices would give them away if they were challenged. She and Girta had waited until long after sunset, hoping the added time would ensure the soldiers would be asleep. The camp looked still, but Dar saw some movement as they approached. She quickened her step and reached the first tents.

"Hey! Why are ye about?"

Dar saw a grizzled soldier stride toward them with the self-important air of a murdant. Girta froze, and Dar had to tug her hand to get her moving.

"Well?" said the murdant, his voice louder.

Dar made an exaggerated shrug and kept walking.

"By Karm's ass, ye'll answer or be flogged!" The murdant bounded after them and grasped Girta's shoulder. She let out a frightened yelp. "A wench?" He grabbed her helmet and tugged. When it came off, golden hair cascaded out.

"Leave her be!" said Dar.

"Karm's milky teats! A pair o' whores!"

Dar slapped the murdant's hand from Girta's shoulder. "Hands off, pig! We're Kol's women."

"Yer lyin'."

"Then tup us both and find out. Just be warned, the general doesn't like to share."

The murdant glared at Dar, but he didn't touch Girta again.

"Since you've stuck your nose in the general's business," said Dar, "you can escort us to his tent."

The murdant stepped back. "Mistress, don't be cross. I was only doin' my duty."

"Escort us, and we won't say a thing," said Dar. "Rosi, put on your helmet."

Girta just stood there, wide-eyed. Dar struck her helmet. "The *helmet*, Rosi!"

Girta quickly put it on.

"Come, Murdant," said Dar. "The general's bed is growing cold."

The murdant walked Girta and Dar to where the blue-and-scarlet tents stood. As Dar suspected, he was relieved when she said they could walk the last few paces alone. As the murdant hastily retreated, Dar saw that one tent bore the royal standard. They headed for it.

A small fire burned in the open area between the royal tents. The space was empty until Girta and Dar stepped into it. Then four guards emerged from the shadows. "Halt!" one shouted.

So close to her goal, Girta found her courage. She threw off her helmet. "I'm Girta, your queen. Don't keep me from my son."

The men stood dumbfounded as Girta strode into the king's tent and woke him. Moments later, mother and son emerged. The boy king, wrapped in his sleeping fur, gazed at Girta in rapturous astonishment. The guards had surrounded Dar with drawn blades, and she waited for what would happen next. Girta spoke. "Lower your swords," she commanded, and the guards did. "The king has been deceived into waging a ruinous war. General Kol is guilty of treason. Seize him!"

As Muth Mauk, Dar had come to expect obedience, and she was surprised when the guards stood their ground.

The occupants of the other tents began to emerge. General Kol appeared, wearing his chain mail. "What sorcery is this?" he demanded.

"No sorcery," replied Girta. "Justice. Guards, seize the general."

The men looked to Kol, as if seeking his permission.

"Do it!" shouted Kregant III.

"Your Majesty," said a high tolum who had just stepped from a tent. "We're at war, and he's our commander."

Kol bowed to the boy. "That corpse looked like your mother. If you seek a deceiver, look to the orcs' queen. This is orcish treachery, not mine."

"Lies!" said Girta. "Your men wounded me. Dar saved my life."

Kol regarded the other officers. "Who do you wish to lead this war? A boy and his mother or me?"

"Consider how well he's led you so far," said Dar. "You've run out of rations, and there's no plunder to replace them. That avalanche sealed the road home. We'll let you surrender for Queen Girta's sake."

"Surrender?" said Kol. "We'll take our chances fighting."

"Do you have six thousand in the hills?" asked Girta. "The orcs do. I've seen them."

"We learned our lesson at the Vale of Pines," said Dar. "Apparently, you didn't. You're camping in a valley."

The officers glanced uneasily at the hills on either side. "The moon will be setting soon," said one. "Orcs favor darkness for attacks."

"I came to save my son from certain and horrible death," said Girta. "If you won't surrender, at least let him depart. He'll give Kol the crown."

Dar laughed. "A lot of good it'll do him."

"We have the orcs' queen," said Kol.

"No you don't," said Girta. "Dar abdicated."

"To the orcs, I'm only an honored memory."

"I surrender!" shouted Kregant III.

"Hear the king," said Girta. "Obey him!"

The high tolum stepped forward. "I'll not go against my king. General, give me your sword."

Kol grasped his sword hilt while his eyes scanned about like those of a cornered animal. The faces of the other officers offered no hope. Several seemed already weighing their chances for promotion. Kol changed his grip to a passive one and surrendered his weapon.

"Your dagger, too."

Kol obeyed.

"The penalty for treason is death," said Girta. "As king, you can show no mercy."

"Kill him," said the boy.

A helmeted guard stepped from the shadows, sword drawn. "I'll take him to the cesspit and return with his head, Yer Majesty."

"Do it," said the boy.

Kol whimpered "No! No!" but the guard seized him roughly and marched him away. Dar watched the pair go, surprised by Kol's sudden meekness and loss of nerve.

General Kol marched submissively in the grip of the guard until they passed beyond the edge of camp. There, a shallow pit had been hacked into the frozen ground. Its odorous contents steamed slightly in the frigid air. The cesspit was an ignoble place to die and a fitting grave for a traitor. As the two men approached it, the guard glanced back toward the dark camp. "Where to, sir?"

"Othar's litter. This isn't over yet."

"Take my dagger, sir," said Wulfar. "Ye shouldn't go unarmed."

Forty-eight

♛

Othar's encampment lay deeper in the valley, apart from the main camp. Everyone was aware of its presence, though everyone tried to ignore it. It consisted of a single, small tent and the litter. The litter's bearers stood unsheltered beside their burden, which presently rested on the ground. The men resembled upright corpses, and seemed as oblivious of suffering. As Kol approached them, he gazed at their pale faces. Balten and Lokung stood among them. Both men's features were constantly twitching, and their chins were coated with frozen drool. General Voltar had perished already. In his place was a strapping soldier who stared as blank-faced as the others.

Gorm emerged from the small tent at the sound of Kol and Wulfar's approach. Kol carefully kept his eyes on him, avoiding the slightest glance toward the enclosed litter. His companion didn't know that trick. When Kol heard a wooden shutter open and a low, rasping voice, he knew Wulfar was doomed.

"What brings you here?" asked Gorm.

"The army's surrendered to the orcs," said Kol.

"What!" replied Gorm. Kol couldn't tell if he sounded more enraged or terrified.

"Dar brought Queen Girta before the king, and turned everyone against me. I was condemned to death. Othar just enslaved the man who saved me." Kol knew that Gorm could free Wulfar's spirit, but when Gorm didn't offer, Kol didn't ask. "Only sorcery can reverse things now."

"And what know you of sorcery?" asked Gorm.

A voice came from the litter, startling Kol with the depth of its enmity. "Dar! I want that bitch! She owes me suffering."

Kol saw his opportunity. "I can deliver her."

"How?" asked the rasping voice.

"I know her. She'll follow me. I'm certain of it."

"You've made promises before," said Gorm, "and have kept none yet."

"Because of Dar," replied Kol. "Always because of Dar."

"Get her," said Othar.

Gorm reflected. "She'd be a prize indeed. Aye, her death might advance our cause." He fixed his gaze on Kol. "Understand, it's all or naught. Hold nothing back."

"I won't. Give me Wulfar. I'll make it look like I killed him in a struggle. Then I'll leave a trail to the burnt hall. Get there by another route. When Dar follows me, Othar can seize her."

"Perhaps they'll send soldiers instead."

"They'll surely do that, but Dar will be with them," said Kol. "We're old adversaries, and hate binds tighter than love."

"Wulfar," said Gorm. "Go with Kol." Wulfar passively joined the man whom he had just saved and who would slay him. Gorm watched the two head for the cesspit. Then he struck his tent and ordered the litter-bearers to lift their burden. Before he led them away, he spoke through the litter's open shutter. "Master, Dar's blood would provide uncommon nourishment."

"And what if Kol fails?" asked Othar.

"Then I'll brew some magic of my own."

The atmosphere about the blue-and-scarlet tents combined joy on Girta and her son's part with a general sense of relief. The war had lost its allure with the hall's destruction. Hunger, harsh weather, and Dar's bluff about an ambush made the officers welcome surrender. In the prevailing mood, the deposed general seemed forgotten by everyone but Dar. It was she who finally asked, "Isn't that man overlong in returning with Kol's head?"

"Probably showing it to his comrades," said an officer.

"Just who was that guard?" asked Dar.

"One of my men," answered Kregant III.

"A *King's* Man?" asked Dar.

"Of course," replied the boy.

"But Kol handpicked all of them! Someone should check what's happened."

"Yes," said Girta. She turned to an officer. "Send some soldiers to the cesspit."

A while later, the soldiers reported back. "The guard is slain and his weapons are missing."

"And the general?" asked Girta. "Where's he?"

"Run off. We followed his tracks awhile. He seems headed for the burnt hall."

"Well, it's stopped snowing, Your Majesty," said an officer, "so he'll be easy to track in the morning. He won't get far."

"Good," replied Girta. "Bring another cot to the royal tent. I'll rest with my son."

"And what about this wench," said the man, gesturing at Dar.

"She can have your tent," replied Girta. "She used to be a queen."

Dar rose at first light, still dressed in the foot soldier's woolen tunic. She donned his leggings, bound her feet in cloth, and slipped on his boots. Omitting the armored tunic, helmet, and sword, she strapped on the dagger, tied on the cloak, and went to investigate the scene at the cesspit. When she arrived there, she saw that the soldiers' account had been incomplete. The guard's body had been dragged away, but it was evident that someone had been slain and his assailant had fled toward the hall. What interested Dar were signs that Kol and his guard had visited another place together and returned.

She followed those tracks and found signs of another camp. Dar studied them awhile. Everything pointed to it being Othar's camp. There were marks where a litter had rested on the snow. There were also footprints of a dozen men who seemed to have stood unnaturally still. They had left sometime in the night, traveling north along the shadowed side of the valley. Dar followed their trail around the mountain until it began to climb the slope. Then she ran back as fast as her clumsy boots allowed.

By the time Dar arrived at camp, jubilation over the surrender had infected the troops. More than once, she had to draw her dagger to discourage a boisterous soldier. But it was her demeanor more than the blade that made the men back down. Dar was intimidating. When she reached the royal tent, she found Girta and the king talking to a young officer.

"Dar," said Girta. "This is Tolum Farnar. His shieldron's going to capture General Kol."

"Are you certain of his loyalty?" asked Dar.

"Absolutely," said Girta. "He's the king's cousin."

"Tolum, you should know that Kol's not alone," said Dar. "A mage has joined him."

"Then we'll kill him, too," said the tolum.

"I'll accompany you," said Dar.

Farnar smiled somewhat disdainfully. "We're seasoned soldiers. We don't need a wench along."

"He's hiding in *my* hall," said Dar. "I know every stone of it. Besides, I have a stake in this. Kol's murdered those close to me."

Farnar shrugged. "Then come. Just don't get in the way."

Dar left with the shieldron soon afterward. Its soldiers were a sharp contrast to those who had served in the orc regiment. The men possessed discipline, and they looked deadly. They were large, fit, and well equipped, and they moved smartly up the road to the hall. Apparently, they had no difficulty following Kol's trail. That worried Dar, for she feared he intended them to find him.

When she reached the mountaintop, Dar was shocked by the state of the hall. Its destruction was far more complete than she had imagined it would be. Blackened stones had collapsed in many areas, reducing familiar places to sooty rubble. As the men clambered over mounds of loose stone, Dar often was unsure where she was. The building had become a roofless maze. Melted snow had refrozen to coat the remaining corridors with ice. The ice, in turn, was covered by a thin layer of snow. This made walking treacherous and left footprints that stood out clearly. However, once inside the hall, Kol had taken care to leave few tracks.

Tolum Farnar ignored Dar until his soldiers were thoroughly lost. Then he was more willing to accept her assistance. While the men halted, Dar shed her clumsy, oversized boots and climbed a partly standing wall like a narrow stairway. Its top afforded a commanding view. From there, Dar saw that the kitchen's roof of vaulted stone was partly intact. Moreover, smoke was issuing from a kitchen chimney. She climbed down. "Tolum, I think I know where your man is. I'll lead you to him."

After putting on her boots, Dar led the men through rubble-strewn hallways toward the kitchen. It lay in the older part of the hall, which seemed to have suffered less damage. Enough of its structure remained that Dar got her bearings. She gestured for the men to halt when she reached a roofless corridor just short of the kitchen's entrance. "Kol could be in the next room," Dar whispered to the tolum "Be warned, he's probably not alone."

"I know," said Farnar.

"The mage has the power to . . ."

"Men," shouted Farnar. "The traitor's ahead. Slay him and all with him. Now move smart."

The shieldron drew swords and rushed into the room. Dar listened for the sounds of combat, but for a while it was ominously quiet. Then she heard confused shouts and ringing swords. Anxious to see what was happening, Dar was about to peek through the doorway when she spied a better vantage point. Near the end of the corridor, a portion of the wall and ceiling had collapsed into a high mound of rubble. From its top, Dar would be out of the way while having a bird's-eye view of the kitchen. She clambered up the pile of stones and peered into the room beyond.

The kitchen was huge. Though much of its floor was covered with fallen stone, a space remained clear. There, a bizarre drama was unfolding. Othar sat atop, not in his litter. Nearby, a large iron cauldron sat upon a fire. A black-robed man stirred it. Judging from the smell, whatever boiled within the vessel was inedible. Kol stood next to him with sword drawn, ready to defend him. He had positioned himself so his back was to Othar. There were other black-robed men, but they lay slain about the floor. Yet there was combat. To Dar's amazement, Farnar's shieldron was fighting itself.

The tolum led the assault against his soldiers. He fought vigorously, but without any sign of emotion. Those men who fought beside him were equally blank-faced as they murdered their comrades. One had an arm that was nearly severed; yet he seemed oblivious of the injury. With a shock, Dar realized that Othar was seizing the spirits of his attackers, transforming them into his protectors. Though outnumbered, Othar's protectors were winning, for their former comrades seemed reluctant to fight them. Quickly, the dead outnumbered the living.

Eventually, the shieldron's remaining men grasped their situation, and they fought with desperate intensity. More died on both sides. Sometimes, a man glanced at Othar, and instantly switched allegiance. Dar watched, appalled yet unable to look away. Soon only a dozen men remained fighting. Then seven. Then five.

Dar became aware that Othar was staring at her. After first spotting him, she had carefully avoided his eyes. Yet even without glancing in his direction, she felt his gaze. It was as immediate as a fire's heat and just as physical. His hatred burned, commanding her to meet it. Dar was gripped by an irrational urge to glance into those scorching eyes. The urge was primal in its intensity, as strong as pain or hate and equally compelling. It took all of Dar's will to resist it.

Another man died. Then another. The floor flowed with blood. A soldier slipped in it. The mishap cost him his life. Two soldiers remained—one expressionless and the other red-faced with fury. The furious man triumphed. He stood dazed and panting in a pool of crimson. Then Kol strode over and downed him with a single stroke. As the man fell with a splash, Kol grinned and gazed up at Dar. "I see you," he said.

Dar scrambled down the pile of stones. Her clunky boots tripped her up, and she fell sprawling onto the blackened rumble. She hurt in half a dozen places, but she bolted upright to half run and half limp away. The walls of the storage rooms that had served the kitchen were still upright. Dar knew which room to enter. She darted into it. As she did, she heard Kol clamber down the rubble.

The room was empty, but it had once stored pashi. Because of this, there were openings in the base of its outer wall for ventilation. They were small, but large enough for Dar to squeeze through. She crouched before one. Its other side was covered with metal mesh. Dar kicked the mesh away, making more noise than she had hoped. Hearing rapid footsteps, she plunged into the opening. It was a tight squeeze. She was almost through when Kol grabbed her ankles. She slipped out of her boots and emerged on the other side of the wall. Discarding her overly long leggings, she hurried down the corridor. It was icy and difficult to negotiate barefoot.

Dar knew Kol couldn't fit through the opening. That forced him to find another route into the corridor, giving her some time, but not much. *I can't outrun him forever*, she thought, *and he has a sword*. Dar knew there was no escape, for Kol would never give up. One of them would have to die. It would be an uneven contest, so Dar concentrated on her few advantages. She knew the hall, and Kol didn't. She also had a dagger. Dar recalled Sevren's lessons: *"There's one time when you have an advantage over a swordsman. With a dagger, you can kill at a distance."* She also remembered his warning: *"You only have one chance."*

An ambush seemed Dar's only hope. Recalling that she had thrown a blade and hit Kol once before, she felt encouraged. Yet Dar was prudent enough to want an escape route if the throw went wide. Thus, she hurried toward the most ancient portion of the hall. The corridors there wiggled like snakes. Dar intended to surprise Kol at a bend, and duck into a room if she missed. The whole area was a warren of hanmuthis interconnected by small rooms and short passageways. Dar knew that maze, for the memories of former queens hadn't faded entirely.

Since she was bait for the ambush, Dar ensured her trail was easy to follow. Being barefoot made her silent. Kol was not. His iron-studded boots gave him sure footing, but their steps were loud. Dar heard them echo between stone walls. As the steps sounded closer, Dar detected a fainter sound, a soft metallic one. *Chain mail!*

I'll have to hit his throat! She was considering fleeing when Kol rounded the curve.

Instinct took over. Without reflection, Dar threw her dagger. It flew from her hand with deadly force. The gleaming blade flipped in the air, a blur of motion. Then it struck hard in the center of Kol's chest. It remained there a moment, then fell to the floor. Kol grinned and bent to pick it up.

Forty-nine

♛

The walls muffled Kol's laughter, but it still seemed loud to Dar. "Do you have another blade or was this your only one?" By the confident sound of Kol's gait, Dar knew he had guessed the answer. "Don't fret. You'll see your blade again. I'll use it to slice off your nose. You're Othar's meat, but appearance doesn't interest him."

Dar crept from one burnt room to another, careful to be silent. She tried to leave no trace, but that was difficult. Open to the sky, the chambers and hallways were brightly lit. Soot and snow often worked together to make her footprints obvious. Dar's feet stung from the cold, making her less agile.

Dar realized that the slain soldiers' weapons were in the kitchen. *But Othar's there also, and he's not alone.* Dar wondered if Kol's plan was to drive her toward him. She speculated on the purpose for the simmering cauldron. *Perhaps it's meant for me!* Images of boiling alive made Dar retreat farther from the kitchen.

Dar was clever prey, but Kol was an accomplished hunter. She eluded him, but he never lost her trail for long. They moved through the desolate hall as a pair, sometimes far apart, sometimes close. Concentration caused Dar to lose track of time. Every movement was crucial, for any misstep left clues. Her icy feet began to bleed, making footprints more conspicuous. She sensed her time was running out.

Dar passed through an archway and was surprised to

see that Muth la's Dome stood intact. *In my vision, it collapsed.* This puzzled her, and she thought it might be significant. The structure stood apart from the surrounding hall, and though a nearby wall had collapsed, the dome was remarkably preserved. Even its wooden door was unscorched. Thinking the dome might offer a refuge, Dar walked over to the door and opened it. She hoped that it might bolt from the inside, but there was only a bolt on its exterior.

Dar turned to leave and saw her footprints leading to the door. The fire had reduced the weedy courtyard to a bed of ash covered by a thin skin of snow. Dar's footsteps had made a dark and bold trail to the doorway. The door swung outward, and Dar opened it all the way to hide the exterior bolt. She stepped into the dome, halting on the stairs leading downward. Then Dar began walking backward, carefully placing her feet into the old footprints.

It was slow, careful work, and Dar was aware that Kol could appear any instant. If he did, she was doomed to an agonizing death. *I can't think of that. These footprints must match.* Dar took the time to make sure they did. She reached the archway and made a few additional conspicuous prints. Afterward, she carefully made her way to where the wall had collapsed, stepping on the fallen stones to avoid leaving prints. Every step was agonizing, but that didn't deter her. Dar hid in the rubble, removing her cloak to wrap around her frozen, bleeding feet. Then she waited. That was all she could do.

Kol had ceased making taunts. Instead, he tried to focus on the chase. It wasn't easy, for rage fought with concentration. He had risen so high—almost within grasp of the crown—and Dar had dashed it from him. Kol was so infuriated that he toyed with the idea of killing her himself. *Forget Othar!* Yet, even as Kol had that thought, he knew he couldn't. Enemies surrounded him. Othar was a dangerous ally, but he was his only ally. *Dar will be my gift to him.*

Nevertheless, Kol kept envisioning using the blade on Dar's face. Other places, too. The images were so compelling that he would lose her trail and have to backtrack. Yet pursuit became easier as time passed. Dar showed signs of wearing out. She left more prints and the prints grew bloody. Though tracks on rubble piles were hard to spot, Dar walked on them ever less frequently. *Too rough on her dainty feet*, thought Kol. As the prospect of her capture drew near, the chase became fun. It reminded him of the sport he had in the orc regiment where the branded women had no chance. *Just like you, Dar. Just like you.*

When Kol passed through an archway and spotted a line of footprints, he knew the game was over. The trail led into the dome but not out of it. He doubted the solitary building had another exit. He strode over to see. *She went inside, all right.* Kol stepped into the dome. A stairway descended into a single room. It was illuminated by a small hole in the center of the ceiling. As his eyes adjusted to the dim light, Kol looked about the room. *There's no way out. She's still in here.* Though the room lacked hiding places, it was shadowy close to the walls. Kol smiled, thinking of Dar sheltered only by darkness. *Not for long. You're mine.* He descended the stairs, relishing the ominous quality of his footsteps. Then the door slammed behind him.

Dar slid the bolt on the door and began piling stones against it. The oak in the door was thicker than a hand's length and hard as iron, but Dar wanted the reassurance of stone. She carried large blocks barefoot through snow, and it was satisfying. Only when a substantial pile pressed against the door did she climb the dome to reach the hole in its roof. The thick stones of the ancient dome had retained some of the fire's heat. They felt soothingly warm to Dar's aching feet.

The interior of the dome looked pitch-black. Dar couldn't see Kol, but she could hear him. He was hacking at the door with his sword. Dar heard the blade snap, and Kol let loose a string of curses. She waited for him to quiet down. "It's no use, *General* Kol," she said, giving the rank a mocking inflection. "You're in sacred space, where the World's Mother is commander."

"Tup your World's Mother!"

"That's not the proper attitude. This dome's for contemplation, and you've much to contemplate."

"Othar will set me free."

"I think not. You were his tool, nothing more. He used you like you used that sword. Who saves a broken blade?"

"I'm not broken yet!"

"You've been broken for years." Dar saw the stone cover for the opening and began to push it over the hole. The heavy cover was hard to move. "Think about those you wronged. Loral. Frey. Twea. All those you sent to the Dark Path." The cover got stuck, and Dar changed position so she could tug it over the opening. She called down the partly covered hole. "Darkness will help you concentrate."

A voice screamed from below, "Dar!"

A dagger flew past Dar's face, nearly grazing it. She flung herself back as the blade lost its momentum and tumbled down, striking the dome and skittering to the ground below. Dar's sudden movement loosened a block at the hole's edge. Perhaps the fire had weakened the stone's mortar; perhaps another force was at work. Either way, the block teetered for a moment, then crashed to the floor below. A second stone fell. Dar's vision had shown her what would happen next. The hole enlarged as the stones encircling it tumbled down. Dar slid down the dome's side and dashed from it before turning to see it crumble. The roar of the dome's collapse was followed by eerie stillness.

Gorm sweated as he stirred the cauldron. Foul steam saturated his sleeves, scalding him. Despite the pain, he continued to stir, certain both his life and soul depended on it. He paused only to scoop blood from the floor with his cupped hands and dump it into the cauldron. That ingredient was new, causing Othar to ask, "What's that for?"

"Shhh!"

"Don't shush me! When did you start doing magic?"

"Long before your mother breeched you."

"What's that brew for?" asked Othar.

"Assurance."

"Against what?"

"Shut up! I need to hear." Gorm cocked his ear, as if listening to a conversation in an adjacent room. After a spell of silence, he said, "Kol has failed." Gorm tensed, as though expecting a sudden blow. After a long moment, he relaxed and assumed the appearance of one who has received a reprieve.

Othar stared at Gorm in puzzlement. "How do you know?"

"I was just told."

"Now what?"

"It was all or naught. Well, it's naught." Gorm resumed stirring. When a loud rumble resounded through the hall, he appeared unsurprised.

"What was that?" asked Othar.

"Kol just died."

"And Dar still lives?"

"Aye."

"Get her! She must die, too!"

"I shall serve my master," replied Gorm.

"Then do it! I want her."

"You were never my master. I told you that. You were only its vessel."

"But your master and I are inseparable."

Gorm reached into his robe and pulled out a black sack, its fabric stitched with spells. "You've been deemed inadequate. My master must retrench." Gorm strode over to the litter and lifted Othar. The mage struggled in his grasp, but feebly with leaden limbs.

"Retrench?" said the mage with rising terror. "What do you mean?"

"It must return to the bones."

"It can't. Dar destroyed them."

"Aye, she did," said Gorm. "But you possess a set." Then he threw the mage into the cauldron.

The mage's dying shriek echoed through the ruined hall. Though horrible, it reassured Dar. She headed for its source with no idea what she would find, but certain her peril had diminished. Nevertheless, she peered through the kitchen's entrance cautiously. She saw that the black-robed man still stirred the cauldron. His hands were bloody. While she watched, he used the metal stirring paddle to fish something from the pot. It was Othar's robe. Dumping the sopping garment on the floor, the man probed its steaming folds and plucked out a bone, which he quickly tossed into the cauldron before it burned his fingers.

Dar stepped into the room. Its blood-puddled floor felt unnaturally warm to her bare feet. "Who are you?" she asked, brandishing the dagger Kol had thrown at her.

The man eyed the blade nonchalantly. "A servant. My name is Gorm."

Dar changed her grip on the dagger to the throwing position. "Othar's servant?"

"Never his."

"Then whose?"

"It doesn't have a name yet. It won't have one for ages."

"Yet it's unholy, I know that."

"Unholy?" said Gorm. "I'm not so sure. Is divinity benign?" He resumed his stirring. "You're thinking of killing me, aren't you?" He smiled. "Can you kill what's in this pot?"

"What's in there?"

"Bones."

"Then they're my enemy," said Dar. "I've been warned."

"They *were* your enemy, but you subdued them."

"By stopping Kol?"

"By stopping war. My master thrives on slaughter."

"I know. He wished to slaughter me."

"That was Othar," said Gorm. "Revenge always goaded him best. Perhaps your death would have reversed his fortunes, perhaps not. Now it's too late to tell."

"So all that remains is to destroy the bones."

"Their power can't perish. You know that. Be content that you've subdued it awhile." Gorm sighed wearily. "A very long while."

"Yet I can't let evil abide."

"The Creator does. Who are you to question her? She made men, and men nourish darkness."

Once again, Dar considered killing the man. *He probably deserves it.* But she sensed he was being truthful; murder was no cure for evil. *Only light banishes darkness.* Dar dropped Kol's dagger in the blood and walked away.

Fifty

♛

Dar found her boots where Kol had thrown them. She retrieved the leggings, wrapped her bloody feet, and put on the footwear. Then she descended the mountain by the same trail that the fleeing mothers had used. She found Skymere and Foeslayer still tied where she and Girta had left them. Dar mounted Skymere and rode toward the orc encampment, leading Foeslayer by his reins.

The idea of facing Girta, her son, or any of the soldiers had no appeal for Dar. She wanted to be alone awhile. Moreover, she felt that Gorm should complete his task unmolested, so he could remove the bones from orcish lands. With certainty that came from Muth la, she knew he would vanish for generations.

Dar rode without triumph, for Kol's death brought no joy. She felt empty, without anything to distract her from that emptiness. She wanted to be among the urkzimmuthi, yet she had misgivings. *I'm dead.* She recalled what happened after she had received the crown. *Muth Mauk said it's unnatural to talk with spirits.* Yet the former queen had spoken to her. *Only briefly.* Dar craved a few final words. *Then what?* She had no idea.

Halfway to the orc encampment, Dar encountered a group of soldiers. She recognized some of them as the officers who served the king. Foremost among them was the high tolum. He, like all the others, bore no weapons as he trudged through the snow. Instead he carried a tree branch, the sign of truce. "Lady Dar!" he called out.

When Dar rode over to him, he bowed graciously. "Lady Dar, what news?"

"The traitor's dead. So is the sorcerer. Tolum Farnar and his men were slain by his magic."

The high tolum made the sign of Karm's Balance. "These are mixed tidings indeed!"

"They are," said Dar. "Please bear them to the king and Queen Girta."

"You haven't spoken with them?"

"My heart was too sore. I've endured much. When you retrieve the bodies of Tolum Farnar and his men, know the hall is now accursed."

Then Dar rode on, not wishing to accompany the men. They would soon be going home, resuming the lives they had left behind. Dar's home was a ruin. She wondered if the hall was truly cursed. *It is for me. And my life? It's gone.*

Dar arrived at the orc encampment before noon. Only Sevren rushed out to greet her, his expression joyful and expectant. But when he saw Dar's face, he grew subdued. She dismounted solemnly, handing Sevren Skymere's reins. "Kol and Othar are dead. The washavokis have surrendered. Truce bearers are approaching." Then, without a further word, Dar went to find her sister.

Muth Mauk was discussing something with Muth-yat, Zor-yat, and the Pah clan matriarch. The conversation halted as soon as Dar approached, and all its participants drifted away from the queen, as though they had suddenly recalled some neglected duty. Dar's sister stood alone, the only one who had met her eyes.

Custom permitted the reigning queen to speak with the former one, but it was viewed more as a séance than a conversation. Muth Mauk bowed to Dar. "Sister, you dwell within me now. I had no idea what you endured."

Dar thought that her sister's eyes glistened. She smiled and embraced her. "Our foes are dead. Washavokis come begging peace. Give them what food you can, then lead them homeward on Old Road. New one is sealed. When spring comes, seal old one also."

"I understand your wisdom. Should we rebuild our hall?"

"You're Muth Mauk," said Dar. "That's for you to decide." She paused, knowing it was the last time they would speak and wondering what to say. *She knows how much I love her; she has my memories.* "Look after Kovok-mah." Then Dar embraced the mother who had once been Nir-yat and held her one last time.

Dar parted from Muth Mauk. To everyone she encountered, she was a beloved memory and just as insubstantial. Thus she was surprised when she felt someone touching her. She turned to see Muth-pah. The matriarch smiled briefly, then averted her eyes. "I wonder what happened to the Trancing Stone," she said, as if speaking to herself.

"I left it with my things," said Dar.

"I hope it's lost forever," said Muth-pah. "I only used it once. Like all matriarchs of my clan, I relived last Pah queen's memories." She sighed heavily. "From inside my rude hanmuthi, I saw Tarathank's wonders. Then all was bitterness. What is past is gone, and longing can poison living. In her wisdom, Muth la has departed spirits forsake their memories. Forsake that stone." Then Muth-pah bowed and departed.

Dar wanted to shed the soldier's garments, but wished that she could wash before she changed. She thought Sevren could find her some warm water and a scrubbing cloth. *At least he doesn't believe I'm dead.* She assumed he would be tending Skymere. The horses had been sheltered in a copse of evergreens, and Dar was headed in that direction when she heard a voice. "Dargu!"

Kovok-mah was hurrying after her.

"Don't you know that it's unnatural to speak to those who are dead?"

"What do sons know of spirits? I only know this: You filled my chest before Dargu-yat was born. I smell your scent. I hear your voice. If I touch you, I'll feel your warmth again."

"You can't."

"Why? Because my muthuri has forbidden it? She can't forbid me to be with spirit."

"You can't because I *am* spirit."

"Perhaps that's so, but we can be together."

"Where? Whose hanmuthi shall I haunt?"

"I'll build you one on land apart from any clan's. I'll grow your food, and tend goats to make hard milk to trade. We'll be alone, but we'll be together."

"Together, but not alone," said Dar. "I can bear daughters. Lorekeeper has told me so."

Kovok-mah grinned. "Daughters!"

"Hai," said Dar, her face serious. "And what latath will bestow their clan tattoos? What son's muthuri will bless ghost mother's children? I would love my daughters, but give them empty lives." Dar caressed Kovok-mah's cheek. "I can't do that."

"Dargu . . ."

"You should go," said Dar as her eyes welled with tears. "I'm sorry, Kovok. You gave me joy, and I've repaid you with sorrow."

"Thwa, Dargu. Not only sorrow."

Dar turned away as she had in the river when she and Kovok-mah parted that summer. She couldn't bear to watch him go, but she listened to every footstep. They were slow and reluctant. Soon they were accompanied by the low, mournful sound of Kovok-mah's weeping. It almost made Dar turn and run to embrace him. She trembled from the effort to resist the impulse and remain silent. Only when the sounds died away did her heart burst from the strain. Then Dar wept bitterly.

*   *   *

Dar washed and changed into her old clothes. She was composed when Zna-yat found her. "I've spoken with Kovok-mah," he said, his expression solemn and loving. "As always, you showed wisdom."

"It tore my chest to do it, Brother."

"Yet you prevented greater sorrows."

"Should you be speaking to me? I'm dead, you know."

"You're same Dargu who bit my neck. My life is still yours."

"Then I give it back to you."

"It's not proper to return gift when it was given lovingly."

"Oh, Zna! What's to happen to me?"

"You'll find your path. You always have."

"Can I stay among urkzimmuthi?"

"Hai," said Zna-yat. "Your home would become shrine. We'd leave you offerings and prayers."

"I'd be honored ghost."

"Hai. Greatly honored."

"And very lonely."

"That, too, I think." Zna-yat was silent awhile. "You might live among washavokis."

"They have little sense."

"Hai, that's surely true. Sev-ron told me they trade land for little bits of yellow iron. He showed me some. They were flat and round." Zna-yat paused. "Perhaps you could get some land."

"I have no yellow iron."

"I think you do." Zna-yat pulled the massive gold pendant from a sack.

Dar smiled for the first time. "And you just happened to be carrying that around?"

"It's natural for mothers to own land."

Dar had already guessed what her brother would say next. "And for sons to farm it. Do you have one to recommend?"

"Sev-ron doesn't altogether lack sense. I know he's wearied of killing. Also, my nose is not unwise. He has feelings for you."

"I know," said Dar. "But I don't for him."

"I smelled no atur about you before we visited Tarathank. It was not same with Kovok-mah."

"My chest is empty."

"Yet it's also big. It won't be empty long. Go to Sev-ron's faraway country. Get some land. See what happens."

"Since when do sons give mothers advice?"

"I'm just talking to some ghost."

Dar took the heavy pendant. "It would be good to work Muth la's breast and see things grow." She sighed. "What will happen to Kovok?"

"He could go back to his goats, but Muth Mauk will need mintaris."

"Might she choose him?"

"I think it likely. She possesses your memories."

A thoughtful look came to Dar's face. "My feelings, too. I saw her eyes make water for first time today." She smiled. "And unlike me, she's pretty."

"Your spirit was always beautiful to those who gained wisdom to see it." Zna-yat smiled. "I'm glad I did."

Epilogue

♛

Dar stepped from her home to enjoy the twilight. Taking off her sandals to feel the newly turned earth, she walked across her fields to view the mere. Averen's shadowed mountains were dark blue, but the lake's calm surface mirrored the pastel sky. As the evening grew darker, the stars came out. Each one had a twin in the water, and Dar felt she was gazing at two heavens, one distant and one within her reach.

A door opened, spilling firelight. Dar heard the sounds of running feet. Small voices cried out joyfully. "Muthuri!" Dar smiled and turned to embrace her daughters.

Acknowledgments

♛

Few journeys are accomplished alone, and mine was not one of them. I wish to thank those people who aided in the creation of Dar's tale: Richard Curtis provided the encouragement to undertake the adventure. Betsy Mitchell, my editor, proved an experienced and skillful sapaha. Diane Gummoe, a true Wise Woman, helped me understand Loral's ordeal. Gerald Burnsteel, Nathaniel Hubbell, and Carol Hubbell provided the insights that only thoughtful readers can. Shashav.

A Glossary of Orcish Terms

♛

armor Orcish armor is strictly functional, being devoid of ornamentation. It is more massive than its human counterpart. The basic item consists of a long, sleeveless tunic made from heavy cloth reinforced with leather and covered with overlapping steel plates. The plates are small and rounded at the lower end to permit ease of movement. The effect is that of fish scales. Its protection is supplemented by additional armor strapped to the arms and legs. A rounded helmet completes an orc's armor. Simple in design, it encloses much of the head. There are small holes opposite the ears, and the area about the face is open to permit good vision and communication. Some helmets have nose guards. Orcs regard their armor as a tool necessary for distasteful work. They take no pride in its appearance, allowing it to rust.

atur noun—The scent indicating love. Also see "sexual practices."

Bah Simi proper noun—Orcish name for Murdant Kol. *(Blue Eye)*

bathing As opposed to humans, orcs bathe frequently. If given the opportunity, they will do so daily. This fondness for cleanliness is probably related to their keen sense of smell. Orc settlements have communal baths where both sexes often bathe together.

biting of neck A practice where one orc voluntarily and

permanently submits to another. The relationship is similar to that of a mistress or master and her or his disciple, although strict obedience is expected from the bitten individual. Also see "mintari."

Blath Urkmuthi proper noun—Orcish name for Urkheit Mountains. *(cloak [of] mothers)*

blessed adjective—Human translation for *vashi*, the Orcish word for "married." The term refers to the fact that an orc couple's union must be approved by both their respective muthuris. In practice, a muthuri will seldom reject her daughter's choice of husband. A son's muthuri is more likely to oppose a marriage. Also see "sexual practices."

breast noun—Human word for *far*. Orcish attitudes toward breasts differ markedly from human ones. In their matriarchal society, breasts symbolize a mother's authority and her nurturing nature. The orc queen colors her nipples as a sign of her sovereignty. Orc mothers seldom cover their breasts except in cold weather.

When a mother wishes to initiate intimacy with a male, she will grab his hand and brush it against her covered or uncovered breast. This action is considered decorous and is often done publicly. Also see "sexual practices."

cape noun—A garment worn by orc males that resembles the kefs worn by orc mothers. It is a sign of leadership that is derived from wisdom. A son who wears a cape lacks the innate authority of a mother, and his leadership extends only over other sons. Also see "military ranks and units—orc leaders."

chest Orcs consider the chest, not the heart, to be the site of emotion. Their expression "to have big chest" means one is brave. A lover would say that his or her beloved "fills my chest."

clan noun—Related orc families that form the principal social unit of orcish society. A mother's offspring belong to her clan, and her daughters will spend their lives in her household. When sons marry, they move into their wife's household, but retain their clan affiliation. Each clan is headed by a matriarch who assumes the name "Muth" upon her election. The matriarchs are subordinate only to the orc queen, and they form a council that occasionally meets to advise her. Every clan has a distinctive tattoo that is marked on the chins of its members when they reach adulthood.

Before the washavoki invasions, the urkzimmuthi had thirteen clans. The ensuing wars reduced the number to nine: the Yat, Mah, Tok, Hak, Goth, Jan, Zut, Smat, and Pah clans. Some clans have acquired a nickname based on a predominant trade or quality. The Yat clan is known as the Queen Clan. The Pah clan was called this before Tarathank fell. Later, it became the Lost Clan. The herding Mah clan is known as the Milk Clan. The respective specialties of stonework, glassmaking, and metallurgy make the Tok clan the Stone Clan, the Hak clan the Fire Clan, and the Jan clan the Iron Clan.

consulting stones This is a voting procedure that the Council of Matriarchs employs to obtain unanimity on contentious issues. When the council cannot agree, they request the queen to "call for stones." Then the matriarchs are given stones of differing colors. The colors represent different outcomes of a vote, usually "yes" or "no." Each matriarch votes secretly by placing her hand in a pottery jar and dropping a stone. Afterward, the queen counts them. The result is called the stones' decision, not the matriarchs', and tradition calls for it to be accepted unanimously. Generally, the council will avoid calling for stones, preferring to avoid acting until agreement can be reached through discussion.

Council of Matriarchs proper noun—An assembly of clan matriarchs that meets periodically to advise the orc queen and assist her in governing. Since the matriarchs have nearly absolute authority over their respective clans, the queen cannot simply dictate to them. Instead, she strives to lead by establishing agreement. When agreement cannot be reached on a pressing matter, a secret voting procedure is employed. (See "consulting stones.")

When a new queen is crowned, the council must meet to affirm her fitness to rule. (Also see "Muth la's Draught.") Otherwise, the council meets when the queen deems it necessary.

crown noun—Human word for *zumuth*, the thin circlet of unadorned gold worn on the orc queen's head.

dargu noun—Weasel.

Dark Path proper noun—The human term for the afterlife. Also known as the Sunless Way, it is conceived as a plane of existence that parallels the living world. Spirits of the dead travel the path on a westward journey to the goddess Karm, leaving their memories behind in the process.

deception Orcs do not have words for any form of deception, such as "trickery," "lying," "betrayal," etc. Sometimes, lying is called "speaking words without meaning," but the understanding of this expression comes closer to "speaking nonsense" than to "lying."

deetpahi noun—This word, which translates as "speaking wood," describes the orcish equivalent of a book. A deetpahi is a very thin board, usually made of birch, that is approximately thirty inches long and five or six inches wide. Writing is burned into it using a heated metal stylus and the board is afterward covered with beeswax. Usually both sides are inscribed.

Temporary records are made on deetpahis covered with a layer of white clay hardened with tree gum. The size of these boards varies according to need. The writing is done in ink, and erasure is accomplished by scraping the clay with a flat stone blade.

falfhissi noun—A potent spirit distilled from fermented pashi and flavored with washuthahi seeds and honey. It is often drunk at the conclusion of a feast. *(laughing water)*

Fathma proper noun—Muth la's gift to the orcs, it is a unique spirit that confers sovereignty. Passed from one queen to the next, Fathma transforms its recipient's spirit by mingling with it. The queen comes to regard all orcs as her children and becomes dedicated to their welfare. She also receives memories from all the past queens. These memories do not constitute an organized body of knowledge. Rather, they are impressions that help unite a queen with her predecessors and her subjects' history.

As a queen approaches death, her ability to perceive the inner qualities of others becomes enhanced. This allows her to choose a worthy successor. Because the queen's spirit and Fathma are intermingled, once she transfers this gift to another, the orcs consider her deceased. Henceforth, they will not openly acknowledge her existence.

Fathma was lost to the orcs when their queen was slain during the fall of Tarathank. For several generations, there was no queen, and the orcs suffered a period of chaos. Fathma returned to the orcs when a child who possessed it was born in the easternmost settlement. She was a member of the Yat clan, and afterward that clan became the Queen Clan.

funeral practices Orcs send the bodies of their dead to Muth la in the same state they entered the world—naked. Corpses are cremated or left upon the ground (*te far Muthz la*—on Muth la's breast). In the latter case, the body is placed within Muth la's Embrace (see separate entry), preferably under a tree.

gabaibuk noun—Thin, soft cloth woven from thistledown.

gatuub noun—An orcish stew made with mutton and dried fruit.

goblin noun—Another human word for "orc." This term is mainly used in the western kingdom.

Goblin Wars proper noun—The human name for the orcs' attempts to retake their lands after the washa-voki invasion. Savagely fought by both sides, this conflict lasted several generations. Most of the fighting was in the form of raids. When it ended, no orc settlements remained south of the Urkheit Mountains.

gold—See "yellow iron."

grandmother noun—The human translation for *muth-muthi*. This term refers only to the maternal grandmother, who is a revered figure in orcish families. The paternal grandmother is called *minmuthi* and is considered a more distant relation.

Great Mother noun and proper noun—As a proper noun, it is the translation of *Muth Mauk*, the orc queen's proper name. It is also used as a term for a queen.

hai adverb—Yes.

hanmuthi noun—A circular room with a central hearth that is the heart of orc family life. Meals are eaten there, and sleeping chambers adjoin it. Its outer walls constitute the Muth la's Embrace. The ranking muthuri heads the hanmuthi and commands the obedience of all its members. (*hearth [of] mother*)

hard milk noun—Orcish term for cheese.

healer noun—An orc who practices healing magic. This "magic" is based on an understanding of the medicinal properties of herbs and other practical therapies. It does not involve sorcery. Both sexes may be healers, though the most skilled healers are mothers.

high murdant—See "military ranks and units."

high tolum—See "military ranks and units."

hiss verb root and noun—To laugh, laughter.

human noun—Human word for *washavoki*.

Karm proper noun—Goddess worshipped by humans. Called the Goddess of the Balance, Karm is supposed to weigh one's deeds after death.

kefs noun—A pair of short capes of slightly differing sizes that are worn by orcish mothers. In warm weather, the smaller cape is worn on top of the larger one so that the breasts are exposed. In cold weather, it covers the chest.

kokuum noun—Avalanche.

latath noun—The mother who bestows the clan tattoo and has other specialized functions as well. She brews falfhissi and makes inks, dyes, and some healing extracts. Within the Yat clan, the latath also makes talmauki and Muth la's Draught. See separate entries.

lorekeeper noun—The mother whose specialized function is to maintain the lore of the clan. A lorekeeper serves for life, and begins her training at an early age. Not all clans possess lorekeepers, and the nature and form of their lore varies among clans. The lorekeeper maintains a **lorechamber**, which resembles a hanmuthi and usually includes a library of deetpahis. These are sometimes copied and given to the lorekeepers of other clans, although every clan possesses its secrets. Tarathank contained a huge **lorehall** with an extensive collection of deetpahis that was maintained by lorekeepers from many different clans.

man noun—There is no equivalent term in Orcish for a human male, although they are sometimes called "hairy-faced washavokis."

military ranks and units Orcs never developed a highly organized military, and all the following terms are of human origin. In the orc regiments, all the officers were human.

> **human ranks** Ranks in ancient armies were less specific than in contemporary ones, and the modern equivalents are only approximations.
>
> **murdant**—A noncommissioned officer, the equivalent of a sergeant.
>
> **high murdant**—The highest-ranking noncommissioned officer. A high murdant reports directly to a general.
>
> **sustolum**—The lowest-ranking officer, the equivalent of a lieutenant.
>
> **tolum**—The equivalent of a captain. Usually commands a shieldron (see below).
>
> **high tolum**—Usually commands a regiment.
>
> **general**—The highest-ranking officer. The general for the orc regiments was called **the Queen's Man** because the orcs believed he derived his authority from their queen.

> **orc leaders** Orcs had no officers or murdants, but did recognize leaders among their own kind. Such leaders lacked the authority of human officers and led by their example and through the use of persuasion. They wore **capes** as a sign of wisdom. These capes were bestowed by the consensus of their comrades and could be taken away in the same manner. The authority of **Wise Sons** derived from the clan matriarchs who appointed them to act in their absence. They guided the orc males in nonmilitary matters. Outside the orc regiments, they had no more authority than ordinary orc males.

military units An orc regiment was composed of orc fighters, commanded by human officers. Human soldiers served support roles, and women served both the orcs and men. A **shieldron** was the basic orc fighting unit. It consisted of thirty-six orcs. The term was also applied to a shieldron of orcs and the humans that commanded and supported them. An orc **regiment** had six shieldrons of orc fighters, accompanied by a human contingent of officers, support troops, and serving women. Units of human foot soldiers were also organized into shieldrons and regiments.

milkstone noun—Marble.

min noun—A male orc, regardless of age. Usually translated as "son."

mintari noun—This word translates as "bitten son." A mintari is a son whose neck has been bitten by the orc queen, which renders his life hers. Mintaris serve the queen by implementing her commands and speaking in her name. Becoming a mintari is considered a great honor. All the clans, with the exception of the Pah clan, send candidates. A queen strives to have mintaris from every clan, with the aforementioned exception, since they will have frequent dealings with the matriarchs.

Mintaris live in the queen's hanmuthi for as long as she reigns. Though only unblessed sons are sent as candidates, they are allowed to marry. The couple must obtain the queen's blessing in addition to that of their respective muthuris. The married couple and their children reside in the royal hanmuthi.

minvashi noun—Husband. *(blessed son)*

mother noun—The human translation for the Orcish word *muth*, although the two terms are not completely equivalent.

murdant—See "military ranks and units."

muth noun—Often translated as "mother," it is the word for any orc female, regardless of age or whether she has borne children. Orcs occasionally use this word to describe human females. Mothers wield the real authority within orc society because Muth la's guidance always comes through them.

Muth proper noun—This is the name a mother assumes when she becomes matriarch of a clan. Thus the head of the Yat clan is always named Muth-yat. The orc queen also assumes this name. However, she is called *Muth Mauk*, which means "Great Mother."

Muth la proper noun—Orcish word for the divine mother who created the world and all living things. Muth la sends guidance to mothers through visions.

Muth la's Draught noun—A drink made by steeping yew seeds in distilled spirits. The resulting beverage is highly poisonous. It is sometimes given to a new queen by the Council of Matriarchs as a test of her fitness to rule. It is believed that the queen will survive if Muth la deems her fit to reign. This test is rarely administered, and no queen has ever passed it.

Muth la's Embrace proper noun—Human translation for *Zum Muthz la*. This sacred circle symbolizes the Divine Mother's presence. It may be temporary or permanent. Orcs always sleep and eat within its confines. A wall, upright sticks, stones, or even a line drawn in the dirt can mark the circle. Orc dwellings always incorporate Muth la's Embrace and tend to be circular for this reason. The Embrace is hallowed ground; the dead are placed within it and worship takes place there. It is said that mothers are more likely to receive visions within Muth la's Embrace.

Muth Mauk noun and proper noun—Translated as "Great Mother," this is both the queen's title and her proper name. The orcs also use its lowercase form or the word *nathmauki* as terms for "queen."

muthuri noun—A mother in the reproductive sense. A muthuri holds strict authority over her offspring. The ranking muthuri heads a hanmuthi. *(giving mother)*

muthtufa noun—A traditional, spicy orcish stew that consists of pashi and other vegetables.

muthvashi noun—Wife. *(blessed mother)*

names Orcish names consist of two parts, the given name and the clan name. Thus, Zna-yat is a member of the Yat clan. In the familiar form of address, the clan part of the name is dropped. This is often done when parents talk to their children, when adult mothers of the same clan converse, or when intimates speak together.

When a mother becomes the clan matriarch, she assumes the given name of "Muth." The orc queen assumes the name "Muth Mauk," *Great Mother*. Her name has no clan part because she is muthuri to all the clans.

nayimgat noun—A healing herb with large, fuzzy leaves that is also a sedative.

neva noun—An article of clothing worn by orcish mothers that resembles a skirt. It may consist of a length of cloth wrapped around the waist or it may be a tailored garment.

orc noun—Human word for *zimmuthi*. The human word derives from the shortening of the orcs' collective name for themselves, *urkzimmuthi*.

orcish adjective—Human word for *urkzimmuthi*.

Orcish language Orcish is the human word for *Pahmuthi*, which translates as "speech [of] mother." Orcish differs from human speech in several ways: The equivalents of the articles "a" and "the" do not exist. Adjectives follow the noun they modify. All personal pronouns are gender-specific when they refer to orcs, with mixed-gender plurals taking the feminine form. Genderless pronouns are used for things, animals, and humans. Plurals are indicated by the prefix *urk*, which translates as "many." Possession is indicated by the addition of a "z" to the end of a noun. Orcish nouns are often formed by the descriptive combination of other words. Example: "Rain," *hafalf*, combines "sky," *ha*, with "water," *falf*. Verbs are conjugated regularly and their roots often function as nouns. Example: *Ma urav ur*—I give gift. **A more extensive treatment of Orcish grammar and vocabulary can be found in the glossary to *King's Property*.**

orcs noun—Human word for *urkzimmuthi*.

Pahmuthi noun—Orcish language. *(speech [of] mother)*
pashi noun—A bland-flavored root that is a staple in orcish cooking. Called "whiteroot" by humans, it is more flavorful when roasted.

Queen's Man—See "military ranks and units."

rebirth noun—Human translation of *themuth*, an ancient orcish ritual that allows a washavoki with "mixed spirits" to become urkzimmuthi. Although physically unchanged, a reborn person becomes the child of the muthuri participating in the ritual, joins her clan, and receives her clan tattoo. There is controversy over whether rebirth involves actual sorcery.
regiment—See "military ranks and units."

sand ice noun—Orcish term for glass. The Hak clan first discovered the secret of its making and still makes it for the other clans and for trade with washavokis.
sapaha noun—A guide.
scabhead noun—Human slang for a newly branded woman serving in the orc regiments.
sexual practices Orcish sexual practices differ markedly

from human ones for two reasons: Females are the dominant sex in orcish society, and orcs can detect the scent of love, which they call "atur." The latter ensures that orcish courtship lacks the bumbling and misunderstandings that often characterize its human counterpart. It also means orcs cannot keep their feelings secret.

Intimacy is always initiated by the female. This is usually done by the mother grasping the son's hand and touching it to her breast. This gesture is the socially proper sign that she is receptive to his attentions. Until he receives permission, a son will not express his desire by word or deed. The orcs believe if a son were to make unwanted advances, Muth la would condemn him to eternal punishment. Thus, despite human claims to the contrary, rape is unknown among orcs.

Sexual intercourse between unblessed (i.e., unmarried) couples is forbidden and carries strict sanctions (see "blessed" and "thwada"). However, any intimacy that falls short of intercourse is considered a proper part of courtship. Orcs call such acts "giving love." A son or a mother at this stage of courtship is called a *velazul*, which loosely translates as "lover." It is not uncommon for mothers to have several velazuls before becoming blessed.

A muthuri will commonly ignore a relationship until it becomes serious. When she shows awareness of a couple's attachment, the muthuri is said to have a "wise nose." Then she is expected to act in the couple's best interests by either facilitating or preventing their permanent union. If a muthuri disapproves of the relationship, she will end it by forbidding her child to see his or her velazul.

shash verb root and noun—To thank, thanks. *Shashav* translates as "thank you."

shieldron—See "military ranks and units."

sleep Orcs sleep sitting upright in a cross-legged position, with only a mat as a cushion. Only babies and the extremely ill rest lying down.

smell Orcs have an especially keen sense of smell, and their language contains many terms for scents that humans cannot distinguish. They are also capable of smelling emotional states and physical conditions. They can detect anger, fear, love, pain, and some forms of sickness. This ability has affected their culture in fundamental ways and may partly explain why orcs do not easily grasp deception. Orcs usually do not speak about those emotions they detect by smell. This is particularly true of the males.

spirit noun—The human word for *fath*. An equivalent term would be "soul." The orcs hold that one's spirit defines one's being. That is why they believe rebirth is possible, since the ritual alters the spirit. Fathma is an additional spirit that passes from orc queen to orc queen. It mingles with the queen's original spirit and transforms it. In the process, it instills the memories of the queen's predecessors.

sukefa noun—A thin, soft garment worn beneath a winter kef. Similar in appearance to a cape, it has two sides with contrasting colors.

sustolum—See "military ranks and units."

tahweriti noun—An orcish delicacy. Doves are stuffed with brak and dried fruit, then slowly roasted overnight over aromatic wood. *(golden bird)*

talmauki noun and adjective—A shade of bluish green that is the royal color and reserved for the orc queen. The queen's kefs and cloak are always dyed this shade. She also uses it to color her claws and nipples. *(great green)*

Tarathank proper noun—An ancient orcish city destroyed

during the washavoki invasion. It was the queen's city in the time when the monarch always came from the Pah clan. Other clans also had their halls in Tarathank. For this reason, it was called the City of Matriarchs. Tarathank was the center of the orcish civilization at its greatest height, and its grace and splendor were never matched. Since orcs of that era were ignorant of warfare, the city lacked defenses.

tava interjection—Hello.

thrim verb root—To have sexual intercourse.

thwa adverb—No, not.

thwada noun—A condition that renders an orcish mother untouchable. There are two kinds of thwada, and they are very different in their cause and nature. The ceremonial thwada is temporary and pertains to mothers about to undergo certain serious spiritual rituals, such as Entering Darkness. Contact with that mother is considered dangerous to all involved. In this state of thwada, the mother cannot eat or associate with sons.

The second form of thwada is a punishment imposed on a mother for having intercourse before she is blessed or continuing in a forbidden relationship. The mother is considered dead, and no member of orc society will have open dealings with her. This form of thwada is permanent. A mother who is thwada leads a ghostlike existence on the outskirts of society, seen but ignored. Though she sometimes dies of hunger and exposure, orcs usually sustain her by "losing" necessities in her vicinity.

It is interesting to note that this punishment is inflicted only on mothers. Offending sons are permanently disgraced, but permitted to remain within society.

tolum—See "military ranks and units."

Trancing Stone noun—A magical object created by Velasa-pah. It allows anyone who holds it to experience the memories discarded by departed spirits. The stone is an heirloom of the Pah clan.

trafpaha noun—A three-dimensional construction of sticks and string that serves as a chart of a rock formation, ridgeline, or mountain. Used only by the Tok clan, it conveys a wide range of information through the shape, color, and material of its various components. *(stone speak)*

Tree Because trees bridge the earth and sky, orcs consider them a manifestation of Muth la. They make a sign for Muth la by pressing a palm upright against the chest and splaying the fingers like branches. This sign is usually made to acknowledge Muth la's presence in an event or deed.

    The yew tree, *Taxu baccata*, is particularly sacred to Muth la because it is evergreen. Its seeds are used to make Muth la's Draught. See separate entry.

tul adjective—Real, having a verifiable existence. This word approaches the meaning of the human expression "true," although the orcs have no term for its opposite.

tuug noun—A cord braided from two differently colored strands of yarn used to tie on a gabaiuk.

urkzimdi noun—An ancient Orcish word for humans. It translates as "second children" and is based on the orcs' belief that Muth la created humans after she created them. The word fell into disuse after the washavoki invasion.

urkzimmuthi noun and adjective—The orc race, also the plural of orc. As an adjective, it means "orcish." *(children [of] mother)*

vash verb root and noun—1. To bless, blessing. 2. To marry, marriage.

vata interjection—Good-bye.

vathem noun—A stone retaining wall used to create a terraced field. After the orcs occupied the Urkheit Mountains, such fields were used extensively.

Velasa-pah proper noun—The name of a human who was reborn before the washavoki invasion and became a great urkzimmuthi wizard. He tried to warn the orc queen of the invasion, but she failed to comprehend the danger or act upon his advice. He was residing in Tarathank when it fell. The orcs tell differing tales about his fate and the import of his prophecies.

Velasa-pah was the orcish wizard (see separate entry) who came closest to the human concept of a sorcerer because the knowledge he received concerned the spiritual realm. He created the Trancing Stone and foretold the future.

velazul noun—Lover. Unlike the human term, it is used only in the chaste sense. *(give love)*

washavoki noun and adjective—Human, either male or female. The word translates as "teeth of dog" and refers to the whiteness of human teeth.

washavoki invasion The first contacts between humans and orcs were peaceful, but that era was ended by the onslaught of human invaders from the east. At that time, orcs were ignorant of warfare and they were easily overwhelmed, despite their superior size and strength. Although orcs quickly learned how to make arms and became ferocious fighters, they never acquired the strategic skills required for victory. They were driven from their lands and survived only in the inhospitable Urkheit Mountains, which they named *Blath Urkmuthi* because they sheltered fleeing mothers.

washuthahi noun—A black, pea-shaped seed that is mildly narcotic and stains the teeth black when chewed. *(teeth pretty)*

weapons Orcs did not make weapons before the washa-voki invasion, and their arms are adapted from human designs. Swords, axes, and maces are primarily used for combat, but orcs also carry daggers and sometimes hatchets. All their weapons are strictly utilitarian in design. They reflect the orcs' strength, being larger and more massive than those humans carry. Spears and pikes are not unknown to orcs, but they are rarely used. Although orcs use bows and arrows for hunting, they do not employ them in combat.

wife noun—Human word for *muthvashi*.

Wise Sons—See "military ranks and units—orc leaders."

Wise Woman noun—A human woman skilled in the healing arts. Wise Women also practice midwifery.

wizard noun—The human translation for *minsi*. Although Muth la speaks to mothers, on rare occasions she imparts special knowledge to sons. This knowledge benefits all urkzimmuthi. Although this may seem magical, it is not derived from sorcery. Renowned wizards include Val-hak, who brought the secret of making sand ice to his clan; Fluuk-jan, who taught his clan how to make steel; and Velasa-pah, who learned how to visit the realm of spirits and foretell events.

woman noun—An orc female is called a *muth*, but the term is not commonly applied to human females. There is no specific term for them in Orcish, although "woe man," a corrupted pronunciation of "woman," is occasionally employed.

yellow iron noun—The human translation for *daumriti*, the Orcish word for gold. Orcs do not prize gold and mainly use it in decorative metalwork and for weights used with scales. The chimneys in hanmuthis sometimes bear designs in gold. Orcs do not wear jewelry or decorate their weapons, so gold is not used for those purposes. Because the metal never tarnishes, orcs consider it a symbol for eternity. That is why their queen's crown is made of gold.

zim noun—Child.
zimmuthi noun—The singular form of "orc." *(child [of] mother)*
zul verb root and noun—To love, love.